THE BOOK *of* RAIN

THE BOOK OF RAIN

of

RAIN

THOMAS WHARTON

Random House Canada

Library and Archives Canada Cataloguing in Publication

Title: The book of rain / Thomas Wharton.
Names: Wharton, Thomas, 1963- author.
Identifiers: Canadiana (print) 20220240825 | Canadiana (ebook)
20220240833 | ISBN 9781039002432 (hardcover) | ISBN 9781039002449 (EPUB)
Classification: LCC PS8595.H28 B66 2023 | DDC C813/.54—dc23

Jacket design: Emma Dolan
Text design: Emma Dolan
Image credits: (water droplets) pinkomelet; (texture) darkbird77;
(bird) Andrew_Howe; all Getty Images

Printed in Canada

10 9 8 7 6 5 4 3 2 1

To the advocates and activists who've shown us that in saving our fellow animals we save ourselves.

Nature see you.

—KOKO THE GORILLA

THE OTHERS

Before we were here, this was their world. They lived their urgent, unstoried lives, each nameless generation passing on without ever knowing the unbroken poem of continuance in their cells. More than once fire, ice, drought, and death from the sky winnowed their numbers to the edge of silence, but they endured, struggled back from the brink, and flourished again, filling the skies, the waters, the land.

Time was an ocean of now. There was no history, no future.

Then we came. And now it's Tuesday afternoon.

Without warning the connections all go down. In the sudden muteness of our devices the chatter in our own heads is deafening. Desperate to escape it we leave our apartments and offices and classrooms and gather on the paths and lawns of the municipal park. There are stalled, silent cars in the street, suggesting that whatever knocked out our signals and screens struck here too. People move slowly, uncertainly, wading like reluctant swimmers in a strange new element. This had been an ordinary working afternoon, but now the rest of the day, the week, has suddenly become unhitched, like a trailer rolling off by itself to the side of a road. All the unfinished projects, the tasks we've been putting off until later, the reports we were supposed to have ready by Friday that we haven't even started yet, and everything else that needs doing before the week's end: the long-postponed checkup and cleaning at the dentist's, the trip to the home reno store to return those light bulbs that were the wrong size, the parent-teacher interview that we hoped would explain how our bright, articulate offspring could be doing so poorly in both math *and* English. It's all still real, and pressing, but somehow now on the other side of an unthinkable chasm no one knows how to cross.

We want to know what's gone wrong. We want to know how long we'll have to wait before things return to normal. Rumours and speculation gush like a punctured oil pipeline, but no one has any real information yet. At first people fret and grumble and curse whoever is responsible for the disruption, but it's clear there isn't much eagerness to return to the heaps of work everyone has waiting for them. The strings that bound us have begun to loosen in the warm afternoon air, the first perfect blue-sky day after what seemed like weeks of grey drizzle. We feel past due for a little relief.

Tentatively we undo a button or two, untuck our shirttails, shrug off our jackets. We don't want to go too far if this isn't going to last. But once we let it start, we keep on sliding slowly out of ourselves. Ties are unknotted, shoes shucked, socks and stockings peeled off. Bare feet touch the grass with a kind of primal shock. People stretch, shake out their limbs, do little dances of relief. They sit or sprawl right out on the grass. Friends and acquaintances find each other in the throng and get to chatting about last night's game and this summer's trips. Someone brings out a soccer ball and strangers begin an impromptu match.

An ice cream van sits stalled at the curb, the driver frantically offering bargain prices before his wares melt. Within minutes young and old are strolling around, licking frozen treats of many colours. A popcorn cart shows up soon after, followed by a man selling balloons and a juggler on a unicycle. People with guitars, horns, and bongo drums appear and start to play. A spur-of-the-moment street party is blossoming before everyone's eyes.

So here we are. How long is an afternoon when you're doing nothing useful? We've forgotten how the hours can unfold themselves into a warm, sleepy country you've always thought about visiting but kept finding reasons not to. In this other kind of time it really seems as if the shadows of the office towers are refusing to lengthen. The commute home will never begin. There's nowhere for the day, for anyone, to go.

But something's missing, something that keeps us from giving in completely, even if we don't know what it is.

Then someone asks, *Where are the birds?*

We look up. We listen. It's true. There's no chirping. No singing. No sparrows darting after each other through the leafy branches. The streetlight poles should have gulls hunkered on them, expectantly waiting for cones and other tidbits to be dropped or tossed aside. You'd expect a crow to flap by, calling to the other crows about this odd thing: humans flocking together at a time when they're usually nowhere in sight.

The perches around us are silent. The sky is empty.

We don't know what to do with this fact. It's a stillness far stranger than the silence from our phones. In the absence of birdsong, we start to notice other things too. The sun is just a little too bright, too warm for this time of year. We become aware that those cheerful rays, right now, are broiling the cells on the surface of our exposed skin.

And the cloud. That one solitary cloud, hanging suspended at the zenith of the sky's faultless blue dome, doesn't look quite right. Or the problem is it looks exactly right. It's the kind of cloud children draw, a bright white cotton ball of cumulus. A cloud too perfectly cloud-like to be real.

Then somebody shouts they've got a signal.

Eagerly we all check. It's true. Our little pocket worlds light up, buzz, tremble in our hands like lost pets who've found their way home. The invisible architecture has reassembled itself around us. And just like that, here comes the rest of the week, moving toward us like a cargo ship carrying all the freight of our lives.

Those of us who bother to look up notice the cloud is gone too. No one remarks on its absence. It was just a cloud, after all. They come and go.

Most of us don't linger another moment. We hurry back to work, to our homes, looking forward to catching the news later so we can find out what happened here and what we should think about it. If we remember the silence in the trees, we decide it was one of those oddities of nature that has a perfectly reasonable explanation, if we bothered to look it up. Someone somewhere knows what it means. It's not our concern. Tomorrow, surely, the birds will be back.

ALEX

He wakes from an Ativan-induced doze to the roar of the plane. The last of the daylight fading on the edge of the world. The window shows him dark stretches of forest, parted now and then by the pale slash of a road, a few lonely yard lights already winking on in the gloom. They must be getting close.

Below him is somewhere he'd lived once. It doesn't feel that way. His adult life has taken place far from here and he'd had no plans to ever return.

Then came the call from his mother, about Amery.

I told her it wasn't her job to make things right, she'd said over the phone.

He tried to be reassuring. Or maybe he just didn't want to be bothered.

I'm sure she's fine, Mom. She probably got busy and just forgot to check in.

No. She never forgets, Alex. We talk every weekend. I insisted and she never misses it. Even if she won't tell me what she's doing, or how she's doing, she always calls. You're sure you haven't heard from her?

I'd remember. I don't think we should jump to conclusions. Maybe she didn't pay her phone bill. We both know she has no money.

I'm not jumping to conclusions. Something's happened to your sister.

The seatbelt sign comes on. The pilot announces they'll be landing in Pine Ridge in ten minutes. The older woman sitting next to Alex puts away her word puzzle book and clasps her hands together in her lap, her thumbs turning over and over each other like some kind of self-propelled mechanism. They haven't spoken the entire flight and it occurs to him they haven't once made eye contact. Or rather, he's avoided making eye contact. He's gotten very good at that the last few years, retreating from humanity to concentrate on his work. The pandemic deepened that inclination into something more like a monastic habit, and even now, as restrictions lift and the world emerges warily into whatever comes after, he has to make an effort to remind himself there's a life outside of his own head.

What had he been dreaming about just now? Sometimes when he dreams he becomes aware that he's dreaming, but this was an ordinary dream, the kind you take to be real, no matter how absurd or impossible its events, until you wake up. He'd been a boy again, out with his father in a boat on a calm lake fringed with a lacy morning mist, the floats of their submerged lures scarcely moving on the water's glassy surface. They'd forgotten to bring the lunch Mom packed for them and they joked about being forced to eat whatever they managed to catch, right there in the boat.

What if it's a rubber boot? he asked his father.

We'll have a lot of chewing to do, said the Ben Hewitt of his dream, far more sage and unflappable than he'd ever been in life.

He looked up then to see the mist thinning. They'd been inside a cloud, he realized in wonder, and now its infinitesimal droplets were dissolving back into invisible vapour. Any moment now these hazy, drifting walls were going to lift like a curtain and all would be revealed. They would see and know where they were.

His voice trembling with excitement, he gripped his father's arm.

You need to watch this, Dad.

Ben Hewitt's eyes stayed fixed on the water, as if he hadn't heard, and Alex had no choice but to look where his father was looking. He glimpsed them then, out of reach in the green, transparent depths. They were of many shapes, hues, and kinds. They moved in the currents of their own unfathomable dreams, dreams that had never imagined an impossible creature like him.

You have to keep quiet, his father said, if you want them to bite.

As the plane descends Alex packs away the notebook, pen, and rubber-banded deck of index cards he'd brought along to distract himself during the flight. It hadn't worked. *The Almanack of Sand* is the most complicated game he's worked on yet, a world in itself with its own laws, customs, history. Now it seems childishly simple compared to what he's returning to—the life of his sister.

He'll check into his hotel and call this Michio Amano, the friend of Amery his mother told him about. He may need to rent a car too, to drive up the highway to River Meadows, or what's left of it. That's where Amery has been spending most of her time, he knows. In the ruins of the place they once lived, now a restricted area. For a long time she denied it, but their mother eventually got the truth from her—that she goes behind the wire. Her one-woman crusade to save the animals.

The runway lights appear, flashing past the window, faster and faster. Alex grips the armrests, tensing into that reckoning with reality that occurs during every landing, when you find yourself reduced to a hurtling object in an equation involving time, space, mass, and gravity, your hopes and plans no factor at all in what's happening.

He passes through the moment, or it passes through him. The plane rattles and shudders down to a human velocity. They've arrived.

The strangest thing about his life, he realizes, is that he can put his finger on the exact point where it diverged from its intended path. This remote part of the world was never supposed to have become their home. His family had only been passing through on their way to somewhere else. Then reality broke one of its own rules.

It was a northern summer evening, the sky a deep pool of blue, still infused with light even at this late hour. They had stopped for the night on their way to a city that still lay three more days of driving away, the big eastern city that would be their new home. They'd found a room at the Lulla-Bear Motel, into which they'd dumped their suitcases, then crossed the highway to get a late dinner at the nearest restaurant that looked to his mother to be halfway family-friendly.

He remembers the sight of their luggage heaped just inside the door of the dingy motel room with its lumpy, narrow beds. The rest of their worldly possessions—their furniture and lamps and cookware, his father's tools and his mother's books, his own comics and action figures and his sister Amery's stuffed animals—were in a moving van roaring through the night that had already fallen over the road ahead and that was just beginning to descend here, in River Meadows, a place he had never been and didn't like the look or the faintly sour smell of. A wave of dizziness swept over him as he imagined the shaking, rumbling van, hurtling headlong through the dark.

Here in this narrow, glaringly lit restaurant by the highway, he felt like they had fallen sideways out of their lives, like something tossed from the window of a speeding car. He was twelve, soon to be thirteen, and angry about having to leave their home and his friends. But when his father had entrusted him with the road map, asking him to keep track of the distances they were covering on their journey across the country, he'd felt a contrary eagerness growing in him. He'd always been fascinated by maps, but it was only after the first two days of tracing roads and checking off the towns they passed that he had truly begun to grasp just how enormous this land was. The names of places they had yet to reach—Portage La Prairie, Lake of the Woods, Manitou Islands—became incantations he would repeat over and over under his breath as they drove along. He looked forward to arriving in these places and seeing for himself whether they lived up to the faraway allure of their names.

The Starlite Diner was nearly empty at this late hour. A bored-looking young woman at the till told them to take any seat they liked. A single elderly couple sat with their heads bent reverently over red ceramic dishes of lasagna as if in prayer. A pale, dark-haired girl about his own age, in a black T-shirt and jeans with holes in the knees, was alone at a table across from theirs. She had a book in front of her, but her gaze was fixed straight ahead and she was chewing industriously at her thumbnail as if that was the meal she'd ordered. Her eyes were emphasized heavily with thick eyeliner. She reminded Alex of someone but he couldn't think who.

As he slid onto the cold, curving plastic bench of the booth, a familiar hollow space opened inside him, a loneliness that could take hold of him even in the presence of his family. The thought occurred to him that eating was something a person always had to do, no matter who you were or where you were going. Even if you were a murderer travelling this highway after you'd killed somebody, you would still have to pull over and put food in yourself like everyone else. When he was older and living on his own, he thought, he might well be driving somewhere and stopping in an unfamiliar little town like this in the evening and wondering what he was doing here, far away from whoever he would be living with in that hazy future time.

Out the restaurant window he could see an illuminated billboard beside the road. It showed three people standing in a green sunlit meadow: a white man in a hunter's cap and camo vest, flanked by a young Asian woman in a lab coat, holding a clipboard, and a Native man with braids, wearing a hard hat and a yellow safety vest. Their upheld faces beamed with quiet pride. Below them large, bold letters proclaimed NORTHFIRE: "WE SHALL NOT CEASE FROM EXPLORING."

Northfire. The unfamiliar word reminded him how far away from home they had already come. They weren't even supposed to be taking this highway, but his father had insisted on driving the longer, out-of-the-way route because his own father had taken him up here once on a fishing trip when he was a boy. They had been hearing all about this unforgettable trip on today's endless drive. Alex's father had even gotten choked up reminiscing about his dad, who'd died when he was still a teenager.

The waitress, a large woman with frizzy ginger hair who introduced herself as Bonnie, brought them glasses of water and took their order. Every time she hurried back into the kitchen they could hear the perky voice of a young boy asking her odd questions.

How does grass know when to grow?

Can a rock have thoughts like people?

Are clouds alive?

Alex's mother guessed it must be the waitress's son, hanging out at the restaurant during his mom's shift and getting her help with his homework.

In a short time Bonnie returned with their meals. They ate quickly, without much in the way of conversation. After a second whole day in the minivan together they were more than a little tired of each other's company. The image of the creased, sunburnt back of his father's neck still hovered unwanted in Alex's head, having been about the only thing he'd had to stare at for hours. Now that his father was facing him across the table, he didn't want to look at this side of him either. Resentment rose in him again. This man had taken them away from their home. He had taken Alex away from his friends. He had done this to all of them.

Even Amery, his bouncy nine-year-old sister, who found it hard to sit still long enough to finish a meal, was unusually quiet. Their mother gently urged her to eat, but after a few half-hearted mouthfuls she abandoned her macaroni and cheese. With a soft sigh, almost a sob, she slid down on the plastic bench and slumped sideways, her head touching the window. It was past her bedtime and she had to be exhausted, as they all were, from a long day cooped up in the car. Alex's mother and father looked at her, then at each other, and shared a fond smile. Alex rolled his eyes.

Bonnie came by to see how they were doing.

"You folks new in town?" she asked.

"Just passing through," his father said. Alex noticed the laid-back drawl he was affecting to match Bonnie's, and it annoyed him. "I was here years ago, as a kid. It's a lot busier now than it was then. I guess with the extraction industry booming and all that."

"All that for sure," Bonnie said with a shake of her head.

The restaurant doors swung open and three high school guys in sports jackets and ball caps came sauntering in. One of them grinned at Bonnie and she gave him a tight-lipped nod, the barest acknowledgement.

"It's not the town it used to be," she said.

"Growth isn't always a good thing," Alex's father said.

"Well, it makes a few people rich and keeps this town running," Bonnie said. "So that's good, I guess."

Two of the young guys had taken a booth while the third— tall, blond, grinning—stood at the counter talking to the young woman, who was laughing and twining her hair around her finger. Alex decided in an instant what kind of guy this was. He'd been pushed around and mocked by enough of them at school.

He turned back to his meal. He'd ordered a cheeseburger and french fries and had wanted a root beer float to go with them, but his mother said it was too close to bedtime for so much sugar and asked Bonnie to bring him a glass of milk instead, like he was a little kid. When the glass of plain white boredom arrived with his food he had sullenly slid it to the edge of the table, determined not to touch it. But having wolfed down his salty meal, he was thirsty. Forgetting his resolve, which was something he did often and without many qualms in those days, he reached for the glass and took a drink, glancing at the dark-haired girl in the corner booth in the hope she wasn't watching.

She wasn't. She was staring at the blond guy at the till, which wasn't what Alex wanted to see either. It bothered him when girls ignored him in favour of someone who didn't deserve their attention. But that feeling vanished in the next moment, when reality turned and showed him its other face.

As the plane rolls toward the terminal at the Pine Ridge airport, he remembers the ripple that had run through things in the diner, the way the air shimmers over asphalt on a hot day. A high-pitched whine started in his ears, like the buzzing of tiny insects. Everything in his field of awareness—the smells of hot grease and charring meat, the grimy window blinds, the posters of dead film legends and rock stars on the walls, the vintage pop music playing from the tinny speakers—it all remained, but for an instant it was changed. Or he was. He was seeing this place from some other place, but this other place was a time. A long time from now. A deep ache rose in him, a longing he could not name, as if a feeling had arrived long before the event that would cause it to be. It stood just beyond the door of his awareness, this thing that would happen, a mountain looming in the dark.

But wherever this was, he wasn't alone. The dark-haired girl was with him. She wasn't looking at him, but from her frozen posture and arrested gaze he knew she was caught in it too, a something that would come to be, unfolding from this moment, even if neither of them could ever know how or when.

Years later, at a puzzle-maker's studio in Prague, Alex would encounter an image blown up on a wall, a woodcut by the artist M. C. Escher titled *Day and Night*. In it, two flocks of birds, ducks or geese perhaps, identical except for the fact that one flock is black and the other white, appear to take shape out of the dark and light spaces between them. The two flocks soar away from their ambiguous point of origin in opposite directions above a landscape that is also a negative mirror image of itself: the same river, fields, and medieval-looking town reflect one another but in opposing shades of light and dark. The white birds fly in a perfect V formation across the nighttime half on the woodcut's right side, while the black birds wing with equal uniformity across the daytime half on the left. What makes the image even more baffling to the eye is that landscape and birds also appear to emerge from one another, the birds and the world they soar above bringing each other into being.

The image stopped his breath. If you took away the austere, mathematical harmony of the composition, that moment in the restaurant had something of this impossible, undecipherable doubling. But to truly replicate the moment you couldn't be simply a detached observer, you would have to be *inside* the image, moving like those birds in a pattern you couldn't grasp, your two selves, the one you are now and the one to come, divided by an unknowable gulf that was also you.

In the diner that evening he had a vision of being one and another at the same time, with the dark-haired girl. And then it was over. The ripple passed. The familiar, singular world was back. Garish fluorescent light, the clatter of plates, smells of hot grease and ketchup.

There were no threads. There was no pattern. Only things as they were.

The girl in the booth was looking at Alex now, her gaze fierce and frightened. Then she scowled, slid out of the booth, and headed for the door.

"Hey, you," Alex's mother said quietly.

She studied him with a hazy expression of concern, as if she'd just woken up, a mother who knows something's not right with one of her children but doesn't know what it is.

She murmured, "You were . . ."

He shook his head.

"No," he said, afraid of what she might tell him. "No, I wasn't."

She looked at him more searchingly, then she laughed softly. "Okay," she said.

Bonnie came by the table with more water.

"How you folks doing?" she asked.

"We're good," Alex's father said, sounding a little unsure. "Hey, just now . . . what was . . ."

"Oh yeah," Bonnie said with a shrug. "We get those here once in a while. The lab coat guys at Northfire call them decoherences. Most folks around here just call them wobbles. They're weird, but harmless. So, you need anything else?"

"Just the damage, thanks."

"I'll leave your check at the front. You can pay when you're ready to leave. Have a great evening."

After Bonnie left, Alex's father took out his wallet with a downtrodden sigh. Anything to do with money had that effect on him.

"Okay, people," he said, rising from the booth. "Time to motor. Alex, wake up your sister."

Amery was curled up in the corner of the booth, her eyes shut, her mouth slightly open. He'd had no awareness of it then, but Amery was a striking child, with fine white-blond hair, milky, almost translucent skin, and large pale blue eyes. To him she was only his little sister, more of an annoyance than anything, especially at times like this. He needed to get out of this place and think over what had happened. By himself, like he always did when life and the world baffled him. Amery, as usual, was holding things up.

"Come on," he said, shaking her arm. "We're going."

"You need to wake her up, honey," his mother said.

"I'm trying."

He gave Amery's arm a harder shake.

"Quit faking and let's go."

His father was at the till, paying. His mother came around to his side of the table, got Alex to scooch out, leaned over her daughter and brushed back her hair. Amery sometimes pretended to be asleep if she didn't feel like participating in some family activity, or if it was late and she had been told to go to bed. She wasn't very good at faking it, though, being such a lively kid. A good nudge or a tickle usually put an end to the act. This time there was no waking her up.

Amery was still asleep, or unconscious, when they brought her to the local hospital. She was taken to an examination room and then given a bed. Alex's mother insisted on staying with her overnight, in case she woke up.

Alex and his father returned to the motel. Ben Hewitt kept going over everything they'd done since they'd arrived in River Meadows. He had to figure this out. Solve this. He'd always had to solve things. Fix them.

"You had a glass of milk with your dinner," he said thickly from the bathroom, talking through a mouth full of toothpaste. "So did Amery, I think. Yeah, she would have. Mom wouldn't have let her have pop this late. No way. The kid's hyper enough as it is."

Alex didn't answer. He was lying down on one of the two beds, his head propped on a folded pillow, watching an episode of *Space Dogs*. It was one he had seen before, but he kept his attention fixed on it because he wanted his father to stop talking and leave him alone. He was worried about Amery too, but he was determined to keep as much distance between himself and his father as he could. After all, this was his fault, for bringing them here.

His father spat into the bathroom sink.

"But milk wouldn't do that to someone," he said, rinsing off his toothbrush. "And neither would food. That's not . . . I mean, what happened to Amery isn't food poisoning. Probably not an allergy, either. Nope, she's never been allergic to anything that I know of. No, that's not it. I've heard things about this town. I mean, this stuff they've been digging up—this ghost ore or whatever they call it. It's pretty rare, I guess, but it's got to be like anything else that comes out of the ground. Coal. Oil. Gas. Right? You get too close to substances like that, or inhale too much, or it gets into your pores, your lungs, it's gonna mess with you. Of course it is. Still, those excavation pits are miles away from this place, so you wouldn't get particulates coming down *here*. How could the ore screw with someone's head *here*? Right? No, that doesn't make sense. We can rule that out too. Then there's those wobbles. What did Bonnie say the scientists call them? Deterrences?"

"Decoherences." Alex couldn't help correcting him.

"Right. She said they're harmless. And nothing happened to the rest of us. So that doesn't really add up. What do you think?"

He came out of the bathroom and started to unpack the rest of his things, still talking, thinking out loud, as he did when there was a problem to solve. Alex knew that his father was struggling to ignore his fears, to remain upbeat and rational during this crisis, working hard to stick to the ordinary things: hold a conversation, brush his teeth, put away his shirts and socks, but he despised him for it—and for the way the dread at the edges of his father's voice was creeping into him too and magnifying his own fear.

"I don't know," Alex finally responded. He kept his gaze on the television screen, on the bright commotion of his favourite animated show, a manic half-hour of cartoon animal slapstick with an edge of satire, not really a children's show even if it looked like one, full of clever rapid-fire pop culture and political references, many of which Alex didn't entirely get, though he often laughed and pretended he did. You had to pay attention in order to keep up.

But he wasn't keeping up. He was still thinking about that moment in the restaurant and wondering if it would happen again, transforming the familiar world into a strange mirror of itself. Him too. And he was terrified that Amery would never wake up. We shouldn't even be here, in this weird, stupid town, he thought. We should be on our way to where we were going. No, we should be turning around and heading home. Yet, at the same time, part of him wanted more than anything to go back to that other reality he had briefly stepped into, to meet his other self again. To find out, if he could, who that girl was to him. Or would be.

"All I felt when the wobble went through was a second or two of *whoa, what the*—" Alex's father said. "That's all. Nothing happened to you, I guess?"

"No."

His father folded back the quilt on his bed. "Your mother said something to you, just before Bonnie came with the water."

"No, she didn't," Alex said.

One of the Space Dogs, Barkley Rover, had gone on a space walk and had fallen into a black hole, which was stretching him like a piece of soft taffy.

"Yeah, she did," his father insisted. "She said something about *you*, didn't she?"

Alex shrugged.

"I don't remember."

Barkley had been rescued from the black hole and lay now in a heap like a limp, coiled mass of canine spaghetti.

Alex's father forced a grin.

"Anyhow, I noticed you checking out that girl in the other booth. She was pretty cute, huh?"

As soon as the words were out of his mouth he frowned and turned away. In trying to lighten the mood, he'd handed Alex a way to get back at him: they did not talk about this stuff. Despite the fact that a new *Space Dogs* episode that he really wanted to see was just starting, he shut off the television, rolled onto his side so that he was facing the door, and pulled the covers over himself. He was stuck with his father in this cramped, stuffy motel room that smelled of cigarette smoke and cleaning solution, but at least he could turn his back on him. The bedsheets were stiff, unfamiliar smelling, not his own sheets. The pillow was rough against his face and at the same time too soft to support his head. Unlike his own pillow, which they'd left in the back seat of the van during all the uproar over Amery. He didn't want to go out and get it, though, because he would have to ask his father for the keys and there was no way he was doing that.

"Yeah, time to turn in," his father said after a long silence. "I'm sure things will be better tomorrow. We just have to stay positive. Everything's going to work itself out."

Alex didn't respond. His father's mattress squeaked and creaked idiotically as he climbed heavily into the other bed and fussed around getting comfortable. He switched off the bedside lamp, then heaved a long sigh. "Night, son," he said.

Alex waited for what seemed a punishing-enough length of time, and then it felt too late to reply at all.

He lay there listening to his father's breathing, keeping still and making his own breathing as quiet as he could. He was determined his father wouldn't even *hear* him, as if the ordinary noises of him falling asleep would have been some kind of concession. Let him hear silence and wonder if he was alone in the room. But at last, the long day and what had happened at the restaurant chipped away at what was left of his sullen determination. Drowsiness began to seep through the cracks and as it did, random, disconnected words and images rose up out of the dark inside him, shards and flashes of the day mixed with flickers of thought that rose and sank so fast he could barely grasp what they had been.

Out of this heaving flotsam a story began to take shape. *Space Dogs*. He and his family were in an episode of *Space Dogs*, his mom and dad and Amery too. They were helping the Rover family after their starship had crashed on the street in front of the motel. Although the motel looked a lot like their old house back home. In fact it *was* their old house, he saw now, the one they lived in before his father lost his job and lined up a new one on the other side of the country. The Rover family was moving in with them, Barkley and Collie Rover and their kids, Fetch and Lulu, and their robot cat, Spam. But something was wrong with Spam. His processors had to be malfunctioning, because his walk was all jerky and wrong, and pieces of metal were falling off of him. Alex followed Spam, picking up what he was leaving in his wake as he lurched and jolted around the room. In his hands the shiny metal pieces turned black and began to smoke, like hot coals. It hurt but he couldn't let go of them. It was up to him to save Spam. Someone asked him if he needed help, and it was the dark-haired girl from the restaurant, but she wasn't quite the same. She was older, and friendly. Alex told her everything was fine but added that he didn't know what was happening to Spam and he was really tired and maybe she could help keep him from falling apart. The girl didn't reply, but she dragged over a folding chair and Alex sat down in it. Then she handed him a glass of water. He dropped the burning pieces of metal in the glass, one after another. The water hissed and steamed as the pieces returned to shiny metallic perfection.

That should take care of it, the girl said.

She had spoken to him. Then he understood.

This is a dream, he said.

He looked up. The girl wasn't there. Everyone else was gone too. Down the hallway was a room he hadn't noticed before. The door was open and the room was full of a wonderful blue light that made him happy just to see it. In the room water was falling, as if the roof was gone and that part of the house was open to the sky.

Then Alex was back in the motel room, wide awake. He heard his father's steady breathing. The neon motel sign cast a blue glow on the window curtain. Outside, in the night, it was raining.

ALL-WEATHER NOTEBOOK No. 25

June 17, 3:10 p.m., Northfire site access road

The downpour isn't letting up. Waiting it out in the abandoned Buick Skyhawk. The doors are gone and there's no glass left in the windows. I'll be able to see or hear anything in time to make an escape if I need to.

When I climbed into the front seat just now I thought of my brother. Wasn't sure why, then remembered: this car was already here before everything went wrong. We'd stumbled across it once when we were kids, the summer we arrived in River Meadows. One of our expeditions. Well, my expeditions. Alex came along because he had to. Our parents insisted he keep an eye on me whenever I went wandering off.

We were excited to find this rusty old wreck. Alex pretended he was driving it, that we were going on vacation. Then we heard that sound from the glove compartment, deep, low humming I could feel in my stomach, my chest. Like it was coming from inside me.

I remember reaching for the compartment latch. Alex shouting at me not to open it. I did anyway. I knew what was making the sound and I wanted to see.

Alex took off running. I stayed.

Not a single bee stung me. They kept on crawling and buzzing in and out of their hive, like they had no idea I was there or it just didn't matter to them. I think that was the first time I ever had that feeling: that there's an entire world around us that doesn't know or care that we're here.

Checked the compartment again just now. Nothing. The bees are long gone.

CLAIRE

As she and the other passengers are disembarking, her drowsy attention is drawn to two people ahead of her in the jet bridge. She hadn't noticed them on the plane—a middle-aged woman and a teenage boy. They're holding hands, which strikes her as odd. The boy's other hand grips the handle of a small animal carrier with something in it. For a moment the moving bodies ahead of her shift and she gets a closer look. It's a tiny dog, head between its paws. The thing hadn't barked or even whined during the entire eleven-hour flight. Then she catches another glimpse—there's something a little too *sculpted* about that sleeping dog—and she realizes it's an unusually lifelike stuffed animal. The boy must have severe travel anxiety, or maybe autism. This is how they keep him calm in unfamiliar, stressful surroundings, by giving him something to look after. It also explains the hand-holding.

Claire wonders what it would be like to travel with someone who depended on you that way, someone you could never let out of your sight or stop worrying about. But she's tired, and besides, it hardly seems worth the effort to imagine an experience she will never have.

———

Through the monorail's droplet-stippled window she looks down into canyons of industrial complexes, open-air markets, a rail yard, the sine curve of a canal. In the brief spaces between crowded apartment blocks she glimpses the sea, an expanse of dull, dinted sheet metal. The track soars over a freeway packed with vehicles that don't appear to be moving, as if time has frozen in the world below her. A shirtless young man dances on the hood of a car, or maybe he's flailing in mad rage—hard to say which from this height.

Too much to look at. To process. She turns from the window, and flips through the barely touched guidebook she brought with her, the one she's here to update. It has everything the contemporary traveller has learned to expect from a guidebook and is convinced they need: glossy pages with ample colour photography, artfully rendered maps at different scales, breezily informative sidebars about interesting local customs, places to visit, flora and fauna. If only such books really prepared you for what happens after you arrive.

One of the sidebars draws her eye.

Some islanders still carry with them a small hollow object called a quith, most often made of clay or copper and worn around the neck on a leather cord. The quith looks something like a small tea-steeping ball, and usually contains a pinch of soil from the region where the wearer was born, although some keep tiny animal bones in theirs, or plant matter like seeds or dried flower petals. The original purpose of the quith is a subject of dispute among ethnographers, but it may have been a talisman against drowning.

She hasn't seen anyone wearing one of these, not yet, but maybe the locals keep them out of sight, to avoid awkward questions from foreigners.

The train glides to a halt sooner than she expects, but it turns out they haven't reached the hotel district yet. The PA system announces that the track past this point has been closed for repairs and all passengers must transfer to shuttle buses.

Claire shuffles out with the others onto a too-small outdoor platform with her wheeled suitcase and backpack. There are signs indicating which shuttle bus to take for which group of hotels, and all is noise and bodies and frayed tempers as people squirm and squeeze and push their way to where they need to go. Claire keeps herself as untouched by it all as she can.

The rest of her journey takes place on a jouncing, mildew-smelling old bus that appears to have been hauled out of storage just for this purpose. Out the streaked windows there's nothing to see but pavements flowing with rivulets of rainwater, and hordes of hunched, faceless people hurrying under umbrellas. It's mid-afternoon but already as dark as twilight.

She sits next to an elderly British man who immediately strikes up a conversation. Wherever she travels people, total strangers, see her as someone to confide in. They sit down next to her in airport lounges, at bus stations, hostels, cafés, and before long they're telling her their stories. Maybe she's gotten too good at being a blank page. If there's nothing here to read, people will write over it.

The elderly man tells her he's come to visit his ex-wife, Abigail. They divorced decades ago and she emigrated here with their son to live with her new husband, a television executive. He was a fine person, a good man, who had died three years earlier of pancreatic cancer. The elderly man and his ex-wife have remained friends over the years. She has Parkinson's now, lives in a care home and no longer travels, although that was something she once loved. The more far-flung and unpredictable the itinerary, the better she liked it. He himself is retired now from the engineering firm he helped found over forty years ago (they did key design work for the Thames Barrier project, which is a whole other story) and he visits Abigail when he can. She's lonely these days. Their son moved to Cape Town, and has a busy, important job in marine law and a young family of his own to look after.

"Abby's roaming days are over," the man says with a sigh. "But she likes to hear about my adventures. That's something at least I can bring her. A good story."

He proceeds to tell Claire one of these stories, from a trip to South Africa a few years back to visit his son and two grandchildren. They had a wonderful time whale-watching out of Hermanus, but after a while the kids really tuckered him out and so he decided to take an excursion by himself to Zimbabwe, to Victoria Falls. After all, it could be his last chance to see this great natural wonder. The old bucket list, right?

He booked a flight to Livingstone and checked in at an old colonial hunting lodge converted into a luxury hotel. It was so close to the falls you could hear the thunderous roaring day and night. You could feel it too, when you put your hand on the paving stones in the hotel courtyard.

One evening, after an astonishing dinner of sizzling kudu and wild boar cutlets, he went out onto to the terrace to have a drink and look at the river. He'd been there just long enough to start nodding off over his sundowner cocktail when someone shouted, *There's an elephant!* Well, that woke him right up. He hadn't seen any wildlife yet on this expensive trip. He looked where everyone else was looking and pointing.

The elephant was in the river.

His fellow tourists leaped out of their lounge chairs and hurried down the well-manicured lawn to the bank, some still carrying their drinks. He went with them, of course, already thinking about how he would turn this into an exciting tale for Abby the next time he saw her.

"And there it was," the elderly man says. "Big as life."

The elephant was wading slowly across the rushing Zambezi, less than the length of a cricket pitch from the cloud and thunder of the greatest cataract in Africa.

The man learned later that the elephant had been attempting to cross into Zambia, the river here marking the border between the two countries. Its goal most likely was to elude poachers, who had increased in number during the last few years of social breakdown and economic hardship (weapons fire from the Zimbabwean side had become a common sound in the area, one of the few noises that could rise above the ever-present roar of the falls). Two smaller, younger elephants waited on the shore for their older, more experienced companion to find the best way across. This was an immemorial elephant fording place, but the river was higher and the current stronger than it had been in years. And on the Zambian side a brand-new five-star hotel had just been built on a formerly much-travelled wildlife corridor, so that animals seeking to cross were forced to divert to less familiar, more risky channels.

The man watched and waited with the other guests, staff, and some wildlife officers who'd appeared when the commotion started. The elephant waded out, backed up and tried again, plunged, floundered, found a secure foothold and then lost it, got swept into the current and battled his way back from the brink. People took pictures, shouted encouragement, angrily declared that someone had to do something. Some wept.

Did the poor beast understand its situation? Did it grasp what lay in store for it if it failed? It must have known, or one assumes it would have just plunged right in and started swimming.

But the elephant didn't do that.

"I think it simply didn't see any choice but to cross there, where humans were watching," the man tells Claire. "Humans without guns, I mean. As if it knew our presence was at least some sort of protection."

Whenever it could clear water from its trunk, the elephant called to the youngsters waiting on the bank, an exhausted bellow, almost a scream, that they answered with their own shrill cries. It might have been warning them to keep out of the river. Or letting them know that it hadn't given up yet.

The elephant made it as far as the last rocky islet before the Zambian shore, and plunged into the final channel that would bring it to safety. People began to applaud and cheer wildly. But the long struggle had taken too great a toll. It had no strength left to fight the current.

They all watched in horror as the elephant was swept helplessly over the brink of the falls and into the churning chaos known as the Boiling Pot.

Days later the elephant's carcass was found downstream, washed up on the Zimbabwean side, stripped of its tusks.

When the elderly man finishes his story, Claire responds with appropriate phrases of regret, though she studies him more closely now that he's shared this tragic tale of an animal's unnecessary death. She wonders if this really is a chance encounter on a hotel shuttle bus or something more.

"Never seen an elephant," she offers blandly, as if it's a gap in her experience she has no interest in filling. "I mean, in person."

"Never?"

"The town I come from didn't have a zoo and I've never visited one."

He asks her where she's from. She names the place truthfully, in case someone really is on her trail. On these trips she's learned it's best to keep the lies to a minimum so you don't get caught in your own tangled web. He's heard of her home town, most people have, even if they're not quite sure where to find it on a map. He blinks, taking in this surprising news, but he shows some restraint and leaves the subject alone.

"So, what brings you to this soggy island?" he asks instead.

"I'm updating a travel guide," Claire says, then decides to offer a little more. "The publisher wants to add material to the new edition, about tourism in dangerous places."

She hopes that's enough. To maintain her cover as a writer she should be talking more effusively, asking questions, even being nosy, but she just can't summon the energy for it right now. Once she gets to where she's going, she'll be more focused. She tells herself she's still in transit, so it doesn't count.

The man's bushy white eyebrows lift.

"Ah, yes. I suppose this *is* a dangerous place, though speaking for myself, I've been coming here for years and it's never crossed my mind. Of course, nowadays no place is really safe, is it? I mean, there are calamities everywhere, all the time, and all of them connected in one way or another. We're all on the same planet now, like it or not. No escaping that. And on top of everything else, there are those clouds. The ones they created out of nanobots, or whatever it was, to fix our broken atmosphere. Dear god. Hackable clouds—that was the brilliant idea. Send them where you like, make them rain when and how much you want, artificially brighten them to bounce light and heat back into space. What could possibly go wrong?"

He snorts.

"Finally, they're admitting that some of them have stopped responding to their controllers. Is anyone surprised? The kite strings have snapped and now these things, these feral clouds as they call them, are wandering the sky, doing whatever they please. They could be causing more storms or making them worse. They could be locking up water vapour or changing the composition of gases in the atmosphere. No one knows."

She's heard rumours of this on her travels but hasn't paid much attention. To her the idea of persistent, undissolving clouds with their own mysterious objectives sounded like yet another lunatic conspiracy theory.

"Of course, I don't understand any of it," the man says. "This whole cloud business is pretty nebulous to me."

He dredges up a chuckle at his own joke, his eyes awash in old man tears.

"Which is not to say," he adds, "that we haven't had some successes in holding back the tides of destruction. One could say the Thames Barrier was prescient in this regard . . ."

He's found a way to bring the conversation around to what is clearly his life's great achievement, and proceeds to describe the famous flood control project's challenges and rewards in mind-numbing detail. By the time he's done, Claire decides this must have been a chance meeting after all.

The lobby of the Trident Regency is hushed, cloister-like. After the damp, rattling ride in, Claire feels as if she's wandered into an enchanted grotto.

The clerk stands poised at the front desk, all in black, head bowed over his computer like a priest absorbed in his prayer book.

As Claire checks in, a rack of tourist maps shimmies across the marble countertop toward her. There's a tinkling sound overhead and she looks up to see the chandelier's crystal droplets shivering. She remembers she's on an island rocked frequently by earthquakes and her heart lurches. She grips the edge of the counter. This is really happening. This could be the *one*.

As the tremor subsides, the clerk says, without even looking up, "Been doing that all week." Claire breathes deliberately, evenly.

He hands her a room key card, along with a flat, square plastic packet that looks like a condom wrapper.

"This is . . . ?"

"A skin patch, ma'am, for you to put on when you get to your room." The clerk's English is inflected with that ambiguous local accent. "It's mandatory now for anyone staying longer than a week. We're sorry for the inconvenience."

"You mean I have to wear this thing. On my body."

"For the duration of your visit, yes. It's perfectly safe. Most people say they don't even notice they have it on after a while. It will help you adjust to the tap water, the particulates in the air. You know, a different environment. Just a precaution. Instructions are on the package."

She's heard vaguely about such things as a possibility in the coming years, as the planet lurches closer to environmental collapse. *Priming*, they call it. She didn't think anyone was actually doing it yet.

She tucks the packet away in her bag, then checks out the rack of maps. Might be a good idea. She takes one.

"Those are out of date," the clerk says. "There've been a lot of changes lately. Some of the coast roads are under."

"Construction?"

"Water."

The island's early civilization collapsed around 4000 BCE as a result of geological and oceanic upheaval. It has been argued that the stratified, imperialist culture hastened its own destruction by stripping the island of trees and other scarce natural resources to pursue endless war against rival sea powers in North Africa and the Mediterranean. Until the major seismic event that briefly inundated much of the island's landmass.

Imagine it: A civilization at the dazzling height of its pride, power, and influence when without warning, utter destruction is unleashed. The earth convulses and buckles. Chasms yawn open, swallowing whole buildings, entire streets. Plumes of fire soar to the heavens, creating feverish pyrocumulonimbus clouds that pour down volleys of hail. The screams of the dying rend the ash-choked air. And when it seems to the few who have survived that the worst has come and gone, the Great Wave. By the time it's all over, a third of the island's former land mass lies forever under the sea.

The only surviving record of this legendary cataclysm exists in two philosophical dialogues by the Greek philosopher Plato, who gives a date for the disaster of 9000 BCE, and mistakenly asserts that the entire landmass sank beneath the waves. Nevertheless, it is true the island remained almost uninhabited for centuries, as a result of ongoing volcanic activity, except for a small population of indigenous u'Yoi on the northern coast. Legends about this lost civilization somewhere in the Atlantic persisted through the classical era, until the island was rediscovered by Portuguese mariners in the fourteenth century, who named it Joia Verde and claimed in it in the name of their king.

Over the succeeding centuries the island became a bargaining chip in a colonial game of musical chairs that saw it fought over, occupied, and renamed in turn by Spain (Tritón), the Netherlands (Inktvis Eiland) and, briefly, France (Jouissance). During the Napoleonic Wars, the two major ports of Atlantische Haven and Asteria were bombed and partially destroyed by the British Navy. In 1821 the island was finally ceded to Britain under the treaty of Corvo, and its original name restored. The colony remained an isolated strategic outpost with a mainly agrarian economy until independence was achieved in 1946 and the pro-development New Emergence party came to power. The economic and technological surge of the last few decades has astonished the world.

And through it all, the recurring quakes, the hurricanes and volcanic eruptions—these ever-present reminders of mortality—have shaped the people, made them who they are. Risk and impermanence give the islanders their keen appreciation of life, their drive to achieve miracles.

"Things falling apart," local celebrity Aphrodaddy Eleganza said recently, "is kind of our religion."

The first thing she does in the privacy of her room is throw up into the toilet. It's the jitters that come at the start of every job. She's trained herself to deal with them right away and move on. She knows what she's here to acquire, but that's all. It could be hours or days before someone makes contact to give her the location and time of the transaction. All she can do is wait and keep herself busy with the guidebook update.

The view from the balcony is fog, with a few red blinking lights on the roofs of unseen towers. She can't see the sea but she hears it, or imagines she does, in the brief lulls of the city's roar. She strains to listen and feels a long ice-cold needle slide into her brain through the top of her skull. Long flights always bring this on. The solution is a hot shower.

In the bathroom she turns on the taps in the stall, and a groan rises from the pipes like the dead waking from slumber. She steps back in alarm. Then moves closer again. The water, coming out in alternating gushes and trickles, has a faint coppery tinge. Or it may just be the oddly dim lighting in this bathroom. She catches some of the splattering water in her palm, sniffs it. Metallic, with a faint briny underscent. She considers calling the desk and asking to have someone come and have a look. In the end she doesn't call, just stands in the unsteady stream of water, keeping it as hot as she can bear.

The blow-dryer is broken. She could ask for a working one but by now she doesn't want even the brief contact of someone at her door to deliver it. While her hair dries, she'll check her email. She stretches out on the bed and opens her laptop, but she can't get a connection. This time she does phone the front desk and is told the Wi-Fi is down. Something about storm damage to an important cable somewhere.

This is a city famous for its technological marvels, and so far she feels like she's come to the back of beyond.

As she's dressing to go get some dinner she remembers the little packet, picks it up off the dresser and squints at the tiny print.

DermAegis
Acclimatizer and Environmental Buffer

Recommended for stays of a week or more. Wash
application area before use. Peel off covering and
apply patch to upper arm, inner thigh, or abdomen.
Do not apply to face or genitals. Do not ingest. Some
temporary discoloration of skin may occur. Do not
remove: patch will fall off on its own in 4 to 6 weeks.

There's no list of ingredients, just a phone number and URL
for more information or in case of allergic reaction.

Allergic reaction. They have got to be kidding. What does
this thing *do*? She tosses the packet on the quilt. Not a chance.
She'll acclimatize the old-fashioned way, by just being here.

When she's finished dressing and is checking her hair in the
bathroom mirror, she glances at the rivulet of coppery water
in the bottom of the shower stall. *You washed in that.* She
finds the packet, tears it open, and takes out the square patch.
One side has a pale blue gel-like surface. She peels off the transparent covering, brings the gel side to her nose and sniffs.
A plastic bandage smell, one of the immemorial scents of childhood that take you right back. Playing outside all day long in
the brief northern summer. Running, jumping, falling off bikes,
scraping knees. Who she was back then, if that was really her.
She can't connect that little girl to the person she is now.

She presses the patch to her upper left arm. It feels cool and
after a moment slightly numbing, like an insect bite cream.

She has dinner in the hotel restaurant, with the travel guide
and a coil-bound notebook open on the table beside her plate,

so she can sketch out an itinerary for the next few days. For a main course she chooses ambarie, which the dignified, greying waiter informs her is the national dish: braised sea anemone stuffed with turbot mousse and rice dyed blue-black with squid ink. It doesn't resemble any food she's ever tried, anywhere, and she eats slowly, pondering what if anything this meal tells her about these people. All that comes to her is an unaccountable sadness, which she suspects is mostly her own contribution. An image floats in her head of a frozen ocean. A sheet of grey ice like solid metal, and underneath it black depths.

She orders a second glass of the house wine. Not like her to do that. To indulge. There's a sidebar in the guidebook that would remind her why she's really here, but she's avoided looking at it since she landed. She doesn't need to—she's read it so often she knows it pretty much by heart.

The remnant of an old growth rainforest on the volcano's west slope is home to the sapphire frog, a rare and beautifully coloured amphibian that lives beside streams and among the damp leaf rot on the forest floor. A species belonging to the Hylidae family, adults are between 3 to 6 centimetres long, with short limbs projecting at right angles from the body, a blunt head, and a vestigial tail that often remains after the tadpole stage. The frog's most notable feature is its deep indigo markings, often dusted with small gold or copper freckles. It has one of the longest life spans of any amphibian, with some specimens thought to have survived twenty-five years or more in the wild.

Already threatened by habitat loss, the sapphire frog has become critically endangered as a result of illegal trafficking in animal parts. The frog's colourful skin (repellent to other animals but only mildly toxic to humans) is prized as an ingredient in traditional medicines in Southeast Asia and elsewhere. Dried, the skins are ground into a powder and added to elixirs that are believed to increase human longevity. As a result the species is in serious decline, despite severe new laws against animal trafficking that in one recent case resulted in a prison sentence of seven years.

Claire notices her heart thumping. She gulps down the rest of the wine, pays the check, and when she returns to the lobby, decides to take an evening walk. Look around, actually talk to people, put in some time on the ostensible job she's here to do, while she waits for further instructions on the other one. In the lobby she remembers she's supposed to call Arthur, her editor, to let him know she arrived.

No signal on her phone.

Claire stands in the middle of the lobby, suddenly adrift. The light from outside is a dull sea-green. She's had too much wine. Or maybe not enough. What time is it? The hour when checking your watch tells you nothing.

Without warning a chasm opens. She teeters on the edge, breathless.

Someone has found out why she's here. What she's come to do. They must know. That man on the shuttle bus and his random story about elephants and poachers. Endangered wildlife and the people who profit from it. That couldn't have been a coincidence. They're probably on her trail right now, watching her every move.

She lowers herself onto one of the red leather sofas. Back straight, feet planted firmly. Eyes closed. *Breathe.*

What the fuck is happening? She gets little attacks of nerves from time to time, and has trained herself to shake them off without a backward glance. But this. Whatever this is keeps coming in rolling waves, one after another. *Breathe.* She's always told herself she *needs* to be a little on edge in order to stay alert and ready. On her first few jobs she took a pill when she got jittery, but she didn't like the way the drug fogged her awareness, slowed her reaction time, made her susceptible to useless daydreaming. She's not carrying any of those pills on this trip. That may have been a mistake.

Watch. Behave normally. *Breathe, damn it.*

A man and a woman enter the lobby from outside. Probably locals, from their clothes and something in the proprietary way they've entered this space, as if it's their own living room and no one else is here. They're arguing in heated undertones: it's fairly certain she didn't want to come in and he won, for now. At the desk he talks to the clerk, pointing out the door and shrugging. Claire can't catch any of what he's saying. The woman stands apart, staring out the windows into the street. She's wearing a long, shimmering green gown, like they've just come from the opera. And maybe they have. The city has a stunning new concert hall, built right on the waterfront, something it occurs to her she should check out, for the guide-book. She's heard that a local composer is doing some sort of human-dolphin collaborative opera. The dolphins are actually creating and performing some of the music.

For some reason, that thought causes another swell of anxiety. She digs her fingernails into the sofa's arm.

The clerk has turned his monitor so he and the man can both see it and he seems to be patiently explaining something, making slow, sweeping gestures, like the frond of an undersea plant waving in the current. The man finally shrugs and stalks back toward the doors without even a glance at the woman. She waits a moment, shooting a glare of angry humiliation at his back, then she follows.

Even the natives get lost . . .

Claire's heart starts hammering again. She needs to think. This place. Facts. Her cover, the guidebook updates. The blog she maintains on the publisher's website. There's legitimate work to do here, no matter what. While she's waiting to be contacted she can get out there and explore, find a couple of good sidebar stories about how the locals cope with the ever-present threat of environmental calamity. She's read about the feverish growth that followed the discovery and mining of vast new orichalcum deposits offshore, and with it the alarming increase in seismic events, flooding, volcanic activity, and deeply weird weather. One positive outcome of the boom is that it led to a blossoming of innovation in science, medicine, art—a renaissance the locals have named the Surge. There have even been rumours of a miraculous new energy technology in secret development. A virtually free source of inexhaustible power. Clearly they're not using it yet for the blow-dryers and the Wi-Fi.

Was that another tremor just now?

She rises so quickly a wave of vertigo sends her lurching sideways. Steadying herself against a pillar she waits while her heart slows again and her breathing settles. People passing through the lobby give her strange looks.

"I'm working on a guidebook," she tells the bartender in the hotel lounge.

He's curly-headed, his eyes an arresting sea-green. The level of good-looking that makes you keep taking glances to confirm what you're actually seeing as much as to enjoy the symmetry of something well made. He's at least ten years younger than she is, she estimates. There's a faint aquamarine tinge to his pale skin, most noticeable along the wrists and the cords of his neck muscles when he turns his head. Which, she remembers from her research, probably means he's one of the rare locals whose DNA goes back to the original inhabitants of the island. Not full-blooded u'Yoi but descended from them.

"So you're a writer," he says, bending his English vowels even more elusively than the desk clerk had. Usually she avoids talking to bartenders and other people in customer service. Such casual conversations end up sounding scripted. Which for her is usually true, it's just that she doesn't want attention drawn to that fact.

"You could say that, I suppose. More of a glorified fact-checker, really. I'm here to update some of the material for a new edition."

"Have you been to the island before?"

"First time. The publisher wanted a different perspective. You know, someone to look at things with fresh eyes. So here I am."

Annoyed at her own nerved-up chattiness, she takes a gulp of the drink she'd hastily ordered from the cocktail menu. A coral sunset, whatever that is. Rum, lime, maybe mango, and an after-hint of something fishy on her tongue. Reminiscent of the water in her shower. It should be a revolting combination, but strangely enough it works, by coming at you in stages like an unfolding memory. And it's doing what she needs it to do. The chasm is still there, but now she can glance down into it without feeling much of anything.

He asks her about the other places she's visited. They chat for a while about her work and his. He's a grad student in applied physics at the university. The bartending helps pay the bills.

When he leans forward to wipe the counter, she glimpses a small, silver quith on a chain around his neck. She wonders what he keeps in it.

He goes to serve another customer, and when he returns to see how she's doing the drink has softened her defences.

"Coral sunset," she says with a grin. "More like coral lights out."

"You want another?"

"Better not."

"I'm Andros," he says, surprising her by taking this beyond anonymity so quickly. Smiling was a mistake, as it usually is.

"Claire."

They shake hands and she pulls her fingers quickly from his confident, cool grip.

"I should probably turn in," she says. "Busy day tomorrow."

There's a look in his eyes for a moment. Alarmed, or no, *sad*. Like he's seen her tomorrow already and it's not going to be good. Then he brightens.

"I'm off work the next couple of days. I'd be happy to show you around, if you like. With all the repairs and the detours it's a real maze out there."

He's only being friendly, she tells herself, and says, "The thing is, I prefer to just dive in on my own. In a new place. Get first impressions, right? But maybe . . ."

"Of course, that makes sense," he says with a shrug. "I hope it goes well for you."

While they've been chatting, three big men in suits have sauntered in, hoisted themselves onto bar stools and are now gazing around with stone-cold eyes, as if scanning for possible threats. Andros goes over to serve them. With thick accents they ask him about what beer is available and debate their choices with one another in what she's pretty sure is Russian.

They look like small-town butchers stuffed awkwardly into expensive clothes, and she decides they must be newly minted petro-millionaires, sniffing out potential investments in the island's red-hot energy sector.

She watches Andros, so slender and fluid before these dour, beefy men and their self-important taking up of space. Even more than his skin, the easy, supple unselfconsciousness of his movements intrigues her. He's so *fresh*, she thinks, surprised at herself. Like a creature that's just climbed out of the ocean to breathe air for the first time.

The local currency rises and falls on seismic readings as much as it does on economic indicators. When the exchange rate is favourable, North Africans, Europeans, and Americans from both hemispheres flock to the island on brief visits known informally as "shop drops."

Get in, do your business, get out quick. Just in case.

The next morning she's awake before sunrise. Like a bird. Whatever had pounced on her is gone. Of course it's gone. She's found her nerve again, like she always does.

After coffee in the hotel restaurant (no text yet about where and when the hand-off will take place), she visits the indoor athletic park next door. To get there she passes through a skywalk that's mostly glass, even under her feet, so that she's surrounded on all sides by mist and rain. In the haze beneath her, the head and taillights of slow-moving cars on the street glow like the lures of anglerfish.

The park's showpiece is the enormous wave pool, said to be the largest in the world. She changes into her bathing suit and walks out into the vast floodlit space. The pool is clearly designed to evoke the island's past: around the perimeter are arranged artfully broken and leaning classical columns and other fragments of antediluvian architecture. Along the walls runs an ancient-looking mosaic depicting leaping dolphins and spouting whales.

Waterslides in bright neon colours loop and spiral down through the fake ruins to the pool, which is already filled with people, mostly little kids and teenagers, bobbing, splashing, shrieking. Along the curve of the concrete beach, painted the colour of warm pinkish sand, young mothers watch over toddlers wading in the shallows and older couples lounge in deck chairs with paperbacks and tropical-looking drinks. A lifeguard perched on a tall chair blows his whistle and points at two kids engaged in a towel-flicking duel. At the far end of the pool rises a massive structure that's been painted to resemble a rock shelf under a storm-blackened sky, shot through with shafts of lightning. Every few minutes the blast of a foghorn ruptures the air and a few moments later the waves surge from under the rock shelf, growing quickly to towering whitecaps. When they've crossed the length of the pool and reached the shallows, the waves subside to a gentle surf.

The whole thing, Claire realizes with a tightening of her chest—the broken columns, the storm-cloud mural, the warning blast, the bodies in the water bobbing and shrieking as the waves engulf them—is a memorial to the long-ago cataclysm that brought the island to its knees. Or a rehearsal for the next one. She thinks of her hometown—how she left just in time, before it suffered its own little apocalypse. She'd taken that close call as a warning. Keep moving. Don't get attached. It's all going up in flames anyhow. Or sinking under the waves. In the meantime do whatever you need to do to stay afloat.

At any rate, this definitely is one for the guidebook. People coming to terms with the end of the world by frolicking in it.

The spent waves rush up to her bare toes and slink back. She takes a few steps, until the water is washing over her feet, her ankles. It's chilly at first, then pleasantly tepid.

She walks into the surf. Up to her knees, her pelvis, to just below her breasts. She pushes on, sweeping her arms to the sides to help propel herself forward, until she's among the bathers with their beach balls, pool noodles, and kickboards, all facing the far end of the pool, eagerly awaiting the horn and the next swell. Claire keeps going, aiming for the dark space underneath the fake rock shelf, a cave mouth where the wave originates.

She reaches the bright yellow rope with floats strung across the width of the pool, a sign hanging from it warning bathers not to swim beyond this point. Claire stops here, bobbing and sweeping her arms. She looks around and sees the lifeguard watching. If she goes any farther there will be a whistle and she'll be ordered back. Not worth it to draw that much attention to herself. She stays where she is.

The deeper water rocks and tugs at her, pushing her off her tiptoes. She feels the urge to just give in, to let this element, so much more powerful than her, move her where it will. She's made up of much the same thing, after all. A human being is mostly just water with a sense of purpose.

The horn sounds, thrumming in her bones. A moment later the choppy surface swells, rises, slides forward, tumbling toward her, seeming to climb itself as it comes, building to a slope, a hill, a mountain, white foam churning at the crest and a gelid green cavern revealed beneath. Children shriek behind her and teenage boys roar like berserkers charging into battle. The wave muscles over her, shoving her backwards and driving her under, into the muted world under the surface. Strange how such peace exists inside tumult. Scrambling and thrashing, she rights herself, kicks upward and surfaces into the after-trough, sputtering and gasping, not sure for a moment which way she's facing and where the next wave is coming from. She finds she's drifted into the midst of other bodies bobbing, twisting, darting, and lunging every which way. Too many others too close.

Enough of this. She's let herself go and the water has rebuked her for forgetting why she's here. She propels herself backwards, away from the rope and into the safer zone among the other bathers, keeping the rock shelf in sight.

She exits the pool, her feet slapping on the wet pink concrete. All she wants to do now is get out of here.

In her hurry she takes the wrong door and finds herself in a place she doesn't recognize—a narrow corridor and a flight of stairs that leads down to another pool, low-ceilinged and windowless, the water lit from underneath by blue subaqueous lights. The air is muggy with steam.

Some of the men and women here are naked. There are no children. No one jumping and splashing in the blue water, so calm and still it looks like some other, more exotic element. People are basking on the wet stone around the pool's rim, young and old alike. Her eyes catch on asymmetries: hunched backs, contorted faces, missing limbs.

She looks more closely and sees that some are caregivers for the others. Holding their hands, encouraging them. Supporting them in the water.

She backs up slowly, feeling like an interloper, a true tourist, but keeps looking. Her gaze stops at last on one older woman with long white hair and serene grey eyes, arms leaning on the pool's edge, her jaw hanging slack.

Claire's heart starts to race.

The woman looks up at Claire and smiles. An automatic, all-purpose smile, just in case this stranger is someone she's supposed to know. Then she slides from the edge into the water, which is up to her waist. She turns and walks forward, and the water rises up her back and arms, her shoulders and neck, her long white hair fans out like the train of a bridal gown, and then she's fully submerged.

They were sitting together in the common room of the long-term care centre. It was at the latter end of the pandemic, and Claire had been allowed in to visit for the first time in months. She'd been grounded for so long and had been going crazy in her tiny apartment, watching her bank account balance tick down.

She remembers the morning sunlight slanting in through the opened blinds of the big bay window. For once her mother didn't burst into tears at the sight of her. She simply sat with a look of uncertain expectation, like someone at a theatre waiting for the curtain to rise without knowing whether she would be onstage or in the audience. Claire held her mother's skeletal hand, felt her pulse keeping soft time, and just noticed things. An old man in the corner was dropping sugar cubes one at a time into the aquarium, glancing around between each plop to make sure the attendants hadn't seen.

Her mother murmured something.

"Sorry, Mom, what?"

Her mother set her other hand gently on Claire's belly.

"When are you due, dear?"

It was her nurse's voice, kind but firmly professional. Claire hadn't heard her use it in years, and it had never been directed at her, not that she could remember. There was really no point in answering the question, but she couldn't help herself.

"I'm not," she said.

"Hmm," her mother said.

A month before, sick of being cooped up by the endless lockdown, Claire had snuck into a nightclub that was defying health orders. She'd met a man there and spent a few insane, frantic minutes with him in the bathroom. An unbelievable breach of her own rules for survival.

Her mother's words were enough for her to buy a test on the way home. A few moments of cold dread while waiting, but negative.

Since then she's been travelling, for over half a year. She hasn't gone back to the care centre in all that time, telling herself it's better that way. It only upsets her mother to see her, or it does when she remembers who Claire is. All the mistakes, the fights, the bad feelings come rushing back. For both of them.

In the elevator back to her room Claire is finally alone. She slumps against the wall, watching the numbers climb, reminding herself what she's been doing all these years and why she has no choice. It's become her story, a script she plays in her head to keep her focused when she has a rare moment of doubt or things threaten to fall apart. It's the story of how it all began, what was done to her, and where it led. Her mother cheating on her father with that creep Ray, who owned a construction business in town and had the time for her that Claire's father didn't. Her father finding out, then leaving them and not coming back. Both her parents checking out on her when she was just a kid, wrapping themselves up in their own lives.

Her mother had tried to make it up to her, or at least distract her, by getting her a puppy. A bright-eyed, scruffy mutt she named Buster. She knew damn well it was a bribe, an emotional ploy, but god she had loved that dog. He slept in her bed. They went everywhere together. Their favourite game was the one where she would toss a rubber ball onto the roof of the house and it would bounce back down and Buster would try to catch it when it dropped off the edge. The stupid dog never knew exactly where the ball was going to be when it dropped, and he would tremble all over and whine until the thing he was so desperate for suddenly appeared, then he would make a mad dash for his prize like his life depended on it. One time she threw the ball really hard on purpose, so that it sailed over the roof and into the front yard. Buster somehow knew it wasn't coming back and tore off after it to the other side of the house. A moment later she heard a squeal and the screech of brakes. She walked slowly around the house to the front yard. She already knew and she didn't want to see, but she had to see. A postal delivery truck was parked wrong, half on the sidewalk. The delivery man was coming up the front walk, crying and carrying her dog in his arms, like a parcel she hadn't been told was on its way to her door.

Kids have to learn life isn't fair, she overheard Ray saying to her Mom that night.

That wasn't long before he started putting the moves on her when her mother was working evening shifts at the hospital.

Well, she'd learned a lesson all right. Everyone and everything you cared about left you, sooner or later. So she would check out too. Out of this crap town with its wobbles, its bad air, its swaggering males obsessed with their trucks, quads, and boats.

The first step in her plan was accumulating enough cash. Babysitting and part-time waitressing weren't going to get her there fast enough, and so she started stealing from Ray, knowing he wouldn't dare accuse her. Taking money from his wallet, a couple of small bills at first. Soon, entire wads. Then she broke into his truck and removed his expensive stereo. He gave her hateful looks over the next few days, guessing that she was the culprit but saying nothing. She'd sold the stereo to a guy in her neighbourhood who paid the full amount she asked, then tried to convince her to go on a night drive with him, to check out the speakers. No chance, pal.

From there she graduated to selling drugs to high school kids, which led her eventually to the man who trafficked bear gallbladders out of the forest and who hired her as a courier. That was way more lucrative, and less risky, than peddling dime bags in school parking lots.

Nature's cruel, the trafficker said to her once. *Survival of the fittest, right?*

Survival of the quickest, anyhow. She'd gotten away with it, all of it, discovering a talent for slipping in and out of tricky situations unnoticed, for staying focused on a goal and shutting everything else off inside her until it was achieved.

Once she'd stockpiled enough cash, she was gone and has never been back. Her mother relocated to Edmonton after the Northfire disaster and the evacuation. Ray was a piece of shit but he was right about one thing: life isn't fair. You have to force it to give you what you want, and you have to be ruthless about it. Once her mother is gone, she will have no ties to anyone other than those she permits, which won't be many.

When she gets low on funds she travels to far-off countries like this one and acquires things no one is supposed to have, animals and parts of animals, and brings them to the people who've paid enormous sums for them. In return she purchases the one thing that matters—the freedom to do what she likes. To go where she likes. To not be beholden to anyone.

The only catch? Freedom is expensive.

THE RIVER MEADOWS ARCHIVE

Build yourself an ark. Time is short—begin it now. If words
are all you have, build it with words.
—RUMI

CHRONOLOGY

175 years ago: On the banks of Conjuring Creek in Canada's
North-Western Territory, an Indigenous hunter whose name
has not been recorded shows Hudson's Bay Company trader
Elijah Bayne a curious-looking outcropping of dark, crumbling
rock. The trader pries a chunk loose to examine it. The hunter
tells him the local name for the strange ore and Bayne notes it
down in his company log entry for the evening, even though
he's not certain he's translated it correctly from the native
tongue: *Ghost dancing in the sky.*

Bayne adds the following note to his entry: *I had some difficulty
finding my way back to my encampment due to an unaccustomed
dullness of wit that came over me after I had handled a piece
of the ore. It gives forth a curious, intoxicating odour like that of
raw mineral spirits. Whatever it may be, I am of the opinion*

that this "ghost" is of no value to the company's enterprises in this land.

130 years ago: Passing references to a dark, viscous mineral nicknamed "ghost" begin to appear in the chronicles of other European explorers and fur traders in the area. If held to a flame, a piece of the raw ore will give off gases that can cause dizziness, a racing heart, even hallucinations.

79 years ago: The Conjuring Creek formation, a large sub-surface stratum of ghost, is discovered near the tiny hamlet of River Meadows, Alberta, formerly a fur trading post.

71 years ago: In the wake of the first big Alberta oil strike in the 1940s, fossil fuel exploration in the region ramps up. Government geologist Ira Solomon, surveying for bitumen deposits like those in the nearby Athabasca tar sands, camps in the bush near Conjuring Creek while he explores the area around River Meadows. He comes across an exposed seep of the ore known locally as "ghost" and brings a sample back to his field lab to run tests on it. Nearly burning down his lab in the process, Solomon discovers the ore has enormous, if risky, potential as a source of energy.

After squinting at a drop of ghost exudate in the lens of his microscope, Solomon notes a strange effect on his perceptions: *A moment's dizziness just now. I felt weirdly small and insignificant. As if I was gazing up into the depths of the night sky, glittering with stars.*

Every Saturday he hitchhikes to the nearby Native village of Fire Narrows to pick up supplies.

There Solomon gets to know an old trapper named Charlie MacKinnon and starts looking forward to their visits. Moved as he rarely is by a desire for human company, Solomon invites Charlie for a weekend fishing trip to nearby Thunder Lake.

After a day of landing some decent-sized cutthroat and wall-eye, the two men build a fire, cook and eat the fish they've caught, and sit talking and drinking bitter tea. Charlie's a born raconteur. As evening falls, he spins his enchanting yarns about fabled moose hunts and men who turn into wolves, and Solomon can't help but think of his grandfather, the legendary anthropologist. On his long-ago expeditions among the Indigenous people of eastern Siberia, he'd gathered stories that he shared years later with young Ira on winter nights by the fire in his drafty old house in Montreal. Heroes battling monstrous fish and outwitting cannibal ogres, entanglements with dangerous shape-changing spirits that could become any animal they wished—goose, narwhal, fox, bear—but who would reward you for treating living things with respect. The one story Ira was never able to extract from his grandfather was the one he most wanted to hear, about the real-life ogre from whom he had fled to a new land across the sea, the monster called Joseph Stalin.

As Charlie weaves his word magic, Solomon thinks he should really be writing these stories down. In case one day he has grandchildren of his own he can tell them to.

But he's not here for stories, no matter how compelling. Solomon decides at last to raise the subject of the ore, something that has been weighing on him since he ignited that sample in his field lab and watched blue and green flames dance above its surface like a tiny aurora borealis. The people here, living more or less like their ancestors did, have no idea what they're sitting on top of. When Charlie at last falls silent, Solomon himself sits quiet for a while, out of respect, then confides in the old man that it's very likely that what he's discovered about ghost will bring more white men here. Many more.

Charlie takes this news without comment. He stretches and tosses the dregs of his tea on the fire. "Not if you don't tell them about it," he finally says.

Solomon laughs. He turns his tin mug around and around in his hands. "I suppose that's true," he says.

In the waning light of dusk something flits between the two men and disappears into the dark under the trees. All that Solomon caught was a flash of surprising blue.

Eager to put the awkwardness behind them, he asks Charlie what bird that was. Charlie replies with a word in his own language that the geologist doesn't know, then adds, "They say that one flies the farthest, to where the birds come from."

"I know a story like that," Solomon says eagerly. "My grandfather told it to me when I was a boy. He heard it from a storyteller he met in the north. Well, north but on the other side of the world, I mean. Not here. This was a long time ago."

"The other side of the world," Charlie says.

"Yes. I don't know where exactly. Or who. But it goes like this . . ."

As he launches in, unsure of himself in front of a master, he regrets having mentioned the story at all. But it's too late to back out. Charlie has shared his lore, and now it's Solomon's turn. In his head he can hear his grandfather's soft, smoky voice in that drafty old house on a winter's night, sweeping him away to a haunted world . . .

Farther than anyone has ever travelled, they say, at the edge of the world, lies a distant ocean. In the deepest stretch of the waters stands a mighty tree towering to the clouds. In the tree is a great hollow, and in that hollow is a sleepless spirit that comes forth and devours any living soul who comes too close. On the far side of that vast, treacherous sea there is another land where no man has ever set foot. The invisible beings who dwell there have made the sky fall to the earth like a great stone that strikes and rebounds, so that sky and earth form a gate that never ceases opening and closing.

This place no living man has seen is the Unattainable Border of the Birds. This gate must be passed if the birds wish to return to their home. But the sky comes down so quickly that many of the birds don't succeed. The unlucky ones are caught in the gate's closing, as in a trap, and all is over for them. The ground before the gate is covered with a layer of crushed birds, greater than the height of a man. In that place of death, feathers are continually floating about, drifting in the wind.

Solomon falls silent. He'd dredged up this gloomy tale without thinking about how it ends, or how it reflects on what he's come here to do. What will happen to this land when the money and the machines follow in his wake? He gazes at the column of fire smoke softly coiling into the darkening sky, dotted with a few faint stars. He's not—or not any longer—someone given to flights of fancy, but for a moment he feels he can almost see the place he's trying to evoke with words. That unattainable country at the end of the earth is not far at all. The dreadful gate is so close, he can hear the whisper of feathers.

Eventually Solomon sends his samples to the government laboratory in Ottawa. The ghost ore is analyzed and his findings confirmed.

Surveying and small-scale extraction of the ore begin.

63 years ago: From an industry report:

> "Ghost" is a semi-fluidic hydrocarbon aggregate with highly unusual molecular lattices. The known deposits are of uncertain origin, possibly from ancient meteor strikes

during the late Mesozoic era, around 70 million years ago. Discovered in trace amounts at various sites around the world and in economically viable concentrations at only three currently known locations: Novaya Zemlya, the Orinoco Belt in Venezuela, and by far the largest deposit, near the town of River Meadows in northwestern Alberta, Canada. At this site, an enormous ore stratum (the Conjuring Creek formation), mixed with a layer of sand, water, and acidic clay, lies several metres under the surface layers of the boreal forest.

54 years ago: The Indigenous community of Fire Narrows has been found to be situated atop a part of the Conjuring Creek formation, now fully surveyed and revealed to be far more extensive than previously thought. Mining operations begin on Crown land that is also claimed by the people of Fire Narrows.

39 years ago: Attempts to make ghost an economically viable commodity had long been stymied by technical problems that render the process of separating the ore from its sand and clay matrix unreliable and dangerous (extraction and refinement must be carried out in immediate sequence, to avoid explosive combustion and the decay of the ore's active properties). After years of setbacks and unprofitability the Northfire Corporation develops a proprietary technology that successfully delivers a safe and reliable supply of refined product. The era of large-scale ghost extraction begins.

The little town of River Meadows undergoes astonishingly rapid growth, as tradespeople and labourers—truck drivers, pipefitters, machinists, welders, boilermakers, electricians, small- and large-engine mechanics, carpenters, glaziers, plumbers, house painters, cooks—flock to the area from far and wide.

28 years ago: River Meadows, the hub of the new industry, has grown to a small but bustling city of fifty thousand, and is projected to keep on growing, as there are estimated to be at least seventy more years of full-capacity ghost extraction in its future. Fully half of the adult population of River Meadows works at the extraction/refining sites or in some subsidiary industry related to the processing and delivery of refined ore.

Over three hundred square kilometres of boreal forest overburden has already either been removed or disturbed by seven large-scale extraction projects.

A gram of ghost is worth twenty-eight times the value of a gram of gold.

Some researchers link ore extraction and refinement to the little-understood phenomenon of decoherence. At unpredictable intervals, the thermal suspension (an intermediate stage between raw and refined ore) emits what scientists have called an ASD (anomalous space-time decoherence) wave, which has been associated with various effects among the local population, including vertigo, disorientation, nervous excitation, and brief visual and auditory hallucinations. Both Northfire spokespersons and government researchers dispute the widespread claim that ASD waves, in the words of one long-time River Meadows resident and anti-extraction activist, are "fucking with reality."

25 years ago: The black-footed ferret. The boreal grouse. The woodland caribou. A count is kept of the animals in the region that have either vanished or that teeter perilously close to the edge due to habitat loss and human activity.

The extraction tailing ponds, filled with a toxic liquid sludge, trap and kill ducks, geese, and other animals by the thousands.

Environmental protesters advocate for an immediate cessation of all extraction activities, citing the immense damage that mining operations are doing to the forest, to the air and water, to biodiversity, and to the ultimate sustainability of life on Earth.

24 years ago: The Hewitt family arrives in River Meadows.

21 years ago: A disastrous accident at one of the largest extraction sites marks what some industry experts foresee as the beginning of the end for the ghost industry. Many homes and businesses in the town are evacuated as a precautionary measure, most people believing the evacuation is temporary and they will soon be able to return.

But the ghost extraction industry is in freefall and a mass exodus from the region has begun.

18 years ago: Several hundred hectares around the excavation sites, including much of the former town of River Meadows, have been cordoned off as an Environmental Reclamation Area and declared unsafe for human habitation. Residents from the evacuated neighbourhoods have never been allowed to return. Most houses and buildings have been left as they were. The forest has begun to take back the town.

Unexplained phenomena are reported to have occurred in the restricted area, although local authorities dismiss these claims.

7 years ago: Amery Hewitt returns to River Meadows.

5 years ago: A newly formed religious group, the Church of the Conjuration, begins holding prayer gatherings outside the Environmental Reclamation Area. They claim the anomalies reported there are signs from God that the world is ending and that a new Eden will be created here, for the faithful. Adherents of the faith flock to the area from around the world to await the day of reckoning.

Now: Alex Hewitt returns to River Meadows.

ALEX

The young man who sits down across from him wears glasses with serious black rims. His hair is cut short, his white cotton shirt and beige chinos pressed. He looks to Alex like someone who goes door to door asking people if they can spare some time to talk about our Lord and Saviour.

"Michio Amano," the young man says.

He and Alex shake hands. Alex takes a closer look and realizes Michio is probably only a year or two younger than he is, likely in his mid-thirties. The boyish voice over the phone misled him.

They're meeting in the Trapline Hotel coffee shop in the forestry town of Pine Ridge, an hour's drive southwest of what remains of River Meadows. Alex's mother gave him Michio's name and number when she asked him to fly to this place he hasn't set foot in for two decades now. She'd insisted a long time ago that if Amery was going to keep doing such dangerous work she had to give her family a name, a number, someone to contact in case something happened to her. And now, it seems, something has.

They order coffee.

"Thanks for meeting with me," Alex says. "My mother is really worried."

Why can't he say that he's worried too? The truth is when his mother asked him to go look for Amery, he had resisted. *I'm sure she's okay, Mom,* he'd tried to reassure her. *She's done this to us before.*

This time is different, Alex. Something's wrong. Please. I need you to do this.

"I mean," Alex adds, "my sister has never been one to communicate much, but it's been three weeks now without a word to my mom."

Michio nods but says nothing. When they'd talked yesterday, the younger man had only said he hadn't seen or heard from Amery either, then suggested that they meet in person. He was clearly unwilling to talk over the phone, and Alex supposed this was because he's aware of Amery's visits to the Environmental Reclamation Area, which is off-limits. A paramilitary detachment of the police keeps watch over the perimeter. Trespassing or even being caught trying to get through the fence can land you in jail. If it doesn't kill you.

Or maybe he wanted to be sure that Alex really is who he claims to be. Just what sort of relationship exists between his sister and Michio Amano is a mystery to him.

"Your mother told me as much," Michio finally says. "She said it's really rare for Amery not to check in with her."

The server brings them their coffee.

"So you haven't heard from Amery either," Alex says.

"No. Not for just over a week. Although that's not so unusual, from my point of view. She's gone days before without getting in touch."

"But . . . this time you think something might have happened?"

"I'm concerned, yes."

"I mean, I have no idea where to start looking," Alex says. "That's why I wanted to meet with you. I don't even know where Amery's living right now."

Another fact that feels like a confession. Every time he opens his mouth, he's making it clearer to Michio—and to himself—how little he knows about his own sister's life.

"She's been staying at my house," Michio says, looking uncomfortable. "She was let go from her janitorial job a few months back and she was having trouble paying the rent."

"I didn't know she'd lost that job," Alex said. "It's not the first. She didn't leave anything at your place that suggests where she's gone?"

"No. Nothing."

Michio takes a careful sip of coffee. He's so quiet and calm, Alex thinks. No, *controlled* is a better way to describe it. He has clearly decided to release as little information as possible, as if this is an interrogation and Alex is someone to be wary of. Which he supposes he must seem to be. Or maybe Amery was a problem for him, with her illegal activities, her hand-to-mouth existence. Maybe he's relieved she's out of his hair and he's trying not to show it.

"Is it possible she left town?" Alex asks. "I mean, Amery was pretty rootless for a few years, before she came back to River Meadows. She travelled all over the place and never stayed anywhere long. Sometimes she'd call my mom out of the blue from Europe, or South America . . . I don't know, maybe she just decided to move on from this place too."

"She would have told me she was leaving," Michio says, as if there's no room for doubt.

A spasm of anger, he's not sure at who, clenches Alex's jaw. His mother is waiting at home for news and this Michio Amano knows it. Why is he covering for Amery? They both know where she goes, that she does this crazy thing she's chosen to make her life's great cause. She hasn't been thinking about what their mother might be going through. Alex just needs to find her so he can make sure she's okay, then get back to his own life.

He glances around first to make sure no one can overhear. There's hardly anyone else in the coffee shop at what should be a busy midmorning hour, which probably says something about the state of the local economy. The few other patrons are busy with their own conversations or absorbed in their phones.

"So I'm guessing you know where Amery goes," Alex says softly. "That she visits the . . ."

He hesitates, feeling a sudden reluctance to name the place, as if by not doing so he can keep it safely not real. Like he's done for years now.

Michio holds his gaze for a long moment. Then he blinks and adjusts his glasses, as if he's trying to get a better look at this person across the table from him. Likely making the decision right now as to whether Alex can be trusted.

"Yes, I know," he finally says. "Around here some people call it the Park."

"The Park. Okay. Anyhow, she doesn't tell us much about her visits there. If you know anything . . ."

"I do," Michio says. "We talked in the morning before I went to work, eight days ago now. She told me she was going in for the day. I haven't heard from her since."

"*Going in.* Maybe it's none of my business, but how do you and my sister know each other exactly? She's never mentioned you to me."

The younger man purses his lips and Alex wonders if he's about to say *she never mentioned you to me either.*

"We've been friends for a few years," Michio says. "That's all we are, in case you're wondering. She came to a talk I gave at the college, about the fuzzy mathematics of weather prediction. She stayed to ask me some really good, thoughtful questions. The *environment* is a dirty word to a lot of people around here. It was . . . refreshing to meet someone who cared about the same things I do. Anyhow, we stayed in touch. Since then, whenever she's planning to make a visit to the Reclamation Area I've asked her to let me know."

"And when she comes back out, she lets you know that too?"

"Usually. Not always. That's why it took a while before I thought something might be wrong. Listen, Mister Hewitt . . ."

"Call me Alex."

"Alex. There are other people who do what Amery does. Who go into the Park to rescue trapped and injured animals. I can't tell you who they are, but they've already searched for her."

"They have? Well . . . when? I mean . . ."

"Three days ago. They searched as thoroughly as you can in a place like that, especially in all the spots they thought she was likely to be. Where she usually goes. They didn't find her."

"Who are these people? I need to contact them."

Michio looks down at the table.

"I'm sorry, I can't give you their names."

"Why not?"

"I can't. That's all. But just because they didn't find her doesn't mean she isn't coming back. Or that she isn't okay. Amery's been gone for long stretches before without getting in touch with anyone."

"Michio, listen, whoever these people are, please ask them if they'll take me. Tell them I *need* to go there. I can pay them a lot of money."

"They won't take your money. It's not about that."

"Then what is it about? Just tell them I want to talk to them. That's all."

"I think it's best now just to wait and—"

Alex throws up his hands.

"Then I guess I'm going to the cops. If you won't help me, if these *people* won't help me, what choice have I got? I don't want to get anyone in trouble, least of all myself, but I can't do this alone."

"Talking to the police won't do any good," Michio says. "They patrol the perimeter and that's it. If they catch someone trying to get in, or coming out, they'll arrest them. But they won't set foot inside the fence. It's off-limits to them too. They'll take your missing person report and that will be it."

Alex glances out the window. Cars and trucks whoosh by on the road in the ordinary light of day. He takes a deep breath, willing himself to a semblance of calm.

"Yeah, I know that," he finally says. "Then I guess I'll do this myself."

Michio blinks and adjusts his glasses again.

"Did Amery ever tell you what it's like in there?"

"Like I said, we never talked about it. Not really."

A memory comes to Alex of the last time he'd seen his sister, years ago now. The three of them had gathered at their mother's condo in the Okanagan for her sixtieth birthday.

Why? he'd asked Amery. A question as much about her return to River Meadows as about the visits she was making to the off-limits area.

I was born there, she had said.

You were born in the maternity ward at Burnaby General, like me.

You know what I mean.

Do I? I don't get why you think it's your job. I mean, what are these animals to you? Creatures die painful, horrible deaths in the wild every day, and they always have, long before we ever showed up. It's just nature.

That place, she had said, actually pointing across the miles of mountain and prairie, that place is not nature. We did that. Humans did that. Somebody has to take responsibility for it.

Alex looks down into the full cup of coffee he has yet to taste. "I don't see that I have any choice. If that's where she's gone, then that's where I'm going."

The younger man studies him as if sizing up his courage, or his determination.

"The authorities have worked very hard to keep people from learning the truth about what happened in River Meadows," Michio says. "They call it the Environmental Reclamation Area because if you name something and the name sticks, it becomes the truth in people's minds. But they aren't reclaiming anything. They just put a fence around it because they don't know how to fix what they've broken and nobody wants to admit that. You lived in that town. I'm sure you remember those blips, those decoherences that came and went. What's happening in the Reclamation Area is like one endless, unpredictable, unstoppable decoherence. You don't have any idea how dangerous it is in there."

Alex swallows. "I'm sure I don't, but I have to find my sister. I have to try."

Michio sits back in his chair. He adjusts his glasses again, a gesture that must be a nervous habit. "I know," he says. "You love her. She's family."

He says it with such simple conviction that he seems even younger, and strangely innocent, as if he lives in a purer world than most people. Alex realizes that Michio reminds him of

Amery as a child. He sees the room at the Lulla-Bear Motel
where he'd stayed with his father while Amery was in the hospital with their mother at her bedside. Ben Hewitt trying so
hard to make the best of it, to reach out to his son, who wouldn't
let him in no matter what. *We just have to stay positive.*

Michio sits up and nudges his coffee cup to one side. He
digs into his backpack, takes out a small coil-bound book with
a pale green cover.

"This is one of Amery's notebooks," he says. "Whenever
she filled one up, she'd give it to me for safekeeping and start
another one. This is the last one she gave me, a few weeks ago."

He slides the book across the table to Alex. He takes it,
examines the soft, wrinkled cover.

Rain-Write
All-Weather Notebook
Patented Water-Shedding Paper

Underneath the printed text Amery had written in black felt
pen, in her meticulous hand, *No. 24.*

Cautiously, as if the thing might be contaminated somehow,
Alex picks the notebook up, opens it to the middle. For a journal whose pages are supposed to shed water, the paper is
severely rippled, brittle, stained. A faint earthy scent rises to his
nostrils—like stones drying in the sun after a rain. He realizes
the book is a testament to how many hours she must have spent
out there, no matter how miserable the conditions.

He flips back to the first page. Her small, neat writing, in
pencil. The first entry is dated a little more than six months
ago. She recorded the time she entered the Park (6:14 a.m.) and
the time she left (7:36 p.m.). More than twelve hours. An entire
day. In between the time entries is a note on the weather and

a list of sightings of animals, including several robins, a yellow warbler, and three white-tailed deer.

He turns pages. She made other kinds of entries too. A chronology of events relating to River Meadows and the extraction industry, organized by year. Facts and anecdotes about human encounters with birds and other animals, attempts to communicate with other species, from history and other places around the world. Stories she must have thought important enough to write down.

Alex flips to the last entry. Another brief record of one of her visits to the Park, with times and animal sightings.

6:47 p.m. Two magpies on the roof of the burnt barn, the breeding pair that's been in this area all summer. The anomaly here, one of the most unpredictable in the Park, doesn't keep them away or seem to concern them, at least not up there. More evidence that it's confined to ground level.

Those new vocalizations again, the short high-pitched triple squawk. They're telling each other something I've never heard them say before. I approached as close as I dared and tried it myself, to see how they'd respond. They ignored me and a few minutes later they flew off. I might not have gotten the pitch or tempo quite right. Or they just don't feel like talking to me.

He looks up at Michio, unsure what to say in the face of his sister's fantasies about birds.

"She used to do this as a kid," he says. "Keep a notebook of her nature explorations. They weren't as . . . detailed as this back then."

"We try to record everything, keep track of everything. Compare notes. There might be patterns we're not able to see day to day, from close up."

"Thanks," Alex says, hefting the book. "I'll look through this. In case . . ."

"I had the same thought. In case there's anything that might provide a clue."

Alex considers asking if he can keep the notebook, then realizes he's thinking that he'll never see her again and this is at least something he can take with him, to show their mother. Proof that he tried.

"Hang on to it, for now," Michio says. "Maybe you'll notice something I missed. If you do, call me. In the meantime, I'll talk to those people and ask them to make another search. If you can just wait, I'll talk to them and get back to you . . ."

"No. That's not good enough. Tell them if they won't help me—"

Michio interrupts.

"Listen to me, Alex. Stay away from the Park. You won't help your sister by going in there on your own. You'll end up missing too. Or worse."

Alex sits back in his chair. He feels numb, exhausted, finished before he's even started.

"I want to talk to them," he says. "Tell them where to find me. Please. Just do that for me."

Back at the hotel Alex goes online, revisiting one of the more credible websites he's found about the River Meadows reclamation zone. He's already pored through this material but maybe there's something useful he missed.

He ignores his latest project, *The Almanack of Sand*, which is sitting, unlooked at for days now, in a folder on his desktop. He's never neglected his work for so long.

Alex sometimes thinks it wasn't really all the superhero comics, TV cartoons, and role-playing games he devoured as a kid that led him to his path in life. It had more to do with what happened at the diner in River Meadows the evening they arrived, when for an instant he grasped a shimmering pattern to everything. Then it was gone, and the world was once more just the world: random, chaotic, any meaning it held always threatening to wash away in the flood of experiences, a flood that had no shape, no edges you could grasp.

If he couldn't find any meaningful pattern in this world he shared with everyone else, he would map out his own. What he didn't expect, when he became a creator of worlds, was that his creations would grow as well, almost beyond him.

His first attempt at a murder mystery game, *Joseph Merrick, Detective*, failed to make much of an impression in the market until it was picked up by the international distributor Cardboard Cosmos. In the alternate Victorian London of Alex's game, Merrick, more familiar to history as the Elephant Man, lives another life as the city's most brilliant detective. Exhibited as a sideshow freak in his youth, Merrick is intimately familiar with the city's carnivalesque underworld, and his long captive solitude has honed his deductive and reasoning powers to an uncanny degree. When puzzled by a case Merrick meditates on it by building replicas of the crime scene out of matchsticks and playing cards. Along with his young accomplices, the boy yogi Rama Sadhu and Fanny Wilkins, the Frog-Faced Girl of Whitechapel, Merrick is often sought out by a desperate Scotland Yard to solve the city's most grotesque and baffling murders.

The marketing team at Cardboard Cosmos loved the concept but wanted to make some changes to the game's look and feel, including grimmer, more lurid artwork than the royalty-free Victorian-era images Alex had used, and an expanded Dickensian rogues' gallery of potential suspects. They made Alex a consultant on the redesign, offering him a fee breathtakingly higher than he'd ever earned for his work. He didn't approve of all their ideas, but at least this way he had some say over what became of his creation.

Encouraged by the team to come up with further background details to enrich gameplay, Alex imagined another game within the game, a card game similar to those that were so enormously popular in the nineteenth century. His initial idea was to create something that players of *The Elephant Man Files*, as the game had been rechristened, could actually play with cards to be included in the box along with the board and pieces, as a kind of diversion from the crime-solving.

The idea took such hold of him that Alex forgot everything else he was supposed to be working on and spent weeks on the card game, tweaking its turn structure and rules. What was meant to be a diversion slowly turned into the key to unlocking the mystery.

A string of particularly gruesome killings has occurred in the East End, Alex wrote in a précis to the design team, *and now someone has been sending Merrick tarot cards that have been altered with pen and paint: instead of the familiar titles and suits, the cards have been renamed for the murder victims (Swords), judges and well-known inspectors on the police force (Staves), members of the upper classes (Cups and Coins), and Merrick's friends and acquaintances (Major Arcana). Then finally one for himself: the card most commonly known as Justice, with the seated potentate's face disfigured with ink to resemble the detective's own. Baffled at first, Merrick eventually gathers his crime-solving accomplices to play these cards with him, like they might spend an evening playing whist or faro, hoping this seemingly innocent parlour pastime will somehow illuminate the events taking place in the back lanes and sordid dens of the city, and lead him to the perpetrator of these horrors. Although he begins to suspect he has become nothing more than a pawn in someone else's game . . .*

The design team liked the idea but wasn't entirely convinced it would fly. There was no way to make the outcomes of shuffling cards lead anywhere but into a labyrinth of sheer randomness. A mystery was meant to lead to a solution, not to a hall of mirrors. In the end, a selection of defaced tarot cards was included to serve as visual clues to the identity of the murderer. You could perhaps come up with a way to play the cards if you wanted to, but it wasn't intrinsic to winning the game.

Still, *The Elephant Man Files* sold well enough that Alex could pursue any project he liked. He next tinkered with a game based on his memories of the Northfire ore-processing complex his father had taken him to see all those years ago. In his reimagined version, its towers and walkways became a maze of secret rooms, dead ends, and lethal traps. In order to survive and eventually escape, the players must uncover the keys to navigating this dark industrial purgatory. You start with only two rules—take turns and keep moving—and collect clues and additional rules as you go. The game would be played on a board that represented the deepest subterranean level of the complex. Players would lay down overlapping, layered tiles, literal stepping stones out of the depths, but also pieces of a puzzle that would enable them to grasp the inner workings of the diabolical mechanism they're caught inside, in order to thwart and escape it.

He called it *The Fortress of Echoes*, but never completed it, being unable to decide whether the players should ultimately find a way out or whether the ladder of tiles should simply recycle itself over and over without end. When he was a little boy he'd been told by his Irish Catholic grandmother, Mary Hewitt, that when he died, he would go to heaven and live there forever. He tried to understand what forever meant, but in his mind's eye it was a kind of spiralling tunnel that went on and on, something like the infinite corridor you saw when you stood between two mirrors facing one another. The idea terrified him. How could you just go on and on, without end? What would you be doing with all that time? Everything had to have an ending.

Two years after the Elephant Man game's success, Alex landed work on *The Almanack of Sand,* an online multiplayer game being developed by Aditi Virtual. The up-and-coming entertainment company was founded by Indian tech genius Suresh Sikandar, who had recently launched his own innovative online ecosystem, VISHNU. This *vast, immersive, self-propagating holistic narrative universe* would, Sikandar claimed, ultimately link all of Aditi's games, data-mining projects, and virtual worlds into what he called an Entanglement. This was the first game Alex worked on that wasn't played on cardboard with plastic tokens. Sikandar wanted him on the team, he learned, because of the details he'd put into the alternate world of his Elephant Man game: the character backstories, the culture and lore, the minutiae of a late-Victorian London that was subtly different from the historical one.

When Alex accepted his contract as a "creative affiliate" on the *Almanack* project, he looked up the history of the company and discovered that Sikandar had named Aditi after his mother, who'd died in poverty when he was a child. The company's logo was a stylized boar with what looked like a mountain balanced on one tusk. The god Vishnu, in his avatar as the great boar Varaha, battled a demon who sank the earth into the depths of the cosmic ocean. Varaha fought with the demon in a titanic contest that lasted a thousand years, finally defeated him, and then restored the earth to its rightful place in the cosmos, carrying it up out of the unfathomable waters on the point of his tusk.

The world of *The Almanack of Sand* was inspired by an obscure collection of ancient legends from the small island nation in the Atlantic known for innovative technology and terrible weather. The island was never actually named in Aditi's industry prospectus, but a number of references to historical events, most notably an ancient volcanic cataclysm, left little doubt about its real-world inspiration. The game was meant to jump around in time and involve a fictional secret society employing magic and technology to protect the island from the forces, both natural and human, that threatened its destruction.

Beyond this vague summary, Alex's inquiries about actual gameplay were politely rebuffed by the Aditi team. They gave Alex only a general overview, explaining that they would consult with him as needed, while in the meantime he was free to play around with the island's history and culture as he pleased. They were happy to consider any ideas he had for filling out the world they were building. Alex next wanted to know if the game featured main characters they could tell him more about, or whether there was a central storyline, even a thread of narrative, that he could attach his ideas to. No one was talking. He was frustrated, but not really surprised—this kind of black boxing was standard in the industry, dealing as it did with intellectual property potentially worth millions.

Alex had never been to the island. He began his research by buying the most recent guidebook he could find. It contained an impressive amount of history along with its breezy write-ups of the local tourist sights. He noticed an odd lack of information for visitors about what to do in case of earthquake or volcanic eruption—mention of such things was consigned for the most part to the depictions of the island's fabled past.

Although Plato was mistaken in believing the island had utterly vanished, he was ultimately proved right about much of its ancient history. As a philosopher, he also found a moral lesson in the island's long-ago catastrophe. In one of his surviving dialogues, Plato described how

> for many generations, as long as the divine nature lasted in them, the race that inhabited that fair isle was obedient to the laws of heaven and pleased the gods. They possessed great spirit, uniting gentleness with wisdom in their dealings with one another, through all the hazards and chances of mortal life. They cared only for virtue and thought little of the possession of gold or property, which seemed to them a needless burden. Luxury did not intoxicate them, nor did wealth deprive them of their self-mastery. They were sober and saw clearly that what is truly good is increased by sharing with all. But when the light in them began to fade, and grosser desires by degrees gained power over them, they ceased to be grateful for their portion and lusted after that which was not theirs to take. They grew mighty in knowledge and force of arms, and through bloody conquest extended their sovereignty

across the seas, making themselves masters of many peoples and nations. To the unwise, the men of the island appeared most glorious and blessed at the very time that they had extinguished all trace of what was divine in them.

At last, the One who Rules from the Cloud, perceiving that a once honourable race had put themselves in a woeful plight, decided to punish them, that they might be chastened and grow again in wisdom. And so, gathering the deathless gods into their most holy dwelling place, which is at the heart of the world and beholds all created things, Zeus spoke to them thus . . .

The text of Plato's dialogue breaks off at this point, although there can be no doubt about how the tale was meant to end.

Moyo Jonathan, the design team lead, sent Alex a copy of the book of legends the game was based on, and slowly, fitfully, he made his way through its forbidding thickness. There were battles, heroes, magical weapons, monsters aplenty in its pages, more than enough to deliver gamers their dopamine fix. As with most ancient epics, the story was painted in broad, mythic strokes, leaving gaps and silences into which he could dream the minutiae of a culture. What would these people eat for breakfast? What pastimes would they indulge in on their days off? What kind of art did they display on their walls? What did they profess to believe in, and what did they *really* believe?

Jess walked out on him just as he started on the *Almanack* project. They'd met at college and had been together since the early days of his career. She had encouraged him, obsessed with him over the minute details, spent hours patiently listening as he talked his way through the roadblocks. He had always believed they were on the same path, toward a destination they would both recognize when they got there. He had thought the success of the Elephant Man game was it, but she had seen something he hadn't, which was that the path he was on had no end point. He was never going to leave his imaginary worlds for the real one, with her.

With the pandemic on the wane, the company flew Alex to London to meet the rest of the *Almanack* development team. The first evening he was there he went to a company party on the rooftop terrace at Aditi's soaring glass and steel headquarters in Shoreditch. At the entrance he quickly downed a glass of champagne, nabbed a second one from the buffet table, then braced himself and waded into the crowd.

People shook his hand and complimented him on the Elephant Man game. Someone praised its meticulous depiction of the city. Alex didn't admit to anyone that he'd never set foot in London until now.

Slowed-down clips of animals from old movies were being projected onto a soaring white wall on endless repeat, silently and in slow motion. Alex stood with his back to the crowd and looked at the images. He recognized the sources of most of them. Those famous few moments from *Old Yeller*. The first attack on Tippi Hedren by the seagull in Hitchcock's *The Birds*. The black dog that shows up halfway through Tarkovsky's *Stalker* and accompanies the human protagonists from then on.

Before he got around to asking anyone what the animal imagery was all about, Sikandar himself appeared, much earlier in the evening than one might have expected of a mogul.

His super-model-statuesque assistant, Vaya, brought Alex over to meet him. Alex had envisioned one of those entrepreneurial dynamos you saw in videos online, aglow with purpose and vision, jacked up on success and talking rapid-fire about the next big idea. He was surprised to be shaking the soft, warm hand of a short, almost pudgy, youngish man dressed in a loose white shirt and jeans, whose voice scarcely rose above a murmur and was nearly lost in the noise of the crowd.

"Alex. Welcome. Call me Suresh, please. *The Elephant Man Files*—very, *very* interesting work. My son Rahul and I played it and enjoyed it very much. The cards that make Merrick suspect he's become a pawn in someone else's game—I loved the self-referential mindfuck of that. Such great fun. I mean, are we all caught up in some mechanism whose rules we don't know? Wonderful. Wonderful. You've already met Moyo and the rest of the team, of course. Good, very good. We're so happy to have you with us on this project, we're excited about the possibilities, and I know Moyo and the rest of the team are eager to get working with you. If there's anything you need, anything at all, you make sure you let Vaya know and she'll take care of it."

After Sikandar made an exit as abrupt as his entrance, Alex relaxed a little. The champagne had kicked in too, and that helped. He moved through the room, chatting with the *Almanack* team members and discovering what else Aditi had in the works. The company's current major—and some critics said impossible—endeavour, he learned, was something called the Forever Ark. It had begun with an augmented reality app— as you walk around your neighbourhood the camera view of your phone is overlaid with animated images of the animals you would have encountered in your part of the world in pre-industrial times, before the great extermination began. Herds of deer quietly grazing. Frogs and salamanders in every roadside puddle. The air alight with bees and butterflies, the skies filled with wheeling flocks of birds. But Sikandar wasn't stopping there. He wanted to build an entire virtual planet, which when completed would contain avatars of each and every currently existing *real* non-domesticated animal on Earth.

The project had already begun with what was felt to be most urgently needed: identifying, tracking, and rendering digital replicas of the world's entire populations of remaining large wild terrestrial carnivores and herbivores—wolves, bears, wildcats, gorillas, zebras, elephants—a shockingly small number of individuals in total compared to the billions of livestock animals caged, processed, and slaughtered in industrial farms.

A second phase would attempt the staggering feat of continuing the process with every animal on Earth larger than a mouse, on land, in the air, and in the sea. Every barn swallow, garter snake, colobus monkey, koala, prairie dog, beluga, musk deer, saw-whet owl, hyrax, okapi, Galapagos penguin, loggerhead sea turtle, dugong, steppe eagle, red fox, Mediterranean monk seal, bonobo, great white shark, ostrich, black caiman, Ethiopian wolf, honey badger, aye-aye, axolotl, orangutan, lyrebird, chameleon, blue whale . . . Eventually, even the crustaceans, the insects, and the creatures of the deep oceans would have their own second life on Sikandar's virtual planet. This would involve monitoring each and every animal in real time, continually collecting and updating data on their movements, migrations, behaviour patterns, births, life cycles, and deaths, as well as developing a conversational algorithm that might one day allow humans to actually speak with other species in the real world. In effect, a universal translator. But most importantly, Sikandar's virtual planet—lush, green, untamed, with an unfucked biosphere—would contain not one single, solitary human.

Moyo Jonathan, the *Almanack* project's shockingly young-looking team lead, explained to Alex how it all fit together: mass entertainment like *The Almanack of Sand* funded Sikandar's real dream, and would give Aditi the edge in innovation to reach for greater things. While other billionaires launched themselves into space hauling a massive payload of ego, Suresh Sikandar was on a crusade to save the planet. In addition to his Forever Ark project, he'd been buying vast tracts of jungle, rainforest, and grassland all over the world, to keep the life in these places safe from his own kind.

The reason humans don't care about preserving the other life on Earth, Moyo went on, is that we don't really know it. "We don't know *them*," he said, charged with evangelical fervour. "Not as individuals. If we could step into the animals' own world and meet *that* female Sumatran tiger, *that* one Yangtze porpoise with the crescent scar on its snout, *that* particular sapphire frog living among the roots of *that* lopsided acacia tree, we would get to know them as single, particular souls, the way we see ourselves, and then we would care about their fate."

He showed Alex to a small white room off the main hall, softly illuminated with recessed track lighting. There was nothing in it but a circular, omnidirectional treadmill, like a small trampoline, and in front of it, a VR headset on a transparent glass stand.

"This is an early alpha," Moyo said, handing Alex the headset. "We've got a long way to go, but it should give you the idea."

Moyo encouraged Alex to take some exploratory steps to get used to the treadmill, then handed him the headset. He put it on. There was only darkness for a moment, then he found himself on a rolling plain of grass at night, the sky a vast pool of the deepest indigo, dotted with faintly luminous clouds drifting silently across a backdrop of glacial stars. In the distance a dark line of trees. He could hear bird calls all around him, the relentless stridulations of insects and lovesick frogs. He felt a cool moisture, like dew, on his forehead, his arms. And that faint sweet scent—was that coming from the meadow around him or was he just imagining it? Could the headset somehow be stimulating his other senses besides sight?

Alarmed, he held up his hands, expecting to see virtual hands appear in his view. They didn't. He looked down. He had no virtual body. The disorientation caused a further flurry of panic and he groped for balance.

He heard Moyo's disembodied voice, as if from another world. *It takes some getting used to. You're doing fine.*

He breathed deeply and calmed himself. This was not a game. No status bar or heads-up display. No quests or opponents, no skills to level up, no need to go around collecting things or meeting non-player characters with helpful information or pointless backstories. Nothing human here except for him, and even he was an invisible interloper, a ghost.

He took a step forward and the treadmill moved under him, and then he was moving through Sikandar's world, a laugh bubbling inside him at the dizzying realness of what he was experiencing. It was like one of those dreams where he knew he was dreaming, only sharper and even more immersive. The things around him persisted, not wavering in and out of existence or shifting shape the way they did in dreams.

This place was alive. Teeming with life in a way the real world no longer was for him. Maybe for anyone. Sikandar wasn't just creating virtual animals. Here was the living breathing Earth as it once had been, the world they had all lost and no longer remembered. It was in his bones, this place. He hadn't expected that when he put on the headset he'd find himself coming home.

He halted on the treadmill and a sob rose from deep inside him, but he caught it in time.

Everything all right? Moyo asked.

"Yeah, good."

He kept walking.

A sound from very close: the heavy snuff of breath of something large. He froze and hunched his shoulders, his body at the mercy of its deepest instincts. There was something out there in the dark—there was no *out there*—and it was aware of him. He searched the starlit shadows and then he saw it. A shape hunkered in the long grass only a leap away, grey fur dimly shining in the starlight. Two pale amber eyes fixed on him.

He whipped off the headset, heart hammering.

"Did you meet her?" Moyo asked.

"Meet who?"

Moyo nodded and clapped Alex on the shoulder.

"Ah, you did."

Later in the evening, his nerves frayed by the inescapable nearness of too many others, he considered trying the headset again, escaping into Sikandar's unpeopled planet, but instead he ended up once more in front of the wall of images.

A woman came up to stand next to him as the silent animals flashed and flickered by. She was about his age, he figured, her hair buzz cut.

"I've got them all figured out except this one," he said, gesturing to the brief, blurry shot of a large dog attacking a burly man in a white mask.

"Nobody else has identified it either," she said. "Not surprising. It's a pretty obscure film."

They introduced themselves. Her name was Josefa Lastres. She was an artist from Mexico City, and the person who had put the cinematic collage together for Sikandar. Later, when Alex looked her up online, he discovered she had also briefly been Sikandar's romantic partner.

"When I was a kid," Josefa told Alex when he asked her about the collage, "I used to go to the cinema with my Auntie Rosa. My mother's younger sister. She was only a few years older than me and looked after me when I wasn't in school. My parents were always busy. My mother was a costume designer for a theatre troupe and my father was a surgeon. I would have been left pretty much on my own if it hadn't been for Auntie Rosa. We would wander the city, go to the park, to the circus, to the movies. Especially the movies. Auntie Rosa had these vague dreams of someday becoming a film star. For her a movie theatre was like a church. She'd sit there, awestruck, worshipping. I caught that bug from her. The movies became like my real life, and everything else was unreal, fictional. We must have seen hundreds of movies together. Including that one." She nodded toward the screen just as the dog lunged once more at the masked man.

"*Santo vs. las Lobas*. Santo versus the She-Wolves. An awful B-grade horror flick, simply awful. But I'm sure you know how these things become part of one's being, whether you want them to or not. The villain in this movie was a woman. They were always pitting Santo against demonic women."

"And Santo was . . . ?"

"Yes, of course. You don't know Santo. He was this legendary luchador, this wrestler who always wore a mask. No one ever saw his face, until he unmasked himself on television after he retired. A few days later he was dead. He was like a god in my country, really. Year after year he starred in these ludicrous movies, fighting monsters and vampires and creatures from outer space, in between bouts in the wrestling ring. Anyhow, in this movie, the villainess is the queen of the werewolves. Tundra is her name."

"*Tundra*? Wonderful."

"Yes. It begins with a disembodied voice luring a young woman through the streets at night. *Venga*, the voice is saying. *Come. . . come. . . .* It's the voice of Tundra, who first appears as a hairy old crone. She takes over the body of the girl, who then stabs the old Tundra to death. The werewolf queen has to renew herself, you see, for the coming battle in which her kind will destroy humanity and rule the earth. After that, things get very confusing. Santo wrestles, gets attacked by werewolves, wrestles some more, and then there is this convoluted plot involving a family of werewolf hunters, some of whom *are* werewolves.

"What stayed with me, haunted me really, were the transformations. The moments when someone would step out of one role into another, a ferocious, uninhibited self, and then run off, out of the frame, to some unimaginable existence. All of these people with shifting identities, and at the centre of it all, like a walking side of beef, this person with no face, no identity. This masked body. So strange. The transformation scenes were very cheaply done, of course, but the way the wolf-people would appear out of nowhere, attack, and then suddenly vanish again—there was something terrifying and very attractive about that. Changing your skin. The possibility of another life. I was a painter before I got into video art, and so I started painting portraits of famous people as werewolves. Frida Kahlo, Gandhi, Elvis. Then people I knew, and then strangers I encountered around the city. Street kids, police officers, prostitutes. I covered them in pelts, gave them fangs and eyes that glowed in the dark. It really took possession of me for a while."

She stood so close, her eye contact so intense, that Alex took a step away from her. She noticed and smiled.

"Have you painted Suresh as a werewolf?" he asked.

"He won't let me. But he did agree to put me into the trial version of his virtual ark. Not *me*, exactly. He gave my name to one of his prototype she-wolves. And my personality too, he says."

He remembered the sleek shape in the grass, those steady watching eyes.

"I think I met her."

"Did you? I haven't yet. I'm afraid I'll be disappointed."

"I don't think you will. So, whose portrait are you working on right now?"

"Actually I've given up painting, at least for the time being. About a year ago somebody broke into my studio and completely turned it upside down. Canvases slashed, paints splattered every-where. I tried to imagine what sort of person would have done this, who this artist of destruction might be, and for the first time in years I thought about those wolf-people in that movie. Suddenly I realized they were all around me, a city full of people changing form, evading definition, identities appearing and dis-appearing. I realized that in a way that was why I moved back there, to find that city I had explored with Auntie Rosa all those years ago. The city that people call 'the monster.' You know pretty early where you belong.

"Anyhow the building owner used her video camera to make a record of the damage, for insurance purposes, and somehow those two things clicked for me. I asked her to send me a copy of the footage. I hadn't used a camera before in my work, so I started slowly, creating collages like this one, with footage shot by others. Something about taking what other people have seen, what they've focused on and put in the frame of the picture, and making something else with it—that appealed to me. Now I have my own camera and I take it with me pretty much everywhere."

"Looking for the wolf-people?"

"To see if I can catch them in the act. In transformation."

"If we were in a horror movie right now," Alex said, "this would be the part where I scoff at the whole idea and then you grow fangs and tear me to bits."

Josefa laughed, a deep, rich laugh that showed her sharp incisors.

"Sure," she said, "but that's just it. I've come to see that these films tell the truth, but they tell it inside out. Or they tell a lie that shows you the truth by accident. We've swallowed the idea that there's this beast inside every one of us, a dangerous, unpredictable animal that civilization barely contains. It's the excuse governments use to assert control, the excuse that we *need* to be controlled because of the wolf under the skin, the wild thing. That's so wrong. As usual, it's the truth turned inside out. The monster's the thing on the outside, walking around in a dream, having forgotten what it really is." She touched a hand to her chest. "It's the animal in here that saves us."

He'd thought of his sister then. She might be trudging through some cold, wet forest right now, following the traces of something's passage. Listening for calls, a rustle in the undergrowth. He remembered their last day in River Meadows, when she'd led him into the woods to show him what she'd found beneath the fallen pine. *There,* she'd said, pointing into the tangled darkness under the branches. *Look there.*

———

When Alex got home to Canada, he revived his dream of a game within a game, one that the players' avatars might actually sit down and play within the pixelated world they inhabit. It wouldn't gain the players any points or increase their skill level. Instead it would be *about* the universe they were in, a meta-game that would reveal to the characters that they were in fact pieces being moved around in a world not of their own making, subject to laws they didn't understand.

The designers, much like the team at Cardboard Cosmos, were skeptical about this kind of self-referentiality, but the directive from Sikandar himself was that Alex be given carte blanche.

The perfect name for it, he thought. He holed up for two weeks in his apartment with a tall stack of blank cards and some dice, pens, and plastic tokens, to see what he could come up with. The meta-game, he decided, should be quick, easy to learn and to play, an intentionally light contrast with the darkly mythic milieu of what he started thinking of as the "outer game." But before long the idea began to spiral away from him. The pile of scribbled-on cards grew, then divided into separate, distinct decks, each with its own role and purpose. He scavenged random tokens and figurines from some of his other works-in-stalled-progress. He started filling a notebook with proliferating rules, turn structures, narrative trees.

Every so often, a forgotten image or episode from his life in River Meadows would pop into his head and he'd write it down on a card as well and set it aside. The big, brand-new house they'd moved into. A family argument at the dinner table. That last long afternoon in River Meadows before they were suddenly homeless, driving out of town with the few belongings they'd had time to gather and no idea whether they'd ever be coming back. What did any of that have to do with this legendary island and its vanished days of glory? He had no idea, but after a while these brief images of his own past were all he was putting down on the cards. And not just memories but episodes in his family's life that he hadn't been there to witness. What had his mother's days really been like? His father's?

Before long he wasn't sure these rescued and imagined fragments of personal history were meant to be part of the game, or whether this was a game at all anymore.

He had been sitting on his floor with cards and tokens scattered all around him when his mother called to tell him she hadn't heard from Amery in weeks.

After meeting with Michio, Alex drives his rental car to the local information centre, where he asks about maps of the region. He is given one that includes the Environmental Reclamation Area. He visits a grocery and loads up on protein bars, instant soup, and trail mix. At the hunting and fishing supply store across the street he buys a large backpack, Thermos, waterproof matches, a heavy-duty flashlight, a pair of hiking boots. He loads these items into his car, stands there thinking for a few moments, then goes back into the store and purchases an ultralight tent and sleeping bag.

Back at the hotel, he lays everything out on the bed and notices with a kind of dull wonder that his hands are shaking. He's really going to do this.

He pours himself a whisky from the bottle he brought with him, sits on the bed, and starts at the beginning of Amery's notebook. After a few entries about bird and animal sightings, and the rescuing of an injured thrush she found lying on a road, he starts flipping pages, looking for his own name. Near the end of the book, he finds it.

At the top of the page is an entry about the fiery holocausts in Australia and Brazil. Below that, a list of other places on the planet that have been abandoned after human-caused catastrophe and became like River Meadows. Involuntary parks where children don't play, where no one gathers for a picnic or an outdoor concert, where no one stretches out on the grass on a summer afternoon and dreamily watches the clouds drift by.

Tikal. Epecuén. Varosha. Shi Cheng. Pripyat. Wittenoom. Namie. Bor. Arkwright. Fukushima. Asteria. River Meadows.

Alex makes impossible worlds. We're making this world impossible for ourselves.

He sets the journal aside, then unfolds the map on the bed. He studies what little detail there is. The red-shaded trapezoid that delineates the Park provides little more than its watercourses and a dotting of small ponds and sloughs. The town's roads, which must still exist in some form, are not shown. The words NO ACCESS are stamped across the restricted area in large, bold letters.

There's a tall electrified fence all the way around the Park, that much is common knowledge, but obviously the people who go in there have found a way—or ways—through. There may be a section of fence cut open that the authorities don't know about. Or more than one. If he walked around the entire perimeter maybe he could find a way in. What is the terrain like, though, just outside the fence? He has no idea. How long would it take him to make that walk? If Michio knows as much about Amery's activities as it seems likely he does, he's probably aware of how Amery gets in and out.

And what about Michio himself. Closed off to intruders, like the Park.

Alex picks up his phone but there's very little to find online. The name Michio Amano—at least the Michio Amano of Pine Ridge—doesn't appear on any social media platforms. He's listed as a part-time instructor in the Pine Ridge College faculty directory, teaching courses in the earth sciences. He's co-authored a couple of papers on weather, complexity theory, and global warming. His name pops up in a list of participants in a recent cancer charity fun run. There's a short clip of him lecturing that a student posted several years ago, titled "A Trippy Talk by My Teacher."

In the shaky poor-quality phone video, Michio stands at a whiteboard covered in what to Alex are incomprehensible numerical hieroglyphics.

Numbers may seem to be cold, indifferent abstractions, one can hear him saying, *but they open a window on a universe of wonder. Of fantastical strangeness. Thanks to numbers we know that reality at heart is nothing but fluctuating, vibrating fields of energy. And that includes us. What emerges from the interplay of these fields is what we call reality: space, time, matter, you and me, everything we take to be solid and real. And numbers also suggest that every instant, as one part of this web of energy entangles with another part, more or less probable versions of our universe branch off from one another. Every instant, another universe. Another you, another me. As far as we know, we can never interact with these other worlds. Never confirm empirically that they exist. But the thing is, the equations . . . the numbers . . . don't expressly rule out the possibility that somehow, one day, we might turn a corner and meet another version of ourselves.*

Alex scrolls a while longer without finding any further evidence of the man. He drops his phone on the bed. The Park is up the highway from here, less than an hour's drive. He shouldn't be sitting here waiting for Michio to call back. He should be heading out there right now.

And if he actually got in, what then?

He packs up the stuff he's bought, gets in his rental car, pulls out onto the highway. The sign at the edge of town that used to say *River Meadows 70 km* has been removed but there's only one way to get there. There's no chance he can miss it.

Amery lay in the hospital bed for seven days after losing consciousness at the diner. She wasn't asleep but she wasn't in a coma either. It was some kind of in-between state that baffled the doctors and wore his parents ragged with worry.

In late afternoon on the seventh day of this vigil, Alex's mother had gone down to the hospital cafeteria to get herself a coffee, readying herself for what was likely to be another long night, leaving Alex to watch his sister.

His father hadn't yet returned from his first shift at the Conjuring Creek extraction site. He'd landed a job with Northfire, driving one of those monster trucks that hauled the ore up out of the excavation pits—arguing that he couldn't just sit here waiting, doing nothing while their money ran out. His cousin down east who owned the construction business wasn't going to wait forever for him to show up. So he'd found work. And it was good work. The pay was amazing. Triple what his cousin had offered him.

As a result of what he'd gone and done without telling her, Alex's mother was barely speaking to him.

Alex didn't yet have a clear picture of what went on out at the Northfire sites, other than the fact that his father would be driving a big truck, as he had always done. The truth was he barely cared. Only after he'd started high school in River Meadows and had been given the assignment of interviewing a parent about their job did he finally see the place for himself. His mother convinced him he should choose his father. It was her way, he understood much later, of trying to bring the two of them closer together.

And so one Saturday morning he sat in silence as his father drove north out of town, joining the unbroken line of trucks and cars heading to the main Northfire excavation site. At one point they passed hard hats nailed to fence posts running along a snow-flecked stubble field, dozens and dozens of hats, white, yellow, green, blue, in a long line. When he asked his father what the hats were there for, Ben looked uncomfortable and then said they were memorials to people who'd died on the job. Alex tried to count the hats, but they were moving too fast and he couldn't keep track. They passed a huge settling pond, covered in stiff yellowish foam, that his father told him was nicknamed Perfume Lake. Before the Northfire site even came into view, the smell of it reached into the cab: a sour, stinging mix of exhaust fumes, churned mud, and rotten eggs.

At the staging yard, Alex was given his own hard hat, safety glasses, and a bright orange vest. He got to climb all the way up to the cab of one of the giant heavy haulers Ben drove, ferrying loads of raw ore from the excavation pits to the extraction facility.

The Fafnir Mark Four, tall as a three-storey building, his father said with obvious pride. Impressive, isn't it?

It was, Alex had had to admit.

Next Ben took him up the clangy spiral stairway of an observation tower. As they climbed above the wall of planted evergreens that veiled the mining operations from the tidy, visitor-friendly office complex, with its cheerful signs displaying images of pristine wetlands and happy canoers, the morning mist began to dissipate. Into view came a startling vision of another world.

Before them an impossibly long, wide, and deep swath of the planet had been stripped, with disturbingly geometric precision, of the dense forest that had covered it and that still grew untouched in the distance on either side. Alex was reminded of a movie he had seen once where the camera zoomed out over Central Park in New York City, revealing a long rectangle of vivid green in the midst of grey city walls and towers. Only here the image was reversed: the green was everything *but* this vast hollowing of dark, churned clay dotted with oily-looking pools.

As it was morning and they were facing east, the excavation was filled with fathomless black shadows, as if this was the hole the night crawled back into when morning came. There were more of the giant yellow trucks down there, looking tiny from here. At the far edge of the site, hazy with distance, rose three huge grey and silver structures, like squarish, misshapen elephants, each with ragged flags of white steam and plumes of darker smoke trailing from their tall chimney stacks. Those were the extractors, his father told him. From inside the observation tower their deep churning reached Alex as a tremor he could feel through the metal railing he clung to. The extractors processed the raw ore, separating the precious fuel from its matrix of sand, water, and clay. Like the excavating itself, that work went on all day, every day, and all night. It only stopped for a few days once a year, when the extractors were shut down so that teams of welders and pipefitters could crawl inside the workings and replace the parts that had been worn away by relentless abrasion and heat.

After they climbed down from the tower, Alex's father took him to a room in a large work trailer. There were men in white coats here, and a small glass tube on a table with something in it—a spherical piece of rock or clump of dirt with a dull wet sheen, like a tiny planet. This is the ore, his father told him. Look what happens when we shine a certain wavelength of light on it.

One of the men in white coats flicked a switch on the side of a machine like a big camera. Alex couldn't see any light coming from it, but something began happening to the sphere in the tube—it was glowing, shimmering, coming alive with every colour there was. Arcing plumes of light like tiny rainbows danced over its surface and held his astonished gaze.

It was the most beautiful thing he had ever seen.

As he sat in a chair by his sister's bedside, that vision was still months away. The River Meadows hospital was small and overcrowded—a huge, brand-new hospital was still under construction—so they'd put Amery in the same room as an old woman recovering from hip surgery. She was asleep right now, but her snoring annoyed Alex, and so he got up and went to the doorway to look up and down the hospital corridor. He noticed a thick black binder on the nursing station desk, on the spine of which someone had placed a sticky note with *Touch This and Die* scrawled in felt pen on it, each word underlined three times.

Nurses hurried past without a glance at him. Except for Reyna, the small Filipina nurse who usually looked after Amery.

"You need something, Alex?" she stopped to ask.

"I'm okay."

"Your sister, she will be fine. Don't worry. I see this before."

"You have?"

Reyna nodded.

"My daughter. She fall asleep sometime, after wobble. Then she wake up. Fifteen minutes maybe. That's all."

"And she's okay after?"

"Yeah, she fine. Amery just sleeping longer. You wait, she come back. She not gone far."

She touched his arm and hurried away.

Alex went back into the room and looked at Amery again, at her calm, untroubled face. He was not used to seeing her like this, silent and unmoving, and the unsettling feeling came over him that he didn't know this person and never had. She was his sister, yes, but who *was* she, really? How much had he ever thought about her, until now? Before this happened to her, who had she been? What had she wondered about or dreamed of?

An icy pit of fear opened in his stomach as he realized he was already forgetting what her voice sounded like.

He sat down and picked up the Mister Mobius comic book he'd already read, a double issue in which Mister Mobius teamed up with Crypto-Girl and Graviteen to face off against the evil cabal known as the Elohim, which had risen again, led by a mystery villain calling himself The Primordian, who turned out to be Mister Mobius's old nemesis, Lord Chroniac, in disguise. Everyone had believed Chroniac was dead, scattered through the space-time continuum several issues ago by his own temporal bomb. But here he was, to the shock of the heroes (even though he had already come back from the dead twice before over the years). There was no suspense left in any of this for Alex—he'd read this particular issue countless times—but he lingered once more over the panels in which Crypto-Girl leapt into battle against Chroniac's beautiful but ruthless female accomplice Nightbird, who had the speed, power, and agility of wild animals at her command.

The girl at the restaurant, he thought with an excited tremor. That's why she had looked so familiar to him. She had the same short dark hair and black-rimmed eyes as the comic book villain. His own eyes ran over the taut curves of Nightbird's hips, the exhilarating outline of her breasts in skin-tight black leather. His father sometimes teased him about still reading comic books. He didn't suspect, or Alex assumed he didn't, the new source of pleasure his son had begun to draw from them.

Alex knew that a few issues later Nightbird would defect to the good guys' side, join the Alliance of Justice, and fight alongside the major players—Macroman, Neutrino, the Beacon—at which point she would get an even more revealing costume, on glorious display in a massive double issue that had been carefully tucked away with the rest of his comics in a box now sitting in a truck somewhere in that eastern city, waiting with all their other possessions to be shipped back here to them. After her shift of allegiance, Nightbird's breasts had been considerably enlarged by the artist to take full advantage of the new costume. But after his initial excitement had worn off, Alex decided he preferred the leaner Nightbird, perhaps because she was still bad and that was more exciting to dream about.

But right now he couldn't linger over these wonderful pages: the old woman, Mrs. Chernik, had woken up, and was talking either to herself or to Alex, it wasn't clear which. Over the last few days she'd chattered his family's collective ear off over how much nicer River Meadows used to be before they started digging up that dirty, awful black gunk, back when she was younger and there weren't all these people from other places who couldn't speak English worth a darn but who expected to get a good job and health care and everything else just handed to them, like they were entitled to it, although you had to admit some of them were very nice people. Like Reyna, of course, who was a real sweetheart, even though she was Filipino, like so many of them were nowadays. But if no one else was willing to do the kind of jobs they were, you couldn't be too picky. And you know, these people work hard, they sacrifice for their families. You had to admit that. Reyna had told her she had four kids and one of them a baby boy not a year old—she'd shown Mrs. Chernik a picture, and he was a cute little thing with his chubby face and shock of black hair.

"They had him plunked down in front of a toy piano," Mrs. Chernik said, "which is starting things a bit early if you ask me, but that's how they like to do it, you know, folks from over there. They make sure their kids get a running start on ours. It's all about money and getting ahead with these people. Anyhow, here Reyna is with a new baby and a houseful of kids and she's already back at work. It's the way things used to be in this country before our young people got so lazy. Filipinos work hard, you have to admire that, even though it's annoying when you have to ask someone to repeat themselves three times."

Alex said nothing. The old woman was lying propped on a buttress of pillows with her eyes still closed, her veiny hands clasped together on her chest. Still he turned the comic book slightly so that Nightbird's revealing anatomy would be less visible if she looked his way.

In the second half of the story Chroniac hurtled Mister Mobius millions of years back to the time of the asteroid that killed off the dinosaurs. He'd also trapped Crypto-Girl and Graviteen in a noctosphere that nullified their powers. Their aging was accelerating too and Chroniac had devoured nearly all the time they had left. There was this great panel where he was licking his creepy blue lips and saying *Mmmm, those minutes were sooooo delicious! May I have seconds?*

Alex wondered what time would taste like. It wasn't something you could see, hear, or touch. Or was it? When you were eating a grilled cheese sandwich, maybe that's what time tasted like at that moment. At another moment it tasted like mashed potatoes, or toothpaste, or even nothing at all. Everything you did *took* time. Listening to Mrs. Chernik and the voices from the nurses' station. Tasting the greasy grilled cheese sandwich from the hospital cafeteria that he'd had for lunch. What did it mean for something to take time? Where did things take it? Could time be used up, like a candle burning down or gas in your car? *I'm sorry, you're out of time. No, I'm just in time.* Time is a something we're all inside of, that's moving around us. Isn't that right? Or we're moving through it. What if people and things weren't in time, what if they were *made of* time? Maybe that's what everything really was, even him. Just time. And that's why nothing ever stayed the same, because time changed everything as it got used up, like gasoline turning into heat and smoke in your car engine.

Time is running out.

Time's up.

He glanced at Amery. When she woke up, he wondered, would it seem to her like no time at all since she fell asleep?

If she woke up.

Mrs. Chernik had moved on to talking about missing her neighbour, Gloria Townsend, who had died a year ago, almost exactly three years to the day after Lyle. She even missed Mrs. Townsend's endless bragging about how much money her investment manager husband made and how her son Tony was an important neurosurgeon in Michigan who performed life-saving operations no one else dared to.

Alex flipped back to the panels where Crypto-Girl was still battling Nightbird, no time having passed for either of them, hoping to distract himself from the woman's voice. Being stuck in this room with her was like being trapped in a noctosphere.

"And wouldn't you know it," Mrs. Chernik said, "she came to see me just last night."

Alex looked up at her. She'd been talking about someone who died, hadn't she? Mrs. Chernik was staring right back at him.

"She did," Mrs. Chernik said, as if Alex had disputed her statement. "She was standing right here, beside my bed, plain as day. She didn't say a word for a change. But I knew what she was thinking. Oh yes. She was thinking she was even more of a big deal now that she'd managed to come back from the dead. Well, I said to her—"

Alex felt a quick, tingly shiver running through reality, like a faint pulse of electrical current. It was happening again, but this time it didn't alter things around him, or himself, it just passed through and then it was over.

The wobble had been enough to halt Mrs. Chernik in mid-sentence, a startled look on her face. So she had felt it too, he was pretty sure, like the dark-haired girl in the restaurant had. This wasn't just him, though Reyna was still the only person who had admitted the decoherences had some kind of impact. (Over the weeks and months to come, whenever one of these wobbles occurred, he watched how other people were affected by them, even though they usually pretended not to be, going about their business as if nothing had happened.)

"Oh my," Mrs. Chernik said, lifting her blanket to take a peep under it. "I think I've . . ."

She lowered the blanket with an anxious sideways glance at Alex and groped for the call bell.

Alex put his head down and picked up the comic book. He had a pretty good idea what her problem was and didn't want to think about it. Although it was a surprise to him. He hadn't realized that could happen to adults.

Then he saw the opportunity—he could ask this old woman about the wobbles. She'd lived here a long time and probably knew more than Reyna did. It would be safe to talk to her about what had happened in the diner because nobody ever really listened to her. He had watched his mother tune her out many times over the last few days.

"So . . . that was weird, right?" he said, a little louder than necessary. "What just happened."

Mrs. Chernik frowned at him, her eyes narrowing. This was the first time he'd made any effort to hold a conversation with her. Then she smiled primly. "We don't talk about that, young man," she said.

"But . . . do you know what it is?"

She tilted her head to one side. "What do *you* think it is?"

He hesitated, suddenly not sure they were talking about the same thing. He was about to try again, when Reyna the nurse came hurrying in.

"You call me?" she said to Mrs. Chernik.

"I did," the old woman said, flustered again. She turned to Alex. "Go get yourself a treat, young man, from the candy machine. Reyna, it wasn't really the boy's fault but I got startled and—"

Reyna gave a little gasp.

"Oh, hello, honey! You are awake!"

It was true. Amery was sitting up in bed, blinking her eyes and clutching her stuffed panda, Shoo-Shoo.

Reyna hurried over, felt Amery's wrist and forehead.

"You all right, sweetie? How you feel?"

Amery's blank gaze roved around the room and found her brother. "Where's Mom?" she asked.

Alex stood up out of his chair but found himself reluctant to go near his sister. As if she, like the old woman's friend, had just come back from the dead.

"She's getting a coffee," he said at last.

"I find Doctor Kapoor," Reyna said. "Alex, you watch your sister for me. I be right back." She hurried from the room.

Amery caught sight of Mrs. Chernik and stared at her without expression. "Who are you?"

"Hello, dear," Mrs. Chernik said with a strained effort at grandmotherly sweetness that only revealed how ruffled she was to have her own predicament ignored in all the commotion. "I'm Ada. Your mommy and daddy are going to be very happy to see—"

She was interrupted again, this time by the arrival of Alex's mother, who, as Mrs. Chernik had foretold, was very happy. So happy she dropped her coffee cup and began to cry.

Amery was checked over by the doctor, and when he couldn't find anything to be concerned about, she was discharged. Alex's father rushed to the hospital from his new job, and they drove back to the motel in the minivan. On the way Alex asked Amery if she remembered anything from just before she passed out in the restaurant. She didn't. All she recalled was sitting in the booth and feeling too tired to eat her dinner, then waking up in a hospital bed with everyone staring at her.

It occurred to Alex then that there had been a wobble in things both when Amery fell unconscious and when she woke up.

The next morning, they checked out of the Lulla-Bear and moved into another motel, in a quiet, evergreen-shaded area near the river, that rented standalone cabins by the month to industry workers. Each cabin had a woman's name on a wood-burnt plaque on the door. Frances. Sarah. Heidi. Kate.

The Hewitt family moved into Frances. Her parents forbade Amery from venturing out of sight and charged Alex with making sure she didn't. The motel's scrubby grounds had a couple of picnic tables, a sandbox with more cigarette butts in it than sand, and the rusty frame of a swing set with no swings. While Alex and Amery listlessly wandered the grounds, look-ing in vain for something to do, their parents shut themselves in the cabin to have it out.

From a distance Alex could hear the sounds of hammering, sawing. The warm, buoyant scent of sawdust drifted to him on the breeze. Somewhere nearby a new house was going up.

He hung around the back porch, eavesdropping through the open screen door. Alex's parents were not loud, passionate arguers. For them to reach the point of yelling took a lot of eva-sive manoeuvres and a slow buildup of tension-filled silence, like a gathering storm cloud.

He knew that his mother had been as upset as he was about having to leave their home, if not more so. She hadn't wanted to move all the way across the country to that big city where they knew almost no one. But now that they were grounded by unexpected circumstances, here in this town in the middle of nowhere, she defended their original destination. She told Alex's father it was a bad idea to pass up his cousin's job offer, because who knew how long this position with Northfire was going to last. If he found himself out of work, he would have burned his bridges with someone who was not only a willing employer but a relative. And what kind of an education or opportunities could their children possibly have in a noisy backwater full of transients?

How can it be noisy *and* a backwater at the same time? Alex's father asked.

I don't mean backwater. You know what I mean.

Do I?

There's a funny smell here.

These cabins are old, yeah, but you gotta—

Not the cabin. This town. Don't tell me you can't smell it.

You think it's the . . . ? Come on. You have to be out at the site to even catch a whiff of the stuff.

Whatever it is, I can smell it on you when you get home.

Well thanks for telling me.

Alex felt childish listening in on all this but couldn't help himself. He wanted to know what they were deciding about his fate, and he was tired of Amery's boring game of collecting and sorting differently coloured rocks gathered from the motel's gravel parking lot.

Since waking up in the hospital, his normally boisterous sister had become weirdly quiet. When she bothered to talk she would often pause in the middle of a sentence, looking blank, and then start up again where she had left off. As if she'd gotten stuck in time while everything else moved on.

There was a big anthill near the back steps of the cabin. Alex sliced through the sandy top of it with a flat piece of wood he'd found in the ditch at the edge of the property, probably a slat from an old fence. As he listened to his parents, he watched the ants come boiling out to engage the invader. It occurred to him to wonder whether the wobble also affected animals. What did an ant feel when a wobble rippled through its lightless city of tunnels? What did an ant feel normally? Did it feel anything at all? Or what about a bird, or a dog? What did the wobbles do to *them*?

With the broken-off end of the slat he carved a zigzag trench down the side of the mound. More ants dutifully scurried out to deal with this new threat. Like little robots in a war zone, they had no choice. They were programmed to fight and die.

The voices in the cabin rose. Alex's father argued that in River Meadows his mother would be closer to her aging parents on the west coast. It was a distance you could drive in a day if you pushed it. Also, his cousin wasn't the kind of guy to take offence if he passed on the job out east. And even if the gig here didn't last at least it would give them time to get on their feet.

Get on our feet? Alex's mother shouted. We *were* on our feet, Ben. Until we ended up in this . . . nightmare.

Oh come on. Amery is okay now and Alex is fine. There's nothing to be concerned about. They know what they're doing out at the site. There's no danger. That's what you told the kids yesterday, remember.

I was trying to cheer Amery up. She's afraid it's going to happen to her again. So am I. The longer we stay here . . .

The doctors told us they can't find anything wrong with her. But I mean, if this did happen because of where we are, then, well, I think it makes sense to stay put. If it happens to her again, they'll have the best shot at figuring out what's going on.

No, that doesn't make sense. And you just said she was fine.

She is. But just in case, right? We should be *here*. Where they know about this . . . thing. They know how to deal with it.

Right, except that they don't.

An ant was crawling up Alex's bare ankle. He watched it rove this strange new terrain, making himself bear the tickle of its tiny legs. To the ant, what was he? It was aware only of a tiny part of him. It didn't know the rest, didn't know he was observing it, that he had the power of life and death over it. One ant alone didn't really have a mind anyhow. In science class he'd learned how an ant colony formed a kind of collective organism, almost like one single animal, each solitary ant like one of its brain cells, not thinking for itself, just obeying the instinctual program that the ant-brain could never deviate from.

He reached down and let the ant crawl onto his fingers. From there he could put it back onto the dirt mound it came from or carry it to the other side of the motel parking lot so it would have to go on an epic journey to find its way back, if it ever could. He could keep it climbing over and over his hand, always moving but getting nowhere. What he did to this one ant would alter that collective mind in some small way that the colony would barely notice. Like a single brain cell winking out.

You don't know what you're talking about, Alex's mother said to his father. You don't know a thing about that stuff they dig up here. You're just making excuses, and not even very good ones.

When the ant crawled to just the right spot Alex squashed it between his thumb and finger. One wipe of his hand on the sandy ground and no ant remained. Like it had never been.

Okay, fine, you're right, his father said. But I know one thing for damn sure: I'm making almost three times as much here as what Gilbert was offering. And the benefits are way better. In a couple of years we can put a down payment on a house. The company helps employees with that—they have a program. Which means we can have our own place, *our own home*, sooner than we ever thought we could. That's what you told me you wanted. What you've always dreamed of. And you know as well as I do it would be good for the kids too. For all of us. A real home.

"What are you doing?" Amery asked. Alex jumped. She was standing right beside him. He hadn't heard her approach.

"Playing with my ant farm," he said. With the slat he took another slice off the top of the decapitated mound.

"You shouldn't do that."

"No?" Alex said. "Why the hell not?"

"You shouldn't hurt the ants. They're not hurting you."

"They're ants. Jesus. They don't know any different and they don't care. They're brainless little nothings."

"This is their home."

"Well, they can go find another one. Just like we did."

He started hacking at the anthill with the slat. Over and over. Dirt and ants went flying. When he saw one crawling on the ground near him he stomped it, aware that Amery was watching him. He hacked a few more times, until she walked away, and then he stopped.

There was silence from inside the cabin. Alex had missed the end of the argument.

Later it became clear that his mother had given in, even if she wasn't completely won over by his father's arguments.

For her River Meadows remained the unplanned rest stop they never should have made. But all of them could see how happy his father was to be working again, how much of his former confidence and optimism he'd regained. And so Ben Hewitt kept climbing into the minivan every morning and driving out to Conjuring Creek and back at the end of the day, looking tired but satisfied, while Alex's mother made the best of it.

By the time their belongings came back on the moving truck, they were able to unload them into a rented bungalow in an older neighbourhood, near the schools that Alex and Amery went to that fall.

———

When classes started, Alex discovered that the dark-haired girl from the diner went to his school, Elijah Bayne Junior/Senior High.

She was in the eighth grade, one year ahead of him. He kept a lookout for her, learned where her locker was, and started taking that hallway between classes and at the end of the day. He got to know the nobody-messes-with-me way she carried herself, her skeptical head tilt and eyebrow lift when gossiping with her friends, the feline way she stretched on tiptoe to put her schoolbooks on the top shelf of her locker. She talked and acted like nothing impressed her and she couldn't care less, but that wasn't who she really was. At the Starlite Diner, for an instant, he had seen someone else.

They didn't have any classes together, but in the hothouse of junior high he couldn't help learning things about her. There were rumours about her mother sleeping around when her husband was away. He was a scientist who studied climate change or something in the Arctic.

Alex caught her eye once in the hallway, but there was no recognition in her passing gaze. He'd clung to the hope that she knew who he was and remembered what had happened that night at the diner, that it mattered to her. But she didn't remember him, that seemed pretty clear.

The school year passed and the next grade began for Alex. He had friends now, with whom he played chess and video games. He'd started making his very first board game, a shameless imitation of Dungeons and Dragons that he abandoned before he got very far. It was far too ambitious and besides, there were other girls he was interested in now who took up most of his time and thought. Like Corrie Velasco. She was the daughter of Reyna, the nurse who'd looked after Amery in the hospital. When Alex discovered that, he'd kept an eye on

Corrie because she was the only other person he'd heard of in this town who'd been affected by the wobbles the way Amery had. But before long his interest in her had changed its focus. She was outgoing and bubbly and had a smile for everyone. She'd even talked to him a few times in the hallway. Pretty much the opposite of Claire Foley.

In late October, a Halloween dance was held at the school. Alex went and stood on the sidelines with two of his friends. He told himself he could ask a girl to dance if he wanted to, he could go right up to Corrie Velasco and ask her, she loved to dance, but he didn't see the point. Why did people do this weird thing, flailing around like idiots, pretending they were enjoying themselves just to get closer to someone they were attracted to? Why did there have to be this dumb ritual everyone obeyed, mindlessly following their programming like those stupid ants? His friends, who also hadn't asked anyone to dance, were shoving each other around like morons and getting on his nerves. Finally, he'd had enough and told his friends he was going home.

Outside on the steps someone called his name.

It was her. Claire Foley.

She was standing on the lawn in a little huddle of her friends. His heart lurched. He didn't know what to do or what he felt, other than confusion. Over the past few months he'd come to harbour a vague hostility toward her, because she was inaccessible to him and hung out with the cool crowd, the rule-breakers, a faction he wasn't part of and never would be.

And now this.

Warily he walked over. He could see from her loose stance and crooked grin that she was drunk. She repeated his name, drawing the syllables out, like the two of them were old pals who hadn't seen each other in ages. He held his breath, every sense on alert, focused on her. What was she going to do?

When she asked him why he was leaving so early, he told her in a voice of carefully cultivated disinterest that the dance was boring and he was going home.

Not until you dance with me, you're not, she said. She took him suddenly by the hands and swung him around and around while her friends laughed. After a few spins he let go and walked away with a shrug, as if this was no big deal.

Goodbye, Alex, she called after him, saying his name over and over like the refrain of a song. *Ahhhlex . . . Ahhhlex . . . Ahhhlex . . .*

When he got home he lay on his bed and replayed the incident over and over in his imagination. How she'd said his name like it was the key to everything. He wanted to believe she'd finally acknowledged him, admitted there was a link between them, that from this point on their lives would converge like he knew they were supposed to.

The next day at school she walked right past him without a glance, the way she had always done. As the days went by, she showed up less often to classes. Eventually she dropped out and disappeared from view, apparently having left town. He understood that what she had been doing that night outside the school, spinning him around like that, wasn't to bring him closer but simply to gain a little extra momentum to fling herself farther away from him and everyone else.

The following September, the Hewitts moved again, to a brand-new blue-and-white split level with a double garage in a brand-new subdivision called Foxhaven, where foxes were eagerly looked for by the neighbourhood kids, but never seen.

THE RIVER MEADOWS ARCHIVE

HISTORY

Early in his career, Richard Burton, the famous Victorian explorer and translator of *The Arabian Nights*, is stationed as an officer of the British East India Company in northern India. He grows tired of living in close quarters with the other men and moves by himself into a house where he collects forty monkeys of many species to be his companions. He gives them names, dresses them in clothes tailored to fit them, and dines with them, even designating one of the female monkeys his wife.

Burton's plan is to learn the language of monkeys, and so he talks with them, practising and imitating the sounds they make. Over time he gathers something like sixty "words" of monkey speech. The experiment is cut short when he is transferred to another posting and has to abandon his monkey household.

Burton's papers from this time are lost when the warehouse where they were kept is destroyed in a fire.

———

In London in the late 1700s, a "learned" pig is exhibited that can spell out words and solve arithmetical problems by picking up cards with its mouth. Hearing of this phenomenon, Samuel Johnson opines that *pigs are a race unjustly calumniated. Pig has, it seems, not been wanting to man, but man to pig. We do not allow time for his education; we kill him at a year old.*

In 2020 a prototype microchip is implanted in the brain of a pig named Gertrude, to read and record her neural activity during such activities as feeding, rooting, and dreaming. The media quickly dub her "Cypork." The experiment, says its creator, is a first step toward a brain-to-machine interface for humans that will allow us to control computers and other devices with our minds. The pig was a natural choice given how similar its cognition and emotions are to those of humans.

In Burlington, Ontario, a transport truck carrying pigs is involved in a traffic accident while on the way to a pork processing plant. The crash occurs close enough to the entrance of the plant that employees are quickly on hand to help bring the surviving animals safely out of the wreckage. Of the 180 pigs in the truck, 138 are rescued, visibly distressed but otherwise unharmed.

The pigs are then herded into the plant for slaughter.

The 2019–20 bushfires in Australia devastated the populations of many birds, including the regent honeyeater, which was already endangered by habitat loss. Now the remaining honeyeaters are so scattered that the young rarely encounter the male adults, whose role it is to teach them the species' mating calls. Scientists fear the honeyeaters are dying out because they are forgetting how to speak their own language.

———

In the 1960s NASA-funded researchers administer doses of
LSD to several captive dolphins as part of an attempt to teach
the animals the rudiments of English. The dolphins become
much more vocal under the influence of the hallucinogen,
although none of the test subjects are ultimately able to learn
and understand English words or phrases.

One of the male dolphins is kept isolated from the others
for three months, his contacts restricted to human researchers.
This dolphin, named Peter, becomes attached to one of the
women scientists and makes sexual advances toward her. To
avoid disruption of the project, the researcher resorts to man-
ually relieving Peter's misdirected urges.

When funding for the project runs out, the dolphins are
transferred to another facility in Miami and no longer have any
contact with the researchers. Peter begins to show the classic
signs of depression noted in his species, such as lack of interest
in food and social interaction. Soon afterward he dies.

China's jet fighters are protected from damage caused by acciden-
tal bird collisions by a squadron of male rhesus macaques (*Macaca
mulatta*) trained to find and destroy bird nests near military airfields around Beijing. The monkeys were not caught in the wild
but previously belonged to itinerant street performers, who had
made them relatively easy to retrain for other purposes by teaching
them to respond to rudimentary spoken and signed commands.

The airfields are located along a migration route known as
the East Asian–Australasian flyway. Huge flocks of migrating
birds, heedless of national borders, pass through the area in
March every year and begin nesting and breeding, which creates
a safety hazard for the jet fighters and their pilots during training manoeuvres.

The People's Liberation Army's Bird Control Division has taught the macaques to scramble up trees and dismantle nests by pulling out twigs. Airbase commander Wang Yuejian told *China Daily*: "Our reconnaissance indicates that two monkeys alone have taken out over 180 nests in the past month."

The star of the primate squadron is a monkey whose speed, intelligence, and enthusiasm for destroying nests is unmatched by any of the others. His admiring handlers name him Sun Wukong, after the monkey king from the classic Chinese novel *Journey to the West*. Sun Wukong begins his career as a demonic figure of rage and chaos, living only to fight and kill, until the suffering of others opens his heart to compassion, and at last he becomes a Buddha.

The handlers claim that Sun Wukong can differentiate between the various species of birds whose nests he is sent to destroy. "When I tell him crane," said one handler, "he goes after only the nests of cranes."

The destruction of the bird nests is deemed necessary so that the valuable and rarely seen fighter jets will be safe and ready for the ceremonies in Beijing marking the seventieth anniversary of Japan's surrender at the end of World War II. The celebration includes a parade of tanks through Tiananmen Square and an airshow.

On his journey up the Orinoco River in the year 1800, the German naturalist Alexander von Humboldt collects birds and monkeys that he keeps in cages on the already overburdened canoes. A mastiff attaches itself to their party during a stay at one of the Catholic missions. Humboldt is grateful for the presence of this large, powerful dog in a jungle teeming with crocodiles, jaguars, and poisonous snakes.

At the village of Maypures, Humboldt is shown a tame parrot that can speak words. Humboldt wishes very much to add this marvellous bird to his menagerie. Through a translator he asks the parrot's owner, an old woman, what the bird is saying.

"We don't know," the old woman tells him. "It speaks the language of the Atures, and they're all gone."

From his native guides Humboldt learns that the Carib people wiped out the Atures tribe some years before. The parrot was one of the spoils of war, but there is no one left alive who can understand it. The bird is the very last speaker of the language known as Maipure.

The villagers will not surrender the bird, but in his journal, Humboldt transcribes the forty words the parrot knows, the last of a vanished people.

Returning to the Venezuelan coast, Humboldt arranges to have his jungle menagerie shipped home across the Atlantic. The animals do not survive the long, arduous sea voyage, but their skins and plumage make it to the Natural History Museum in Paris, where Humboldt is able to view them again four years later, after his return to Europe.

In 1997 an American artist and a bird behaviourist team up to teach a group of parrots to speak the forty surviving words of Maipure. The birds are kept in a small aviary made of opaque plastic that amplifies and echoes their speech, while they themselves remain obscured from view.

Studies have shown that birds experience REM sleep much as mammals do, which suggests that they dream.

The great auk (*Pinguinus impennis*) is driven to extinction in the modern era by Europeans who hunt and kill the bird for its down, used to make pillows. The bird's demise is hastened further by its own increasing rarity, as museums and collectors are willing to pay enticing sums for specimens, money that proves irresistible to poor fishers and sheepherders.

The very last colony of great auks survives until the middle of the nineteenth century, on the nearly inaccessible island of Eldey, off the coast of Iceland. On July 3, 1844, three men sent in search of great auks by a wealthy collector find what is possibly the very last breeding pair of great auks in the world, incubating a single egg. One of the men, Sigurður Ísleifsson, later described what took place:

> The rocks were covered with blackbirds and then we saw the geirfuglana (the auks) . . . They walked slowly. Jón Brandsson crept up with his arms open. The bird that Jón got went into a corner but mine was going to the edge of the cliff. It walked like a man . . . but moved its feet quickly. I caught it close to the edge, a precipice many fathoms deep. Its wings lay close to the sides, not hanging out. I took him by the neck and he flapped his wings. He made no cry. I strangled him.

The third man, Ketil Ketilsson, finds the nest and, acting on a familiar human impulse that has yet to be fully understood, smashes the egg with his boot. That night, he and his companions return home from their long, exhausting day and fall asleep quickly, their heads filling with phantom people and scenes that vanish into nothingness and are left unrecorded when they wake.

From this night on there are no more great auk dreams.

———

In response to increasing Soviet presence in Arctic waters, the US Navy begins a program in the early 1980s to train whales to detect underwater mines and retrieve sunken test torpedoes. Belugas, with their friendly, trusting nature, turn out to be the ideal subjects for training. A young male beluga named Noc is caught as a calf and spends most of his life in captivity, interacting with humans.

The divers who train the whales talk to their onshore supervisor through an underwater communications device called a wet phone. One day a diver hears an order to get out of the water that he thinks has come from his supervisor. When the supervisor denies having given the order, they discover that Noc has learned to imitate human speech. From this point on, recordings are made of Noc's burbled strings of human-sounding chatter, and his vocal abilities tested, in order to determine if this is a real attempt at speech or only mindless mimicry. Belugas, like all whales, have their own complex forms of auditory communication. Noc babbles only around humans, and not with the others of his own species in captivity. It's suggested by some expert observers that Noc resorts to mimicry out of boredom, or perhaps even mockery of what he considers meaningless human noise.

Four years after Noc is first overheard speaking, he abruptly stops making human sounds. For some reason, after that, the researchers no longer call him Noc, and he is known from then on only as "beluga."

Some words for animals in languages that no longer have native speakers:

fish, Ubykh: psa
fox, Woccon: tauh-he
mouse, Thracian: argilos
worm, Anglo-Norman: achée
turtle, Kansa: ke
cattle, Norn: kye
hummingbird, Taino: colibri
wolf, Old English: wulf
lion, Vaal-Orange: !hoeti
frog, u'Yoi: mana
horse, Phoenician: ss
dog, Mbabaram: dog

1558: Aboard the ship bringing Jean de Léry home from
Brazil, the "Land of Parrots," an eerie silence now prevails.
All through the voyage the crowded decks have resounded
with the calls, grunts, hoots, and seasick whimpers of the
exotic animals de Léry has collected during his brief sojourn
in the New World and that he hopes to present as gifts to
noble patrons upon his return to France. But the worm-eaten
old hulk of a ship has been plagued by constant leaking and
driven far off course by a hurricane. The provisions have long
run out, and with starvation looming the crew has turned to
de Léry's menagerie for salvation. Into the cooking pot, one
after another, have gone monkeys, lizards, birds feathered in
every colour of the rainbow, and other creatures with no
names as yet in the tongues of civilized men.

A shoemaker by trade, young Jean de Léry joined a band of
fifteen French Calvinists who had sailed across the Atlantic
only a year earlier with the dream of establishing their perse-
cuted new faith on this virgin continent. Back home in Europe

countless lives had been lost to fire and sword in the ferocious religious wars of the age. The colonists hoped that here, in this untouched paradise, men might remember they were all brothers and live in peace.

The hope was short-lived. The governor of the fledgling French colony they'd joined maintained that the consecrated bread given out at Mass was, by the mysterious grace of God, both real bread and Christ's actual flesh. De Léry and the other new arrivals, firm in the rational principles of the Reformation, disagreed. They followed John Calvin's teaching that the sacrament of the Eucharist was a kind of spiritual sustenance only. The notion that the Saviour transports himself down from heaven every Sunday to be divided up into tidbits and nibbled on was grotesque, a fantasy imposed on the credulous by a corrupt and superstition-encrusted Church.

The Calvinists were banished from the colony for their heresy and sought shelter among the Tupinambá people. They were cannibals, it was true, but they dined only on the captured warriors of a neighbouring tribe and had no interest in the flesh of Frenchmen. And soon de Léry had to admit he found these naked savages more charitable and good-natured than many of his own countrymen. One rarely saw them without smiles on their faces. They shared what little they had with the exiles, teaching them which plants were safe to eat or good for ailments. They took childlike delight in the few cheap trinkets de Léry and his companions offered them in return. But with war almost unceasing between the Tupinambá and their ancestral enemies (not to mention the Portuguese, staking their own claim to the newfound riches of Brazil), the Frenchmen lived in constant fear for their lives. When an outgoing merchant vessel offered them return passage to France, they hastily accepted.

For weeks now the ship has been lost upon the trackless ocean, and nearly all of de Léry's animals have been devoured. What he fancied as his own little ark is dying, and himself with it. And yet miraculously he has managed to keep his most cherished specimen alive and hidden from the crew, a magnificently plumed parrot, blue as the heavens and as big as a goose. De Léry has already taught the bird a few simple prayers and polite phrases for the day he finds it a new berth in some rich man's menagerie. Each morning, after his companions crawl out on deck to strain their bloodshot eyes for any sight of land, he feeds the parrot a few seeds from the remaining handful he has squirrelled away, and he and the bird hold a conversation.

And what is your name, my fine fellow?

I am called Jacques. Pleased to meet you.

I am glad to make your acquaintance as well. My name is Jean.

But at last, nearly mad with hunger and fearful of what will happen when the others discover what he has been keeping from them, de Léry knows he must surrender his prize.

Good morning, my fine fellow, and what is your name? he asks the bird one last time as it perches on his arm.

I am called Jacques, the parrot says. *Pleased to meet you. It looks like rain.*

It does indeed. And how are you this morning?

Jacques is hungry. Jacques wishes to dine.

I know it, my friend. I wish that too. Shall we say our prayers?

The parrot doesn't answer. Instead it preens what remains of its fading plumage.

Shall we say our prayers? de Léry asks again.

Father of all, the parrot croaks out at last. *Bless us this day. Through Jesus your Son. Amen.*

It occurs to de Léry that what truly separates mankind from the beasts is not our power of speech, the cunning of our devices, or the reach of our intellect. It's much simpler than that. Men lose the innocence they are born with. The animals do not.

De Léry brings the parrot up on deck, where it is swiftly strangled, plucked, boiled, and devoured in grim silence. Every scrap is eaten, even the hooked beak, the tripe, the scaly feet. Taking a few sinewy morsels of the bird's flesh for himself, de Léry thinks of Noah. There must have come a day aboard the Ark when they ran out of provisions and had to decide which of their precious cargo would be sacrificed to save the last of humanity. The fated chosen erased forever from the roll of God's creation. We no longer know their names or what voices they had. The guoto. The malabee. The speckled orotain.

This bountiful earth teems from pole to pole with living things, de Léry muses in awe, but here on the ship there is nothing left for the men to eat. Except one another.

Five days after the parrot falls silent forever, when it seems they will have no choice but to sample that last forbidden flesh, the lookout sights the coast of Brittany.

The decks resound once more as the men shout, sob, and cry to the heavens in gratitude for their deliverance.

In the later stages of the global COVID-19 pandemic, many people insist that during the relative quiet of the lockdowns, the birds sounded different.

Researchers eventually confirm it: as vehicle traffic, large machinery, and humans themselves became scarcer in urban and rural areas, the birds' calls and songs changed. Many birds sang more loudly, to defend their territory or attract mates, while the calls of some species became softer, as the absence of human noise allowed their voices to carry farther.

In all species that were studied, one finding was the same: as peace descended, the birds' songs became more melodious, skilled, and beautiful.

CLAIRE

In the morning she finds something halfway familiar to eat at the breakfast buffet, a plate of overcooked scrambled eggs and a kind of snail-shell-shaped roll filled with a tart blue jelly. Then she heads outside. Yesterday's fog and drizzle is maybe a little less thick. She can actually see a block or two around her, and at least a couple of storeys upward. She strolls the already bustling streets, making notes, taking pictures with her digital camera, asking questions of shopkeepers and people on their way to work. It's not up to her to do anything except be ready and play her part.

Her contact could be someone she's already met. She's rarely told ahead of time who to look for or when and where the encounter will happen, and she prefers to be kept mostly in the dark. All she knows is that she will be picking up an empty piece of luggage to take home with her. A large canvas messenger bag she can fill with whatever she likes when she's ready to leave—souvenirs, magazines, dirty clothes, it doesn't matter. The authorities check for illegal items hidden *in* one's luggage, not *as* one's luggage. It's the bag itself that's worth all her trouble and risk, because of what the inner lining is made from.

The stitched-together skins of an animal so rare it would mean prison to possess them. How long it took to collect enough skins, or how many of them were needed to line the bag, she doesn't know. Maybe all that are left on the island.

If the species was already on its way out, she reflects, some-one might as well profit from its swan song.

The perfect concentric rings of the ancient city have long since been pierced and altered and rearranged, but at ground level she finds many partial iterations of that primeval pattern: curving streets, traffic circles, a domed shopping complex like a huge glass sunflower, parks laid out as mandalas. Almost all of it is new, paid for with energy money. *Just built* is the phrase she hears most often. The tallest structure in the city is the soar-ing Spire of the Aetherean, a silver needle snagging the clouds. Just built. There's the Museum of Time, only a year old but closed for repairs because of a leaking roof. Next to it, the Theatre of Sounds—the entrance a giant human ear made of riveted metal plates—just built. Something to check out later, maybe. There's the new airport too, of course, all soaring glass and light, but she was so eager for the journey to be over she barely noticed it on her way out the doors. She'll have to pay more attention on her return. Although by then they'll likely have built a new airport.

The one thing that doesn't exist is a centre. The traffic and the curving, banking thoroughfares all seem to be orbiting around one, and it's supposed to be where the tower of the sea god stood in ancient times. Yet whenever she thinks she's about to arrive at the hub, there's a twist or a turn and the street flings her outward again, toward the periphery, like a sailboat driven off course by a contrary wind.

This city must have a heart. Every city does, and not necessarily at the geographical centre. It's a metaphor she always has at the back of her mind, something she looks for. Sometimes, in some cities, the location of the heart surprises her. With this city and its atavistic ring structure, you'd expect that spot would be right in the very bull's eye.

But it seems you can't get there.

There are enormous video screens everywhere with scrolling messages about weather conditions, tropical storm watches, and traffic updates about which roads are currently closed and where the detours are.

There seems to be a lot of police presence. *But then,* she reminds herself, *you're always looking for them.*

Her phone buzzes. A brief, anonymous text: *nice morning for a walk,* accompanied by a shared map location. A public square not far from where she's standing. She takes a moment to gaze around, as if undecided where to go next, then heads in the direction of the square.

The fog lifts. The sky is still clouded over but the city's heights are unveiled at last. She discovers she's been wandering at the bottom of an abyss of steel and glass, watched over by distantly towering cranes. Vertigo returns, and a deep churn of unease that threatens to grow into something much worse. If she lets herself think about the restless tectonic plates underneath these streets, dread washes up over her feet.

Here's the square. She'd passed through it once already this morning. It's busy, loud, surrounded by three lanes of slowly orbiting traffic. There's some kind of rally happening on the far side. A milling knot of people with banners and signs she can't read from here. A speaker on a platform, with a megaphone.

Shouts and whistles from the crowd, and curious onlookers drifting over to see what's going on.

Nothing to do with her, but whatever it is should be enough to divert attention from a canvas bag changing hands. Good choice of time and location. She needs to get this over with and then she can get back to the hotel. She scans the people around her, while pretending to consult a fold-out map in the guidebook.

Then she sees him.

He's as unremarkable as he should be. Just another scruffy-bearded young guy in jeans and a hoodie, hunched over his phone on a bus-stop bench, a large canvas messenger bag beside him, forest green with a sticker of a smiling cartoon planet Earth on the front flap, the identifying mark she was told to watch for. He looks like an exchange student, or someone not long out of high school on a cheap hostelling vacation, his great solo adventure before some nondescript career claims the rest of his life. Nobody you'd glance at twice.

She's a few dozen steps from the bus stop. A matter of seconds. She heads in his direction at a casual stroll, still making a show of consulting the map while figuring out the best approach and looking for promising escape routes in case she's got the wrong guy or this is a trap.

He glances up, notices her, holds her gaze for an instant, then glances down quickly again at his own phone.

She's only a few steps away when Andros pulls up beside her on a sleek silver and blue scooter. All she can do is stand there and stare at him. She avoids glancing at the guy on the bench. Andros drops the scooter's kickstand.

"You look lost," Andros says.

She shrugs.

"I am lost," she says, and laughs, flushing not from any embarrassment but from the sudden, sharp braking of what was just in motion. Though Andros isn't going to know that.

"That happens a lot here," he says. "Sometimes to me too."

"It's like the city wants to keep you going in circles." Grinning, she spins around once to illustrate her point, giving her a chance to check the bus-stop bench. Her contact is already gone.

"Well, if you've had enough of circles, the offer is still open," Andros says.

While she tilts her head, appearing to ponder this, she calms herself with a long, slow breath. She knows from experience that the right thing to do is to get away from the hand-off spot as fast and as far as possible.

"Sure, why not."

"Great. Where would you like to go?"

"I really don't know. Surprise me."

"Ah, okay. A challenge. Let's see . . ."

"First thing that comes to mind."

"I have an idea." He pats the scooter's seat. "Hop on."

She settles herself uneasily behind him, and he says, "Hold on tight."

She puts her arms around him, feels the lean muscles of his midsection. There's no way to maintain any distance on one of these things, she realizes too late.

The tires hum on the sand-coloured pavement, but if this vehicle actually has a motor, it's whisper quiet, and there isn't the faintest whiff of fuel. The scooter stops, starts, changes speed with a smoothness she's never experienced before. Is it electric? There are no dials, gauges, switches. She remembers the rumours about the mysterious new power source.

They weave their way out of the downtown congestion, take a soaring off-ramp onto the coastal expressway. This is not what she expected. She might get a text any minute now, giving her a new location for a retry, and she'll be too far away to make it there in time. But it's too late to tell Andros to turn around.

The scooter's quiet hum means they can talk as they drive. He tells her he's doing his graduate practicum on time crystal dynamics at the island's energy research facility. This means nothing to her.

"And on your time off? Other than helping clueless tourists."

He plays the llir, the traditional native version of the guitar. His parents are musicians in the national orchestra, and they insisted he have music in his repertoire.

"But they don't like the kind of music I ended up playing," he says with a laugh. "It's a local version of what you might call jazz. My mother calls it pots and pans falling down a flight of stairs."

Claire's mother was a nurse, but her passion was the piano. She tried to teach Claire, but it only frustrated them both.

You have to let the music in, her mother would insist as Claire plunked hopelessly at the keys. *You* are *the music, Clairey.*

So Claire tried to be the music. She really tried, her eyes brimming with frustrated tears. She didn't understand what she was being asked to do. She couldn't get to the place her mother did when she closed her eyes and her fingers flowed over the keys, so she started avoiding the piano. She retreated to books, to writing awful poetry, to hiding in her room. Eventually her mother stopped trying.

Claire doesn't tell Andros any of this. Instead she talks about other travel writers she knows, tells him semi-anonymous stories of their odd rituals, their messy lives, their misadventures. A good half of it at least is true. The rest she makes up as she goes along.

Andros merges onto another highway with a long, banking curve that takes them inward again, toward the central volcano.

Its pale blue cone stays distant and doubtful no matter how many kilometres they eat up, and then, suddenly, around a bare, rocky hillside here it is: looming over them, sharply defined, real at last. A thin white cloud of steam, like a frayed ribbon, trails from the snow-capped summit. The wind is stronger here, making it harder for them to talk.

"Is this safe?" she shouts in his ear.

"For now," he shouts back. "I thought you were looking for the dangerous stuff."

"Yeah, I was just hoping to keep a respectful distance."

The highway rounds the base and then winds under the volcano's long, ash-covered north slope. Ahead Claire glimpses pylons, a ski lift, tiny figures slaloming downhill trailing plumes of dust.

"You've got to be kidding," she breathes.

"We've had more ash than usual the last few years. So they put it to use."

They park, then climb with others up a steep pathway to the Nordic-looking chalet at the base of the chair lift. There's a faint sulphurous reek in the air but nobody seems concerned about it. While Andros is buying their passes, her phone buzzes in her pocket.

Hope you won't have to cut your trip short.

Translation: fuck this up again and there will be consequences. A second message follows a minute later. *Not today.* So she's in the clear for now.

Andros returns with the passes. "You ready?" he asks, grinning like a little boy. The scariness of what they're about to do helps her channel the shaky energy brought on by the text. "I am so ready," she shouts over the wind.

He does a double take, not expecting this sudden enthusiasm, then laughs. "Okay."

The slope looks much steeper from above than it did from below. Neither of them has much experience with skis or snow-boards, so they play it safe by renting toboggans. They're given yellow haz-mat-looking suits and gloves and goggles, then they ride the chair lift to the sledding hill.

On their first run, they slither and jounce down the hill side by side, until he leans too far sideways and rolls into the ash.

At the bottom of the slope she waits for him and laughs when she sees his chimney-sweep face.

"Sorry."

"No, that was funny," he says, dusting himself off.

Claire squints up the dark slope, at the other sledders rock-eting down, their distant shrieks and whoops, people riding the lift chairs, the peaked roof of the chalet. It's like she's looking at a photographic negative of a fine winter's day on the slopes. Skiing in hell. She digs her gloved hand into the grey dust and glittery flakes of rock and scoops up a ball that shivers apart in the wind. Her nervous energy has drained out and she feels the shakes coming on.

Pointlessness.

"I did ask you to surprise me," she says.

On the way back he takes her to the energy research facility. It's in the middle of a scrubby field that seems as far from the sea as one can get on this small island, and looks like a squat, white-washed industrial bunker. She's reminded of the Arctic field station her father spent so much time at when she was a teen-ager, the photos he sent her of it, a group of huddled trailers on a featureless tundra. He was gone so long her mother found someone to keep her company. Ray. She remembers the chunk of stone with the lichen living inside it that her father sent her from

Ellesmere. Her mother sent him back a letter saying he needn't bother coming home. Claire knows her father returned from that trip so he could see her again before he walked out of their life, but the details have slipped away. A blessing, probably, given that she does remember how much she once missed him. It is as if he'd stayed out on the ice forever.

She still has the stone and his last letter to her, in the self-storage unit where she keeps the few remaining artifacts of her past.

"In case anyone asks," Andros says just before they reach the gate in the tall chain-link fence, "you're not a writer. You're a visiting researcher."

This increases her interest, and eagerness. She's not supposed to be here.

Andros shows his security pass and they're allowed through. Inside, the facility is a humming, hissing labyrinth of corridors lined with ducts and pipes. Andros takes her past what looks to be a glassed-in control room, busy with people monitoring screens, and shows his pass to a guard stationed at another door, a woman he chats with briefly about her recent vacation to Costa Rica. The woman glances inquisitively at Claire, but Andros doesn't introduce her and they move on.

They take an elevator deeper into the complex, then walk down a long, sloping passageway to the door of another room that Andros uses his pass to unlock. The long, low room is like a bunker or a cell, holding only a table and a couple of folding chairs. On one wall there's a narrow horizontal window, reinforced with wire mesh.

Claire can feel a faint vibration rising from the floor through her shoes and into her bones. And along with it, a low throb of sound, like the slow grating of some enormous *thing* against another.

Andros gestures to her to have a look through the window. She looks.

The space on the other side of the glass is a floodlit cave carved out of dark, wet rock. In the floor, a circular hole, at least twenty metres across, opens into darkness. A catwalk runs across its mouth, and wires snake in and out of it.

"What is this?" she asks, startled to feel disappointment. After coming all this way she'd been expecting something more awe-inspiring.

"Our oldest stories say we lived under the sea once, and that's where we'll return, when the gods finally punish us for our arrogance. They gave us a warning once before, but this time they'll finish us off for good."

"You don't believe that," she says. "That the whole island's just going to disappear one day."

"It *is* disappearing," he says. "It's sinking right now."

"Well, yeah. Geologically speaking."

"No. *Now* speaking."

"What do you mean? We've got, like, a matter of hours?"

"Or days. Weeks. Years. Nobody knows. The most recent readings show an acceleration of tectonic activity, subduction at a rate no one's ever seen. The jury is still out on whether it has anything to do with all the offshore mining and fracking, but it means we *will* have an unprecedented seismic event, on a catastrophic level. We just don't know when."

Claire places a hand against the wall to steady herself. She's deep underground, miles from the ocean. Are they safer down here, or just the opposite?

"I'll tell you what *now* means," Andros says. "The government's hired a Japanese engineering firm to secretly build artificial floating islands offshore, in preparation for the possibility of mass evacuation. That's where things are at. *Our* experiment is about finding a way to keep any of that from happening. The prototype for our solution is down there."

"In that hole."

"There's a chamber at the bottom for building up a special kind of wave. Not the liquid kind. It's difficult to explain, but you could say the wave opens up alternate paths in space-time. Other ways that reality could be. If the theory behind our work is right, then you and I and everything else exist at the end of one of these countless paths, with countless branchings lying before us that lead to countless possible futures. There are realities other than this one, where the island really did sink under the waves thousands of years ago like the Greek philosopher said it did. On another path, our island is located somewhere else, or it never even existed."

"Well, for centuries people thought Plato made this place up."

"Yes, and in some realities maybe that's all we are: a cautionary tale in somebody's book. Most of the paths, though, exhibit only barely perceptible differences from the reality we know. The probability of our universe taking any one of these paths can, at least theoretically, be changed. That's what we're hoping anyhow. The intense pressure and heat down there give us the optimal conditions for the attempt. Basically we're looking to create a small, local deviation in our path. To nudge probability just a little. If we can tune the wave just right, we can make a catastrophic outcome a possibility rather than a certainty."

"I've heard of these waves before," she says, then finds herself telling him where she comes from, River Meadows, and how they used a similar process to extract what they were after from the toxic black ore it was embedded in. She's not confessing to anything she shouldn't, but it feels as if she is.

"We studied that early method in one of our classes," Andros says. "It caused more problems than it solved."

She nods. "A lot of weird things happened in that town. Mostly to little kids and teenagers. Blacking out. Visions. Strange illnesses. People disappearing for hours and then showing up with no memory of where they'd been. Nobody could ever prove it was the waves causing any of it or got very far taking the corporation to court. The industry basically ran the town. They had the government in their pocket, and everybody was making heaps of money, so it was *damn the torpedoes, full speed ahead*. And now it's a disaster area they're still trying to figure out how to clean up."

"That will not happen here," Andros says. "It can't. The technology has advanced a long way since then."

"So, are you getting anywhere?"

He taps a finger on the window glass.

"We're not sure yet."

When he delivers her to the Trident that evening, she's fairly certain she's going to let happen what they both clearly want to happen. It has its risks, but she's gotten away with it before, and in more than one tricky situation it likely even helped with her cover. She's learned it can't hurt sometimes to appear a little reckless, even stupid.

She's going to invite him up to her room for a drink, but whether it's a late spasm of caution on her part or something else, when she climbs off the scooter and meets his unwary gaze, the words don't come. Instead she says a quick and awkward goodnight outside the main entrance. Once she's in the lobby she turns and watches him through the glass doors. He climbs slowly back onto the scooter. Just before he drives off he looks up to see her watching.

He smiles and waves. She smiles and waves.

Before she presses the elevator button, she looks around the lobby, in case her contact is here to try again. But no, what is she thinking? They said not today, and anyhow no one would be foolish enough to set foot where she's staying. She's only wishing for that, she has to admit, because she wants desperately to be done with this.

Undressing for bed, she checks the patch. It looks flatter and the edges are more irregular, almost as if it's spreading out, amoeba-like.

It's a custom in many households even today to pour a few drops of saltwater on the floor after the evening meal, in honour of the sea gods. These deities are said to visit islanders most often in their sleep, bringing them counsel, and warnings.

Whenever she's on one of these jobs she dreams more than usual, or the dreams themselves are more memorable. She's gotten used to this, night theatre of a meticulous detail and coherence, holding on to a setting, an intention, a trajectory in a way one's dreaming rarely does. Most of the dreams follow a similar script. They begin in the mundane—she's cooking a meal in her kitchen back home, she's going for the mail, she's shopping—and she'll suddenly realize she's forgotten something, or someone, and has to go look for whatever or whoever it is, and this urgent quest will take her farther away from her familiar surroundings, sometimes into very strange places, alternate realities of drama and disorder, where she finds herself caught up in a story already in progress involving characters her dreaming mind summons out of oblivion as if they have been waiting all her life for their moment onstage. Some of these phantom people become so vital to her dreaming self that they stay with her in her waking life, so that she aches to see them again: friends, rivals, lovers.

Tonight, she dreams she's where she really is, at the Trident, being awarded a prize in one of the conference rooms. She's just published the definitive guidebook to the island, a thick tome filled with facts and dates and arcana. She's proud of her accomplishment, but there's a big crowd applauding and she's uncomfortable with all the attention. Then she remembers the child. Yes, the child she was supposed to be looking after while she was here, her older sister's little girl, who came with her to the wave pool this morning (in waking life she has no siblings, but in the dream an entire history constructs itself from this conjured sister). They had fun splashing in the shallows and getting ice cream cones from the snack bar, but then she left the child there—she forgot her. How could she have done that? She has to go back and find her before something terrible happens.

She walks out of the conference room without a backward glance and hurries across the skywalk into the pool complex. It's nighttime and the place is dark, but there are still people walking along the shore under the stars. The stars? There's no roof—the pool is open to the sky.

She notices a man about her age, standing at the water's edge, who looks out of place here, where everyone's in beach clothes and swimwear—he's wearing a heavy red flannel shirt, dirty jeans with grass stains on the knees, and hiking boots. The man stares at her as she goes by and she thinks he looks familiar, that he might be someone she knew years ago, but she doesn't have time to think about it because farther down the shore is the child, digging in the sand.

The horn blasts. The wave is about to come. The final wave, the one that will drown everything.

Claire gathers the little girl up in her arms, and she's tiny now, the size of a newborn kitten. But she's not an infant, just a perfect miniature girl, and Claire loves this impossible being with her entire self and always has. She murmurs, *I've got you now, I'm so sorry, I won't let you go again, I promise.* She wraps the doll-child in a towel and hurries with her back the way she came. As they're crossing the skywalk, she notices a glimmer in the blackness outside the window, a flickering ripple. She looks more closely and it's something alive, no, it's many living things, a school of shiny silver fish darting and shifting course together in the dark.

Too late. She's too late. The skywalk is under water now.

She pauses at the glass. A vast shape swims out of the night. As it passes it regards her with a curious blue eye.

Andros is working at the research facility all day, so she's on her own. Which is good, she tells herself. She moves outward from the hotel, fact-checking, making notes of minor details the guidebook got wrong, her own mental map starting to take shape like writing in invisible ink that slowly appears on a sheet of paper. For short periods of time she actually manages to forget the hand-off hasn't happened yet.

At midday, a slab of cloud closes down over the city, bringing wind-whipped drizzle and a twilight gloom. She returns to the hotel in the late afternoon, drenched, deciding to avoid the bar and Andros.

As she's waiting for her room service dinner the fear makes a sneak attack. She curls up on the bed, clutching the pillow, moaning.

What *is* this?

The patch.

She sits up, switches on the bedside lamp, checks her arm. No longer any form of square, the patch has spread even more, reaching out pseudopods, or peninsulas. It's also turned almost the same colour as her own skin.

This must be what's fucking her up. The city is seeping into her. Claiming her. She'll be damned if she's going to let it.

She tries to peel it up. She can't catch an edge. She pinches at it. Scratches it.

This thing is not coming off.

She hurries to the pharmacy she'd noticed at the end of the block. She shows the pharmacist the patch and asks about side effects. He asks her which type she's wearing. Derm something, she says. She can't remember and she threw out the packet. He tells her not to worry, that the patches can take some getting used to. That's what they're *for*, she protests. All he can suggest is that if she's really concerned she could try one of the twenty-four-hour walk-in clinics.

Heading back to the hotel she considers taking his advice, but it will mean hours under fluorescent light in a crowded waiting room full of curious strangers. And for sure her personal information will get uploaded into some official database somewhere and somebody will flag it and cross-reference it and discover a pattern to her travels that she's tried hard to obscure. Okay, maybe that's just paranoia but who knows. And anyhow if she goes to a clinic it means there really is something wrong with her. And there can't be. She's got something to do and then she's getting out of here.

———

Crossing the lobby she runs into Andros. He beams when he sees her, tells her he managed to get two tickets for a performance happening tonight that she should not miss. A special event that takes place only once a year. Like Christmas.

"In a way it's kind of related to what you came here for," he says.

She's going to say no. She says yes.

The new concert hall rises from the harbour in a pearlescent spiral, like a giant conch shell. To get there they cross a footbridge over the water, joining a crowd that's strangely sombre for people on a night out. Andros hasn't told her much about the so-called event. He says it's best for her to experience it without any prior knowledge.

It turns out to be an opera based on a collection of ancient legends called *The Almanack of Sand,* which apparently has the status of a national myth. The opera is performed in the native tongue, and frustratingly there are no English surtitles— only a brief summary in the program. One of the lead players is a celebrated u'Yoi drag performer and pop singer, Aphrodaddy Eleganza. White pancake makeup, arched eyebrows, turquoise lips—if the photo in the program is current, this person is maybe sixteen at most, still a kid.

From the raising of the curtain on, she struggles to follow what's going on. It begins with a storm at sea and eerie offstage voices singing above the roar of the wind and waves. Then there's a shipwrecked traveller, a kind of female Odysseus, Claire gathers, who washes ashore and is taken in and sheltered by a village of the indigenous islanders, the u'Yoi. The oldest among them, a blind woman, tells the traveller stories of her people, which are acted out by other performers. Beyond that, Claire has little understanding. A water spirit is caught and tamed, she thinks, there's a struggle between siblings for the throne, and a sea god has a love affair with a mortal woman. Scientists—or magicians—build a device that powers ships and makes armour invulnerable, but it also apparently angers the volcano spirit, and a group of rebels, it seems, conspire to destroy the machine before it's too late. Often several of the characters are talking or chanting at the same time, or moaning and gesticulating off by themselves in corners while seemingly more crucial things are claiming one's attention at centre stage. Some players appear to take on major importance in the saga, then are gone and never return. The seats Andros got them are pretty far back, which makes it all the harder to interpret what's going on.

"There's Aphrodaddy," Andros whispers in her ear.

She sees a small figure crossing the stage in a long purple robe, bald, arms outstretched, holding one long high note. The other performers make way for them.

"Who are they supposed to be?" she whispers back.

"The ocean," Andros says.

Just before the intermission some sort of tentacled sea beast, a giant squid perhaps, rises through a panel in the floor and coils itself around a man and woman who are standing alone onstage, holding hands. The creature is embarrassingly fake-looking, its mechanism creaking loudly. The players slowly sink out of sight in its deep blue-black folds, still declaiming their lines as if they haven't noticed what's happening to them. It's an absurd mash-up of Shakespeare and a fifties horror flick, and Claire has to stifle a laugh. The same thing happened to her the first time she heard a diva mewling like a cat in heat at the traditional opera in Shanghai.

She glances at Andros and is shocked to see tears sliding down his face. He's not the only one. She hears sniffles, glimpses tissues and handkerchiefs coming out, stricken faces, and then she feels it, like a physical force: a tide of deep emotion rolling through this gathering of otherwise sane-looking people. Andros turns to her, gives her an *it's okay* smile, and takes her hand in his.

And then it gets weirder. In the third act, halfway through a musical number, a large piece of the backdrop, painted to look like the facade of an ancient temple, suddenly topples backwards, ripping down a hanging screen as it goes, and hits the boards with a rude bang. Claire gasps at this catastrophic malfunction, but the players carry on without missing a beat. She looks at Andros. He's still rapt, transported.

She feels a cold drop on her wrist and looks up at the vaulted ceiling. Is the goddamn roof leaking now, or is this also part of the show?

There are no more drops, but onstage even weirder things begin to happen. Only Claire seems to find them strange. Muffled thumps from the wings. Unidentifiable pieces of stage machinery appear—edges of things that hover or slide behind the set for a moment and are gone. A stirring of possible bodies not quite seen, behind the translucent curtains meant to represent rippling waves. And underneath it all, she's certain her ears detect another faint sound, a low, grating drone, like some vast thing ponderously revolving, that she knows she's heard before but can't place. Then she remembers: it's the sound from the underground bunker at the research facility, when Andros showed her the wave experiment.

She can feel the vibrations in the floor, in the arms of her chair. Can't anyone else? Players and audience, all of these oblivious people, carry on as if there's no difference between being onstage and being down here in the seats. They're all caught up in the story, whatever that is. But she grows more and more convinced that there's some larger spectacle going on behind this one, that what she's seeing are just slices, hints, the faint nudgings of a vast event unfolding on another scale and in its own time, a gradual, inexorable process or coming-to-be, like the advance of an ice sheet, that nobody here can grasp in its entirety or admit is happening. She's the only one who sees through all this play-acting to what's really going on.

She whispers an apology to Andros and hurries up the aisle, brushing past an usher who gives her a stern look, as if she's walking out in the middle of some sacred rite. She heads across the lobby and into the drizzly night, walks up and down the courtyard, rubbing the arm with the patch and whispering to herself that she's being stupid and to get back in there. *Stop drawing attention to yourself, idiot.*

She goes back inside and orders a scotch at the lobby bar, downs it quickly. Andros finds her. He gives her a sheepish grin, but the catharsis or whatever these people were going through in there is still in his eyes.

"Not what you were expecting, I guess," he asks, touching her shoulder. "Are you okay?"

"I'll be fine. I think I need to get back to the hotel, though."

"Let me walk you there. I can explain more about the performance if you—"

She takes his hand.

"No, thanks. Let's not talk about that. Anything but that."

Claire wakes before dawn. Beside her Andros is still asleep. They're both lying naked on top of the covers. Despite the storm it was warm in the room all night and they spent most of it in each other's arms.

She touches the silver quith hanging from its chain around his neck. If she pried it open, what would she find? What does he keep so close to himself?

She slips out of bed in the dark and pads to the bathroom for a shower. As she's towelling off she examines the patch again. She pinches it, then lets it go. Until it comes off on its own, she's stuck with this thing. It can do with her as it pleases. But she won't let it win.

When she comes back into the bedroom he says, "It's a secret."

"What?"

"You were wondering what I keep in this," he says, flicking the quith.

"Was I?"

He grins. "Maybe I'll tell you some time."

"That's all right. Everybody should have at least one secret."

After she and Andros have breakfast together in the hotel restaurant, not talking very much or feeling the need to, he gives her a kiss on the cheek and leaves for the research facility, where he'll be all day.

Claire goes up to her room to get her notebook and camera. When she comes back down the desk clerk calls her over and tells her she might want to avoid going out if she can help it. There was some serious flooding last night, and the streets around the hotel are nearly impassable.

She wonders if Andros made it to work. She's got his phone number and could text him on one of her burners to find out, but that would be unlike her. When she's in the middle of a job she tries to avoid using phones. Even to call home and see how her mother is doing. They are lines of connection that can be traced, mapped, zoomed out so that someone can survey the entire intricate web of her travels. Her life. In fact, what does she think she's doing letting this thing with Andros happen? A call could come at any moment. A new plan. Directions to a meeting place. Any of this could happen while he's with her and then she'll have fucked up again.

You've had your fun. Time to cut it off.

Outside the front doors it looks like a river's been diverted through the middle of downtown. She hesitates, then returns to her room. After a few minutes of standing at the window look-ing out at nothing, she switches on the lamp and spreads her notes and maps on the desk. She tries to do some work on the updates, but pretty soon discovers she can't muster enough concentration to string ideas together. Outside, the storm thrashes on. She has the balcony door shut tight but there's still a low moan of wind and a rattle in the frame.

What is she going to do, stay in here all day? The patch doesn't seem to care whether she's out there or in here. And she knows her contact is not going to come knock on her hotel room door. They may be downstairs right how, pretending to read a magazine in the lobby, wondering where the hell she is.

She checks the time, doesn't register the number, checks it again.

Maybe Andros actually knows why she's here and has been assigned to watch her. To apprehend her when she picks up the bag. No. That doesn't make sense. He showed up and inter-rupted her just before the hand-off. If he was working for the authorities he would've let it happen, right? He showed up before it went down. Yes, but *just* before.

Too restless to concentrate, she lies down on the bed and switches on the flat-screen TV on the opposite wall.

She finds a channel in English, where a documentary about evolution and genetics is just getting started, hosted by a scientist with wispy white hair, who holds forth like someone religiously convinced of the truth of what he's saying.

A human being, the scientist declares, is really a support system for a complex molecule, deoxyribonucleic acid, whose sole purpose is to replicate itself. Although of course, he adds, this molecule has no actual *purpose*, in the sense of a conscious, deliberate intention, being simply a mindless chemical process that is itself caught up in another mindless process, known as natural selection, taking place on a time scale beyond imagining. There follows a panoramic shot of seals or sea lions or whatever they are, a vast conglomeration on some godforsaken grey shore, huddled against a pelting rain. Then a close-up of one of them with its snout raised to the sky, bleating mournfully. *This is life? This sucks,* it seems to be saying.

Other images follow in swift succession. A twinkling galaxy of stars that resolves itself into a vast flock of white birds on a shore at dusk, swelling and sagging like a country with a feverishly disputed border. A seething mass of furiously busy ants. Luminous single-celled things spinning and colliding in a glittering darkness that could be a drop of water or the emptiness of outer space.

We're a species of clever primate that might never have been, the scientist insists cheerfully as he picks his way across the black lava field of a volcanic island, waves detonating on rocks in the background, his professorially unkempt white hair flung around by the sea breeze. We were not destined to be here, nor are we destined to remain.

She starts clicking through the channels, eventually settling on a cooking show where four intense people in aprons are competing to make the most extravagant dessert. The heart-warming backstories, the contrived ingredient challenges, the epic life-or-death struggle for culinary supremacy compels what's left of her attention for quite a while, until it suddenly doesn't, and she begins to drift sleepily into thoughts of what she and Andros would likely be doing if he was here with her now. An image takes hold of their bodies entwined. This is agreeable, but then, as if a plug has been pulled, the carnal charge drains and she might be looking at an animated graphic of some mechanical process, a four-stroke engine or something, the two of them nothing more than thrusting, pumping *things*. Wired meat, going at it. Shlup shlup shlup.

She looks down at herself.

I'm a cunt, she thinks. A cunt with accessories.

On the cooking show a contestant's soufflé collapses and the contestant does too, in tears.

Something that feels like an external force drives Claire off the bed. She should get herself downstairs, give her contact every opportunity. Even hanging out in the lobby would be better than holing up here. She could work at one of the little tables, make herself visible. She doesn't understand her reluctance. It's unlike her, and dangerous. They don't mess around, these people. She's already blown it once, and any more screwing with their operation would be very bad.

The guidebook's still lying on the floor next to the bed, where Andros had dropped it after briefly flipping through it, laughing at the inaccuracies he'd found. She picks the book up and opens it to the section about the new concert hall. There's no mention of the performance she fled. She tries the index, searching for a word that might describe—

Something strikes the glass door of the balcony with a thump loud enough to jolt her upright, braced for violence.

A wet splotch has appeared in the middle of the floor-to-ceiling pane. She can see something lying on the bare concrete slab of the balcony floor. An unidentifiable white something that wasn't there before.

Taking a few cautious steps toward the glass, she realizes that the white thing is almost certainly a bird. A large gull, perhaps, lying on its side, one wet, ragged wing splayed. It likely broke its neck colliding with the reflection it took for more rain-veiled, empty air. She considers sliding open the door and stepping out to make sure but decides against it. The bird could still be alive. Who knows what it might do.

Claire squats on the balls of her feet, touching the tips of her fingers to the cold glass to steady herself. The thing is bigger than a seagull, probably. It's hard to be certain. How carefully has she ever looked at a seagull?

She notices the long, tapering fuselage of the chest faintly swelling and subsiding. The bird is definitely alive. Faint shirrs of iridescence glimmer in the spread wings. She wonders if that's natural, or whether the gull or gannet or whatever it is got caught in an oil slick.

The bird suddenly spasms and she jerks away from the glass, tumbling backwards onto the carpet. The wings shoot out, startlingly wide and flapping madly as the creature scrambles up onto its long, stick-like legs. It stands there blinking its eyes in that oddly mechanical way birds do, like a camera shutter, its long, dark bill snapping open and shut.

A crane, Claire guesses, able now to see the long, curving neck and the head in profile. She knows very little about birds, but that's the word that bobs immediately to the surface of her mind, probably from some long-ago picture in a school textbook.

The storm is still gusting in from the sea, but the balcony is deep, more of a battlement really, and sheltered from the elements by its overhang. She wonders if the crane has simply dropped in for a rest and to dry its feathers before casting off again into the wind and wet. Or maybe it really likes wind and wet, maybe that's its element, but it needs time to recover from hitting the glass. Either way, Claire thinks, a wild bird isn't likely to feel safe in this enclosed, unnatural space, with a human in close proximity. It will probably take off any moment now.

The crane turns its head and the angry red stone of its eye fixes on her.

ALL-WEATHER NOTEBOOK No. 25

July 21, 6:37 p.m., dry slough 0.3 km southwest of trainyard

Web of an orb weaver, spun between cattail stalks. Milky-yellow butterfly caught in it, wings vibrating helplessly. Spider had its head between the butterfly's head and thorax, as if giving it an intimate kiss. Either delivering a paralyzing bite or already sucking out the juices.

So there are still spiders. And butterflies. See them so rarely now. Used to be terrified of spiders. Of a lot of things. Then I met Bone Girl.

The sound started after we moved into the new house in River Meadows. It was coming from inside the walls, that much I knew for sure. Mom set out mousetraps, but this wasn't a skittering or a chewing. More of a slow, fluid rasping, very faint but sometimes growing louder. The traps remained empty.

We had gone to be with Grandma Hewitt on the coast earlier that year, when she was dying. The sound in the walls reminded me of the thin, constricted way she'd breathed, lying in her hospital bed.

Sometimes there would be a sudden thump or a knock, followed by a long silence before the barely audible rasping began once more. As if whatever was moving through the walls was trying to remain unheard, and sometimes failing.

If it was happening in Alex's room too, he didn't say anything.

Worse than the noises in the walls was the fact that my closet door had creaked open by itself three nights running. The first time I screamed for Mom, but Dad came instead and told me I was too old to be scared of the dark. After that I knew I would have to endure this on my own, whatever this was.

Only, how?

The next night I burrowed deep under the covers and imagined I was a caterpillar wrapped up in its cocoon and just beginning to turn into a butterfly. I curled up and squirmed like my dazzling metamorphosis was not far off. I imagined a pair of delicate wet wings stickily beginning to unfold from my shoulder blades, in anticipation of the moment I'd be leaving my snug, warm sanctuary and crawling out into the sunlight. What bright colours would I be when I emerged? What beautiful, never-before-seen pattern would my wings reveal to the world? I'd painted a picture of a great big butterfly in art class, just a few weeks earlier. It was bigger, brighter, and had more colours in it than anybody else's. I was proud of it. Even if everyone said they liked Shawna's the best because she'd made hers jet black with red veins in the wings and announced to everyone that it was a vampire butterfly.

The caterpillar game worked for a while, but my thoughts kept jumping back to the closet. Hiding like this under the blankets was making me more afraid, but I knew if I poked my head out, I might find myself face to face with whatever liked opening and closing doors.

In the hot, prickly envelope under the blankets my left eye started getting itchy. I reached up and rubbed the tender lid. That felt good—or at least kept me distracted—so I went on doing it. Then my finger found and felt, really noticed for the first time, that hard, unyielding ridge of bone that ran around my eyeball. My own eye lying nestled and vulnerable within it like a soft-boiled egg in a ceramic cup. I circled both eye sockets, again and again, then ran my finger along my cheekbone to my jaw.

With both hands now, in the dark, I got to know that other face underneath the flesh. The one made of white bone. This face didn't blush or sweat. It never looked surprised, or sad, or gave away what it felt about anything. If it felt at all. It wore the same expression no matter what life threw at it: a lipless grin, cold as outer space. Who was that? How could that be me?

It was Bone Girl, I decided. The ultimate badass, the monster that hunts monsters. She had been there, inside me, all this time. The shivering, terrified kid named Amery Hewitt was merely Bone Girl's outermost layer. Her suit and glasses. Her Clark Kent. I thought about the vampire butterfly with the blood red veins that Shawna had painted, and now I understood why.

Bone Girl was death, and death was right here, growing and waiting, inside its cocoon.

After that night, there wasn't much that frightened me anymore.

ALEX

He returns to the hotel in Pine Ridge in the evening, his face scratched, his hair matted with sweat and his clothes filthy.

He'd known the new highway took a long, curving detour that bypassed River Meadows, but he'd hoped to find an old industry access road that would at least bring him to within walking distance of the Park fence. He did finally come across one that was still open and drove along it until it abruptly ended at a deep, steep-sided ditch, an unexpected obstacle not marked on his map. The ditch must have been dug to keep vehicles from getting any closer. On its far side a large sign read in huge letters CAUTION RESTRICTED AREA. Beside it stood a tall pole with a surveillance camera mounted at the top. There was no sign of the fence.

He got out of the car and walked to the edge of the ditch. It was full of dark, standing water, but it wasn't that wide. He could probably leap it. He listened—birds were chittering and calling in the distance, and he could just make out the far-off roar of the highway. There was a faint smell of rot, of vegetation steeping in the cool dampness of early fall. He eyed the camera on the pole. Was it actually on, recording his features, his vehicle? Could he expect a visit from the police when he returned to town?

To hell with them.

He shouted his sister's name. Once, twice, three times.

Amery! It's Alex! I'm here!

He waited a few minutes, listening, then turned and walked back to the car. This was foolish—it wasn't going to help her if he got himself arrested. Driving back out to the end of the access road, he spent the next several hours making a slow, convoluted circumnavigation of the Park on the few roads he could find that weren't closed off. He parked several times in patches of trees, out of sight of any traffic that happened to come by, and walked in the direction he was sure the Park perimeter had to be. He pushed his way through head-high snagging brush, stumbling into hollows and scrambling out again, never once coming within sight of the fence.

He drops onto the bed, intending to close his eyes only for a minute before taking a shower and heading out to get some dinner at the fast-food place next door. The next thing he knows he's outside, on a shore of wet sand under the night sky, waves washing over his boots.

He's standing at the edge of a large body of water that stretches away into darkness. There's a shimmering blue glow below the choppy surface, rising from bioluminescent sea creatures, he thinks. In the bathic light he can see rocky islets and the ruins of ancient-looking columned structures just offshore. There are people in bathing suits strolling along the sand and wading in the surf.

Then he sees a woman. Coming toward him along the shore. Claire Foley.

She's older, taller, but the way she carries herself, the tight-lipped set of her mouth—this couldn't be anyone else.

Her gaze locks with his for a moment, then darts past. She's looking for someone, and it's not him.

This is a dream, he says out loud. The deep blast of a horn shatters the quiet, and he wakes.

It's dark out. He gets up groggily and stands at the window, rehearsing what he will tell his mother when he calls her in the morning to check in. How bright a gloss can he put on what little he's accomplished without her realizing he's doing it? When he'd called her after his flight landed, he could tell she'd been crying.

She gives us nothing, she'd said. The people who've loved and cared for her all her life. She shuts us out.

I'll find her, Mom. Don't worry.

Just stay safe. Okay? Don't do anything . . . you know.

I won't.

He couldn't find a way into the Park and now he has no plan at all. He can't tell his mother that. Not yet, anyhow. But if he tries playing down the hopelessness of what he's facing she'll hear it in his voice and worry even more.

With nothing else coming to mind he rewatches the video clip of Michio Amano teaching.

When he gets to the part where the quiet, reserved science teacher says that *somehow, one day, we might turn a corner and meet another version of ourselves,* he pauses the video and calls Michio's number.

"Hello, Alex."

"It's you. You're the one who searched for Amery. You're the one who goes in there with her."

A long silence.

"I'll take you tomorrow morning," Michio says at last. "We'll be starting before dawn, so get some sleep. We'll go together and make another search."

"Okay. Okay, good. Thank you. I've been researching the Park, and I've got a pretty good idea of what to expect. I bought some supplies too. I should be prepared, I think."

Another silence.

"Amery told me that you make games for a living," Michio says at last.

"Yes, that's what I do. What about it?"

"I need you to understand one thing. This isn't a game."

THE RIVER MEADOWS ARCHIVE

MEMORY

Decoherence is a tabletop role-playing adventure for four players. You and three others will take on the roles of inhabitants of River Meadows, struggling to deal with the uncanny disturbances that have troubled your happy and prosperous town. You will gather evidence, solve puzzles, and deal with eerie encounters while trying to survive and achieve your goals, which will vary depending on which of the included Scenarios you play and the cards you draw randomly from the Story Deck. The virtually endless combinations of chosen Scenario and random card draws means that *Decoherence* can be played again and again, with new twists and unexpected outcomes each time, similar to the way we all retell our pasts over and over again, imagining how things might have been different.

   All four players must remain alive and together as a cohesive group to the conclusion of the final round of play. The death or disappearance of one of the characters ends the game.

COMPONENTS:

1 game board.

1 map of River Meadows and surroundings.

1 "Surviving Decoherence" manual, which you're reading right now.

6 Scenario booklets.

11 two-sided Settings tiles (Day-side and Dream-side).

4 Character tokens (the pieces shaped like people).

1 Creature token (the piece shaped vaguely like an animal).

4 Character sheets.

Story Deck (40 cards).

Life Event Deck (18 cards).

12 Decoherence markers (3 types: Wobble, Trap, Anomaly).

4 Action dice (yellow, six-sided).

4 Damage tokens (the red cubes).

If this is your first time playing *Decoherence* it's recommended you start with the tutorial Scenario, "Family Ties," which is outlined below.

SETUP:

Place the game board in the middle of the table, within easy reach of all players.

In regular Scenario play, players choose their Character by drawing a random Character sheet. For the "Family Ties" tutorial scenario, the Characters are pre-selected for you, as follows.

Player 1: Alex Hewitt (the Son).
Player 2: Amery Hewitt (the Daughter).
Player 3: Beth Hewitt (the Mother).
Player 4: Ben Hewitt (the Father).

The appropriate Character sheet should be placed face up beside the corresponding Character. Each player should also take a Character token in the colour of their choice (white, yellow, green, red) and one Damage token, which they place on the leftmost space of their character's Damage Tracker on the game board. In *Decoherence* players always begin a Scenario with one existing point of prior damage.

Shuffle the Life Event cards, select four of them at random, and place them face up in the appropriate Life Event spaces on the game board. Shuffle the remaining Life Event cards and place them face down near the game board, creating the "Alternate Histories" deck.

Separate the 12 Decoherence markers into three sets according to the symbols on their backs (Wobble, Trap, Anomaly). Shuffle each set and place them face down next to the appropriate Action fields on the game board.

Place the Setting tile "Home" so that it is Day-side up (the side with the image of the Intact House) on the indicated space on the game board. All four players now place their Character token on that tile, and each takes one Action die.

The Creature token is kept to one side for now. It will come into play later.

The goal of the "Family Ties" Scenario is for the Hewitt family to stay together and safe during the strange and unsettling events that occur in River Meadows as the game unfolds. For the purpose of best illustrating how a Scenario should progress, we will describe a sequence of narrated gameplay, with the players in their roles as Alex, Amery, Beth, and Ben: the Hewitt family.

The shiny new neighbourhood of Foxhaven is almost treeless. The lawns are perfectly groomed and the freshly paved streets run in smooth unbroken curves, but only small saplings, recently planted, grow along the sidewalks.

Alex is fourteen. Amery is eleven.

Foxhaven is in the northwest corner of River Meadows, the closest subdivision to Conjuring Creek and the extraction sites. The neighbourhood is so new that at the end of the Hewitts' street there's uncleared bush. The creek is out there somewhere. Beth doesn't want Alex and Amery going into the woods by themselves, in case there are bears, or god knows what, but they often do.

Every morning Ben drives his new half-ton to the main Northfire site, twenty-five minutes down the highway from town. Beth continues to drive the old minivan, the vehicle that brought them here, to her clerking job at the town office. Ben sometimes gives her a ride to work and picks her up on the way home. He doesn't like her to drive when the streets are icy and visibility is poor, because she once had a minor accident in such conditions. Beth is not entirely happy with his cautious, protective attitude, but she goes along with it because, on those winter days when Ben picks her up from work, they can be alone together for a while to talk about whatever needs to be talked about. Which is usually the kids and how they're adjusting to life here.

The children have had no worrying health issues since the incident at the diner. Amery has had her tonsils removed. She hated the cream of wheat porridge they served her in the hospital after the operation. She said it tasted worse than tapioca pudding and made her want to throw up.

Alex's second toe on his right foot is deformed: a tiny rounded stump. He showed it to his friends at school once, in the city where they used to live. When a new girl named Virginia O'Brien came to class, Alex's friends dragged her over to have a look at the mutant toe, to gross her out. Since coming to River Meadows, Alex has kept his misshapen digit hidden from his new friends.

When Alex and Amery started school that first fall, they walked together in the mornings and then back home in the afternoons. This was when they were still living in the cramped rented bungalow in an older neighbourhood. The elementary and junior/senior high schools were next to each other, separated by a playground. Beth insisted on coming with them on the first day of classes, despite Alex's protests. After that she stayed home, but reminded her son every morning that it was his job to make sure his little sister got there and back safely.

Alex obeyed, but as the weeks went by and he got to know other kids, he started ditching Amery in the mornings before they came in sight of the schools. After they'd gone a few blocks he would walk quickly ahead of her so that his friends wouldn't see him arriving with his little sister in tow. He would do the same thing after school, ducking out as early as he could and waiting for Amery a few blocks down the street.

One afternoon he waited for her at the usual spot but she didn't appear. He walked back. Amery wasn't outside the school. She wasn't in the playground. Alex walked all the way around the two schools, waited a good, long while by the doors of the elementary school, and then reluctantly made his way home, dreading what would happen when he told his mother he'd lost his sister.

But when he came in the front door Amery was there. After school she'd followed somebody's cat and got turned around for a bit, but then found a different way home. This was how Beth discovered Alex had been shirking his duty.

We don't know this town yet, Beth reminded him. We don't know anybody here. We have to stick together.

Ben operates one of the mammoth trucks that haul the raw ore out of the excavation pits.

They're removing the boreal forest in neat rectangular chunks, like date squares from a pan. Peeling away a soggy carpet of muskeg to scoop out what has been steeping here for a hundred million years, the sour black honey of time.

There's a coker plant on the site, which he thinks is funny. *This whole place is a coker plant.* One of the guys Ben gets to know had been a crack addict who cleaned himself up after his friends staged an intervention: they broke all of his crack pipes and beat the shit out of him. When he tells Ben the story he adds, *And when I got out of the hospital, I thanked them for it, and we're still friends. Those guys saved my life.*

Only two women work at the excavation sites. Every guy on the shift knows exactly where these women are at all times. Most of this attention is your typical slack-jawed scoping of the ladies, but in a few cases the surveillance is clearly hostile. Some men do not want women in their domain.

Everything about the operation is orderly, methodical, streamlined. If you don't count some of the yahoos working the machines. The marathon shifts they pull have some of the younger crew on a slow smoulder all the time, as if the toxic fuel they're clawing out of the earth has leached into their veins and started combusting. Ben stays well away from those guys. He is here for his family. That's what this is all about. It's up to him to be orderly, methodical, streamlined too. But once in a long while his new friends talk him into a drink after work, and it's hard to say no. Some of the younger guys, the loose cannons, go with them, and at the bar they're soon primed and ready to go apeshit on anyone who looks at them sideways.

One weekend his new friends invite him to go quadding with them, somewhere the bush wasn't yet stripped bare.

They quad to a remote campsite, get a fire going, and bring out the beer cooler. Their laughter grows louder as the daylight fades. When Ben was young and single, he lived for this kind of thing. Now he just feels restless, wondering how soon he can turn in without getting razzed about it. All of a sudden it's night. It gives him a strange feeling, watching the embers whirl up into the dark and being so far from home, his wife, his kids.

They don't talk about the wobbles in school.

Alex is sitting in social studies, the first class of the morning, barely paying attention, as usual, doodling cartoon faces and superhero costumes in the margins of his scribbler. His teacher, Mrs. Kishka, has projected a map of the Americas onto the smartboard and is talking about Cortez and the fall of the Aztec empire when a decoherence ripples through the room.

For an instant the map has changed: the large island in the middle of the Atlantic that's had so many names throughout history isn't there. Where it used to be, nothing but blue ocean. Then the screen goes dark and flickers to life again and the island is back where it belongs.

Mrs. Kishka gives a flustered little laugh, then returns to her story of how the conquistadors brought about the end of barbarous human sacrifice.

The Hewitts subscribe to the local paper, to *Time,* and for Amery, to *Owl.* An owl can turn its head all the way around, almost. It has big yellow eyes like moons. There's one in that tree, or there was, maybe, you think so, but it's getting dark and the light is bad and you're not really sure.

The toaster's on the fritz again. The handle goes down but sticks there. Beth makes French toast on the griddle as a treat for Amery, then she gets Ben's lunch together.

He likes thick cucumber slices, and cheddar sliced thick too. Not too much mayo; it makes the bread soggy if the sandwich sits too long, and sometimes he doesn't get his actual lunch break until later in the afternoon. Beth adds a couple of cherry tomatoes and a dill pickle to the sandwich container and presses it shut. Amery is pouring herself a glass of orange juice.

No sign of your brother? Beth asks.

He doesn't want to go to school today. He says he's not feeling well.

Oh yeah? What's he doing right now?

Drawing comics. Does he get to stay home?

Beth snorts.

In a pig's eye.

Amery is the tallest girl in her class. She tells her mother that the boys are scared of her. Beth knows she thinks it's because

of her height, but it's probably not just that. It's all of her.
She's become beautiful in an almost uncanny way. Ben always
says she's pretty like her mom, but pretty isn't the right word
for her severely angelic face, the sharp cheekbones, those deep,
serious eyes that hardly seem to blink. Where did such a face
come from? Beth can see a little of Ben in the set of Amery's
mouth, but nothing of herself. Alex takes after his parents, but
Amery looks like there might have been another being altogether involved in her creation, a third parent, celestially
winged and light-filled, from a higher sphere.

Beth brings two cups of lemon ginger tea down to the carpeted
family room, where Ben is watching the late news. He takes one
from her. They watch the news together, sipping their tea, not
talking. The cold snap is supposed to break tomorrow. When
the news is over, Ben yawns. I'm bushed, he says, rubbing his
neck, and heads up the stairs. Good night.

Once she's finished her tea, Beth switches off the television.
She collects both tea cups and is about to go to bed too, then
looks around the finished basement, unsure for an instant
where she is or how she got here. It's not a decoherence. It's just
one of those moments when it catches up with her that they left
their home and came to this town and stayed. Some part of her
has never quite believed that really happened.

Ben's exhausted but tonight he can't get to sleep. The lines of
his favourite poem—Robert Frost's "The Road Not Taken"—
tread their soft cadence, over and over, through his thoughts.
He recited the poem at a talent festival when he was in grade
six. He didn't win. The girl who came onstage after him recited

a poem called "A Cry from an Indian Wife" in a loud, dramatic voice. Ben hated her perfect diction and stagy hand gestures, but the judges loved her.

One day he chose a different road and they ended up here. What would their life be like if he'd stayed on the main highway instead of chasing a memory of his old man?

Amery wakes often at night and cries out for her mother. She insists there's something in her room. It makes noises, like it's moving around in the walls. Sometimes her closet door opens by itself. Beth and Ben find nothing. Ben tells his daughter it's a new house and it's just settling, that's all. She doesn't need to wake them up for that. She's a big girl now.

The truth is they've all noticed the same things: odd noises, clunks and rattles, doors opening and closing by themselves, but they don't want to frighten Amery, or themselves.

Beth sides reluctantly with Ben, but secretly she wants to go on comforting her child, in the hope of staying close to her. Amery is so distant now. She doesn't talk much at all, not since the night they first came to River Meadows. About all that Beth knows about what's going on inside her is that she loves animals. These days she's outside more than she's in the house, wandering for hours and coming home with grass stains on her jeans, her hair tangled, having followed a cat or gone crawling around looking at bugs.

When she was younger Amery used to have terrible nightmares, mostly about witches. Beth would hug her and tell her not to be afraid—she had it on good authority that the last witch died a long, long time ago, just faded away like mist and was never seen again, because nobody believed in her anymore.

But what if I believe her *back?* Amery had asked her one night after a dream had woken her. Beth was sitting on the bed beside her, stroking her hair.

You're just one kid, Beth told her. An amazing kid, but still. That's not enough belief power to bring back a whole witch. Maybe just her pinky finger. But then you can stomp on it. Boom! One squishy witch pinky.

Amery laughed and repeated Beth's words: *one squishy witch pinky.*

It becomes a catchphrase the two of them share for years, whenever there's some problem, big or small, that one of them can't tackle on her own.

Amery burrowed under the covers and Beth wished her a good sleep and got up to leave. At the door of the room Beth turned and had a vision of a beautiful young witch at the window, looking in at them, her long, flowing hair the colour of moonlight.

On weekends Amery wanders into the woods near their house, and Alex, obeying his mother's wishes, goes with her. Amery has begun keeping a notebook about the bugs, birds, and plants she finds, intently scribbling notes and drawing sketches that Alex has to admit aren't half bad. Ben and Beth look on this development positively, as a hobby that might turn into a career for their intense and studious daughter. Forest management is a big thing in the region, where wildfires can spark the evacuation of entire towns.

As he follows Amery on one of her expeditions, Alex wonders where the dividing point is, exactly, between the town and the wilderness that surrounds it. He's sure there has to be such a boundary, though he's never sure when they've crossed it. He tells himself that if they're still on the non-wild side of the boundary, they can't be attacked by a bear.

If you take even a few steps away from the paved streets, you're already heading into the wilderness, but when do you actually arrive there? The bush around the town is threaded with trails that look old and well used, and of course there are always nearby roads, power lines, abandoned vehicles, and other markers of human presence. Can one even really call it a wilderness? It even seems odd to Alex to say that one is heading *into* the forest. As if the outside is somehow also an interior.

But the town isn't completely non-wild, either. Living in River Meadows is a bit like living in a house with all the doors and windows wide open. Deer graze on lawns in the evenings, and coyotes are an ever-present menace to neighbourhood pets. One summer they heard that a mountain lion had been found living under a house in the trailer park, preying on dogs to feed her cubs.

Then there's Amery herself. With her far-off stare and her ease with spending hours outside in the heat and the rain, she seems to live now on that invisible boundary, if she hasn't already crossed it.

One night both kids are at friends' houses for sleepovers, and Ben strolls into the bedroom with the video camera. He points it at Beth and offers the observation that they could score some easy extra cash by making their own home porn flick. Beth, lying in bra and panties on the bed, throws the mystery novel she's been reading at him and yells *get out of here with that thing*. She's never liked having her picture taken, although everyone tells her how photogenic she is. She cut her long, dark hair not long after she had her first child and has never let it grow back to the length Ben always loved.

Ben leaves, as ordered, but comes back a few minutes later, minus the camera and his clothes. He and Beth make loud, passionate, endearment-filled love for the first time in many weeks.

Beth is an accomplished amateur photographer. She has won second prize in two national photo contests, and several honourable mentions. Some of her best shots, usually candid photos at family gatherings, are displayed in frames around the house. A picture of Alex and Amery at Trailblazer Days, the local summer festival, munching on two enormous blossoms of pink cotton candy, hangs above the key table in the front hall.

Their new house's main floor bathroom boasts two deep porcelain sinks, the first time they've had this luxury, with countertops finished in lavender Formica. A specimen of bark art, depicting a northern forest scene, hangs on the wall above the towel rack, a wedding gift from a relative—both Ben and Beth have forgotten who. Alex was in the bathroom once, on the toilet, when a wobble occurred and he thought he saw, in the tangled, shadowy midst of the tiny bark forest, a dark figure making its way toward him.

Ben would like to buy and install a hot tub in the backyard, where a struggling Nanking cherry tree now stands. Beth argues that it's more than they can really afford, even now. The truth is, she thinks hot tubs reek of brainless self-indulgence.

By the gate in the white backyard fence is a wooden toolshed Ben built, with a gently sloping shingle roof. Alex likes to climb up there to be alone and draw on summer afternoons, making his own comic books about superheroes in a futuristic metropolis called Megacity. Towerman. Helium. The Goshawk. Payload. And their enemies, the supervillains: Doctor Bedlam. The Pain Artist. Pathogen. Mandrill. Something he enjoys more than actually drawing their adventures is coming up with their origin stories, and making charts of their powers and their relative ratings in terms of parameters like strength, speed, endurance, intelligence, or reality manipulation. Figuring out with diagrams and dice rolls who would win in a match-up against who, rather than going to all the trouble of actually drawing the battle.

He's been working on a sidekick for the heroes: Kid Quantum. Teenager Chris Callender gains the power to stop time, jump instantly between distant places, and other cool abilities Alex hasn't quite worked out yet. The problem is that Chris is young and inexperienced, still learning how to control his awesome powers so that they don't cause more harm than good. But how did Chris get his powers? What's his origin story? Alex remembers the glowing sphere in the lab at his father's workplace. Maybe Chris lives in River Meadows. Maybe what happened to Alex at the diner could be what happens to Chris. Only worse. Or better.

Except that superheroes don't live in places like this.

It's a hot one, there hasn't been rain in a few weeks, and Ben has set up the sprinkler on the front lawn, which is looking patchy and parched. He thought the kids might want to put on their bathing suits and jump through the spray while he's got it going. But Alex is holed up in his room and Amery was home a minute ago but now she's gone off somewhere, probably roaming the neighbourhood on her bike. Alone, as usual. Ben remembers when a sprinkler and a popsicle were all the kids needed on a summer afternoon. He sees them as they were then, shrieking and laughing as they leap through the chittering spray.

Ben sits by himself on the front steps, timing the sprinkler, moving it every so often, to cover the entire lawn. Beth appears with a tray laden with plastic tumblers, a tall pitcher of lemonade flashing in the sun.

Where's Amery?

She was just here.

Well, there's lemonade for whoever wants it.

Ben looks into the hollow of Beth's shirt as she bends to set down the tray on the folding table beside him. He admires as he always does what he glimpses there. They'd met at his high school grad party, on Jericho Beach. Beth Leitner. She was someone else's date, from another school, but by the end of the evening she was with him, walking along the sand away from the bonfire, sharing with each other what they wanted to do with their lives. Or at least she had done the sharing. She wanted to be a photographer and travel the world taking pictures of people and places. In those days he didn't have any idea what he might do with himself—he never thought beyond working at his uncle's body shop and tinkering with engines. But he couldn't say that to this pretty, spirited girl walking so close to him, so he'd looked up at the night sky, the few stars they could see, and told her he wanted to be a pilot, even maybe an astronaut one day, having no idea where that came from and hoping she would never bring it up again. A few dates later he was unbuttoning her blouse in the back seat of his old Mustang. The first time he'd unbuttoned anyone's blouse, if he was being honest.

Ben smiles to think how close he came to crying then, for the joy and terror of it. The first time you do a thing that you know will change everything.

Beth goes back inside, and a few minutes later Ben hears the front door open again.

To his surprise it's Alex. His son stands at the top of the steps, looking out over the street.

Time for some fresh air? Ben says, and the words sound forced and awkward to his own ears.

Mom wants me to look for Amery, Alex says sullenly.

Ah, give her a few minutes, Ben says with a shrug. She'll be back.

He pats the step beside him.

Have a seat while you wait.

After a long pause, Alex sits down.

There's lemonade.

No, thanks.

So, Ben says, searching for something to add. Working on a new game?

Yeah.

What's it about?

Time travel.

Cool. Very cool. *Back to the Future* sort of thing?

Not really.

Oh well. No flux carburetor or whatever, I guess.

Alex rises.

I'd better go find Amery.

Sure, Ben says. Then, because he can't say what he really wants to, he adds, Good luck.

Alex gets his bike from where it's parked beside the garage door and pedals off down the street. Ben watches him go.

One January afternoon at the gleaming new Save-On-Foods, Beth is inspecting the packages of chicken breast, searching for one that will feed the four of them without blowing the dinner budget for the week, when she remembers they have money now.

She can have anything in this store that she wants. Well, within reason, but still, it's a new sensation to have this kind of buying power. It makes her catch her breath and take a step back. She looks up and down the meat section at the abundance of pink and red and white flesh on display. Beef, ham, pork, chicken, turkey, veal, lamb, salmon, tuna, crab, lobster. Steaks, briskets, ribs, chops, drumsticks, thighs, tongue, shanks, loins, fillets.

She picks up the biggest, most expensive cut she can find: a giant slab of wagyu. The price makes her heart race a little. Her impulse is to drop the thing and move away before anyone notices. Instead, she holds the package closer. Inside its wrapper the exquisitely marbled meat glistens like it's just been touched with morning dew. What part of the cow is this from? She heard somewhere they feed these animals beer or milk or something and that's what makes the flesh such a delicacy. Like the way they fatten up those sumo wrestlers maybe. She wonders what Ben would say if she served this up to him. He's been so busy with his job lately, taking extra shifts whenever they're offered, she wonders if he would even notice.

A tremor in the air. Beth is able to ignore them most days, they don't mean anything, but for a moment she feels like a tree in a great wind, toppling.

The decoherence passes.

She buys the steak and brings it home. When she's got the meat out of its wrapper and it's lying there on a cutting board in the kitchen, raw and pink, she wonders what she was thinking. It's the middle of winter, a rock solid twenty below outside, and this is something you slap on the barbecue on a summer afternoon and let sizzle. How does she think she's going to cook it?

She looks again and, in her mind's eye, the blade of an electric saw buzzes down, cutting into a trunk of hanging flesh that
swings open like a door.

Early fall, a Saturday afternoon. Alex and Amery are walking
along the railroad tracks at the edge of town. Alex is tired of
being Amery's bodyguard but his mother still insists on it. If
he isn't busy with his friends, he has to look after his wayward
sister. That's the law.

Alex glimpses something in the trees alongside the tracks.

Hey, look, he says.

He breaks into a run, down through the ditch and up the
other side into a stand of poplars. Amery follows.

Alex has spotted an abandoned car half-buried in tall grass. It
was maybe green once but now it's pretty much rust brown all
over. He thinks it looks like a big, brown metallic turd dumped
here by a giant rusty robot and files the idea away for one of his
homemade comic books. Robots that digest metal and poop scrap.

Most of the car's windows are busted and gone. A couple
of the doors too. The tires are flat or missing, the seats split
open, the yellow stuffing bulging out like giant bug guts.

Alex climbs into the driver's seat. Amery, after some hesitation, climbs in on the other side.

It smells funny in the car. Not bad, exactly. Just . . . funny.
Like cinnamon sprinkled over musty old clothes.

The game Alex comes up with is to pretend they're on vacation. For once Amery plays along. They bounce up and down
on the creaking seats. They point out the windows and ooh and
ahh at imaginary sights like stupid tourists, really hamming it
up. Wow, look, it's the Grand Canyon. There's the Eiffel Tower.
Is that the Taj Mahal?

Then Alex pretends he's driving drunk, slurring his words and lolling his head around.

What are you doing? Amery asks. She sounds really concerned, although she might still be in the game. It's hard to tell what she's thinking most of the time.

I'm driving, what does it fucking look like? Now shut up and quit distracting me before I drive us off a cliff. No, you know what, I *am* going to drive us off a cliff. You hear me? I'm sick of this life and I'm sick of you and I'm going to end it all.

Alex cranks the wheel.

Here we go . . .

Amery gasps. Alex thinks she's really getting into this, then he sees the bee. Look out, he shouts, ducking down in his seat. The bee buzzes around their heads, bumps against the roof, frantic, then it zips out one of the glassless windows and it's gone.

Holy shit, Alex says.

Other than the gasp, Amery hasn't reacted.

Wait, she says. Listen.

There's a humming from somewhere. It's muffled, but Alex knows what it is: that angry sound made by a whole swarm.

Where's that coming from? he says.

He knows what Amery's going to do even before she reaches for the latch of the glove compartment. He tries to stop her with a shout but it's too late.

The compartment is crawling, seething, alive with bees. Alex is out the door in an instant and bolting. Then he stops and looks back.

Amery's still in the car. She hasn't moved.

Ben is in the truck cab one afternoon, climbing out of the pit with a load of ore, when the hammering starts. At first, he thinks it's coming from somewhere on the other side of the shatterproof windows, but it's his heart banging to get out. He manages to brake just before something huge pins him to the seat so that he can't move or breathe. A dark planet has rolled over the earth and is crushing the air and the light out of him, out of everything.

He's pretty much gone except for one thought. The kids. He sees them as they were when they were little, and after a while notices his hand moving the way it did when he stroked their hair, after one of them had woken up after a bad dream. That's what gets him through. When it passes, whatever *it* was, he can finally answer the voice freaking out on the radio.

He makes up a story about the instrument panel going wacky, warning lights blinking like a Christmas tree. They garage the truck and run it through every test in the book. They don't find a thing, of course. Wrong piece of equipment hooked up to the monitor.

It wasn't a decoherence, he knows that much for certain. It hadn't felt like one of those at all, and anyhow the wobbles never happen at the excavation sites. Some townspeople said that proved the decoherences had nothing to do with ghost extraction, while the environmentalists argued it was an eye-of-the-hurricane type of situation.

Whatever it was, where did it come from, he wonders, and why had it sucker punched him now? Things are good. His job is paying the bills and then some. A lot of *and then some*. Beth has the part-time position at the town office. There's no question about what they're working their butts off for, or who.

He's a father. There really isn't anything better a man can be, is there?

He doesn't say anything to Beth. He's hoping this was some freak one-time thing, a momentary glitch, but the next three days, when he shows up for work, the fear does too, with bells on. His knees turn to jelly before he sets a foot on the ladder to the cab. An hour in, he's sure this is death perching on his shoulder.

The next morning he drives to the site and parks, but instead of heading straight in as usual he takes a stroll around the perimeter of the lot. His hands are shaking, his walk all jerky and wrong like a marionette's. At the far end, nearest the exit, a skinny guy leaning against a sky-blue Camaro sees him coming his way and waves, as if he's been waiting for him. Ben has never met the guy but he knows who he is by reputation. Some of the crew call this end of the parking lot the candy store. Easier than ordering a pizza.

Hey, the guy says. I think I just saw a bear.

A bear?

The guy nods toward the trees at the edge of the gravel. They stand there all leafy and uninterested, like this is any other morning.

In there, man. I mean, a *big* bear. Maybe a grizzly, I don't know. It was right there.

What's it doing, do you think? Ben asks, squinting and shielding his eyes with his hand. He's really straining to see that bear. He needs to see it.

Taking a shit probably, the guy says. That's what they do in the woods, right?

Ben laughs but it comes out sounding like he's jogging downhill.

The guy's eyes widen. Whoa, that kind of day, huh?

Yeah, that kind. Are you Jarod Sawchuk?

None other.

Okay, Ben says.

Okay indeed, Jarod Sawchuk says. What'll it be?

Ben looks at the Camaro. Then at the trees. He raises a hand.

You know what, forget it. I'm good.

Well, I would say not.

Ben heads for the gate. In the staging compound he finds Dylan Chaudiere, the shift foreman, and tells him he must've come down with the stomach flu or something. Dylan looks at his chalky, sweating face and backs away, ordering him the fuck home.

He goes home, and stays there, spending his next three shifts on the sofa, making queasy faces whenever Beth is looking. Eventually she realizes there's something going on here other than some flu bug.

He's getting himself a bowl of cereal at two in the afternoon when she finally confronts him about it.

We need to talk, she says.

About what?

Her eyes travel down to the grubby terrycloth housecoat he's wearing.

If something's wrong . . . I mean, is it the work? You've been putting in a lot of overtime.

It's not the overtime.

But something *is* wrong.

I'm handling it.

Are you? I want to help. Let me.

Beth finally convinces Ben to see his doctor, who listens without asking many questions, as if he's heard this tale before, then asks him if he's ever considered changing jobs.

He hasn't, actually. The doctor writes him a prescription for something that should help with the anxiety. Ben picks up the medication but never opens the bottle. The doctor's question has pointed him to a door he hadn't seen was always standing open.

He talks to some of the guys he's gotten to know who work elsewhere at Northfire. Lyle Butterfield, whom Ben met at a Northfire Christmas party last December and hit it off with over their shared love of old westerns, manages maintenance and safety inspections for Extractor No. 2. Ben takes him out for a beer one evening and broaches the subject of finding other work. Lyle is enthusiastic: there's a new position opening up next week on his team. Ben would have to start at a lower salary than he's bringing in now, but after a few months, with some extra training courses under his belt, there's no reason he couldn't move up to a supervisory position.

Ben and Beth stay up late that night to talk it through.

The next morning Ben gives Dylan Chaudiere his notice.

He thinks sometimes it was the sheer scale of things that got to him. The magnitude of what they were doing to the earth. Burning through millions of years to light our cities for a day. Turning the past into fuel to rocket ourselves full throttle into the future. *This isn't real,* he said to himself some days as the truck plummeted into the pit like the space rock that wasted the dinosaurs. *This can't be real.* Like a boy playing with matches who looks up and sees he's started the whole forest on fire, maybe it was too much for the mind to take in. And then there was the way everything around you—the robot-monster excavators, the giant tires of your own truck, the pit like a drained seabed—made you small. Even the eye-popping bottom line on your paycheque could do that. There was no way a number that big could have anything to do with *you.*

Extractor No. 2 is huge too, a behemoth of pipes and cat-walks and soaring vent stacks. But here he doesn't have to take in the big picture. He leans in close to the gauges on the control panel he's monitoring, watching the needles twitch faintly. Here where the ore is transmuted into power and wealth they keep their eye on the little things that gesture to what's going on elsewhere, with the big things.

Their third summer in River Meadows, the Hewitts join the Butterfield family on a camping vacation in the Rockies. Amery and Heather Butterfield are about the same age. Beth and Maureen Butterfield expected the girls to become fast friends on this trip, and are puzzled and disappointed when it doesn't happen. Amery and Heather refuse to bond, despite all of their mothers' gentle coaxing and attempts to come up with activities they can do together.

She's weird, Mom, Alex overhears Heather complaining to her mother on the steps of their motorhome, brand new and nearly twice the size of the Hewitts' camper.

She's just shy, honey.

No she's not. She's weird. She makes bird noises.

Bird noises?

When she hears birds chirping, she chirps back.

Alex knows it's true. He's caught Amery whistling and chittering to the birds like she's carrying on a conversation with them. It makes him angry, both that she does something so crazy, and that somebody else has noticed. And also that people are talking about his family this way.

Amery finally seems to catch on that she's not delivering on something they're all expecting of her. The next morning she's her old chatty, bouncy self, the Amery she'd been before they came to River Meadows. Alex wonders if anyone else can see how hard she's having to work at it.

We should climb a mountain today, she says to Heather as everyone is tucking into the sausages and eggs that Ben cooked for breakfast. I bet we could get to the top of one easy.

That's a good idea, Beth says, beaming at Amery. Let's all climb a mountain.

Really? Ben asks, incredulous.

Let's do this, Lyle Butterfield says, pumping a fist.

I don't know, Maureen Butterfield says.

We don't have to go all the way to the top, Beth qualifies, and points beyond the roof of their camper. There's a trail that climbs to that ridge, right there. I saw it on the notice board on the way in. It takes about an hour and it's not too steep.

So they climb a mountain. Alex fumes at first—he'd planned to spend the day in the camper with his comics and sketchpad, away from everyone else—but it isn't long before he's started to enjoy himself. There's a feeling of adventure out here, of something unknown waiting to be discovered around the next turn of the trail or over the next rise. He's read plenty of fantasy novels, and played games with his friends set in places he'd imagined being much like this. He fills his lungs with the crisp air, breathes in the warm, sunny fragrance of high alpine juniper and fir. Through the trees he catches glimpses of the river and their campsite far below, the flash of sunlight on cars and motorhomes crawling along on the distant highway. When they stop to catch their breath at a bend in the trail with a lookout bench, he closes his eyes and listens to the wind approaching from the slopes below them, rushing through miles and miles of spruce and pine.

Amery keeps up a steady stream of chatter—about school, about other kids at school, about her favourite TV shows—and Heather chatters right back. But Amery can't keep it up, and when she finally goes quiet, so does Heather. Soon they're not walking side by side but far apart.

They come out into an open, sloping meadow of grass and flowers, under a mountain wall down which a thin white cascade is falling, far enough away that its sound doesn't reach them over the roar of wind. This is the end of the trail. Alex is disappointed the climb is over. He wants to keep going, up into the wind and light.

It's so peaceful here, Beth says.

Alex guesses what she really means—there are no wobbles. Everything is just what it is.

They bring out the lunch Ben and Lyle carried up in their packs. The two families sit a little bit apart, nobody saying much. Amery gets up and wanders off. Heather doesn't follow.

They lounge in the sun for a while and the warm air lulls them. Before anyone is fully aware, there's a prow of dark, threatening cloud edging over the cliff above them. The wind chills and a few needle droplets touch their arms and necks.

Here comes the rain, right on cue, Ben says. If you don't like the weather in the mountains, wait five minutes.

We should probably get back, Maureen says, putting her arm around Heather.

As heavier drops start to patter on their heads and shoulders, they hurry to pack up. When Alex looks around for her he sees Amery at the forest's edge, looking into its dark green depths. He runs over to her.

Come on, he says, unable to keep the annoyance out of his voice. For some reason he wants to blame her for the change in the weather.

She turns and looks at him.

I'm coming back here, she says with certainty in her voice and not a trace of wistfulness.

What are you talking about?

I'm coming back here. To climb this mountain.

Okay, sure. Whatever. Tomorrow?

No. A long time from now.

Why don't you just stay here, he says offhandedly. Nobody wants you around anyhow.

He walks away, not waiting to see if his words have struck a blow.

As far as Alex can recall, they never went on another trip with the Butterfields.

It's been two weeks since they returned from the mountains. They're at the table having dinner when there's a soft thump from upstairs, followed by another.

When one door closes, Ben says with a tired shrug, another one opens. Every time.

No one laughs. The dad joke has already gotten old.

I didn't hear anything, Alex says.

Come on, Ben says. That was the upstairs linen closet just now, right after your little sister's bedroom door. You can go check if you like.

Beth takes a deep breath and keeps her eyes on her plate. It's not important, she says softly.

It is, Ben says, bristling. We have to keep track of these things, Beth. You know that. We bought this place on the not unreasonable assumption that you get what you pay for. And we paid good money for quality. And craftsmanship. And now we find out the place was apparently slapped together by incompetents.

Beth says, It might not be the house . . .

No? First the teeter-totter flooring in the front hall. Then the mysterious smells. And now, hey, how cool is this feature? Self-operating doors. *That's* why we have to keep track. We need an accurate, detailed record of everything that's wrong with this place, right down to the last floorboard creak, because to me it's looking increasingly like we have no choice but to take the goddamn builder to court.

His voice has risen and he's clearly in one of his moods. Money weighs on him more now than it did when they didn't have any. When he's like this Alex has to fight the impulse to get up from the table and walk away. He knows from experience that will only make it worse, but sometimes that's what he wants— for things to blow up. Tonight, something in his mother's strained tone holds him back. Making his father angry is a thing he seems compelled to do. Making his mother angry is the forbidden zone.

It's like people don't take any pride in their work anymore, Ben goes on. Somebody's always trying to rip you off or scam you, and we all just go along with it, like *oh well, that's the way things are.* Well it's not the way things used to be, and it's not the way things should be.

It wasn't mine, Amery says.

What's that, honey? Beth asks. Hearing from Amery at the dinner table these days is an even rarer event than Ben losing his temper.

That wasn't my door, Amery says. It was Alex's.

Bullshit, Alex says.

Alex, Beth says.

Well, she's wrong.

I'm not. I can tell the difference.

Alex has to admit she's probably right, though he's not going to agree with her. Amery is much more sensitive to these things than the rest of them, that's obvious. Which makes sense if what's happening to their house is somehow related to the decoherences.

Can we get back on topic here? Ben says, addressing the light fixture above the table. And, as if on cue, it starts flickering.

A wobble is passing through, such a familiar event now no one even comments.

You know the contractor's coming to have a look next week, Beth says. In the meantime, there's nothing we can do. So why don't we just—

I can think of something to do, Ben mutters, pushing his plate away. Something involving my foot and a certain contractor's fat ass.

Beth rubs her eyes. It's a good house. We'll get things put right.

She didn't want to stay here, Alex thinks. Why is she defending this place?

Ray, the contractor, runs his hand along the kitchen wall, then knocks on it softly, cocking his ear to listen.

Oh yeah, he murmurs, nodding.

Yeah what? Beth asks.

It happens with some of the new builds, Ray says. Out of the blue. Doesn't seem to pick one house over another for any particular reason.

It's the decoherences, then?

Well, hard to say for sure. I'm not the expert on that. Could just be the ground shifting.

Is there anything we can do?

Ray leans his ear close to the wall, knocks softly and listens.

Oh sure, you've still got time, he says. We caught this in the early stages.

That's good, Beth says. That means you can fix it, right?

I can bring my team in, probably like . . . three to six weeks. Have to check the schedule. But no worries, we'll straighten things out. No problemo.

He pats the door frame.

The place will be good as new.

It *is* new, Beth says.

Ray chuckles.

Right, he says, and winks at her. Better than new.

On a chilly Saturday afternoon in early spring, ridges of dirty snow still clinging to the edges of lawns, Beth comes home from shopping to a silent house. She heads upstairs, finds Amery's room empty. Alex is in his room, drawing comics as usual.

Where's your sister?

I don't know.

What do you mean you don't know?

I'm not following her around anymore, Mom. Why do I have to keep babysitting her when she's not a baby? It's not fair. I've got things of my own to do.

They hold each other's gaze, neither backing down. Beth swallows an angry retort and walks away. Alex's shout follows her down the stairs.

She's fine! She belongs out there! You know that!

Beth isn't sleeping well. No one in the family is. Well, except Ben. He never has any trouble passing right out, no matter what.

Cucumber slices, but no cheddar left. Just the processed slices, not Ben's favourite, but she forgot to buy the good kind last night at the store. She hears Alex hollering at Amery through the bathroom door to hurry up.

I'm picking up some extra hours at the office today, Beth says to Ben, who's looking through today's *River Meadows*

Record-Gazette. Reading at the table, just like he's told Alex not to do.

Oh yeah? You doing all right? You look tired.

I'm fine.

Ben nods, folds the paper closed. He gets up, touches her shoulder.

I'll call you at lunch.

Okay.

The bathroom door opens, and she hears Alex say, About flipping time.

Amery wanders into the kitchen, gets herself a bowl and spoon, brings them over to the table and pours herself some cereal. Beth watches her without trying to make it obvious she's watching her. Amery hasn't said anything for weeks now about the scary noises and doors opening by themselves. Maybe she's finally gotten used to it. She may have to, if that contractor never shows up again. But Beth feels it's more than just the weird stuff with the house. Amery is so calm and deliberate now, in everything she does. Nothing seems to bother her. There was that thunderstorm the other night, that rattled the windows and had them practically jumping out of their skin with every tremendous *boom*. Except for Amery, who used to be terrified of thunder.

Ben is out the door. Both kids are eating breakfast now. Half day today, Beth remembers. They'll be on their own at home all afternoon.

Was there something in the room with her last night? Did she dream it? A faint, smeary shimmer in the dark, a moving-ness, or maybe just those tiny explosions of phosphenes in her eyes, the vibrating circle of red dots she sometimes sees, hovering in the gloom wherever she turns her gaze, when she's lying there wide awake and it's late at night and she knows she won't fall asleep now.

Beth remembers where she is and glances up. Amery is looking out the window, as she often does these days. Then she turns and stares at her mother. A long, steady, unreadable look. The urge boils up in Beth to shout at her child, *Please just be a normal kid for once!* Instead she smiles.

So, you two, she says brightly, what have you got planned for your half day of freedom?

Alex looks up from his bowl of Cybercrunch, surprised by this unexpected query. He shrugs, regarding his mother warily, like he suspects she's about to assign him some chore that will eat up his afternoon. I don't know, he says at last. Drawing and stuff I guess.

And how about you? Beth asks Amery, still smiling but hearing the tremor in her voice. Is she actually afraid of her own child?

Amery puts on a smile. It's an eerie sight.

I'll probably go over to Shawna's, she says. If that's okay.

They both know it's not true.

Alex is in his room that afternoon working on his new Kid Quantum comic book when Amery appears in the doorway. He's surprised—she's been gone for hours, wherever it is she goes these days. Usually she returns from one of her forays without anyone noticing. They just suddenly find her there, in her room or wherever, as if she'd never left.

Amery stands there, not saying anything.

What is it?

There's something . . . I need you to come see.

Come see what?

Just . . . I'll show you. It's in the woods.

Of course it's in the woods.

I need your help. Please.

Thirty minutes later they've reached the bank of the creek. They can hear River Meadows behind them, the soft, distant murmur of a working town. This is in late May, but it's been a dry spring and the water in the creek bed is little more than a trickle. They cross on the little three-log bridge that someone built there, maybe a long time ago. On the far side, they walk through a stand of poplars and come out into a long, straight open area, like a cutline, only narrower than the ones Alex saw when Ben tried to get him interested in snowshoeing one winter.

This odd corridor through the bush is full of knee-high grass, most of it still pale and withered from winter, and clinging plants that clutch at clothes and scratch bare limbs. There are rusted metal posts with numbers on them, spaced a long way apart, that must have something to do with the extraction industry, Alex thinks. He's come out here a couple of times with his friends to explore and goof around. They found shotgun shells, cigarette butts, beer bottles, but never stayed long. There's something creepy about this place. It smells faintly of burnt rubber or melted electrical wiring. He's felt a strange tingling along his arms and the back of his neck out here. And once he and his friends heard a low, staticky hum that seemed to be coming from under the ground.

Where are we going? he asks his sister for at least the fourth time. She hasn't told him anything.

They walk for another few minutes until they near a huge pine that has fallen into the path. Its branches are still thick with needles but they're brown.

Amery comes to a stop.

Alex looks around.

You brought me out here to look at a dead tree?

No, she whispers, pointing at the pine. *There. Look there.*

He squints. Half-concealed in the tangle of shadows beneath the branches there's an animal. Alex is so startled he nearly jumps back. It's a small dog, he thinks at first, then he notices the patchy dark-rust shade of the fur, the pointed black-tipped ears and sharp snout, and realizes this must be a fox.

It's tensed, heeled forward as if it had frozen in place while darting into a run. The wind is catching and flicking stray tufts of its fur. The pale amber gems of its eyes are fixed straight ahead.

A feeling like a frenzy of ants crawls across the back of Alex's neck. You never see wild animals just stand there like this when people are around. As soon as they catch sight of a human, they're gone. Something is very wrong here.

It's stuck, Amery says. Her tone is matter-of-fact, simply stating how things are. She doesn't sound scared or upset or anything. Alex feels a cold dread in his stomach, a fear either of the animal or his sister, he's not sure.

What do you mean stuck?

It's trapped.

I don't see any trap.

You can't see it, but it's there.

He doesn't know what she's talking about. He searches the ground and finds a dead branch as long as his arm, slender enough that he can grip it easily, but with a good solid heft to it. Holding the stick at the ready, he dares another step toward the fox, then another. Amery follows.

No, it's a stuffed animal or something, Alex whispers. It's not alive. This is some kind of trick. Did you do this?

It's alive, Amery says. Look at its face.

Alex edges closer. He can just make out a tremor along the fox's muzzle. After a further moment of careful observation, he sees the same almost imperceptible trembling in its forelegs. The ribs pressing against taut skin, the quick rise and fall of breath.

It looks like it's starving, Alex says. It must have been stuck here a long time.

It's in pain, Amery says. It's really hurting.

How do you know that?

Its eyes.

It's afraid of us, he says. That's all. It can't move for some reason and it's scared shitless.

No, it's dying, Amery says, because it can't escape. We have to help it.

Alex turns to her.

That thing'll bite us for sure if we go anywhere near it. It probably has rabies. And I don't want to get stuck like that.

You won't, Amery says.

How do you know?

I got stuck here too.

You *what?*

The last time I came here. I went up to the tree and I felt something holding my arms and legs. Something I couldn't see. I pulled really hard and I got away. I don't think the trap is strong enough to catch animals as big as us.

We're not animals.

Yes, we are.

I'm not touching that thing, he says.

We have to do something.

Alex glances down at the stick in his hand.

There's one thing, he says.

Amery looks at the stick and back up at her brother.

Don't do it, she says, and for the first time in a long time he can hear emotion in her voice, see it in her eyes. Not fear or disbelief. Something more like disappointment in him.

He remembers the cabin they lived in when they first came to this town, the anthill, the stick he wielded without giving it a second thought. With shame in his heart and anger at his sister he understands that some part of him is looking forward to what he's about to do.

You got any better ideas?

She shakes her head.

He edges slowly toward the fox, holding the stick out in front of him. When he's a couple steps from it he stops. He can smell the animal now, a pungent reek like wet dog and rotting leaves, and a sharp metallic odour that reminds him of the smell of his own blood.

He looks back at Amery. Her face is expressionless again. She isn't looking away.

On the car radio on Beth's way home from work two loud obnoxious announcers are setting up a joke. *Knock knock. Who's there? Don. Don who? Don miss the incredible twenty-four-hour stuff-yourself-silly buffet at Banquet World!*

Her body feels like a stone that someone dropped off a bridge. She can barely blink her aching eyes. It's a struggle to concentrate on the road and on the other vehicles pressing in on all sides, jockeying impatiently to get ahead. She glances at the drivers lunging past: some impassive behind the wheel, some slack-jawed, some glowering. She's coming up on the off-ramp to their neighbourhood, but she has to squeeze into the

far right lane and it's tight but she makes it. A little powder
blue sports car darts in front of her to get onto the ramp first.
Its licence plate reads XS CASH.

On Foxhaven Drive the convoy of homebound commuters
grinds to a glacial crawl. She's never seen it this busy. There's
a turn-off coming up. It's not one she ever uses, but she knows
it's an alternate route to her street. As she inches the car
closer she debates taking the exit. It doesn't look anywhere
near as busy.

There's a ripple of air around her and the radio cuts out
for a moment then returns . . . *now with all-you-can-eat bone-
less wings!* This happens sometimes when there's a wobble:
electronics giving a hiccup. It's a weird one, though, because
for an instant there she could swear she heard Ben's voice
underneath the announcer's chatter, saying *turn here.*

Beth finally reaches the turnoff and exits. She's out of the
traffic jam and on her way.

The radio is still clamouring for her attention. She switches
it off, but meaningless phrases echo in her head. *How many
girls can carry their heads in their hands? All you can-can? Yes,
we can-can. At the dancity banquest of the knock-knock man.*

Her mind feels like a torn-open envelope. Whatever was
inside it is important, but gone. All she has is what's written on
the envelope. Which is her own name and address. As if this
letter was returned.

When Beth finally gets home the house is silent. Amery is
outside in the backyard, sitting in the grass. She isn't facing
the house and from the kitchen window Beth can't tell what
she's doing, if she's doing anything at all. Once in a while she
still goes blank like this and doesn't move for minutes at a
time. Alex's door is shut and she assumes he's in there. Has
he started to do *that* yet? she wonders, not for the first time.

He must have, he's fifteen. It's normal, it's fine, even if she doesn't want to think about it.

But no, something's not right. Even though one of her kids spends all of his time in his room and the other hardly ever talks, there's the usual quiet and then there's this level of quiet. Like invisible radiation in the air. She needs to talk to her children, to gently coax whatever it is out of them if she can, but she's so tired. She'll have a glass of wine, then start getting dinner ready. She'll wait for them to open up to her. Sooner or later they will. They always have. Or that's how it used to be. Amery would come to her and say those words and she'd know something was wrong. It's been a long time since Beth has heard them. *One squishy witch pinky.*

Beth sits in the sunroom with a glass of shiraz, taking in the last of the sun as it sets over the rooftops of Foxhaven. September and already starting to get dark so early. Something she's never gotten used to. When the wine is finished she sighs, gets up, and goes into the kitchen. Choosing a classic rock mix on the music player, she starts washing and cutting vegetables for a pot of chili. Singing along with old songs she loves. *I want to ride my bicycle. I want to ride my bike.* She remembers Ben laughing as he clumsily peddled Amery's tricycle around the driveway.

He's been distant too, lately, like his daughter. Is he still having trouble at work, even after changing jobs? He told her he's happy now, but the truth is they haven't talked about what happened to him, not since that first time. They always used to talk things through, keeping in the loop of each other's lives. It seems like there's never any time now. Or maybe she just doesn't want to know how he's doing, maybe she's still angry with him for bringing them here. If it's been hard on him too, well, now he knows what it's like to have your life disrupted, uprooted.

That's not fair. She thinks of the way her mother used to complain about her father and his woolly-headed ideas, his lack of practicality. She vowed never to be that kind of wife.

She's gone for a while, in a memory of her father, how he would come home from his failing camera shop—Leitner's Photo & Lens—and she would climb on him after he collapsed into his armchair and check his pockets. Sometimes, most times, she would find gum or candy that he put there just for her. If there was nothing in the "magic pocket" he'd shake his head sadly. *Sorry, bug.* Bug. One of his many nicknames for her. *Bethaboo. Lizzy-Bear.*

Sure, he was idealistic and absent-minded, dreaming and bumbling his way through life—her mother wasn't wrong—but Beth loved him for it. That time he was hanging a big family photo on the wall, and he stepped back to appraise the hole he'd drilled for the drywall anchor and put his foot right through the frame.

Rinsing carrots under the tap, Beth laughs. *Oh Daddy.*

She remembers the vacation they took to Vancouver Island the summer she turned thirteen, the towering firs in Cathedral Grove and her father standing there looking up in awe. *What a planet this is*, he says, hands on his hips. *What a planet.* Oblivious to the teenage boy from another tourist family who was staring at her, not at the trees, like she was the wonder.

She comes back, realizes she's still cutting vegetables without paying attention and could so easily have cut herself. Lucky. She puts the big pot on the stove, drizzles in some olive oil, turns on the heat, then surveys the ingredients she's laid out on the counter. This should do it. Just in time for another glass of wine.

As she's refilling her glass there's a sound of tires pulling up on the driveway. She glances out the window, surprised that Ben is home so early.

It's not Ben's truck. The car is a police cruiser.

Beth's arms and legs go cold as if they've been plunged into freezing water. Her heart constricts, the pain so great she groans out loud.

A young man in uniform climbs out of the vehicle. He glances warily at the house, takes his hat off, and runs a hand through his hair.

On their first wedding anniversary in River Meadows, Ben came home from work early and told Beth he was taking her somewhere special. She wanted to know where, but he said it was a secret.

The kids were old enough to be left on their own. Ben drove out of town, to one of the new excavation sites. A friend of his working evening shift on security let them through the gate.

They parked near the edge of the pit and climbed out of the car.

What are we doing *here?* Beth asked. Ben gave her that boyish smile she had fallen for when they'd first met and hadn't seen for a long time.

The sky was on fire with a northern sunset. The pit looked like the black hole that night was coming from—the night of all the time before they were here and all the time to come after they were gone. Their lives brief flashes in the dark. Ben set up a folding table with a tablecloth and put out a candle, a bottle of wine, and two glasses. He queued up some slow tunes on the portable music player and pressed play. Then he took Beth's hand in his and slid his arm around her waist. On the edge of that dark lake, for a little while, they danced.

ALL-WEATHER NOTEBOOK No. 25

Sept. 5, 8:49 p.m., Foxhaven Drive

Encounter with one of *them*. Started with a low drone that had no apparent source. A metallic edge to it like an electric shaver, coming from all around. My head went in a long, loopy circle and I had to get down on the pavement. Then something else, a vacancy, an emptying, I don't know. I might have blacked out for a moment.

The next thing I knew, he was there. Walking toward me up the road. Walking slowly and I couldn't really make out his features because it was getting dark and he had the last of the light behind him. But I knew that walk. Coming to find me at the end of the day, to see what I was up to and bring me home, my hand in his, just like it used to be.

I was so sure it was him. I nearly called out.

It wasn't him, of course.

Then he wasn't there anymore. It wasn't there. It just vanished, like they do.

I miss him. I miss all of them. It doesn't hit me very often but it's always waiting. Some days it catches up to me.

CLAIRE

When she returns to the room the crane is gone.

The balcony is empty, the rain still flurrying sideways in the near dark of this sunless day. That's over with, then, Claire thinks, and feels a twinge of disappointment. She drops into the chair, looks over the notes she'd been transcribing from her journal onto her computer.

She'd gone downstairs and out into the street, then sat in a nearby coffee shop for over an hour. She told herself she had to give them every opportunity to hand over the bag if this was the day they decided to try again. But she knew she was mostly avoiding the bird. The last thing she wanted to share her room with was an animal.

She remembers the supreme fuck-up last year in Thailand. Those little bats. She'd held one cupped in her palms, a tiny, trembling thing not much bigger than a bumblebee, before the smuggler showed her how to hide them inside the tube of a roll of toilet paper. At the airport she took a risk and looked them up online: Kitti's hog-nosed bat, thought to be the world's smallest mammal, discovered only in the late twentieth century by the naturalist they named the species after. *An adult bat weighs less than a copper penny. The species is capable of hovering, like a hummingbird.*

When she got off the plane in Dubai her luggage didn't show up on the carousel. The airline apologized and said they would find it. She went to her hotel room and waited, pacing and breaking out in a sweat despite the Arctic-level air conditioning.

That evening someone finally brought her bags up to her room. The bats were still inside the toilet rolls, all of them dead.

After that she drew a line: no more live animals.

As she glances up absent-mindedly from her screen toward the balcony, trying to rope in a phrase, the crane drops shakily out of the storm, like a pilot bailing from a lethal dogfight.

It's come back.

Something is hanging from the bird's beak, a ragged pale blue mass. The shredded remains of an Ikea bag, by the look of it. Claire doesn't move from her chair. She stays as still as possible. The crane takes slow, deliberate steps up and down the balcony, looking this way and that, like a fussy homeowner deciding where best to place an expensive new piece of furniture. Finally, it chooses a corner, and gets to work wadding and shaping the material it's brought, pulling and plucking at the frayed fibres, its red-crested head juddering like a machine.

It's making a nest. Over the next hour Claire types infrequently and looks up often as the bird takes off and returns several times with more nesting material: wet twigs and shaggy bundles of straw, limp straggles of newsprint and dirty plastic sheeting, a ribbon of neon orange warning tape. With its long bill, it prods, pokes, and threads this miscellaneous refuse into the weave of its new home. There is something wonderfully uninhibited about all these random colours and textures twined together, she has to admit, as if, rather than submitting to instinct, the bird is creating art.

Underneath the calm veneer of her thoughts a thin, manic voice has begun whispering *abort*. This is just too strange. Could the bird have been trained by someone to land *here*, on *her* balcony? That's crazy, but then again, in a place like this, is it? Another part of her mind is simply observing, as serene and unmoved as the bird appears to be, aware that her panic-button reaction is excessive, and can probably be blamed on the patch. She does a round of steadying box breathing, pours herself a vodka from the mini-bar, and waits.

When evening comes, she keeps the lights off. There's enough illumination from the city's sleepless glow to allow her to move easily around the room in the dark, although she's had to learn to do that too, for jobs that required her to carry out her activities at night.

Claire sits on a chair near the glass. If there's already an egg under the bird, then what she's doing now is brooding. That's the correct term for it, she's fairly certain. She carries a sharp splinter of memory from her days in River Meadows. She must have been seven or eight when her mother took her to some old woman's property deep in the bush. She doesn't remember if she was ever told the woman's name or who she was. She used to wonder if she'd only dreamed it, but it really happened. The woman was a psychic, a friend of Claire's grandmother. Her mother was into astrology, tarot, palm reading—the kind of stuff that made her father roll his eyes. That's why she'd taken Claire out there. One of many *fuck yous* to everything her father believed in.

An evening in early fall, yellow and gold poplar leaves shivering all around them. The smell of woodsmoke, damp grass.

A decrepit mobile home hunkered in the middle of a field of dry stubble. The old woman was standing at the open door of an old shed, in a padded down jacket with the stuffing coming out of it, smoking a cigarette. Inside, several white and russet chickens were nestled in crude plywood boxes stuffed with straw. Claire remembers gaping in awe at the unfamiliar creatures. The woman had said to her *they're brooding*. Or *they're broody*. Claire wasn't sure which. Then she tossed aside her cigarette, gestured for Claire to come closer. When she did, the woman reached out and took her hand. Claire pulled back but she was held in an iron grip. The woman turned Claire's hand palm upward and studied it. She gave off a sharp scent of tobacco smoke. *Let me go*, Claire shouted, furious with her mother. The old woman released her grip, then looked up at her mother and said, *Just try keeping this one in a cage.*

The crane's eyes remain closed. Its breathing rises and falls. This kind of brooding, Claire thinks, is the opposite of what it means when humans brood. The crane looks utterly at peace in the shelter it has made for itself. As if it's come home.

Watching the bird, she realizes that the fear has completely vanished. She feels alert, but calm.

Around nine she receives a text from Andros, who wants to know if she feels like joining him for a drink. There's a nightclub she should check out for the guidebook. What gives the place an aura of danger is the part of town it's in, the stretch of sleazy bars and strip joints near the docks.

She decides it's late enough that she can ignore the text. If he asks in the morning she'll tell him she was already asleep.

As the island can experience extreme weather events and unexpected seismic activity, it's wise to come prepared. Before leaving on your trip, put together an emergency kit that includes thermal and waterproof clothing, a flashlight and back-up batteries, and a basic first aid kit with pain medication, bandages, and disinfectant. The likelihood is slim, but in case you are directed to seek shelter at one of the island's emergency centres, make sure you bring something for entertainment that doesn't need to be plugged in, like a travel chess set, or a book. If you have any concerns, or you aren't sure what to do should a serious weather or seismic event occur, don't be afraid to ask for help. The locals are friendly and approachable.

The bird is still in the nest the next morning, a quiescent white mass. Claire orders breakfast from room service. The storm has made the Wi-Fi laggy and intermittent, but she manages to look up local bird species on the internet. This is not her assignment. It's not either of her assignments.

She finds what she is almost certain has to be the correct species. *Grus poseidonis.* Its range stretches all the way from these shores to western North America. Or used to. The red tinge of the crest, the fiery opal eye, the gunmetal beak: nothing else on the official identification website resembles what's out there on the balcony. If only the bird would get up again and walk around, give her another look at its camera tripod legs, she could confirm it.

The thing is, this particular crane is rare. Extremely rare and critically endangered. There may be only a single breeding pair left in the wild. And only here, on the island. Nowhere else on the planet.

Out there on her balcony is one of them. Probably the female.

She lets herself imagine what it might be worth to the right person.

Stepping outside the room, with a quick glance up and down the corridor, she hangs the DO NOT DISTURB sign on the door. Andros texts later in the morning, *Hey how are you?*

Not so great, she texts back. *Staying in today.*

Can I get you anything? What can I do?

I'll be fine thanks. Better if you stay away. I don't know what this is.

Okay. I'll check in with you later.

With a burner phone she sends another text, off-island. A short message, with a photograph. Half an hour later there's a reply.

Will respond. Stick with original itinerary.

The "original itinerary" is the hand-off she still hasn't completed. At least they're giving her another chance.

She holds the cleaning staff, and Andros, at bay for another twelve hours. That night he texts that he's worried about her. He doesn't want to be a pain, but she should think about going to see a doctor. She says she's feeling better, she just needs another decent night's sleep and she should be good to go in the morning.

Quite late there's a soft knock at the door. It's him.

She cracks the door open.

"I know this is bad, showing up here like this," he says. "I'm sorry, I was worried about you. Tell me to fuck off and I'll go."

"I don't want you to fuck off," she says, "but I do want you to go."

He's taller than her and easily looks over her head, into the room, squinting.

"What is *that*?"

"Look at her," Andros says, crouched at the glass. "I thought they were extinct."

It's nearly midnight. Claire still has all the lights in the room off. The bird remains huddled into itself.

"You can't tell anyone about this," she says.

"But people will want to—"

"Exactly. If this is *that* bird, it'll be a big deal. There will be media all over it in no time. They'll disturb her, maybe chase her off. They could ruin this."

"The conservation people need to know. They could help make sure—"

She thinks quickly.

"I'll let them know. I will. I just want a chance to write about this first. To have it to myself for a little while before the frenzy starts. You understand, don't you? I mean, this could be a breakthrough for my career. I could get an article in *Planet Geographic* out of this."

He looks at the bird, then at her. She sees in his eyes that he's aware of a layer to her he hadn't suspected.

"I see. All right."

He stands then and gazes out over the galaxy of his own city, the whorls of lights shimmering and twinkling in the droplets streaking down the panes.

"When did they build that?" he murmurs. She's standing close behind him, not wanting to ask what he's seen that he doesn't recognize. Not wanting to speak at all or have him talk either. The whole time he's been in her room she's been stealing glances at him. Since she decided to let this thing with the crane unfold there's been another feeling growing stronger. It's so not like her, this ache of desire. This eagerness to surrender. Her role has always been to move briskly along the periphery, scoop up the quarry, and get out. Not *dissolve into*.

"You can get closer," Claire urges him in a reassuring whisper. "Right up to the glass if you like. It's okay, she's sleeping. It won't bother her."

He does as he's told. Let him fall in love with it. Get attached. Then he'll want to protect it. He'll be an accomplice.

"Hello," Andros says in a soft, lilting voice. "I never thought I'd be meeting *you*."

She gives him the moment, then touches his shoulder. He turns and looks at her, blinking.

"Oh," he says at last, and grins. "Do you think we can . . . I mean, would it bother her . . . ?"

Well after midnight Claire opens her eyes and sits up. Something has changed. Then she knows what it is.

It's not storming anymore. The air outside is calm, not whipping around in a wet frenzy. It almost makes her dizzy, such stillness. The crane lifts its head too, as if it's also been disturbed by the quiet. It regards her with a dark, fathomless eye. The night breeze lifts its russet crest and gently settles it back in place.

Beside her Andros breathes evenly.

She can still make this work, even with him involved. It will be difficult but she's up for it. If the bird itself is simply not a possibility, she'll focus on what it made the nest for. The precious thing it may already be keeping warm and safe underneath itself. An egg from such a bird might be worth as much or more than what she was sent here to get.

They've curled up, almost asleep again when her phone hums. Blindly she gropes the bedside table.

It's her editor. For a moment she mixes them up: this gentle, long-suffering man who's been waiting for updates from her, who's always waiting for updates from her, and the one she spoke to briefly over the phone before she left, anonymous and terse.

"Claire? Arthur. Sorry about the time. How are you?"

"I'm fine. Good."

"So you're *there?*"

"I'm here. I am."

"Good, good. We haven't heard from you. Listen, I wanted to call . . . the thing is . . . let you know . . ."

"What? Sorry, Arthur, I didn't catch that. What?"

". . . tell us . . . home . . . return . . ."

"Sorry, what? Could you say that again. Hello?"

No bars on the screen. No signal.

She sinks back onto the pillow. Andros stirs and slides his arm over her hip. All that that broken conversation has succeeded in doing is to put an image in her head that won't leave: her mother's tiny room at the care centre. What is it now, six months? Seven. Arthur wouldn't have been calling about that. The people at the care centre would've gotten in touch if there was anything . . .

She'll try Arthur's number in the morning.

———

Before dawn she wakes to find Andros sitting naked and cross-legged on the end of the bed, watching the bird. Again, she wonders at the way she's abandoned her caution. That woman who clutched her hand as a child: she hasn't let anyone else do that to her since. She remembers Arthur's late call, decides to hold off for now on calling back.

"We should give her a name," Andros says.

"Like what?"

"How about Artemis? The moon goddess."

"Why a moon goddess?"

She can hear the annoyance in her voice, the impatience for him to be gone. The pause before he speaks again tells her he can too.

"Her colour, I guess. And she looks so serene."

"Have you seen videos of these things catching fish? You can tell they're descended from dinosaurs. I'll bet a velociraptor mother looked serene sitting on her eggs too."

Andros fetches them breakfast from the restaurant downstairs. Then he has to head off again to the research facility.

"Have a good day, honey," he says in a pretty good American drawl as he's heading out the door. She actually laughs.

After he's gone, she gets up off the bed and takes pictures of the bird from various angles. She feels a sudden desire to open the sliding door and step out onto the balcony. To be closer to her new companion, not on the other side of a glass wall. She knows this would be an unforgivable breach on her part. The bird wouldn't welcome her. It wouldn't understand why she's violated its space. Not that she would, either.

She's bent over her work again when light floods the room. She looks up, blinking. The sun. The actual sun, after so long. The bird is still tightly huddled. In the dazzling light it resembles a mound of late spring snow.

She ventures down to the lobby and outside, carrying the guidebook. There are still a few places to visit on her checklist. Museums. Galleries. Archives. All public places with enough human traffic to hide a hand-off in plain sight.

The wet pavements are steaming, people have their jackets off and their umbrellas closed, and they're smiling, strolling rather than hurrying, sitting at the outdoor tables of cafés, chatting and laughing and having a good time. She finds a vacant chair outside a café, orders an iced tea, watches the passersby. This is normal. This is what you do when the sun is out. She's enjoying the day like everyone else.

No, it won't go away. Nice try. It's wrong here too. She stirs her tea and the light catches her spoon. She squints into the sky. That blazing orb up there—we never think about what it really is, an explosion, a billion-year kaboom that's still going on, still blowing up. Good old Mister Sun: a violence, a cataclysm. One day that gorgeous annihilating light will eat everything.

She gets up, walks farther along the street. Finds a little park tucked between two gleaming obsidian office fronts. Sits on a bench under a shade tree, a living green parasol. It's no use. She heads back in the direction of the hotel. She needs to check on the bird. Who knows what she might be missing. What if this change in the weather is what it's been waiting for, and it decides to fly off and find a better nesting site?

A half-hour after she's returned to the room her phone buzzes. Another text from off-island.

Both. Fires today. The Sounds. 1 hour.

Fires? It has to be an autocorrect error for *first,* meaning the messenger bag. The sender was typing fast and didn't stop to double-check—rare for her employers. Or did somebody else send this text, someone other than her usual fixer. What if it's not even from the people who hired her?

No. She can't start second-guessing everything. It's just a typo.

What about *The Sounds*? They must mean that new attraction. It's downtown, near the square where the contact was waiting with the bag. That has to be it. So a second attempt will happen today, in one hour, at the Theatre of Sounds.

They've decided it's worth the risk to try for both. She knew they would, since it's mostly her risk, not theirs. How she's going to get a large, pissed-off crane out of the hotel without anyone noticing remains to be seen. Anyhow, one thing at a time. Let them think through the logistics of that for now while she concentrates on completing the job she was hired for. No fuck-ups this time.

The first outfit she worked for, years ago now, gave everyone code names for security—picked from some old superhero comic she's never read. Hers was Nightbird, which she hated. It made her sound like she was involved in something glamorous and sexy, as if it was about something more than money. For her it was *only* about the money. You do a job and if you don't mess up you get paid, you move on, and do another one. The people who pay you don't care about you, as long as you get them what they want. For them it's only about the money too. No misunderstandings that way.

The Theatre of Sounds is dimly lit, with channels of soft lights set in the floors to guide visitors through the semi-darkened halls and corridors. The building has been ingeniously designed so that each sound occupies only a small contained area, a kind of "audio bubble." As you make your way through the halls and galleries you pass in and out of these spheres of sound, which are marked with a ring of luminous paint on the floor.

The first exhibit space you enter is the Hall of Contemporary Background Noise. The buzzings, ringings, and low, metallic drones gathered in this room are simply those of the familiar outside world—only here they have been disentangled and made to stand apart from one another. You encounter each sound on its own, and can only marvel at how many different auditory projectiles make up the relentless bombardment that assaults us everywhere we go.

The Zoophonic Garden features many of the animal noises we're already familiar with, along with a few delightful surprises, like the squishy burbling of squid sex or the heartbeat of a chimp in love with its keeper. One section of the Garden is devoted to Microsounds: the crepitation of soil fungi, the burbling of pond amoeba undergoing cell division, the tiny crickle-crackle of demodex mites bushwhacking through the forest of your eyebrows.

Things become more disconcerting in the Conservatory of the Body, which features amplified versions of the many unglamorous gurgles, pops, and whistles we all utter (this gallery is unsurprisingly very popular with children). One of the larger audio bubbles picks up and enhances the bodily noises of anyone who stands within it, no matter how faint and usually unnoticed. Enveloped in your own corporeal cacophony—the blood rushing through your arteries and veins like a river, the pumping of your heart magnified into a thunderous drumbeat, even the soft, eerie whisper of your hair growing—you discover yourself to be a kind of flesh-and-blood musical instrument, if not an entire orchestra.

The Auditorium of the Earth takes you on a humbling journey into the realm of our planet's own life. Haunting drones and whistles from the depths of the ocean, unexplained wails and rhythmic booms recorded in various far-flung places around the globe, the eerie, staticky whispering, like voices conspiring, inside clouds just before a thunderstorm . . .

In the Cosmic Cathedral you stand under a roof of glimmering stars and listen to faint radio signals from other planets and distant galaxies.

Be sure to save some time for the Hall of Silence, where a scientifically engineered pattern of acoustic interference envelops you in what experts agree is the quietest quiet on Earth. If you're looking for an escape from the hustle and bustle of the city this is the place to be.

Claire wanders slowly through the rooms, trying the headphones stationed at each exhibit, keeping an eye out for anyone with a messenger bag over their shoulder. She does the whole circuit, including the Hall of Silence, which astonishes her. In this dim, cone-shaped room she can't even hear the familiar hiss of air on her eardrums. For a moment she lets herself sink into this utter absence of noise. Her racing thoughts go still as if they've found the place where they can finally lie down to rest.

In the Auditorium of the Earth she puts on a pair of headphones and hears what the informational plaque describes as the low, plaintive moan of the tectonic plates beneath the island, grinding over one another.

It's the same sound she heard in the depths of the research facility, and during the opera.

She flees, heart thudding, and finds herself in the gift shop. Here she lingers, calming herself, picking up and examining T-shirts and trinkets. A top that whistles the national anthem as it spins. A kit for making your own parabolic microphone. A mug with the saying *How does a coffee sound?*

People come and go around her. No one approaches. She stays long enough to draw attention from the gift shop staff. She's growing anxious again, but it's not because of her no-show contact, she realizes, it's about leaving the crane alone all this time.

One of the staff, an older woman with a librarian's frown, comes over to where she is and starts pointedly reshelving things. Claire grabs the first item at hand, a Mystery Sound Box (*creepy unexplained noises from around the world*) and pays for it with cash.

Outside the entrance, under the curve of the giant metal ear, she wonders with a jolt if she was supposed to have gone in at all. Maybe they meant for the hand-off to happen out here. Or maybe they didn't mean the theatre at all. She may have just fucked up royally.

No, this *was* the place, it had to be. And they wouldn't have chosen a conspicuous spot like the front entrance. They must have intended for her to meet the contact in those darkened halls.

But still, that doesn't explain why the hand-off didn't happen.

Nothing on her phone. A prickle of fear at the back of her neck. She imagines a police car screeching up to the curb beside her, then reminds herself that a no-show isn't all that rare. These transactions get called off at the last second for all kinds of reasons, sometimes just because of a gut feeling, a hunch, an internal alarm. The other party decides the timing or the surroundings don't smell right, or they suspect they're under surveillance. Better safe than sitting in a holding cell.

That must have been it. Like the first failed attempt, this wasn't really her fault.

As she's going up in the elevator to her floor, a text.

Not today. Stay put. Soon.

Back in the hotel room, the crane is still in its nest, apparently asleep. Claire has the odd feeling it's a replica, switched out for the real crane while she was wandering the Theatre of Sounds. A lifelike fake, like the boy's stuffed therapy dog at the airport. She resists the urge to step out onto the balcony and check. Standing between her and the bird is her own reflection.

"So," she says, "what am I going to do with you?"

THE RIVER MEADOWS ARCHIVE

BIOLOGY

Three years after his discovery of the properties of ghost ore, Ira Solomon returns to River Meadows, this time with a survey crew of thirty. He considers a visit to Fire Narrows to see how Charlie MacKinnon is doing, but he decides against it. What would he say to him? What he prophesied—the arrival of more white men—is coming true, mostly thanks to Charlie's old fishing buddy.

Solomon sets up his field lab in a canvas tent that he pitches at a good distance from the noise and squalor of the all-male survey camp.

Within days, he has taken an interest in a pack of timber wolves whose den is just over a ridge from his lab, astonished to discover a coyote living among them.

He hikes up and over the ridge every morning, before beginning the day's work on the ore samples the surveyors dig up for him. He's not here to study animal behaviour, but he knows researchers back home in the biology department who are sure to be interested in what he's found. He knows enough, too, not to say anything about his discovery to the other members of the crew. This is their territory now—they'd be over the ridge in no time at all with poison and dynamite.

Solomon is pretty sure that what he's seeing through his high-powered binoculars is unheard-of behaviour. Wolf packs are known to kill any coyotes they find encroaching on their territory. Although the coyote is clearly an adult male, it frequently displays playful, ingratiating behaviours, such as mock pouncing, hopping, and rolling around in the grass. These, Solomon surmises, are deliberate attempts to appear puppy-like and therefore harmless. The wolves not only tolerate these antics, they seem to enjoy them and sometimes even "play back," as if the coyote has earned its place in the pack by making itself a source of entertainment.

Solomon finds himself enjoying the coyote's games. He starts keeping daily notes. He refers to the coyote as "Danny Boy," after the comedian Danny Kaye, even though he tells himself repeatedly not to make it personal. *Don't get attached*, he writes in the margin beside one day's entry. Still he can't help imagining what that moment must have been like when the coyote found himself encircled by his enemies and made the choice neither to run nor to fight, but to put on a performance. To disarm the merciless ring closing in on him with a show.

One day, when the pack brings down a moose calf, Danny Boy waits unobtrusively on the sidelines until the wolves have eaten their fill and abandoned the carcass, and only then moves in, stealthily, to scavenge what remains. Another time, when an unknown coyote appears near the wolves' main den, Danny Boy joins his fellow pack members in chasing the interloper away. At such moments it's clear to Solomon that the coyote's clownish demeanour is an act—a strategy Danny Boy has employed to survive among the larger, stronger wolves. *His essential, wary, clever coyoteness appears at such times*, Solomon writes in undisguised admiration, then speculates as to why the coyote might have joined the wolves in the first place. Perhaps he lost or was driven away from his own pack, and the instinct—the deep *need* to be part of a group, even one made up of mortal enemies—was too imperative to resist.

Solomon watches, keeping his distance. He doesn't want the wolves to get spooked and leave the area. He doesn't know enough about these animals to predict what they're likely to do if he gets too close. Anyhow it's easy for him to pretend he's not really here. He's done that around people all his life.

His father used to take him grouse hunting in the lake country north of Montreal when he was a boy. The part he loved best was when they moved apart from one another through the trees, out of eyesight and sometimes earshot. Usually that happened by accident, but once in a while he would deliberately wander farther away.

When his father was nowhere to be seen or heard he could pretend he was lost and alone in the bush, far from home. He would move as quietly as possible and stop often, listening to bird call and leaf hiss, sounds that were outside of him but somehow inside him too. In the solitude he would have thoughts so strange and unexpected they would stop him in his tracks. He would wonder if this was a dream he was having, or if someone else was dreaming him. It was usually the crack of his father's rifle that brought him back to himself.

In the years since, his field work as a geologist has been mostly solitary, from choice as much as anything. Out here in the wild he sometimes feels close to being nobody at all. More and more he finds he likes that feeling.

But he knows the wolves know he's there. In his journal he wonders whether his own disruptive presence has compelled the entire pack to start performing for *him*. Perhaps the wolves merely tolerate the coyote because this other strange mammal in their midst is the larger concern. The real threat.

Perhaps, he thinks, everyone involved—including himself— is playing a role, like actors in an unscripted theatre piece, ad libbing their parts, not knowing how the story will unfold.

It's Danny Boy—the most obvious performer—who becomes the main character in Solomon's journal. In playing the part of a wolf, and even turning against his own kind, it's unclear what the coyote has become, or how long he can sustain the masquerade of goofy court jester before the lords of the realm tire of him.

When the pack's pregnant alpha female retires to her den to give birth, Solomon speculates about what might happen when the young wolves grow up with a coyote in their midst. He wonders if Danny Boy might become a kind of big brother or babysitter for them while their parents go hunting. It could be valuable data for ethologists to discover whether the young ones accept Danny Boy as one of their own, knowing no different, a situation that could change the way the next generation of wolves from this pack react to other coyotes. However this turns out, Solomon thinks eagerly, he will be the sole witness.

One afternoon while collecting scat in the forest for his study of the wolves' diet, Solomon finds Danny Boy's body lying in a dry streambed.

The coyote has been torn apart, very recently it appears, and all the signs indicate the killers are wolves. There are no other packs, or lone wolves, in the area, and so it must've been Danny

Boy's own pack that has done this to him. Perhaps the killing is an instinctual response to the recent arrival of the defenceless cubs, still mewling in the den and as yet unseen. Or the realization may have dawned on the wolves that *these* are their real young, not this clowning pretender. The worst thought for Solomon is that it's him—the human—whose presence destabilized the situation. How can he be sure this isn't somehow his doing?

In his imagination Solomon sees Danny Boy again the way he first pictured him, hopping, tumbling, frolicking desperately, while the deadly ring closes in on him. He's shocked to find himself on his knees, weeping for this animal.

It's an unusually warm spring day. Swollen sacks of cloud have piled on the horizon and the air is growing muggy, weighted with the impending threat of rain. Solomon knows he should get back to his camp before the sky lets loose, but he stays with the body for some time to take detailed notes. For posterity, or whoever might be interested one day.

The ants have already discovered the bounty in their midst, and soon the flies and crows will too. All of them will come to the body and take away some of its coyoteness, which will become antness and flyness and crowness.

And where will that leave him, the human? He'll be taking away something with him too, even if he can't quite give it a name.

Danny Boy, Solomon writes at the top of the page, along with the date. Then he scratches the name out.

Back home in Montreal, while he continues his research on the ore, Solomon starts to turn his notes about the coyote into an essay. The essay grows into a book, a meditation on animal life and the deep connection to it that human beings once had and have lost. He also uses the book to report his findings on ghost ore, and its possible harmful effects on living tissue and the natural world.

Solomon's book expresses a deep astonishment, even a kind of spiritual dread, at the strange fact that there should be not just one living thing in the world but many. He understands the genetic basis of heredity, but still allows himself to speculate that the evolution of new species proceeds through a kind of dreaming. Life, a singular, unitary entity, desires new expressions of itself and brings them into being, much as we dream ever-shifting, alternate lives for ourselves when we sleep. Human beings are the animals that have come closest to dreaming lucidly, that is, understanding that we are Life dreaming itself into new forms. When a species disappears, when an animal goes silent forever, it may not matter to us, but the truth is we have lost some part of ourselves.

Listen to the birds outside your window, Solomon writes. *Their calling and singing. What is it but a language? Simply one we don't understand. But their language and ours must descend from a common ancestor, just as birds and humans themselves did before our evolutionary journeys branched off from one another and took different paths. It may even be a language that the universe spoke before Life itself even began. We have begun to trace the story of our species' descent, from the "ape-men" all the way back down the tree of evolution to the earliest living creatures. I believe that humanity will also one day seek out, and learn to speak, that primeval language.*

If that day comes, we will recover the oldest wisdom, and all living things will speak to each other, in a chorus of voices, and know themselves to be One.

The book is eventually published by a small press in New York specializing in esoteric knowledge. Almost no one reads it, but word gets out to Solomon's colleagues in the department. There's an uproar, and an official censure. He's asked by the dean to take a sabbatical. His wild speculations have discredited the university and the profession. Instead, he resigns. The few friends he has left advise him to get help. They gently suggest he may have spent too much time in the bush.

Many years later, after Ira Solomon is long dead, Amery Hewitt finds a copy of his book in a second-hand shop in Pine Ridge, in a pile of old library cast-offs. She takes it home and reads it with a pen in hand, underlining passages and making marginal notes.

MICHIO

The spring after his first year of college he answered an ad in the local paper for a trail walker. He wasn't sure what that meant but it intrigued him, so he called the number. The person he spoke to, a man with a Newfoundland accent, asked him a few questions—how old he was, where he lived, what kind of physical shape he was in—then gave him a rural address and a time to meet next Saturday morning. The man also told him to bring some decent hiking boots.

The place was several kilometres out of town in an area that was mostly trackless bush, in between the town and the ore extraction sites. The long dirt driveway looked like it had been hacked out of the forest yesterday. Michio pulled his dad's old van into a circular gravel parking area in front of a huge unfinished log cabin, once he got a good look at it, more a mansion than a cabin, with stone frontage, a wide wraparound veranda, and a towering front window like something you'd see on a cathedral.

He was a few minutes late, taking a wrong turn at one point and having to backtrack. There were already three other young guys about his age waiting around outside their own vehicles.

A grader, a backhoe, and a big skid-steer brush cutter were parked nearby. A construction trailer sat in the yard.

Michio introduced himself awkwardly to the others, none of whom he knew: Tyler and Sean, who were friends, and Marvin, a lanky guy in a trucker hat.

A balding middle-aged man with an impressive beer gut came out of the trailer. This was Ray, the man Michio had spoken to on the phone. He was not the owner, it turned out, but the contractor for the building project. The owner was some bigshot Northfire executive who had bought this huge parcel of land with a creek running through it and a lake in the middle and was building himself a palatial summer hideaway, using mostly local materials, rock and repurposed wood. He wanted everything to be aged-looking and rustic and *real* (while at the same time featuring state-of-the-art luxury amenities like a gym and a hot tub). He'd had Ray's crew cut a rough set of trails out of the bush with their heavy equipment and now he wanted some fit, energetic young people to walk them.

"I told him my guys could groom the trails for him," Ray said to Michio and the others. "But he didn't want it done that way. He wants the trails *walked* into shape by people feeling every foot of the ground they walk on. So that's the plan. That's what you'll be doing. He wants it so that when he comes out here it'll be like the trails have always been there. Like they're authentic Indian trails or something, I guess."

"Why doesn't he get authentic Indians to walk them then?" Tyler asked, smirking at his buddy Sean like he'd said something really clever.

"He got *one*," Marvin said.

Tyler grinned and said, "Shit, sorry, man."

"So that's what you'll be doing," Ray said, ignoring the awkward moment. "He wants you out here every day except

Sundays, just walking. No partying, no girls, no booze, no drugs. Just walking."

"Why not Sundays?" Sean asked.

"Day of rest. I guess it matters to him."

"So," Michio said, "do you need references or . . . ?"

Ray shrugged. "You showed up. You got the job. This isn't brain surgery."

He named a generous hourly wage, better than they'd get anywhere else as unskilled labour over the summer. The four of them looked at each other like they'd hit the jackpot. Ray handed around a waiver for them to sign. If they injured themselves on the job they couldn't sue the owner. Michio hesitated over this, having yet to see what condition the trails were in, but when the other guys signed, he did too.

The owner had given Ray a long list of rules for them to read and sign as well, then he handed each of them a copy, along with a map, in a red plastic folder.

The rules stipulated they had to walk for a minimum of seven hours every day. They could set their own hours, but it was best if they didn't do any walking after dark. They could go at any pace they chose but were expected to complete at least one full circuit of all the trails each day. Walking in groups was fine, as was walking alone. They were not allowed to bring anyone out here who had not been hired as a trail walker. No pets either. No bicycles or motorized vehicles. The list specified what items they could carry with them—walking stick, knife, snacks, juice and soft drinks, reading material for their breaks—but whatever they brought in had to leave with them, including all food wrappers and other garbage. They were not permitted to carry firearms, under any circumstances. Urinating and defecating were not allowed on the trails—there was a portable toilet in the yard they could use. They were expected to log the daily distance they covered—a pedometer would be supplied to them along with bottled water, mosquito repellent, protein bars, and first aid items, all of which were stored in the construction trailer for them to access as needed. If they came across any large obstructions such as fallen logs, they were to inform Ray, who would get his crew to deal with them. They were not to move, remove, or damage any tree or plant material in any way. They were not allowed to walk anywhere on the property that was not a designated trail. The house and its environs, including the rock garden, stable, and riding arena, were strictly off-limits. Any walker found in these areas would have their employment terminated immediately.

There was one last rule: *If during your walks you see anything that you think the owner should be made aware of, report it to Ray.*

"Any questions?" Ray asked when they'd all browsed through the dos and don'ts.

"Yeah, I got one," said Tyler. "What does *anything you think the owner should be aware of* mean?"

"He didn't provide details," Ray said. "I think he meant like if you see any big animals, or someone on the property who shouldn't be here. Trespassers, that kind of thing."

"So big animals . . . like bears?"

"Well, they're out here, for sure. Black bears. My guys and I have seen them. The owner's interested in knowing what's available to hunt, for sure. And there are cougars too, most likely, though we haven't seen any of those. With all the noise my guys will be making you shouldn't have to worry. You'll be getting a can of bear spray to carry with you just in case, though, and a whistle."

Ray gave each of them these items, along with a large bottle of water and a small day pack to carry everything in. With that it was time to begin. The trailhead was some thirty metres or so from the house and plunged immediately into the trees. Before they set out, they all shook hands with one another, which Michio found odd. It wasn't as if they were heading out on some dangerous mission. He then wondered why no young women had been hired. Maybe none had answered the ad. Maybe the thought of being out here alone was enough to scare them off. Or more likely the thought of *not* being alone out here.

Tyler and Sean headed off down the trail first, together, at a good clip, like this was a test of their fitness. Marvin went next, by himself. Michio had considered asking Marvin if he'd like to walk together but held back, worried about how the invitation might come across, and then it was too late.

The trail was a little wider than his outstretched arms and very rough, more so than he'd expected. Roots and jagged sapling ends stuck up from the ground in lots of places, and there were plenty of broken branches, twigs, and other tree litter that must have been left after Ray and his crew chewed through here with their big mower. There was a wounded, desolate feel in the air, like a violence had been done. Michio was reminded of footage he'd seen on TV about the clear-cutting of the Amazon rainforest.

As he walked, he consulted the map. A main trail wound a serpentine course through the property, with shorter loops branching off from it. The trails had been numbered but not named, which Michio thought strange. If you were going to put this much effort into making "authentic" trails through the woods, you think you'd want to give them names that sounded old, like people had been walking them for ages. Maybe the naming would come later, he thought, when the owner had had a chance to walk here himself. But Michio liked the numbers. They lent a logical, unambiguous feel to the task at hand. The map showed that one of the trails circled the small lake, and bridges spanned the narrow creek where the trails crossed it in several places. It reminded him of one of those geometry puzzles he used to love as a kid. *Can you walk across each of these bridges only once...*

The first half-hour or so Michio spent completely on his own. But because each of the walkers could choose how they wanted to complete the loops, he started meeting the others every once in a while. They would say hello and keep on going. Nobody seemed to want to stop and chat. It was as if everyone was treating this as a competition, even though they were all getting paid the same amount for the same work.

It was a morning in late May with a chill in the air. The sun would vanish behind a cloud and then suddenly come out again, like someone had flipped a switch. It didn't get too hot, which was good, because it took some effort to walk without stumbling over this tricky, lumpy ground. Before long he'd worked up a sweat. The mosquitoes weren't bad yet, but if they got some decent rain that plague was sure to come.

The small lake, not much more than a pond, was fringed with the green shoots of new cattails, and there were a few ducks floating around on it, near the reeds on the far side. As Michio walked along the shore a red-winged blackbird swooped low over his head, loudly scolding him.

He crossed all of the split-log bridges over the creek, checking each one off on the map. Near one of the crossings there was an ugly hole blown out of the bank on both sides. Michio learned later this was where Ray's crew had dynamited a beaver dam and trapped out the beaver. They would be cleaning up the mess later in the year.

Michio completed the entire trail system with all of its loops in an hour and three-quarters. The pedometer told him he had walked a little less than eight kilometres. He was surprised and even a little disappointed. Looking at the map he had thought it would take longer.

He took a half-hour break to eat the bento lunch his father had prepared for him, then he got going again.

Michio was an only child and had never had any problem being on his own. It was peaceful out here in the woods and he was free to think his thoughts, dream his daydreams, imagine the future, just as he always had been with just him and his dad at home. When he was younger his dad would pose him a logic puzzle or brain teaser and he could spend all day by himself, rolling the puzzle around in his head, looking at it from all angles, before coming up with the solution or finally giving up and going to his dad for the answer. *I left my campsite and walked three miles east, south, and north, and when I got back to my camp a bear was sleeping in my tent. What colour was the bear?*

At the end of that first day's trail walk he was confident he'd made a good choice when he answered the ad. There was only one thing that made it less than ideal.

That evening Michio called Ethan to tell him about his new job. Like Michio, Ethan had moved back home at the end of the school term to work so he could save up for next year. The problem was his parents lived on a cattle ranch a nine-hour drive away near Longview, in the foothills. Michio would hardly get to see Ethan all summer. Maybe on one or two Sundays, but they had to be careful. Ethan's parents didn't know he had a boyfriend and if they found out it would mean trouble. They were severely Christian, and from what Ethan had told Michio, intolerant of pretty much everything outside their carefully curated little bubble of what was right and good.

Ethan had fed them a story that Michio was his partner for a summer project their computing science instructor had assigned them, which was why he and Michio had to text and talk on the phone so much. So far his parents seemed to have bought it. According to Ethan, they were glad to learn that Michio was Japanese—Ethan's mom had said that was great because Asians were good with numbers, but she hoped Michio's English was okay. Michio and Ethan had laughed about that, but it bothered Michio afterward. He wondered if it would make any difference to Ethan's mom that he was born here and his dad went to a Baptist church. But if she ever discovered how he and her son really felt about each other, that would cancel out everything else.

"I wish you could walk out here with me," Michio told Ethan. "They said we can't bring anyone else."

"Nobody would even see me," Ethan said. "I can make myself invisible when I need to. It's one of the survival skills you learn in a cowboy town."

"I'm only walking during the day. I've got the nights free. You could come out next weekend."

"I can't," Ethan said. "Dad needs my help tagging the new calves."

"Maybe the weekend after that, then."

"We'll see."

The next few days of walking were uneventful, and Michio began to see that the biggest occupational hazards would be boredom and blisters. Marvin shared some strips of moleskin with him and that helped with his feet. He was getting to know the trails so well that he'd begun to recognize individual trees and had even given some of the more noteworthy ones names.

Old Moss. The Great Birch. Pinetop Perkins. In town he bought a used field guide to local birds, by a guy with the somewhat fitting last name of Acorn, and a blank journal with a picture of a moose on the cover in which he started keeping a record of the wildlife he encountered, including time and location of sighting. In addition to the ducks and blackbirds he identified swifts, woodpeckers, grouse, warblers, blue jays, hawks, and once even a huge horned owl he was surprised to see in daylight. There were squirrels everywhere, and he caught sight once of a mouse scurrying through the underbrush alongside the path. He didn't see any deer, although he did come across a pile of their droppings one afternoon, looking like those caffeinated chocolate beans you could buy at the college coffee shop to keep you awake while you were studying for exams. He reported this to Ray, whose response was a shrug.

He never saw a bear, but that was okay. *The bear was white! My campsite was at the North Pole!*

One afternoon he was walking along on autopilot, wrapped up in thoughts of Ethan, when he stopped in his tracks. His pulse, he noticed in surprise, had started galloping and his breath was coming in shallow gasps. What was he doing out here? What was this place? Maybe everything—buildings, roads, civilization, Ethan—had vanished and he was now truly and utterly alone in the world.

It only lasted a moment but afterward he tried walking with the others more often. Marvin was a nice enough guy, but he was pretty quiet and clearly wasn't here to make friends. They walked together a few times and Michio learned that Marvin was from the Fire Narrows First Nation. He had just started college too, working toward a law degree so that someday he could help his people with their land claims. Michio also walked with Tyler and Sean a few times. They yakked a lot about cars and trucks and their muddy adventures tearing up the backcountry on their quads, none of which Michio had any interest in. After a couple of circuits with those two, he decided he preferred walking alone. After a while he noticed Tyler and Sean walking apart from each other more often than not, and he wondered if they had finally gotten tired of each other's bullshit too.

After four weeks it was clear their daily presence was having an effect. The trails looked more tamped down, trodden upon, in use. More like actual paths you'd want to take a leisurely nature stroll on than ragged swaths of cleared bush.

Eventually, to Michio's surprise, his daily circuits began to feel like an essential part of his life. He realized he would miss the walking when the summer was over. He had admitted this to Ethan the last time they'd talked. That conversation hadn't gone well. Ethan seemed distant and there were awkward silences. He finally agreed to come see Michio the following weekend, then had said a hurried goodbye. Michio hadn't found the right moment to ask what was bothering him. Or maybe he hadn't wanted to know. It was selfish of him, he knew, but he didn't want anything spoiling their plans. Ethan was sure to get over whatever it was by the time they saw each other again.

The next morning there was a young couple waiting in the parking area, Lorna and Ted. Ray explained that the owner had come out to inspect the trails the previous Sunday and had decided that more boots on the ground were needed to get them into shape by the time the house was scheduled to be finished, in early fall.

"Will we ever meet him?" Tyler asked after everyone had been introduced to Lorna and Ted.

"Meet who?" Ray asked.

"Our boss. The guy who owns this place."

"Buddy, *I'm* your boss. Let's keep that straight. As for the owner, I've only met him twice myself, so I'd say your chances are pretty slim."

The addition of two more trail walkers changed the dynamic more dramatically than Michio would have guessed. Now it seemed he was always running into someone. Lorna and Ted were chatty and often stopped to talk with him when they met on the trails. Lorna had a thick paperback copy of *The Lord of the Rings* with her that she would read when she and Ted took breaks.

"Is that a good book?" Michio asked her when he joined them one afternoon. He had never read it or even seen the movies. He had no use for made-up stories about things that could never happen.

"It's the *best* book," Lorna said, her eyes lighting up. "Especially out here. You know, you kind of remind me of one of the characters. Legolas."

"Is he Asian?" Michio asked, then felt bad for putting her on the spot. That comment by Ethan's mother was still on his mind. Lorna stared at him, blinking. He grinned, to show her it was only a joke.

"He's an elf," she said, still flustered. "He's just . . . he's good at walking."

The presence of an attractive young woman also had an effect on Tyler and Sean. They went unusually quiet whenever Lorna was around and Michio saw them eyeing her appreciatively when Ted wasn't looking. But sometimes Ted was looking, and he soon took an obvious dislike to the both of them.

Marvin got into the habit of singing old country songs as he walked. You could hear him coming from a long way off, belting out Johnny Cash and Marty Robbins. Soon Michio's refuge of peace and solitude was becoming like every other place did when enough people were around: all the human stuff—the talk, the tensions, the cross-purposes, the fields of attraction and repulsion—started to drown out everything else.

Then one hot, drowsy afternoon he got lost.

It seemed impossible. He knew these trails now as well as he knew the streets of his neighbourhood, his childhood home, his own room. At night he'd started dreaming he was walking the trails. He knew every bend, and what was around every bend. He knew every rise and every hollow. He knew when to take an extra-long stride to avoid a stone jutting out of the path, and when to lower his head to avoid the overhanging limb of the bent old fir that Lorna had named the Entwife after Michio had pointed out its strange shape to her. He knew where the mud puddles would be when it rained and where to step to avoid them. He knew where he would pass through the biggest swarms of mosquitoes, and where the best shade was on hot days. He could have walked the trails with a blindfold on, he sometimes thought, though he never tried it.

He had just finished his lunch, sitting on a pine stump at the top of a sunny rise before the trail plunged back down into a stand of black spruce. But the stand of spruce didn't end where it was supposed to end. He was supposed to come out after two and a half minutes into a sunlit glade filled with tall grass, flowers, and the hum of bees, where one of the log bridges crossed the burbling creek. But the stand of dark spruce went on and on, snaking through the woods, up and down, an entirely new and different path that held no landmarks he recognized.

He stopped, heart pounding, and checked his watch. He thought about turning around and going back to the rise. The only thing he could think was that Ray and his guys had come out here recently and blazed another trail without telling any of the walkers. But this didn't look like the trails did right after they'd been hacked out by the mower's huge circular blades. This trail had been *walked*. It felt and looked and even smelled just like the other trails he knew and had helped create with his own two feet.

Were the other walkers breaking the rules? Making new trails without telling anyone? Not possible, he reasoned. They couldn't have accomplished this much without him noticing.

He went still and listened. He would have given anything to hear Marvin's off-key rendition of "El Paso" right about now.

Birdsong. Insect buzz. Leaves stirring faintly in the breeze. Some days when it was really still he would catch the faint roar of big trucks on the highway to the extraction sites. There wasn't a trace of that now.

Michio turned and walked back a little way, then swore at himself, turned around and kept on the way he'd been going, under the gloomy shade of the spruce. There were crows here. He had seen crows before on his walks, but never paid them much attention because they were so ubiquitous in town. Now it seemed to him that there were more crows than usual in the trees, and that they were calling to one another as he passed, as if alerting each other to his presence. Maybe they were even following him. Every time he stopped and looked up into the dark, needled branches, the crows would go quiet. They didn't seem to be watching him, but it was really hard to say for sure with birds. They took a lot of interest in some things and ignored others, but not always the same things as humans did.

After a few more stomach-churning minutes he finally heard the creek and came out of the trees at the bridge. The rest of the twenty-minute walk back to the parking area was exactly the way it had always been.

He considered saying something to Ray, but what would he say? When he thought about it, he realized he hadn't been lost. Not exactly. He had still been on a trail. It just wasn't any of the trails he knew.

The next two days, Friday and Saturday, were like any other. The trails stayed as he knew them. He decided he must have been affected by the heat the day he got lost. He probably hadn't drunk enough water, and his sense of time or distance had gotten foggy. That had happened to him once before, when he had taken a drag on a joint at a party for the first and last time. He checked his pedometer late Friday afternoon and saw that he hadn't racked up any more mileage than usual. Which meant he must have imagined the whole thing.

That Sunday was a day Michio had been looking forward to all summer. His father was taking his boat to Thunder Lake for three days of fishing, and Ethan was finally driving up to River Meadows. The two of them would have the rest of the day and all night together with no one else around.

Early Sunday morning Michio texted Ethan to wish him a good trip. Ethan didn't immediately text back, which was unusual for him. Michio ate his breakfast with his phone right beside him. It didn't buzz the whole time. He figured that Ethan had probably already left. Still, he called again a little later but there was no answer. Just before noon, when he was starting to get really worried, his phone finally buzzed.

I can't work with you on this project anymore. Don't contact me again.

On Monday morning Michio called Ray and told him he wouldn't be coming in because of a personal matter he needed to deal with.

He'd hardly been able to sleep since Ethan's text. He considered just quitting, but after the second night of staring at his bedroom ceiling he'd realized that the walking was the only thing he had left. He typed out reply after reply but didn't send any of them. He wouldn't risk getting Ethan in trouble with his parents by saying what he really felt, what he needed to say, but he couldn't keep up the lie that this was only about a school project.

On Tuesday he showed up at the trailhead early and waited until Lorna and Ted arrived, then joined them when they set off. If that thing with the trails happened while he was with them, he would know for sure it wasn't just him. He stuck with the couple so doggedly that it wasn't long before they started glancing at each other as if to ask *what is with this guy today?*

Eventually he slackened his pace and let them pull ahead. They were quickly out of sight. He walked on alone, trying not to think about Ethan but failing utterly. The words in that unbelievable text came into his head again and again, no matter how he tried to shut them out. *Don't contact me again.*

Ethan's parents must have been standing over him, making sure he typed what they told him to. Making sure he was the son they wanted him to be and not who he really was. Those intolerant fucking assholes. Was finding out they had a gay son the unforgivable thing, or was it the *Japanese* boyfriend? But Ethan could have stood up to them if he had really wanted to. If they really meant to one another what Michio was sure they did. But he hadn't. He'd gone along with it. How could Ethan have let them win? How could he sit there and type those words? *Don't contact me again.* Michio took the statement apart, turned it over and over, looked at it from different angles like one of his dad's old logic puzzles, only this one had no solution.

It had to be a mistake, or some kind of joke. But Ethan didn't joke around like that. And how could it be a mistake?

No, he convinced himself, Ethan had done it for a reason. A good reason. Michio finally decided the message was actually meant to warn him off, because Ethan's parents must have either found out or suspected the truth, and now they had their son under constant surveillance so that he had no chance to get a message to Michio. That had to be it. He would hear from Ethan again when it was safe. After his parents thought they'd won, and the heat was off. In a few days, or a week, maybe even a month, Ethan would find a way to get in touch. He'd tell Michio he was sorry, he'd had no choice, but nothing would ever stop them from being together. The best thing Michio could do in the meantime was wait. No texts. No trying to get in touch. Just wait and trust.

By Friday there was still nothing from Ethan.

That day Ted had to drive to Edmonton to visit his mom, who was in and out of hospital with some kind of stomach problem, so Lorna came to work on her own. At first, she seemed happy enough to have Michio walk with her, but he was too anxious to make conversation and stuck so close to her that after three hours she started shooting him uneasy looks out of the corner of her eye. When they stopped for lunch, he ate quickly and then told Lorna he was going to try a faster pace to see if he could beat his best time to the next trail junction. When he waved and said *catch you later* she looked relieved.

Pretty soon Michio was so lost in thought he stopped noticing where he was. Time passed but he paid no attention to his watch or the sun's position in the sky. He broke out of his spiralling thoughts at last to see he had come once again to the stand of black spruce. It was the middle of the afternoon.

He checked his phone. Reception was iffy out here, but he was sometimes able to pick up and send texts. The phone registered a weak signal, but there were no messages.

He took a photo of the trail ahead and sent it to his father with the message: *The deep dark forest.* A few minutes later his father texted back: *Watch out for talking wolves.*

His father knew who he really was and had never spoken a disapproving word. He might not be able to come right out and say he loved and accepted his son, but Michio had never doubted it.

Out of nowhere he was crying. He sank to his knees, choking and gasping. There was never going to be another message from Ethan. He knew that with the same certainty as the solutions to the equations in his math classes.

Don't contact me again $= 0$. No hidden variables.

He got up, wiped his eyes, and got moving again, afraid one of the others might come along and see him like this.

He walked through the stand of spruce and crossed the creek and it was fine. What remained was the last stretch of twenty minutes on mostly flat and easy ground, and he'd be back at the parking area again. He would call it a day then. Take off early, go home, and help his father in the garden.

When he came around the next bend he saw Sean's red Honda Civic at the end of a tunnel of trees, seventeen minutes before it should have appeared. He checked his watch.

It was half past five.

When he'd left Lorna, only a few minutes ago, it had been a little after three.

By the time he reached the parking area his legs were trembling and he was having trouble getting enough air into his lungs. Tyler and Sean were just climbing into their car. Sean cheerily flipped him the bird, then they peeled off, tires spitting dirt and gravel. Lorna's little white Hyundai was already gone. Even Ray and his crew had left for the day.

He opened the driver's door of his father's van, got in, and sat for a while. He put the key in the ignition but he didn't turn it. Finally, he removed the key, climbed back out of the truck, and stood in the yard. The wind rose and fell in the flickering leaves of the poplars, making that boundless oceanic sound he'd always loved. Today it sounded like the trees were passing messages to one another, making their own secret plans.

Let them. He was going to make sense of this. Solve this.

No matter how long it took.

Taking out his notebook he wrote a message for Ray, tore the page out and placed it under a rock on the log mansion's stone steps. Then he went over to the construction trailer, punched in the key code, and stocked his day pack with three extra water bottles, half a dozen protein bars, and a first aid kit, which he checked to make sure had an emergency blanket, in case he was caught out in the middle of nowhere at night without any shelter.

He walked over to the trailhead and stood there a while, blinking up at the sky, thinking it might be a good idea to soak up a little more of that cloudless blue before he plunged in under the trees. There was no telling how long this was going to take, but he would keep going until he'd sorted it all out. Until he'd made these trails his own. It was the height of the northern summer and he figured there were still a good five hours or maybe more until it started getting dark.

ALEX

"This is good right here," Michio says to the driver, a lanky man in a trucker's hat and jean jacket, whose name Alex hasn't been told. Since the man picked them up at Alex's hotel before dawn in his nondescript late-model car, he hasn't said a word, only hummed old country and western tunes under his breath. Michio hasn't said a word either. Alex assumes the silence is deliberate—the less he knows about the people involved in this the better for everyone.

The man slows the car and pulls over to the side of the dirt track.

"Tomorrow, ten o'clock, the train crossing," Michio says.

"Train crossing at ten," the man says. "Don't be late."

"We won't be."

"That's what you always say."

Alex and Michio climb out of the car and take their packs from the trunk. When they're ready Michio pats the hood twice and the man drives away.

It's not yet daylight. The world is pale and cold, but there's birdsong in the stand of poplars alongside the track. Alex can hear the distant rumble and snort of a semi picking up speed on the highway bypass.

"This is where we go in," Michio says.

"What about the fence?"

"There's a way through. Amery found it."

The clouds are now reddish on their undersides and there's a damp chill in the air. An early fall morning like those Alex remembers from his years here. Getting out of bed in the near dark, getting ready for school still half in the possession of sleep. He feels a kind of dizziness come over him as he remembers the decoherences back then and what they used to do to him. He can't tell for sure whether what he's feeling is coming from outside of him or from a memory lodged deep in his nerves, stirring to life again.

Before they set off, Michio has Alex empty his pack, and examines the contents with his pocket flashlight. He hefts the handgun Alex brought with him from home, safely locked in a metal case in his checked baggage. For the first time Alex sees an emotion disrupt Michio's mask of cool detachment—anger.

"This won't help."

"It can't hurt."

"Guns are a mistake out here. They make you think you're safer than you are. Is it loaded?"

"No."

"You're sure?"

"Yes."

"Keep it that way."

Michio holds up the bottle of Ativan.

"Also a bad idea. Have you taken one?"

"Not today."

"Don't. We have to be on alert the whole time we're in there. If I tell you to move, you need to be able to respond without hesitating."

When Michio is finished his inspection, they set off, wading through a field of tall, wet grass, toward a wall of spruce and fir that stands black against the dim sky. It's very quiet here, without even the birdsong he heard at the edge of the road. Alex's neck feels itchy, and he wonders if this is an effect of the Park or whether he's conjuring up symptoms out of fear.

"You teach science classes at the college, I guess," Alex says, to distract himself. "I saw that video on YouTube."

Michio grimaces.

"I've seen it too. That was from my seminar on complexity theory and climate change. I may have gotten a little bit off track. The way I see it, if we're going to save ourselves from our own stupidity, we have to completely transform the way we look at what's around us, starting with what our best theories tell us is actually real. It won't be easy. Maybe impossible."

"Were you born in River Meadows?"

"No, we came here when I was a teenager, for my dad's work. He was an agricultural chemist for the government, monitoring and improving livestock feed, that kind of thing. He moved back south to Picture Butte a few years ago, after he retired. He missed the big skies down there, the wide-open prairie. That's where I was born, and where my mom died, when I was seven."

"That must have been tough. My dad died here, in an accident at one of the extraction sites. I was fifteen."

"Amery told me."

"I thought for a long time that's why she came back here after we moved away. And maybe it was, at first. I don't know."

After a few minutes Alex can see the wire of the fence shining faintly in the dim light. When they reach it, Michio crouches and creeps along the fence line, then stops.

"This is the place," he says.

Alex can't see any break or gap. Michio walks forward, and an instant later he's on the other side, looking at Alex through the wire mesh.

"Just walk straight toward me," he says.

Alex does. The mesh goes hazy for a moment, as if he's too close for his eyes to focus on it. Then he's through.

"How could you tell that was the spot?" he asks.

"You learn, if you come here often enough. And survive."

The ground beneath them is soft and mossy. Alex can smell the early damp rising from the earth. It brings to mind camping trips when he was a kid, waking up outdoors and away from home, the freedom and at the same time the uneasiness. He wasn't sure what he was expecting on this side of the fence. Something more obvious, perhaps—a scent or a feeling that screamed *stay away*.

Michio reaches out a hand and flicks something off Alex's neck.

"Biter," he says.

"Thanks. I did bring bug repellent. Are they bad here?"

"Not inside the fence."

"Well, that's one good thing."

"Is it?"

Alex isn't sure what that means. He realizes he's not eager to move forward.

"Stay a couple of paces behind me," Michio says. "Don't lag behind. If I raise my hand, stop and wait for me to say it's okay to move again. If you see me drop my hand, that means crouch down. We can talk, for now, but keep your voice down."

Alex takes his phone from his jacket pocket. He'd called his mother first thing in the morning, to tell her he was getting help looking for Amery and that he had some promising leads to try. He said nothing about going into the Park himself. He debates sending her an update now, to reassure her that something is being done.

"You won't get much from that here," Michio says.

Alex puts the phone away.

"In this place you don't check your devices," Michio says. "You check your senses. All of them, over and over. Sight. Sound. Smell. Balance. How things feel, on your skin and in your gut. Keep checking in with all of that. Cycle through it every few minutes. Sight, sound, smell . . . It's easy to get distracted and not notice that something has changed. There might only be a tiny shift, but it could mean your life."

Alex nods, too dismayed to speak. For an instant he wants to bolt for the fence. Could he even get back through on his own?

Michio is already moving on.

He has to follow. He has to see this through.

"Have you ever watched a grouse step through the underbrush?" Michio asks in a gentler tone.

"No."

"Or the way a moose or a lynx will stop and watch and wait until it feels safe to move again. That's how we need to move in here. Like the animals. Like every step we take means life or death."

They wade through a patch of chest-high thistles and move slowly into the trees. On their right the ground falls away into a long, low trench, natural or artificial he can't tell, filled with shocks of thick grass and stunted willows. A tangle of green where something could easily be hiding, waiting to spring out at them. He forces his thoughts back to what he was told to concentrate on: focusing a few seconds at a time on what's coming to him through his eyes, ears, nostrils, skin . . . There's no difference between the world on the other side of the fence and here, as far as anything his senses are telling him. It's the same damp, resinous darkness. In his head he keeps seeing Amery as the little girl she was, before River Meadows. Full of beans. Happy, laughing. He imagines she's going to jump out from behind a tree at any moment and shout *Ha! Gotcha!*

But it's no good. He can't shake this dread roiling through him. And now it's found its point of attack.

He stops. Michio turns.

"What is it?"

"I have to . . . I went this morning, at the hotel, before we left, but . . ."

Michio nods, looks around. He gestures to the ditch beside them.

"Down there," he says. "We're still close to the perimeter. It should be safe."

"Yeah?"

"Or I could just turn my back."

"No, down there is good."

When he's finished, he clambers back up the side of the ditch, hot with shame over his body's humiliating betrayal. His unfamiliar new boots slip on the wet grass and Michio helps him up.

"Are you going to be okay?" Michio asks.

"Yeah. Yeah, I think so."

"You sure you want to keep going?"

"Yes."

They start walking again in silence. Alex has noticed that since they got inside the fence, Michio seems less tightly wound, despite his sombre warnings to remain vigilant. His gait is easier, his tone less clipped. He's lost his nervous habit of adjusting his glasses and abandoned his crisp, fashionable clothes—a disguise, Alex now understands—for a dark green sweatshirt and a pair of jeans. As if the Michio who lives *out there* has been shed along with the pressed shirt and chinos, and this is where he can truly be himself.

"Does anyone else come here?" Alex asks. "Or is it just you and Amery?"

"There've been others. Scavengers, mostly. Looters. A few thrill-seekers too, looking to challenge themselves. They stopped coming after a few years."

"Because of the dangers?"

"For some, yeah. I think for most of them, it just became obvious that whatever they were hoping to find here, they wouldn't get. Or other things became more important."

The way he hesitates gives Alex another illumination.

"You gave it up, didn't you?"

Michio looks over his shoulder at him. He seems surprised Alex has figured this out.

"My weather research was starting to get somewhere, and I needed to focus on it. I told Amery almost a year ago that I was done and stopped coming with her. I felt guilty about it, like I was abandoning her, and scared for her too. So I came with her one last time, not long before she went missing. I tried convincing her to walk away while she still could. We both knew the Park had changed—it had become less predictable, more dangerous—but she wouldn't listen."

"More dangerous how?"

"More anomalies, but also because of the Church. They started harassing us a couple of years ago."

"The Church of the Conjuration."

"You know about them."

"Only what I could find online. There's a lot of wild speculation about this place, but I'm sure you know that. I found a site dedicated to proving the ore was planted in the ground eons ago by aliens, who knew we'd dig it up one day and use it to destroy ourselves. That was their plan, get rid of the competition before they become a real threat. But this Church . . . they're even crazier. They believe God is building some kind of sanctuary here for the chosen few, right?"

"Something like that. They're convinced that after the world ends this will be the site of God's new earthly paradise, just for them, the true believers. They've decided it's theirs alone and they don't want anyone else messing with the Almighty's grand plan for them. At first they were friendly, or pretended to be. They approached us, asked for our help to guide them in and out. When we said no, they were not happy. Some of them come in here on their own now, with guns. They shoot any animals they find. Their way of intimidating us, I guess. Scaring us off. It hasn't worked on Amery."

Alex considers this. "Do you think it's possible . . ."

He can't say it.

"I don't think so," Michio says after a silence. "They haven't gone that far. They only shoot the creatures they think their god has put here for their use. Or entertainment."

He raises a hand and stops. Alex stops too. Michio looks slowly around. Then he turns to Alex, his eyes alive with emotion in a way Alex hasn't seen before.

"I don't understand how they think. What they do. They believe in a creator who made everything out of love. Then they come here and kill anything that moves."

Alex gives a dry laugh. "How well do you know your religious history?"

They walk on. The light grows, the clouds brighten and lose

their blush, and Alex can see farther ahead. They come out onto what was a road, lined with leaning and fallen power poles, the asphalt like old bone, cracked, spongy, and rotting in places, patchily carpeted with tufts of grass and leafy stalks, even a few small trees. The sun is rising above the black palisades of the evergreens. It looks like it's going to be a lovely fall day. He reminds himself to cycle through his sensations again. What's changing around him. The light. The heat. Sounds of birds and wind in the leaves.

Then it strikes him: how peaceful it is here.

He shrugs off his jacket, breathes deeply, feels his footsteps on the earth. He remembers Sikandar's virtual world, the unforeseen ache of homecoming he felt there, and thinks he might understand Amery a little better.

"I've heard about the ghosts," Alex says. "Will we see any of them?"

"They aren't ghosts," Michio says. "There are no ghosts here, other than the ore. Some call them the Visitors, but Amery never liked that name. She says they're not the visitors—we are. Anyhow, they might look like people or animals, but they don't have actual physical bodies, not like us anyhow. They behave more like some form of energy we don't yet understand."

"Some would say that's what ghosts are."

"Well, I don't know about that. It's true the Visitors sometimes resemble people who've died. But Amery and I have seen more than one who looked like someone who lived here before the town was evacuated, but who's still alive."

"They're dangerous, right? That's what I've heard. That even if they're someone you know, they can be hostile."

"*Hostile* isn't the right word. Usually they just seem to be wandering aimlessly, and they flicker in and out of sight pretty quickly. But sometimes one of them will come right at you, like they've seen you and they want something from you. Maybe they do. Or maybe they're just curious and don't mean any harm. I have my own theory about what they are."

"Which is?"

"I think they're our creation. They're the feral clouds."

"You mean those escaped clouds that are supposedly intelligent."

"It's just a theory. Not even Amery is convinced I'm right. Anyhow, whatever they are, the ones that approach people are dangerous, even if they don't really intend to hurt anyone. You can't let them get near you, even if they look like someone you know. One touch can stop your heart."

Alex walks on, taking this in. He glances around apprehensively. He's studied his map, but he still hasn't got his bearings.

"Did Amery ever show you where our house used to be?" he asks.

"She did," Michio says. "She was terrible at staying organized, at keeping track of things, other than what she put in her journals, so I started an archive. Every scrap of information we gather, in case some day someone can find the patterns. I come from a long line of obsessive record keepers. Paper hoarders. I thought maybe one day we could make sense of all of this, if there's sense to be made. Anyhow, on our maps we give each site the name of who lived there when the place was abandoned. So yours is the Hewitt house. At a normal walking pace, in a direct line, it would take us maybe thirty minutes to get there from here. We'll head in that direction, but we won't be going at a normal walking pace, and we won't be going in a straight line."

"You've spent a lot of time in here."

"I started doing this before they closed it off. I had a job out here one summer, when the extraction industry was still thriving, helping break in some trails in the bush. Things were already getting strange then. I got lost on those trails once. I knew them like the back of my hand, but I still got lost."

"For how long?"

"Seven days."

"Jesus. Maybe that's what happened to Amery."

Michio shakes his head. "No. I know it isn't. She and I have walked those trails many times since. Whatever occurred there happened only to me, that one time. Never again. The thing is, this place, sometimes it seems to *react* to a person. The puzzles, the traps . . . it's like the Park is defending itself, like your body does when something foreign gets in. It sounds crazy, I suppose."

Alex remembers the evening at the Starlite Diner. "No," he says. "Not really."

Michio stops, raises a hand. Alex freezes.

Michio turns in a slow circle. When he seems satisfied nothing is wrong, he starts walking again.

"You come to learn," he says, "that even though things here stick to you, or follow you, or bend themselves around you, none of it is *about* you. That's what makes the Park so dangerous—not understanding that. We bring our stories with us, we can't help doing that. Who we are, what we desire, what we're afraid of. Then everything you see, everything that happens, becomes part of the story you've been telling yourself all your life about who you are and where you're going. It's easy to believe that what the Park is showing you is meant for you, that there's a message here just for you. That's what gets you into real trouble. Anyhow, it's not possible to get lost on those trails anymore. I checked them out the other day when I went looking for Amery, just to be sure. Didn't find anything out of the ordinary. I know that's not what happened to her."

"When you got lost, how did you get out?"

"I just did. Suddenly I was back in the parking lot I started from. It was like the trails were just . . . finished with me."

"And you kept coming back here."

"Not for a long time. I left town to go back to school. Then I worked for a while in Calgary, teaching at a college there. A few years ago, a position came up in Pine Ridge and I took it. My field is atmospheric science, and some strange things were happening around here with the weather. I wanted to be closer to that. When I wasn't working, I started sneaking into the Park. Mostly at night, which was unbelievably stupid. I still don't know what I was doing or thinking. Then I met your sister. She'd come back too."

"Yeah, but I don't understand why. I mean, I know why, but I still don't get it."

"All I can say is neither of us was done with this place. Or it wasn't done with us. For Amery there was something she needed to do here. Something nobody else was going to do. She asked me if I'd help her. I said yes."

Alex takes a sip of water and checks his watch. The churning dread has returned.

"We should stop talking," Michio says. "I need to concentrate on our route."

The house rises before them out of the grass like a surfacing whale. Much of the roof appears to be gone or collapsed inward.

Alex and Michio stand together in front of the black crevasse that was once the big bay window.

True to his word Michio brought them here by a series of winding paths, stopping often and silently observing before moving on again, without telling Alex what he might have seen or sensed. It's taken them over two hours. Michio often seemed to be hearing something that Alex wasn't picking up on, but so far they haven't encountered any of the things that make the Reclamation Area so dangerous. The sudden broils of superheated air that scald flesh. The invisible knots of pressure, some of them powerful enough to crack bones. The memory holes that scramble your brains for hours, or permanently. He doesn't know which of these things are only internet rumours and which are real, and he's begun to wonder if the dangers have been exaggerated, to keep people away for some other reason that's never been revealed. So far he and Michio haven't encountered anything you wouldn't expect to find in a place that had been abandoned like this. What if it's all a hoax, he wonders. Some crazy game of make-believe Michio and Amery like to play. What proof does he have, really, of anything Michio's been telling him?

For the last hour, a fine drizzle has been falling. Michio had planned ahead, unsurprisingly, bringing light rain ponchos for both of them.

As they approach Alex's old house, Michio says in an undertone, "Amery sometimes camped here, if she stayed late and couldn't get out before dark. I searched it the other day."

Alex tries to imagine her staying in this ruin of their past life. Out here alone, at night. This is his sister, so it isn't difficult. He remembers a conversation long after they'd moved away from River Meadows. He'd just put out his first board game, *Temporal Defenders*, and Amery had actually come to the launch at a gaming store in downtown Vancouver. Afterward they'd gone out together for Indian food—butter chicken, paneer tikka, rajma chawal, chur chur naan—a feast that Amery tucked into as if she hadn't eaten in days and that she let Alex pay for without protest. He'd gotten to talking about the house in

Foxhaven, about things they'd had to leave behind during the evacuation—bikes, toys, mementoes he'd assumed he would never see again. That's when Amery told him she was living in Pine Ridge now and making trips to River Meadows. She admitted she'd gone into the Reclamation Area several times already and that she would find his stuff for him if he liked. He concealed his shock and told her not to worry about it. Back then he wasn't even sure he believed her. You spend the first indelible years of your life with someone, then you go your separate ways and one day you meet again thinking they're who they always were and you discover you're talking to a stranger.

You used to be frightened of that house, he'd said to her at the restaurant, trying to invoke the sister he remembered. When we first moved in, you cried for Mom almost every night.

I was a scared little kid, yeah, she told him. Then I met Bone Girl.

Bone Girl?

You weren't the only one inventing superheroes, she said, and told him the story about what happened to her that night.

He stands beside Michio in front of his old house, swallowing back tears. Where has Bone Girl taken his fearless sister this time?

"Can we go in?" he asks in a whisper.

"We can but be ready to leave suddenly. And stay close."

They ascend the wet, crumbling concrete of the front steps to the porch. Alex suddenly feels awkward with this man he doesn't really know, like they're two strangers who've accidentally arrived at the same time to a house party.

The door is furred with bright green moss. He remembers hearing somewhere that green is the only wavelength of light that plants can't use to make energy, so it gets reflected back. It's the rejected light we see and think of as the colour of life. If trees absorbed the entire spectrum, they would appear black. But of course, if the world was like that, no one would think it strange.

"What would Amery usually do when she came here?" Alex asks.

"Wait," Michio says. "Listen."

He can't tell if Michio is answering his question or issuing a command. He decides to obey, in case it was an order, but very soon he's having trouble keeping still. He needs to be doing something. All of the circling around and stopping and waiting has charged him with nervous energy he can't use. He wants to be far away from this place and its unsettling quiet. He feels a hot, despairing surge of anger at something, someone, and then he realizes it's Amery. She gave up everything, any kind of life she might have had, to keep coming out here. She thought it was her responsibility. And now she's made herself *his* responsibility.

He reaches toward the lid of the rusted mailbox.

Michio grabs his wrist and whispers, "The last time I was here something was living in there."

Alex steps back, thinking of whatever might be nesting in the mailbox leaping out at him, all claws and fangs. He's ashamed of his own reaction. He doesn't want to show fear again in front of Michio, so he extends a defiant finger and presses the doorbell. To his shock he hears it chime faintly, somewhere deep in the house.

"You shouldn't have done that," Michio says. He sounds so like a disappointed child that Alex feels a delirious laugh bubbling up. He stifles it.

"There's still power out here?"

"Of a kind, yes."

"What does that mean?"

Michio doesn't answer. He shifts to one side, looking into the blackness of the bay window. Then he leans close to the door, which looks to Alex like it has been shut tight for centuries.

"Can we go in?" Alex whispers.

"It should be safe."

Led by Michio's bobbing flashlight beam, they move through the front room, with its rotting furniture. The kitchen. The back hall. Up the stairs to the second-floor bedrooms.

Amery's door is the only one open. Alex steps cautiously inside while Michio waits in the hallway. A pungent musk of decay hits him. The walls bulge and sag inward where drywall has swollen with water. The bed frame has been upended and the mattress is lying on the floor.

"This is where she sleeps when she stays here, I guess," he says to Michio.

"It would seem so. You can go farther in. I think it's okay."

Her desk still has books and other reminders of her old life on it, blurred with dust. A jar of sand from the beach back home on the coast. A shelf of pocket-sized stuffed animals. A photo of Amery when she was nine, dressed as Red Riding Hood for a school play. If she's been back here many times, to this room, then she just left all of this stuff where it sat, as if all of these mementoes of her past had no meaning for her anymore.

He crosses the room and picks up the photo, examines it closely. Then he slips it into his pack, for his mother.

Michio allows him time to look in his room.

His own desk seems to have receded much farther from the door than he remembers, as if the room has somehow expanded during the years of his absence. He spots the mix CD he made for a girl at school that he liked. Corrie Velasco. A gift he'd held off giving her, convinced there was no chance she felt the same way about him. Then without warning life here came to an end and it was too late.

He's long forgotten what songs he put on the CD, and all at once he's curious to remember his younger self and the path he thought he was on.

Taking slow, cautious steps he makes it halfway across the remains of the carpet, then freezes in his tracks. He'd already noticed that the space under his desk was filled with a tangle of shredded paper with a dark hollow at its centre, but he had been too caught up in his memories to consider what this meant. The shiver that crawls up his back tells him that this once familiar spot where he had sat and done homework, drawn comic books, and played computer games has become something's lair.

He'd been expecting a nostalgic flood of memory, but this is no longer his room. It's not even really a room at all.

The mind always hurries in first, then the body follows and faces facts.

After descending to check the basement, with its lake of dark, reeking water, Alex and Michio return to the porch. The drizzle has drawn off and the sky is clearing to a crisp iceberg blue.

Michio insisted there are no ghosts here. He was wrong.

Alex remembers a summer afternoon, his father running the sprinkler in the front yard, sitting on the steps by himself. Alex had come outside to go look for Amery, and Ben had invited him to sit down and talk. He knows this wasn't the last time he spoke to his father, but it's the last memory he has of the two of them alone together.

He takes one last look at the front door and it occurs to him that he was the one who shut it, all those years ago, and walked away. *When one door closes*, his father used to say, that corny old joke he never tired of. Somewhere, Alex realizes, another door is still standing open, waiting for him. One day, no matter how far from this place his exile takes him, he will have to walk through it.

Alex and Michio take off their rain ponchos, and sip coffee from a Thermos.

"When Amery told me what she doing here, rescuing animals," Alex says, "I thought she would do it for a little while and then move on. I mean, you'd think the animals would eventually learn to stay away so they wouldn't get trapped."

"Neither of us thought we would still be coming here after all this time," Michio says. "We figured once we'd rescued all the lost pets and the strays that wandered in here from nearby farms, that would be it. We thought the same thing, that the wild animals would stay away, that their instincts would warn them off. But it didn't happen that way. Wildlife had mostly vanished from the area, then eight years ago, before Amery and I started coming, one of the feral clouds stayed over the Park for a long time."

"So you did you see them here."

Michio blows softly on the steam rising from the Thermos.

"It's why I came back to the area. Scientists have been trying to re-establish communication with the clouds, but we're going about it all wrong. I believe there is a way we can speak to them again, if we learn how they see the world, how they experience it, rather than simply expecting them to obey us."

"You really believe these things . . . *think*."

"We could debate what that word means all day. The point is, one solitary cloud stayed over the Park for a week, and it rained an unusual amount during that time." He looks up at the sky. "We say *it's raining* without thinking about what we mean by *it*. That's something we humans have to consider now. What—or *who*—is doing the raining? Anyhow, not long after the cloud vanished, the animals started coming back. It's dangerous for them here, just like it is for us, but we see more of them every year."

"Do you know why?"

"Amery says it's because there are no people here, or almost no people. I agree with her. You take the people away from a place and the animals will move in, whether it's safe for them or not. We're a worse calamity than anything the Reclamation Area can do to them."

"But they must get caught in the traps and run into the other things, the anomalies."

"They do, and sometimes they die. If they were human, we would consider the losses unacceptable. But the animals can take these losses and survive, even thrive in some cases. Still, no creature should have to suffer because of what we've done. That's why we come here. If there's any way we can save at least some of them, we will."

Alex remembers the fox. How he raised the stick and brought it down on the animal's skull. At the first blow, too hesitant, the fox shivered a little, maybe even made a sound, Alex wasn't sure. After the second, harder blow its eyes glazed over, soft and unfocused, like it was drifting into a dreamy slumber. After the fifth or sixth blow there was blood. Lots of it. The neck went limp, the limbs buckled as much as the trap would let them, and there was no fox anymore. What made it a fox had leaked out, gone somewhere or nowhere. It was just a dead thing.

He wonders if this was the moment that showed Amery the path she would travel in life. The action he'd taken that day, easily, even eagerly, might have led here, to this moment. To his sister becoming stuck, like the fox, unable to tear herself away because he'd failed her—failed them both. He wonders if she told Michio about that day.

"I read something in Amery's notebook," he says. "Something about birds—magpies—making sounds she'd never heard before. She tried speaking to them."

"She had a theory," Michio says, and Alex notices the past tense. Michio seems to have noticed too. He blinks and hesitates before continuing. "She believes the birds are developing new ways to communicate with one another. New sounds. New behaviours. It's not just a random mutation or anything like that. It's cultural. New *words,* she says, are being passed down through the generations. New ideas. And it's happening because of the adaptations they have to make to the pressure we put on them. Their speech, you could say, is becoming more sophisticated, to help them navigate the dangers here. They're learning to say new things. Even to communicate across species."

"Different species talking to each other. I don't know what to think about that."

"It's a thing some animals have always done, but science has only recently managed to see it. Accept it. I mean if we've learned to talk with gorillas and parrots why can't other animals talk to each other, right? We think we're the only animals who speak, Amery says, but it's our endless talk that keeps us from hearing theirs. And now the behaviour seems to be accelerating. Here and in other places that have been turned into no-go zones. It happens where animals are under intense stress, because of us. Amery's journals are full of details like this. She even started using symbols, like musical notation, for the different vocalizations and new gestures the birds are making."

"Has she ever told anybody? I mean scientists. There are people who would want to know about this."

"Some do already. Researchers have been petitioning the government to let them into the Park to do field research. We've brought a few of them in, secretly. Nobody's corroborated what Amery's been saying. Not yet."

They both realize it's time to move on. At the end of the front walk, they stop while Michio looks around. Alex glances back. He supposes he'll never come back here again. But who knows? He imagines himself moving back into this house, living here. A home at the heart of his own lethal little kingdom, hidden from everyone else, where he can invent games about his own past that no one will ever play.

"We'll make a circuit of the town and then head northeast," Michio says. "We can stay the night at a place I know that's safe. Tomorrow morning we'll reach the opposite side from where we came in and meet our pickup outside the fence."

The street takes a slow, curving rise, as Alex remembers. That shipwreck over there missing part of its roof was the Henderson house. And there's the Fliegers' ostentatious chateau, as his father mockingly called it, not looking so grand now. And farther down the street, only partly visible in a cloud of foliage, is where the Velascos lived. The mother, Reyna, sometimes stopped by over the years to see how Amery was doing. Alex had walked or biked by their place often, keeping a lookout for Corrie, hoping for a chance to talk with her. Often in the evenings, looking in their front window, he'd see her little brother studiously bent over the piano. He tries to recall the boy's name, and then it occurs to him he'd be grown up now.

They leave the street and Michio follows a faint trail through the woods. It takes them to another, wider road that Alex guesses might be the old main highway in and out of River Meadows.

The pavement shines with the recent drizzle. Faint curls of vapour rise from it.

After they've walked for some time, Michio stops. Alex has been plodding along with his head down, sifting through memories, forgetting to check his senses or his surroundings. He looks up to see that Michio is standing still, gazing around as he has done so often during their time in this place.

A speedboat lies beached by the side of the road, its hull cracked and peeling.

Alex wonders what time it is. Early afternoon, he would guess. He resists taking out his phone.

"Where are we?" he asks, then he recognizes the building. It's half buried in trees and undergrowth, and the big rotating sign has fallen from its pole into the tall grass at the curb, but the shape of the place is burned into his memory. The Starlite Diner.

Beside it, the billboard he noticed the first night they arrived in this town is still standing, but the Northfire ad is long gone. Across the bleached, shredding paper someone has spray-painted in large red letters PLANET RAPERS.

He looks across the road to a dark wall of green. If the Lulla-Bear Motel is still standing after all these years, it's buried deep.

"Can we search the diner?" he asks.

"Not a good idea. Right now it's one of the hot spots."

"Right now?"

"The anomalies, the most unstable areas . . . they don't always stay in the same place. They grow and shrink and show up where they weren't before. We don't know why. I think that when we broke this place it allowed something to leak through. Something we can never see the edges of is moving through the world, through us, with its own purpose, on its own time scale. It's happening everywhere, but in the Park we can see it more clearly because here our fragile reality has been scraped so thin. Maybe to whatever's passing through we're the anomalies, the brief little blips, the decoherences that come and go without meaning. Or maybe this thing doesn't even know we're here."

Alex has no reply.

"Amery warned me about the diner a while ago," Michio says. "She said that if you spend even a few minutes in there, you'll carry out a headache that will leave you helpless for three days."

"So no chance she'd be inside."

"We can check, but I doubt it. She's never found animals in the place. They avoid it too. They usually have more sense than we do. Let's go up to the door. We can see from there."

Alex follows Michio across the road and into the Starlite parking lot. The diner's full-length windows are intact but blackened with grime, the doors wide open, bent out of true and missing their panes. Michio and Alex reach the entrance and stand looking in. It's too dark to make out much of anything. There's a faint sound coming from somewhere in the interior, like the hiss of a radio tuned between stations, playing nothing but static.

"What is that?" Alex asks.

"Whatever it is, Amery says it's what gives you the headache."

Alex listens. Then he calls his sister's name. Calls it again, louder this time. No answer.

He closes his eyes, struck with the memory of what he's always thought of as the last afternoon of his childhood. Coming home after what he did to the fox, hiding his blood-flecked T-shirt in the back of a dresser drawer until he could safely get rid of it. And then the police at their door, telling them that Ben Hewitt had been killed along with several other people at the extraction site. Telling them—gently but with no room for argument—that they had to pack a few essentials *right*

now and get to the emergency shelter at the hockey arena. There
had been an explosion at Extractor No. 2 and a leak of contam-
inants that hadn't been contained yet, so for everyone's safety
the town was being temporarily evacuated. They did as they
were told, numb from shock, along with their neighbours, along
with everyone else, not entirely believing this was happening.
Only later, staying at a motel in Pine Ridge, did Alex's mother
get the details, on the phone, from someone at the hospital. His
father had been standing on a catwalk outside the venting stack
when the explosion occurred. A ruptured pressure relief valve
struck him on the temple and he fell three storeys.

You turn a corner and here's what has to be someone else's
life, only it's yours.

Alex has understood for a long time why he makes other
worlds, why he invents rules for how these worlds work and
then lets them play out. There has to be an order to things,
something behind the random events that brought him and his
family to this place, that set his sister onto her strange path,
that killed his father. The rule-bound little worlds he's invented
have never given him the answer. This place might.

He opens his eyes.

"I'm going in," he says.

"Let me check it out first."

"No, I need to do this myself."

He steps across the threshold, pauses to let his eyes get used
to the dim light. The warped and stained tile floor, buckled into
ridges and troughs like frozen waves, is covered in dead leaves,
oily puddles, shards of glass that crunch under his boots. There's
a pungent reek of rot. There's a slow drip of water from the
roof and where it hits the floor a ring of bright green moss has
grown, like a tiny tropical island. The dead American celebrities
framed on the walls are faded to pale revenants of themselves.

There it is. The booth where he sat with his sister and his parents, none of them suspecting what was about to send them hurtling off the track of their lives.

He crosses the floor, his new hiking boots crunching on broken glass. He stops in front of the booth, then slides onto the seat, facing the front counter, the exact spot he remembers sitting all those years ago. It's like no time has gone by at all.

He lets his gaze rest on the booth across the aisle, where Claire Foley sat chewing her fingernails, sullen and alone.

And Amery. She had been beside him, picking at her food. Then the ripple passed through their lives and the next time he looked she was slumped in the corner, head against the window, eyes closed.

Everything they've lost.

Maybe what he experienced in the diner that evening had nothing to do with Claire. Maybe they both just happened to be there, and what he'd felt was a preview of *this* moment right now. Finding himself sitting again in this booth in the Starlite Diner, his father long dead and his sister vanished without a trace.

He turns to look at the corner beside him where Amery had sat. After a blank moment he realizes the cracked beige vinyl seat is free of the dust that coats everything else. The pale, ashy film on the tabletop has been disturbed too. There's a clear patch, like the half circle left on a dirty car windshield by a wiper, where an arm or an elbow might have swept away the dust.

Someone was sitting here not very long ago.

He's about to call for Michio but holds back. Instead he slides over into Amery's spot. Immediately the staticky hiss ceases. He's enveloped in an absolute quiet that stops his breath.

Claire was there. And Amery was here. Years ago. Maybe moments ago. What would bring her back here?

He's got it wrong. He's always had it wrong. Amery hadn't been sitting beside him. He'd been sitting beside her.

He sees it now. Whatever happened that evening had nothing to do with him. He had been only a bystander.

Alex slides carefully out of the booth and walks to the door. He blinks in the sudden light.

"Amery was here," he tells Michio. "She was in the diner."

"How do you know that?"

A bright stab of pain shoots through Alex's right temple, advance notice of the headache Michio warned him about. He explains the traces he found in the dust.

Michio considers this.

"I'll have a look."

He goes inside the diner and a minute later returns.

"You're right. Someone was sitting there recently. I found what could be a couple of her boot prints. Hard to say for sure, or where she went from here if it was her. I'm going to make a circuit of the building in case she left any other traces or anything behind. You stay here. This could be tricky."

"What does that mean?"

"It's just better if you stay here. I mean *right here*. Don't go wandering off."

"I wasn't planning on it."

"I'll be back as soon as I can."

Taking his usual slow, careful steps, Michio is soon out of sight around the side of the building.

Alex looks up and down the street. Something across the road snags his gaze and drags it back before he's even aware of what he's seen. He searches, heart racing, and finds it again: perched on the limb of a tall pine and nearly invisible against its reddish-grey bark, an owl is watching him. He doesn't know what species, but it's very large, with jutting ear tufts, its plumage blending in almost perfectly with the tree. He only spotted it because of the eyes—yellow, steady, piercing. As it strikes him that this is the first animal he's seen since they entered the Park, the owl lifts off from its perch and away over the treetops, until it's out of sight.

Alex notices how dry his mouth is and sips from his water bottle. He checks his watch, not sure how long it's been since Michio left. A flutter of panic rises and he settles it by taking several slow, deep breaths, counting the way that counsellor taught him to do a few years ago when he began, inexplicably, to have panic attacks.

The fear starts to subside, but he can't help wondering if something's happened to Michio. Something might have gone wrong, and now he's here by himself, with no idea how to make his way back out.

I can't do this alone, he'd told Michio when they first met.

Why can't you? he asks himself now. Amery did. Does.

He needs to move, to do something other than stand around helplessly. He could search the parking lot for clues. He takes a couple of steps when he hears a rustle nearby. Michio emerges from the tangle of bushes on the other side of the diner.

"That took a while," Alex says, both relieved and angry. "Did you find anything?"

Michio shakes his head.

"Just some footprints in the dirt back there, but I can't be sure they were hers." He studies Alex's face. "Did something happen while I was gone?"

"No. Not really. There was an owl."

"Where?"

Alex points. "It flew off that way. Spooked me, that's all. Waiting just isn't something I'm good at."

"You get used to it in here."

"I suppose. Where should we go now?"

He notices Michio is staring past him. He turns.

Two people are walking toward them up the street. A man and a woman. The man is carrying a rifle on a strap over his shoulder.

"Are they—" he begins.

"I'll do the talking," Michio murmurs.

The couple stops about ten metres away. The man is bearded. He's wearing a hunting vest and jeans, work boots. There's a big sheathed knife on his belt. The woman is dressed in a similar way, her greying hair tied back in a ponytail. They're both in their late forties, Alex guesses. The man is smiling but the woman's eyes are narrowed.

"Well, this is a surprise," the man says to Michio, his gaze flicking to Alex and back. "I thought you were done here, Professor Amano. I thought you'd come to your senses and packed it in for good. And anyhow, don't you have classes to teach this time of year?"

His tone is casual, but Alex senses the tension in Michio and braces himself for whatever might come next.

"We're just leaving," Michio says.

"Are you? Funny, I seem to recall that's what you said the last time we ran into each other in here. Do you remember that day?"

"I remember."

"Good. Good. I thought maybe you'd forgotten. Because I believe we came to an understanding that day. Was I wrong?"

Michio says nothing.

"Who's your friend?" the man asks.

"We're going now," Michio says. "The place is all yours."

The woman snickers.

"I asked you who your friend is," the man says, still smiling. "The polite thing would be to introduce us."

When Michio doesn't reply, Alex steps forward.

"We're looking for someone," he says. Michio stiffens beside him. "My name's Alex Hewitt. Amery, my sister, came in a couple of weeks ago and we haven't heard from her since. Maybe you've seen her."

The man and the woman exchange a glance. "We know who she is," the woman says. "We haven't seen her. Best thing for you to do is turn around and get going right now."

"Hang on a minute, Jean," the man says. "You know, I think there's an opportunity here. For all of us. Alex, is it? Alex, you're looking for your sister and we've got somewhere we want to get to. We can travel together, look out for each other. Your friend Michio knows the area so well, after all. Better than just about anybody, they say."

"They don't belong here," the woman says.

"Well this could be a way for us to show them that. Really get the point across. What do you say, Alex?"

"Amery's brother has never been here before," Michio says carefully. "We've finished our search and it's my responsibility to get him safely out of the Park."

"Don't call it that," the woman says, shaking her head. "It's not a *park*. You have no idea what it is."

"Maybe not," the man says with a shrug. "But they don't have to understand what we're doing in order to help us."

"You're looking for a way to the burnt barn," Michio says quietly. "If you want to go there, that's your choice. Leave us out of it. We're done here and you won't see us again."

The man sighs.

"Yeah, I'd really like to believe you," he says. "The thing is, I've got a pretty good idea that you're intending to keep on searching after we're out of sight. You need to rethink that idea, professor. I thought you'd gotten the message, even if your friend Amery hasn't. *We* decide what happens here. We make the rules, not you. Did you think we were joking about that?"

Michio slowly shakes his head.

"Jean and I are going to the burnt barn, we can use a guide, and here you are. When we're done with what we need to do, we'll escort you to the fence. And who knows, maybe we'll find Amery, too, and she can join us."

Alex can feel Michio's anger on his own skin like a kind of radiation. He's angry too, and frightened. He pictures the handgun, unloaded and tucked into its holster in the bottom of his pack. Out of reach.

He's tried, for his mother's sake. She can't expect anything more from him than that. Then he remembers the fox. The blood spattering his shirt, his shoes, the bare limbs of the pine. The stricken look on his sister's face when he walked back to her after what he'd done.

He raises his hands slowly to signal he's no threat, and takes a slow step forward.

"I'll go with you," he says to the man, then turns to Michio. "I'm not leaving yet. I'm not finished here."

Michio stares at him. "This is a mistake," he mutters. "But fine. We'll all go."

"That's more like it," the man says, beaming. "You can keep looking for your sister, Mister Hewitt, and the professor can look out for all of us. Sounds like a win-win to me."

Michio shoulders his pack without another glance at Alex and starts walking. Alex follows, with the man and the woman close behind him.

CLAIRE

The island's official languages: English, Dutch, Portuguese, Atlan. There is a substantial Asian population, mostly descendants of Chinese and Japanese labourers who reconstructed the ancient canal system in the nineteenth century under British rule and built the Circumferential Railway.

During the excavations for this latter project a royal tomb was discovered that contained the bodies of four hundred mummified horses posed in full gallop, the famous Mares of Amphitrite, which are now on display at the Museum of the Ocean.

Perhaps the most enigmatic surviving relic of ancient art was unearthed during the building of a storm surge barrier in the harbour at Asteria: a naked ten-metre-tall figure with the body of a woman and the head of a bull, holding an axe. Dubbed the Minotauress, it resides now in the National Museum of Antiquities. Fragmentary lines of poetry found inscribed on a stele also recovered from the harbour refer to the Minotauress and to a laby-rinth with a devouring monster at the centre. Whether the bull-woman was the monster or the champion who ventured into the labyrinth to destroy it remains a mystery.

Stay put, the message read. *Soon.*

Fine. She can do that. She has plenty of work to finish on the guidebook updates, and she can keep an eye on the crane and think through the possibilities. Unless they want her to stay put because the operation has been fatally compromised and she's been thrown to the dogs. She can't name anyone higher up in the outfit that sent her here—she knows only aliases. They might have decided to cut their losses. Namely her.

No. It's just this place, the patch, the two near misses. She drops down onto the bed, suddenly aware that the last couple of hours of hair-trigger alertness have drained her. She'd like to crawl into a nest too and curl up around herself for a week. Or a year.

A firm knock at the door jolts her back to her feet.

It's the hotel's assistant manager, accompanied by a sombre-faced, greying older man in a rain-soaked pale green uniform. He identifies himself as a field investigator from the national conservation office.

Calmly Claire observes the increase in her heart rate, the slight sweat breaking out on the back of her neck. It's not like the night she first arrived—she's looking into an abyss again, but this one is familiar, almost comforting. She's been here often enough.

"May we have a moment of your time, please?" the manager asks in an undertone, as if there's something unseemly to discuss.

She steps aside to let them in. The cold wet outdoors billows off the conservation officer's soaked uniform and seems to chill the room.

"One of the household staff informed us there may be . . ." the manager begins, then stops dead at the sight of the bird. The conservation officer seems stunned into immobility as well, then he quickly crosses the room and drops to one knee near the glass.

"She's here," he breathes, fogging the pane. "She's really here."

With a pocket camera the conservation officer takes pictures of the bird in its nest, then scribbles furiously in a weather-beaten notebook.

"You know what it is?" the assistant manager asks the conservation officer, keeping a safe distance from the glass. The officer names the species Claire herself had identified. Her guess wasn't wrong. It really is the golden goose.

"There wasn't another one?" the conservation officer asks Claire. "A second crane didn't help build the nest? Or visit it?"

Claire shakes her head. "I didn't see another one. I was gone part of the morning, but no, I think she's alone."

The conservation officer rubs his grizzled chin. He can't keep his eyes off the bird. "Something may have happened to her mate," he murmurs. "That's not good. If she's on her own looking after the eggs that's not good at all. And in a place like this. Why here?"

He turns to the assistant manager.

"We can't move her, not now. She *must* stay where she is."

"We would be happy to find you another room, ma'am," the assistant manager says to Claire.

It's only much later that Claire realizes this was the turning point, even if she had no suspicion of it at the time.

"No, thank you," she says. "I'm good right here." She's supposed to be a writer, looking for new and surprising stories to tell about the places she visits. No one else in her position would walk away from an opportunity like this. She glances at the conservation officer and adds with a shrug, "I don't like being moved either."

He studies her coldly, as if searching for some irreparable flaw in her character that would allow him to deny her.

"I need to talk to my superior," he says at last. "You're not to disturb her while I'm gone. Do you understand?"

"I haven't gone near her."

"That means no noise. No music. No partying."

"I didn't come here to party."

The conservation officer glances out at the darkening afternoon. Another storm on its way.

"Keep the lights off too," he says. "I will be back very soon."

It's a warning, Claire understands, not a reassurance.

She needs to be ready for a sudden departure and starts packing her carry-on. While she's cleaning her things out of the bathroom, she rolls up her sleeve and checks the patch in the mirror.

It's gone. Just bare skin, as always, without a mark or trace to show that the patch had ever been there. Does that mean it fell off, way ahead of schedule, or did it finally complete the process of disappearing into her—*becoming* her?

She doesn't have time to get sidetracked over that. When her carry-on is packed she asks herself, why wait? Make a preemptive getaway. There's still a chance she can extract herself, hang on to her freedom, at least for a while, even if it means she's done with the people who sent her here. And maybe finished with this business altogether.

Claire is already heading to the door when she takes a last look at the crane. To her surprise its head is up and it's watching her. She freezes. At least she thinks it's watching her. Hard to say what it can see through the glass, but she can't help but feel the bird is aware of her, of what she's about to do, and is waiting to see if she'll go through with it.

She sees her hands poised above the keys of the piano, all those years ago. Her mother's voice in her ear.

Take your time, Clairey. When you're ready.

She sets the carry-on by the door and returns to the desk.

Later, another knock, soft but official, demonstrating just a hint of unwillingness to disturb, telling Claire that this is not someone come at last to arrest her.

The assistant manager is back, with the conservation officer.

"My department will be setting up in here first thing in the morning," the conservation officer announces after he's confirmed the crane remains unharmed. "There will be people coming and going. You have to understand that this is an extremely rare event. A precious once-in-a-lifetime opportunity. For our whole country. Where she's chosen to nest, and the fact that her mate's abandoned her or he's dead—it makes her extremely vulnerable. It puts everything at risk, and for you to act like you've got some right—"

"Which is why," the assistant manager interrupts, "we feel it's best that we find you another room. For your own convenience and privacy. At a half rate, for your trouble, and we would also like to offer you a complimentary dinner tomorrow evening at our restaurant."

He knows she works for a travel publisher. Claire smiles and shakes her head.

"I'm staying," she says. She can almost feel it, the humming swarm about to converge on this hotel room and flow back out again into the ether. Algorithms, search histories, servers, data extraction—an ozone of information coming from everywhere, spreading everywhere, beyond her control. But this thing has already gone far beyond her control, hasn't it?

The conservation officer laughs.

"Staying for what? If she's sitting on an egg right now, she won't be moving for three weeks at least. There isn't going to be much for you to see in the meantime. It's pointless."

"I'm staying," Claire says.

"This is not acceptable," he says, glaring not at Claire but at the wall beside her.

"I understand how important this is, because it's important to me too," Claire says, gesturing to the notes and papers spread over her desk. "People all over the planet are going to want to know about this, and I'm the one who can tell them."

"You're not putting this up on the internet," the conservation officer says. "That's the last thing this situation needs."

"I didn't say I was going to—"

"This will not happen." The conservation officer turns to the assistant manager. "Doesn't your hotel have some kind of policy about rooms that are no longer safe to occupy?"

"Ah, well, it's possible there may be . . ." the assistant manager stammers.

Claire laughs. "How is it not safe for me here?"

"For *her*," the conservation officer growls. He rubs his unshaven chin, mutters something in his own language, then says, "I suggest, ma'am, you get yourself prepared to leave."

I am, she thinks. *I have been all my life.*

———

At dawn a different conservation officer appears at the door, a neatly groomed and smartly dressed younger man with two junior colleagues. Claire has just finished her morning coffee. She's ready. She's feeling calmer and more in charge than she has since before she arrived. Long before.

"You are welcome to stay here for as long as you like," the new conservation officer informs her with a bow. "We will try to bother you as little as possible, you and the Messenger. Everything is taken care of."

"The Messenger?"

"The crane."

"That's kind of you," Claire says. "Thank you."

"I am not the one to thank. It was the Arahant who permitted it."

The term is familiar, from the guidebook.

"You mean the . . ."

"The Holy One. He has been told what has happened, and he said that if the Messenger has come here, to *your* room, then this wonderful event is meant not only for us, the people, but for you as well, an honoured guest in our country. So he wishes you to remain."

She's standing still but in some other dimension she feels herself moving at breakneck speed. There's no backing out of this now. Too late to run. Whatever happens, she has to remember she's never been anything to her employers but a disposable asset. When this ends she may discover what disposable really means.

"Well, please tell the Arahant thank you from me. That's very generous of him."

"You can thank him yourself, ma'am. The Holy One will be coming to see the Messenger for himself."

The young conservation officer and his colleagues make a quick observation of the crane, snapping pictures and scribbling notes, talking softly but excitedly on their phones all the while, sometimes in English but more often in their own soft, sibilant language. One of them asks to take a picture of Claire. She declines.

"This isn't about me," she mutters, surprised to find herself blushing.

When they're done, they let Claire know the Arahant will arrive some time later today. They're sorry they can't be more specific. The Arahant's daily itinerary is a carefully guarded secret. Then the conservation officers take their leave, their young leader bowing to Claire from the doorway.

The most commonly practised religion is Eshafani ("extinction" or more literally "snuffing out a candle"), said to have been secretly passed down through the ages from the original inhabitants who worshipped the sea as a god, although syncretic elements of Christianity, Islam, and Buddhism have had their influence. A primary tenet of the faith teaches that all phenomena are waves in the infinite ocean of the universe. Like waves, each one of us briefly rises to life and consciousness and then subsides again, back into the ocean that itself rolls on forever, boundless and eternal.

The faith's spiritual leader is known as the Arahant ("revealer of hidden things"), revered by millions as an incarnation of the spirit of divine wisdom.

The next arrival, early in the afternoon, is a middle-aged woman in a saffron-coloured robe. Her head is completely shaven.

"I have been sent by the Holy One," she tells Claire, "to pre-
pare for his visit, which he would like to take place one hour
from now. If that is convenient for you."

Her name is Alala. She's the public relations secretary for
the Arahant. Something about her otherworldly serenity, or
her steady, unflinching gaze, sets off Claire's internal alarm.
For an instant she's braced to fight or bolt. Then old habit
kicks in, and with three deep breaths, she has slipped into a
state of relaxed alertness.

"The Holy One is to be greeted with a bow," the woman
continues, "although you may also shake his hand if you wish.
There is no requirement, other than politeness, for you to wait
for him to speak before you do."

"What should I call him?" Claire asks. "I mean, when I
address him."

The woman's eyes shine like the young conservation officer's. "As an incarnation of the one pure light that pervades
this universe, the Arahant is to be addressed at all times as
Your Holiness."

"*Your Holiness*. Sure."

She didn't mean the echo to sound quite so skeptical—it
doesn't fit with her cover. In the blog posts she writes for the
guidebook publisher's website she plays up the mystique of
the places she visits in gushing, impassioned prose. A voice
that isn't like her at all, but it serves her interests to cultivate
a reputation as a romantic. Who would suspect someone
who writes like that to be guilty of the things she's done?

The woman asks, her eyes still shining, if she might see the
Messenger before she goes. Claire invites her in. After a few
moments silently contemplating the nesting crane, the woman
turns from the glass, looking sombre and strained, as if the

sight of the crane has hefted a burdensome weight onto her shoulders.

"I did not know she would be so beautiful," she says. "I did not know—" She breaks off, her eyes wet.

"She's really something," Claire says.

The woman gives her a tight smile. In her eyes Claire is a tourist, a clueless foreigner like all the rest. Let her think that.

"I will inform His Holiness that the visit may proceed."

Claire Bear,

I hope you like the enclosed gift. I know it looks like just the cracked-off half of a round stone, but on the broken face, if you look carefully, you'll see a hair-thin band of green running through the dark grey. That thread of green is actually a living thing, a kind of lichen called a cryptoendolith.

I found the stone here at the field station, in the main lab. I have a personal rule against removing specimens from the places I visit, but I ignored it just this once because the rock, I was told, had already been sitting on a windowsill at the station for years, and no one seemed to mind my claiming it.

You might be wondering what I do here all day. Well, I roam around looking at plants, lichens, moss, that kind of thing, measuring them and marking their locations, while keeping one eye out for polar bears. In the evenings I hang out with the other researchers. We play chess, poker, and backgammon and watch old VHS tapes of hockey games and comedy shows. It's nice to have other people here but still it can be really lonely some days. Every time I passed that windowsill I saw the rock sitting there, a little bit of life in the endless grey of the tundra outside the window. It always made me think of you. I miss you a lot, punkin.

So, the science: a lichen is a symbiotic colony formed by bacteria and algae. But this lichen is a little different from the rest: it lives inside rocks.

It's amazing to think how life can carve out a niche for itself, even in the harshest place. The cryptoendolith grows just under the translucent surface of a rock, where there's enough light and trapped humidity for photosynthesis to take place. When the climate takes a turn for the worse the colony goes into suspended animation, literally freezes, sometimes for hundreds of years, until conditions become favourable again for life and growth.

We now believe this is a lot like how life on Earth survived the first billion years or so of its existence. Hidden in undersea hydrothermal vents, far below the toxic atmosphere on the surface, the first living collections of cells waited and waited through eons for conditions to change enough so that they could escape and begin to colonize the rest of the planet, and one day evolve into us.

Care of the cryptoendolith is simple. Just leave it on your bedside table or on a bookshelf. It will draw moisture from the air. The rock has a lot more patience than I do. I can't wait to see you again.

Kiss your mom for me.

Love, Dad.

She used to bring the letter with her when she travelled, until it
got too soft and fragile from being unfolded and read so many
times. She knows its contents by heart, anyhow. She would
bring the stone with her too. She'd hold it up to the light, look
at that thin emerald ribbon, and think about how far the lichen
had travelled. Like her, it was far from home but still alive, still
thriving. It had everything it needed. Then one day she packed
the stone and the letter away with her other belongings. In her
line of work, you couldn't afford to be sentimental about a little
bit of green.

The Arahant is u'Yoi, the first one she's met. He's a teenager of
perhaps sixteen (the details of his birth, as Claire discovered
online while waiting, are shrouded in mystery: he was found as
a young child surviving alone on the streets and his parents
have never come forward). His head is shaved like Alala's, his
skin pale, almost albinic. He wears a robe of the same russet
colour as the crane's ragged crest. A ripe pimple adorns his
plump, downy chin.

It occurs to her he looks just like the actor from the event
the other night. Aphro-something. It can't be. Can it? She
has the terrifying thought that the performance has been continuing all this time, it's been going on around her, it involves
her, and only now has she realized she's one of the actors.

The woman, Alala, has accompanied the Arahant, along
with two other attendants in similar dress, an older man and
a very young woman with beautiful, placid eyes, her face
disfigured by terrible burns. The Arahant smiles brightly at
Claire and returns her bow, but he can't keep his attention
from straying past her to the wonder waiting beyond the balcony glass.

"May I?" he asks, still in the doorway. His English is more heavily accented than anyone else's she has met here.

"Please, Your Holiness." It occurs to her she's enjoying this whole production more than is advisable. But then again *advisable* flew out the window a while ago.

The Arahant crosses to the window with surprisingly deft, nimble steps for a teenage boy in a floor-length robe. His attendants station themselves a couple of paces back. The boy gazes at the brooding crane without speaking for a long time, then he gives the bird the same deep, slow bow he made to Claire. When Claire catches Alala's calm, unwavering eye, her alarm bells go off again, but now she understands what she's been responding to. This person is ready to give her life to protect the Arahant. And very likely kill for him too.

"The snowy messenger," the Arahant murmurs. "The moon shining in dark water."

He turns again to Claire. Now he is just a boy, awkwardly at a loss for words.

"Thank you, Miss Claire," he says with difficulty at last, and another bow. "For . . . being here. The first one to greet the Messenger. Someone else might have frightened her away. Or worse."

"I'm glad I could help, Your Holiness."

"This is a difficult time for my country. We cannot hold back what we know is coming. Many things are changing. Not for the better, it seems. People have been losing hope. For the Messenger to come now . . . it is a blessing. Miss Claire, your . . . your thoughtfulness is . . ."

He appears to struggle with the limitations of his English.

"I haven't done anything," Claire hurries to say, and now she also fumbles for words. "Your Holiness, I should be thanking you. You are . . . you . . ."

To her surprise the boy giggles.

"Listen to us," he says, and laughs again. "Sometimes words just get in the way, I think. I used to read a lot, when I was learning English. My teachers gave me American comic books to practice with. *Scooby-Doo. Archie. Space Dogs.* And children's books. I liked *The Little Prince* best because the words were not hard. The talking fox in that book, it was foolish of me but I wished him to be my friend. I wished him to be real. There were so many duties for me, so much to learn. Stories gave me a place to go for a little while."

He shoots a playful scowl at his attendants.

"They do not allow me time to read anymore. But Alala read to me one of your blog posts, Miss Claire. You are a good writer. I am sure that if you write about the Messenger you will be faithful to her."

"Thank you," Claire says. She feels a strange letting go and at the same time a quickening of her pulse, as if she had passed a crucial, perhaps even mortal examination.

"What will happen now, Your Holiness?" she asks. "With the crane, I mean."

"In the oldest stories of our people, the Messenger comes from the faraway country of the birds, beyond the Whirling Mountain, near where the sky meets the earth, bearing a gift. We no longer believe this. Or not in the same way. But we still hope she brings us . . . something long wished for. Something only she can give."

"Something. . . ?" Claire isn't sure what the boy is talking about. Some kind of religious mumbo jumbo, she guesses.

Alala steps up and whispers in the Arahant's ear. He listens and then nods.

"Alala tells me I am not making myself clear. I apologize. We are waiting and hoping that the Messenger will do what

she has come here to do. The researchers who know about
these matters tell me this is possible. If she is left in peace. Do
you understand, Miss Claire?"

"Yes, I see. She's nesting, so you're waiting for . . ."

"That is it. She is precious, Miss Claire. She may be the last
of her kind. And time is short. She reminds us that everyone,
each one of us who . . . draws breath on this planet, is also precious, a being whose life . . ." He pauses, searching for words.
"Whose life can be no other's."

Claire feels something welling up that she isn't sure is coming from her or from the person the boy believes she is. He
studies her now with the same eerie calm as his acolyte. It's like
he's looking *into* her, as if through a window, at a nameless,
churning disarray that he nevertheless seems to recognize.

He turns to his attendants.

"I wish to speak to Miss Claire alone, please," he says with
sudden, brisk authority. "And Alala . . ."

The woman hands him some sort of folded embroidered
fabric. No, now Claire sees it's a book, the cover made of thick
sea-green cloth adorned with spiralling shapes and flowing
characters she doesn't recognize. After an uneasy hesitation, the
three attendants bow and exit the room, shutting the door
behind them. For an instant the thought slams into her that she's
been caught at last—that this baby-faced boy is her opposite
number, the agent charged with apprehending her, who started
on his own tightening orbit around hers the moment she set
foot on the island.

"Do you see it, Miss Claire?" the Arahant says in an urgent
whisper that puts her even further on her guard.

"What am I supposed to see?" For an instant she thinks
he means some literal object in the room, like a bug or hidden
camera. It occurs to her she's forgotten the honorific address,

but the formal mood of the situation seems to have vanished with the boy's question. The two of them are in a different space now, a disorienting one for Claire, like a room whose roof has lifted without warning into the sky.

"This is her home," the boy says. "She will not leave it. That is her freedom. We do not have a home. Not any longer. None of us do. That is our freedom, even if it does not seem that way."

"I don't understand."

"We do not have much time," the boy says, and she's not sure if he means the two of them, or the island itself. Perhaps both. "*She* is what you are here for. What you have come to find. Do you see it?"

For some reason Claire thinks of the trafficker she took over from when she started on this road, the older man she thought of as her trainer. He told her, *Someday you're going to find yourself in a situation where your ass is riding on what you do in the next five seconds. Bet on it. If you're really lucky and the moment is right, something's going to click into place for you. It'll be like you just fitted in the last piece of a jigsaw puzzle you didn't even know you'd been working on. But this puzzle—it's you. Okay? It's you. Everything else will fall away and you'll see. Things can still go south even then, oh yeah, it's no magical guarantee against fucking up, but you will understand for the first time what you're truly capable of.*

On every job she's been waiting for just this moment, hoping to coax it out of the circumstances, skating a tight circle on the thinnest ice, leaning into the risk factors like someone poking at a wasp nest with a stick. In some of the worst do-or-die moments she's even believed she'd finally got there, but she was never entirely certain.

At last, like the trafficker predicted, she knows.

She remembers her dog tearing hell-bent for leather out of the yard, chasing after a stupid, pointless ball as if it was everything, the only thing. He'd done it because she'd thrown the ball too hard on purpose in order to find out what would happen. She found out, that's for sure.

Another memory flashes across her inner screen, from a couple of years later, at that all-night diner on the main drag. It was late and she was sitting alone, not wanting to go home because her mother was working the graveyard shift at the hospital and only Ray would be there. She knew that when she walked in the door he would pat the sofa beside him, invite her in his carefully offhand way to plunk herself down and watch the hockey game with him. And when she did, he would edge close, sometimes stretch and yawn and brush up against her as if by accident. He hadn't dared anything more. Yet.

No, she couldn't go home and she had nowhere else to go.

There had been a family sitting in a booth across from her. A boy about her age—he went to her high school but she can't remember his name now—and a girl, his little sister probably. And then a decoherence rolled like a wave through things, and for an instant the girl wasn't there, none of them were. There was a woman sitting alone in the booth, a young woman with long white-blond hair, just like the girl. No, it *was* the girl. It was her when she was older, or would be. Claire knew one thing with certainty: she was on her way there too, no matter what she did, to this place—no, this *time*—where this young woman was already waiting. Wanting something from her? No, but aware of her, surprised to see her, wondering who she was and what she was going to do. Claire understood that she could flee to the ends of the earth—that's just what she'd done, wasn't it—but wherever she ran, this lay ahead of her.

Then it was over. The girl was just some kid slumped in the corner of her family's booth, eyes closed. The boy beside her caught Claire's stunned gaze and stared back at her like his life depended on what she did next. She didn't know him, and she didn't want to. It didn't matter what she'd just seen. It didn't mean anything. Nobody was going to trap her, make their claim on her. She'd gotten up and walked out of the diner, and when she got home and saw Ray passed out drunk on the sofa she found his wallet and took a fifty, confident that even if he suspected, he wouldn't dare say a word, knowing she could turn the tables on him in a second with her mother. One soft, well-trafficked fifty. The very first installment in her freedom account.

She ran. Just like that stupid dog, like it was life or death. She's been running ever since, pursuing this threadbare sham of a life to punish the people who were supposed to love her and care for her more than anything, not abandon her. Maybe she's been running to punish herself too, charging into the path of whatever careening wheels will crush her at last.

"The Messenger is here for all of us," the Arahant says to her when she doesn't answer his question. "That means you too, Miss Claire. But there are some on this island who do not want her here. Some who would harm her, because of what she is. What she stands for. And there are others who hope to profit from her. I have never understood these people, how they think, but they are a danger to her. There is so much at risk. Everything is . . . fragile. And so I am asking you for your help."

To her surprise, Claire asks, "What can I do?"

"You may stay in this room, in our country, as long as is needed for the Messenger's task to be finished. I have made sure that you will not be disturbed. But if something goes wrong, if the Messenger should be forced to flee . . ." He sees her incomprehension and smiles. "What I mean is that we want *you* to have the gift she brings. If it comes to that. We want you to take it with you. There is a safe place, not on the island. Another of her kind is being kept hidden. This may be the only way. The only way to make sure that one day another one like her may come again, to someone other than us. To bring a message they need to hear."

Claire closes her eyes. She is no longer in the room. She is no longer anywhere. In some other place rain is falling from a depthless sky into churning grey waves. She opens her eyes.

"Your Holiness, I have to tell you something. I'm here to . . ."

The boy leans forward.

"Yes, I know what you came to our island to do. I know that you have . . . *skills* that can help us."

He places the book in her hands. A warm fragrance of sandalwood rises from it, and something else, an elusive scent like a sea breeze that vanishes before she can name it.

"This is for you," he says. "One last deception is needed, I'm afraid. This box has been made to resemble our oldest scripture. No one will ask you about it, when they see my seal. No one will take it from you or dare to open it while you are still in my country. The book will keep the gift safe and hidden until you leave. Until you can pass it on to those who are waiting for it."

Claire glances toward the door. She knows Alala is on the other side, ready to rush in at a moment's notice.

"Why can't you find someone else? Why me?"

"If we chose someone else," the Arahant says, "you would never get your answer to that question."

"These people waiting. How do I find them?"

"They will find you."

———

After the boy and his entourage are gone, she opens the book. It's hollow inside, as she guessed, the empty space softly padded and inviting. A safe place for something or someone to sleep and dream. She wonders how it can make any difference to save the life of one animal, when entire species are vanishing every day. Then she considers that she has only one life too, which might also be worth saving.

Andros texts her that evening from downstairs, asking her if it's all right to come up. She leaves the text unanswered for a long time. Long enough that her phone buzzes again with another message from him.

How is she doing?

She hesitates, then replies.

She's fine.

And you? I heard about the visit from the Arahant. Wow. Sounds like it was quite a day for you.

It was.

Okay if I come up?

She considers this.

Opening the back of the phone she's been using for her texts with him she pries the card out and flushes it down the toilet. Then she undresses, down to her bra and panties, and sits at the end of the bed to watch the bird. The lights in the room have been off for some time and her eyes are already well adjusted to the dark.

That night, not long after she manages to calm the quake inside her enough to drop into something resembling sleep, a frantic squawking jolts her out of bed. She stumbles to the window and slides open the balcony door, blinking the fog out of her eyes, just in time to register two simultaneous events: the crane flapping frantically away through the billowing scrims of rain, and a camera drone coptering off in the opposite direction, bucking a wet crosswind then bouncing down through the layers of bewildered air, into the liquid shatter of the city's light.

In the nest are a few white feathers, and a large, perfectly white egg.

Claire steps all the way out onto the balcony. The thrashing air carries a tang of brine. She crouches and cautiously reaches into the nest's intricately whorled hollow. The egg lies at its heart but she's not ready to touch her new charge just yet. Instead she rests her hand on the nest's soft floor, feeling the animal warmth there that is already seeping away.

REYNA

Luggage lies scattered over the meadow. Most of the suitcases are splayed open, their contents strewn across the grass. Reyna ignores these. She stops and crouches only by the intact cases, unzips or unlatches each one and digs inside, emptying it of its clothing and gadgets and toiletries, rooting to the bottom and in all the pockets until it's empty.

A few of the suitcases have locks. Some are made of hard plastic. The ones she can't open she puts her ear to, closes her eyes, and listens. After a few moments she gets up and moves on to another case.

Only while she's walking from one to the next does she look up. On the other side of a road, in a field of tall sunflowers, there's a large, jagged shape she won't let herself focus on. People are milling around it, some in jackets with yellow Xs that flash when they catch the sunlight. She tells herself that what they're doing isn't her business, even though lifelong habit urges her to go and help, if she can. Instead she watches the other people nearer to her, the ones wading slowly through the sunflowers in her direction, carrying bundles of sticks with ragged white ribbons that flutter like pennants in the wind.

Their heads are bent always to the earth, like the monks back home in the Philippines who walk in meditation through the streets. She remembers the soft-spoken monk who came to talk with her when her mother died, all those years ago. The monk had told her that when a loved one leaves us, it can feel like they're playing hide and seek. We're sure we can find them if we just look hard enough. And maybe we can, if we know where to look. Or how.

Every so often one of these slow walkers anchors a stick with a white ribbon in the ground and moves on.

They haven't seen her yet. They're coming her way but haven't cast their attention that far ahead. They still have to finish with the sunflower field before they cross the road and start in on the meadow.

She empties another case, rises and hurries to the next. It's so hushed here. Peaceful. The warm, lazy buzzing of bees. Lush grass and so many flowers, so many scents of growing things. She's thankful for that. The reek of burning barely reaches her. There's a stand of trees nearby with little round leaves that shiver and whisper when the wind moves through them, with a sound like the soft rain of home.

She first heard the name of this country as a girl in school, years ago. Before she left home and came to Canada. Her teacher showed the class an old film. The steppe ribboned with great rivers. Brightly painted churches with domes like a sultan's palace in the Arabian Nights. Wind-rippled wheat fields under a towering sky. So strange to her then. A fairy-tale country, not a place where real people lived real lives.

When she was told by the woman from the airline that his flight had been shot down here, over this faraway land, those pictures came back to her. She saw a domed church, a sea of waving golden grain, and the airplane gently settling there, like a bird come to rest. Just one small hole in its wing. A tiny hole trailing a thin line of smoke, and a man in the distance with a gun, a dog at his side. A mistake. That's what they were telling her. The plane had come down, she understood that, but everything would be sorted out quickly and he would be on his way home.

The people with sticks are coming closer. She must hurry if she's going to get to every case. In his last phone call, he told her he'd had to buy a second suitcase, a used one, to carry all the presents he was bringing everyone. She hadn't thought to ask him what kind of suitcase or what colour. It could be any of these.

The next is full of expensive clothing. A grey silk jacket and burgundy tie. Polished black shoes. He used to say, *you'll never catch me in one of those monkey suits*. Still, he let her buy him a new shirt and dress pants for the trip, to make a good impression when he got to the school. She bought him a warm coat too, because she'd heard it got almost as cold in the north of that country as it did in Canada. She'd looked forward to sitting with him on the back porch in the evening after he got home, like they used to, him telling her about his adventures, the people he'd met, the things he'd seen. His eyes lighting up, his animated gestures, her laughter. Before them a curtain of soft rain.

The wind comes back and the little round leaves shiver.

She empties the suitcase and moves on to the next, and the next, unpacking all these hopes and secrets tucked so carefully away. Women's lacy underthings. Stuffed animals. Pill boxes, prescription drugs. As a nurse it bothers her to think of these people not getting their medication on time, then she remembers they won't be needing it anymore. And yes, these are things she has no business touching, but she does anyway because she knows their owners would understand. They would have done the same if it was them here instead of her. Someone who sat with her after she got the news mentioned that there were doctors on board the plane, as if that was something to be hopeful about. Doctors on their way to a conference. There had been a doctor sitting with her for a while too, who gave her a shot and held her hand and told her to rest. When had that been? Just before she came to the meadow, although she can't remember how she got here . . .

And then it's strange because she's back home in Pine Ridge, lying in her bed, in the house they moved to after they were forced to leave River Meadows. It's raining outside, and her husband and her daughter are beside her, and she's telling them she needs to go back, she's not finished yet, and her daughter is crying and saying, *Mom, no, no, the airplane's on the other side of the world. You're here with us.* She wants to tell them they're wrong, she's found her way to where he is, but then they're gone, along with the rain, and she's back in the meadow.

She returns to the task at hand, empties another case of its contents, and then the one lying next to it.

When she moves on she glances up and freezes in her tracks. The people with sticks are out of the sunflower field now and standing in the road. They're huddled in a group, a few of them smoking. She doesn't think they've seen her yet, but she crouches anyway. A tall man among them gestures with his arms, making slow sweeping motions that include the meadow.

Soon there will be sticks planted here too.

So many suitcases still to go. She should have been keeping better track, should have done this in some kind of order. No time now.

She turns in a circle, once, twice, and then she sees it. A squarish shape, apart from the others, in a hollow near the shelter of the trees. She hadn't seen it earlier because it's a light shade of brown that blends in with dappled shadows, as if it hadn't fallen from the sky but belonged here.

Some of the searchers are coming this way now. She hurries to the suitcase, keeping her head low, then drops to her knees in front of it.

It's a big case. Maybe the biggest one yet. But it's whole. Nothing's touched it. Nothing's torn or broken.

A large blue dragonfly is perched on one of the latches, motionless. Gently she brushes the insect aside. It whirs away into the air.

The case is not locked. The latches click open easily. She raises the lid.

On top is a glossy, folded fabric. Bright red stippled with gold. The flag of the country that he travelled to for his music studies.

She sweeps away the cool, thin cloth and here he is.

It's him.

Where he had to be all along.

He's curled up with his earphones in and his music player in his hand. His eyes are closed and there's a hint of a smile on his face, like he's deep inside a good dream. She catches a faint, tinny drone of strings rising and falling. That slow, stately music of another time and people that took him so far from home.

When he was little he used to hide from her in the funniest places. Cabinets. Drawers. In the bottom of the laundry basket. He'd been small for his age and could curl up almost anywhere. It was their favourite game. His muffled call, *Mama, come find me!* He would never budge until she finally did. That's how she knew where to look this time, where he would think to be when the plane was falling out of the sky. Thinking of her and knowing he had to stay hidden because she would keep searching until she found him.

He's been waiting for her, like always, but it took her so long to find him this time that he's fallen asleep.

Carefully she reaches out and touches his shoulder. His eyes flicker open and when he recognizes her his face breaks into that familiar lopsided morning grin. Then his eyebrows knit in confusion and she knows he's wondering if maybe he's still dreaming.

She takes his arm to help him as he climbs unsteadily out of that cramped space, and it's almost funny because he's so much taller and stronger than her now. He's even grown some, she realizes, since he left home. He gazes around, not quite sure what's happening or where they are, that's to be expected, but he's still smiling. *You found me.* She wants to speak to him, hear his voice, his laughter, but they'll have time to talk later, nothing but time once they've left this place and they're back home again. And they must go, now, before the people come with their sticks, parting the grass, looking for bodies and finding them. Finding nothing but bodies and parts of bodies.

She takes his hand and they walk together through the long grass, away from the dark shape and the searchers, toward the sound of rain.

Dusk is falling and most of the searchers have gone home for the day when a man comes to the meadow. He lives in a town not far away and has paid the right person a lot of money—money he himself was given only yesterday—for an emergency worker's pass and jacket, and to make sure no one will ask any questions. He wears a backpack, which none of the other searchers do.

He walks slowly through the meadow, pausing from time to time to squat down and examine various pieces of luggage. It doesn't take him long at all to find what he's after: a large dark green messenger bag, its front flap torn open by the crash. He crouches, opens the bag, finds it empty inside. He runs his fingers over the unusual inner lining: the dark, iridescent blue and the odd stippled texture are exactly right—they're what he was told to look for.

The man glances around. None of the few searchers left at the site this late in the day are looking in his direction. And even if they do, this is none of their concern. The plane unfortunately strayed into the crossfire of a conflict that has nothing to do with what the man has come to retrieve. From what he's been told that smoking wreck over there is just the latest snag in an operation that had already run into some major foul-ups. The poor guy who ended up boarding this flight was a last-minute replacement, brought in to finish the job after the original courier went rogue and vanished with something even more valuable than what's lying here in this meadow. She's cheated the Reaper, whoever she was, but she had better hope their employer doesn't catch up with her.

The man slips off his backpack and sets it beside him.

With a large box cutter he proceeds to slice the bag into pieces. When he's done he carefully rolls up each piece and tucks it away in the backpack, including the strap and buckles. Then he stands, looks around, and walks back the way he came, pulling his jean jacket tighter around him against the chill wind that's picking up now as night falls. A car is waiting for him down the road, just out of sight beyond the meadow's gently sloping rise, to take him back to town.

ALEX

In a cul-de-sac at what used to be the wealthiest end of Foxhaven, three gabled, stone-fronted edifices stare back at them through the empty sockets of their windows. Behind the abandoned houses rises the forest, mostly dark, shaggy spruce and steel blue fir. This is the original woodland, the boreal forest that was here before the town, before the new subdivisions were carved out of it. Where Amery used to go on her expeditions and he would follow, bored and fed up with being his sister's keeper.

Michio leads the way down a roughly trodden path through the tall grass between two of the houses. He stops every now and then to cock his head and listen.

"I'm Daniel," the man says to Alex after they've walked for a while in silence. "You're not from around here, I guess."

"We used to live in River Meadows when I was a kid," Alex says without looking behind him. "But no, I'm not from here."

"I'm not either," the man says. "I came to find work, years ago. I was an angry person in those days. No direction in my life. No purpose. I hurt someone I cared about, someone it was my duty to cherish and look after, and then I left. I just ran away, went back east. But it wasn't right, and I came back to see if I could make it right. Make up for what my anger made me do. Turns out I couldn't. But then I met Jean. She opened my eyes to the wonderful thing that's happening here. Sure, I was skeptical at first, like most people. It's so easy not to believe in anything. I even mocked her. That's how ignorant I was. But things change in this life. They can change for the good when you least expect it. I've been given another chance and I am truly grateful for that. Grace can find a person. Even when they don't deserve it. That's what grace does."

Michio comes to a sudden halt and turns.

"You need to stop talking," he says to Daniel.

"And why's that?"

"When you're talking, you're not listening. You're not paying attention. You want to make it out of here, you have to keep quiet."

Daniel laughs softly.

"Okay, professor. But you've got one thing wrong. This isn't a place we want to get away from. I mean, we know it's not possible for us to stay here for long, not yet. We're not stupid. One day it will be, though. One day this will be our home. The only home there is. But sure, I'll work with you on this." He puts a finger to his lips.

They start walking again with Michio in the lead. Daniel stays quiet. After a few minutes Jean, who's close behind Alex, whispers, "Your dad was Ben Hewitt, right?"

Alex turns his head, startled to see that Daniel has unshouldered his rifle and is cradle carrying it.

"Yes," Alex says.

"I worked for one of the other outfits in those days," Jean says. "Not Northfire. But I heard what happened to him, and the others. I'm sorry for your loss."

"Thanks."

"It was a terrible thing," Daniel says, "but you should know, Mister Hewitt, they didn't die for nothing."

"What's that supposed to mean?"

"Well, the professor wants me to stay quiet. We'll get a chance to talk later, you and I."

They climb up and over a dome-like rise and come down out of the woods onto the remains of a gravel road. A waist-high picket of ferns and loosestrife runs between two deep ruts. They stop here for a rest, and everyone takes a drink of water except for Daniel. He keeps the rifle cradled in his arms like an infant.

"Where are we?" Daniel asks Michio.

"This was an access road to the main Northfire site," Michio says. "It's the quickest way to the barn but you'll have to do exactly what I tell you."

Jean takes a protein bar from one of the pockets of her vest. She unwraps it, breaks it in half, and shares it with Daniel. Once they've eaten, they bow their heads together a moment. Daniel takes a deep breath.

"A good day," he says, then nods toward Alex. "You should eat. Both of you. You must've brought something in those packs."

"We're good," Michio says.

"Suit yourself."

Michio leads them on. They walk without speaking as the road begins to climb. When they reach the top of the rise Michio halts them again.

"Hot work for sure," Daniel says, touching his jacket sleeve to his forehead.

Michio drops onto his haunches and appears to be examining the ground. Alex wonders if he's found something connected to Amery. He's about to ask when the woman says *hey* sharply under her breath.

Alex looks up. She's pointing to something below them on the far side of the rise and to the left of the road, in the ditch full of tall grass at the edge of the woods. After a moment's searching Alex spots what she has seen. A deer, its tawny coat dappled by tree shade, its head nodding up and down as it grazes.

Daniel goes down on one knee, brings up the rifle. Jean crouches beside him.

"Don't do it," Michio says.

The deer moves forward a step, flicking its tail and ears, then its slender head comes up, alert. At the same instant the rifle fires with a crack that makes Alex jump. The deer buckles, drops out of sight into the grass.

The echoes of the shot gallop away in the shocked air.

Daniel climbs to his feet. Jean reaches out and grips his arm, her face alight with some emotion Alex doesn't understand.

"Thank you," Daniel murmurs, his head bowed.

Michio gets up and walks back to Alex.

"I'm going now," he says, his face set. "Are you coming with me?"

Before Alex can reply, Daniel interrupts.

"Now you're the one not listening," he says, setting the butt of the rifle on the pavement. "I told you things have changed. We're not making accommodations anymore. You're staying with us until we're back at the fence. These are the new rules— nobody comes in here without the Church's permission. So let's keep this friendly and move on, and hopefully we'll all get what we want today."

Michio stares at the ground, breathing hard.

"You should think about your sister," Jean says to Alex in a softer voice than he's heard from her yet. "I mean, this could be why she's gone missing. So it would bring you back here, to meet us. We can't always see the good in bad things when they happen. All we can do is have faith that one day we *will* see. We'll know as we are known. It might help you to think about it that way."

It's Alex's turn to swallow his rage. Again, he pictures the handgun at the bottom of his pack.

He turns to Michio. "I'm sorry I got you into this."

"You don't need to be sorry, Alex," Daniel says. "Jean is right. You have to take some things on faith."

Michio locks eyes with Alex for a long moment. He slides his glasses back up his nose, but this time Alex sees his fingers trembling.

They set off again, down the slope of the road. No one speaks. When they reach the place where the deer went down, Jean steps off the road into the grass. She crouches out of sight, then stands up again, nods at Daniel.

"Clean," she says.

"Mark it," Daniel says.

"What for?" Michio says. "You can't carry that out."

"Maybe not," Daniel says. "But it lets others know we were here."

Jean looks around, then breaks a branch off a nearby dead willow and shoves its jagged end into the ground. She takes a roll of neon red tape from her pack, ties a strip around the top of the branch and knots it. When she comes back out onto the road she glares defiantly at Michio, as if daring him to comment. Michio says nothing.

Half an hour later they stop for a rest on a truss bridge over a dry streambed. They sit on the rusted guard rails, Alex and Michio on one side of the narrow single-lane span and the couple on the other. The twinge in Alex's temple has billowed into a dark aurora dancing across his skull, like nothing he's ever felt. The glare off the sunlit metal bridge supports pummels his eyes. He's reaching into his pack for his water and the bottle of painkillers he'd brought when the man raises a hand.

"Hold on there, Alex," he says. "You can just set that down."

"I'm getting some water."

"We'll share our water with you from now on. We brought plenty, don't worry about that. Just set your pack down. You too, professor. Right in front of you."

He gestures at the pavement with the muzzle of the rifle, in case the point isn't clear.

Alex looks at Michio and reads the thought in his eyes. There will be no way to hide the handgun. He sets his pack down where Daniel indicated, and Michio does the same.

"Another of the new rules," Daniel says. "That's just how it is. Jean, have a look please."

The woman gets up and comes toward them. She's focused on the packs, not looking at Alex or Michio, but Alex can see she's nervous, braced for anything. She picks up the packs, carries them over to the other side of the bridge, and dumps out Michio's first. A portable camp stove, dehydrated food packets, a first aid kit, and other things spill out over the road and she has to reach for some of them. She's more careful with Alex's pack. She leans forward, checking all the pockets, rummaging carefully before she takes anything out.

She shows Daniel the photo of Amery that Alex brought with him from her bedroom.

"Your daughter?" he asks Alex.

"My sister."

"So that's Amery. Cute kid. Little Red Riding Hood . . . lost in the woods."

Jean takes out Amery's all-weather notebook, studies the cover a moment, then tosses it on the road.

"What's that?" Daniel asks.

"Her diary, I think."

Daniel reaches out a hand. "Let's hang on to that. Look through it later." He glances at Alex. "Could be interesting reading."

"That's not yours to take," Alex says.

Daniel shrugs, tilting his head apologetically. He tucks the notebook into an inside pocket of his jacket. "You don't have a say about it, I'm afraid."

Digging in the pack again Jean grunts softly in surprise and lifts out the handgun in its holster and the pouch with the bullets.

"I thought you didn't approve of these things," Daniel says to Michio. "Did you know your friend here was carrying?"

Jean takes the gun from its holster, deftly pops out the magazine and slides back the action, eyes the chamber. She's had a lot of experience with weapons, Alex realizes. Much more than he ever has or wants. A friend who knows firearms picked out the gun for him and gave him one short lesson in loading and firing it.

"We'll hang on to that too," Daniel says. "Wouldn't want anyone getting hurt."

Jean loads the magazine, holsters the gun, and clips it to her belt.

"Well, let's get back to it," Daniel says, climbing to his feet. "Your packs stay here. You can pick them up on the way back."

"We're not coming back this way," Michio says.

"You don't really have a say about that either."

"We may need what's in those packs. All of us. In case we can't get out before nightfall."

The man sighs.

"Professor Amano, you have to learn to trust there's a power here looking after everything."

"*Not a sparrow falls*," Jean murmurs.

Michio gestures to the rifle. "Then you don't need one of those."

"Actually, we do," the man says. "For now at least. When the time comes, when the work is done, we'll be able to put them down."

They start walking again, across the bridge and up a sharp slope of the road. On the far side they pass a sign on a leaning metal pole. Whatever message the sign once held has been worn or perhaps scratched away, leaving a few unreadable marks, like hieroglyphs from the world after this one.

Just past the sign Michio halts again and glances around, tilting his head as if trying to hear better.

"What is it?" Daniel says.

Michio raises a hand for silence. He sniffs the air. A bird calls from the trees on one side of the road, a quick, sharp run of chittering like a lawn sprinkler. Another bird answers with the same call from somewhere on the other side.

A frown crosses Michio's face. For the first time he seems unsure of his next move. They wait, keeping still and listening, until at last Daniel speaks again, this time in a whisper.

"What's the plan, professor?"

Michio squats on his haunches, sets a palm flat on the pavement. He stays like that for a long time. Then he stands again.

"We have to leave the road," he says.

"You're sure about that?"

"I'm sure."

"I hope you are. For your sake."

"You want to get to the barn? This has to be the way. And you should know, I may not be able to get you there, not all the way there, taking this route. I'll take you as far as it's safe to go."

"We'll decide how far is far enough. Let's get moving."

They turn aside from the road and plunge into the woods. The sun is high in the sky now and the air is growing hot. There's some shade under the towering poplars but it's muggier here, the air more close. Before long Alex is sweating and stumbling over roots and uneven ground. The pain in his head has become a steady throb.

They cross the overgrown remnant of a dirt track. A rusting pickup truck sits parked here, its driver's door hanging open, as if the owner just hopped out for a stretch and might be somewhere nearby.

"Where does the track go?" Daniel asks.

Michio doesn't answer.

"I said where does it go?"

Michio stops and turns to him.

"It doesn't matter where it goes. We're not going that way."

"You know, it might help you to understand what we're doing here."

"I don't care what you're doing here."

Jean laughs. "You will."

"Killing things seems to be all you've accomplished so far."

Daniel fixes Michio with a cold stare. His hand tightens on the rifle's stock.

"Keep walking."

They start off again, Michio in the lead, but he's moving even more slowly now than before, and stops often to wait and listen. During one of these halts Daniel starts to speak but Michio raises a hand to cut him off. Then Alex hears it beneath the whisper of the wind in the leaves. A low, almost inaudible hum that reminds him of the sound he once heard coming from an electrical transmission tower they were walking near, on one of Amery's expeditions into the woods.

"It's moving," Michio murmurs. "Coming this way, I think. Everybody get down."

"What is?" Jean asks, whirling around. "I don't see anything."

"Keep quiet. Crouch down and don't move."

Alex hunches beside Michio. Jean starts to drop, then she sees Daniel hasn't moved.

"Shouldn't we . . ." she murmurs.

"It's okay," Daniel says to her. "You go ahead."

She crouches beside Alex. Daniel remains standing.

"*Get down*," Michio says in a sharp whisper.

Daniel regards him without expression. He bends slightly and lowers his head, gripping his rifle, but drops no farther.

Alex tries to keep perfectly still but he can't help moving his head at flickering leaf shadows and light in the periphery of his vision. The hum doesn't seem to be coming from anywhere in particular, and as far as he can tell it's not getting any louder or softer.

Then it stops. Alex strains to listen.

Nothing.

Michio remains crouched a while longer, then he rises slowly and turns in a circle. Finally, he lets out a breath.

"It's gone. We can keep going."

Alex and Jean climb to their feet. She glares at him defiantly, but her face has gone pale.

"How does your science explain that?" Daniel asks.

"If you want to get yourself killed," Michio mutters, "that's your problem. Don't endanger the rest of us."

Daniel smiles serenely.

"We won't hide from what's happening here."

"Then you don't need me," Michio says, walking away before Daniel can reply.

They follow for a time in silence. Then Daniel gives a soft laugh. He clearly can't let it go.

"You think you've got it all figured out, don't you, professor," he says. "This place. What it means. You call it the *Park* to mock it, because you don't understand and you're afraid of what you don't understand. You think if you measure something, if you turn it into numbers, then you'll know all there is to know. Your *science* will explain everything. There's so much you miss. So much you don't see. Or hear. There's something speaking in this place, to all of us. Some*one*."

"*They heard Him walking in the garden in the cool of the day,*" Jean says. "*His voice was the sound of many waters.*"

"You can't hear it, it won't speak to you, when your heart is shut," Daniel says. "You'll never . . . know . . ."

His voice trails off. The trees have given way to an open meadow of sparse yellow grass. In the middle of the meadow, on the other side of a fallen, half-buried barbed wire fence, stands a large, dark structure.

The large central doorway gapes open. The long walls, the peaked roof, the timbers and posts have all been blackened as if by fire but are still intact. It's as if the building had gone up in a great blaze, but when the flames had burned themselves out nothing had been consumed.

Around the barn the poplar leaves shiver in the faintly moving air.

"There it is, Jean," Daniel says in a choked voice. "Just like I told you."

"That's really it?"

"That's it."

He slips off his pack and sets it down. He hangs on to the rifle. Jean takes off her pack as well. They quickly embrace and let go.

"You've been helpful, Professor Amano," Daniel says. "And you too, Alex. You held up your end of things. We can't let you go just yet, though. Like I said, we're staying together until we're back at the fence."

Michio doesn't reply. His gaze hasn't left the barn.

"Did you hear me?"

Michio finally tears his eyes from the building. He looks at the man as if he's surprised to find anyone here other than himself. "I heard you," he says.

"Then I need you to cross that wire just ahead of us. You too, Mister Hewitt. Don't go too far. Just the other side of the wire. We'll be right behind you."

"Alex can stay here," Michio says. "You don't need both of us."

"We don't need either of you now, really. But this is non-negotiable."

"It's all right," Alex says. "Let's get this over with."

Michio hesitates, then walks to the fence and steps over the sagging, twisted length of knee-high wire. Alex follows, then the man and the woman. It seems to Alex now as if the barn has drawn much closer. It's less than thirty metres away, he figures, and appears to be empty, though he can't say for certain. All he can make out of the interior are bright slivers where sunlight shines between the vertical slats of the far wall. The charred posts and boards, the roofline, everything is perfectly straight and true, as if the barn was raised yesterday. As if whatever fire tore through its timbers had only tempered it, made it stronger.

Something without a name has come into the world here. Something invisible but powerful has gathered itself around this building, or it's the building itself, as if the barn wasn't built by human hands but was always in this place, older than the grass, the trees, the earth itself, waiting through eternity for the four of them to come. Alex can't even say for sure which of his senses is telling him so. It may be a sense he never knew he possessed until this place drew a response from him. He has no name for the information he's getting. All he can say for sure is that the pain in his head has vanished, as if the top of his skull has opened to the air.

He thinks of the day his father showed him the chunk of ghost ore at the extraction site. How they shone an invisible beam of light on it and the ore came alive and rippled with colour and he'd thought it the most beautiful thing he'd ever seen. That feeling returns to him now, stronger than before. This meadow he's never set foot in before has become the centre of everything. He and the others have arrived where they were always meant to be.

Jean's lips are moving as if she's speaking under her breath. Daniel has drawn himself to his full height, his chin raised, his eyes fixed on the barn. Even Michio seems wonderstruck.

They take a few more steps and then Daniel says, "That's good."

Michio halts. Alex nearly bumps into him.

The couple comes up beside them.

"This is it, Jean," Daniel says. "We made it."

Jean turns to him, places a hand on his arm.

"You're sure, Daniel?"

"Can't you feel it? It was just like this the last time I was here. I *knew* I'd found what we've been looking for."

"Yes, I can feel it," Jean says. "I just think we should wait."

"Wait? For what?"

"We should make sure, before we do anything."

Daniel shakes his head. "We can't make sure. That's the whole point. You know that as well as I do."

Jean's eyes glisten with tears.

"*Because you have withheld nothing,*" she murmurs, "*your descendants will be as numerous as the stars . . .*"

"*And take possession of the cities of your enemies,*" Daniel finishes. "That was the promise. If we hesitate now, if we don't trust, if we wait until we *know*, then it's not a real test."

Jean nods toward Alex and Michio.

"We could send them in first. Let them try it before we do."

"Jean, no. We can't. That's not how it's meant to work. If we did that it would mean we don't have faith."

"I know that. Yes. Yes, you're right. But . . ."

The woman's eyes dart around, as if she's looking for a way out.

"You're afraid and that's okay," Daniel says. "I understand. That's what happened to me last time. I thought I was ready, but fear was still hiding in my heart. My faith wasn't strong enough. But you're here with me now, Jean. I wouldn't have made it this far without you. You're the one who showed me the way. Remember how we prayed together for this day to come."

"I remember."

"This is what we wanted."

"It was."

"It is."

Daniel takes her hand.

"We'll do this together. You and me. Together, we won't fail."

Jean shakes her head, pulls her hand away.

"Wait," she says. "It's not right. We have to stop and think about this."

Anger flashes in Daniel's eyes.

"What is there to think about?"

"We have to leave the guns behind," Jean says quickly. "For it to be a true test we can't bring weapons. It's like you said. To show we're not afraid, we leave everything and go forward without fear. It's how we prove our faith."

Daniel blinks. He drops his head and stares at the ground, his jaw working. Then he looks up again, this time at the sky. "*Not by the power of arms but by My Spirit*. That was part of the promise too. You're right. We have to leave them behind."

"But we can't both go and leave the guns here."

Daniel frowns. He darts a glance at Alex and Michio, looks down at his rifle, then up at Alex and Michio again. For a terrible moment Alex thinks he's arrived at the most efficient solution and tenses himself to lunge for the weapon.

Then Daniel nods.

"No, you're right, Jean. I wasn't thinking. We can't take the guns and we can't leave them here."

He holds the rifle out to her.

"I'll go first," he says. "Then you."

"Are you sure?" The relief in the woman's voice is unmistakable.

"I'm sure. I wanted it to be both of us, together. But this way I can show you. I can help you with your doubt, like you helped me with mine. We make each other stronger. That's what we do."

Daniel shrugs off his jacket and lays it in the grass. He stands still a moment, his head bowed, then starts taking slow, steady, deliberate steps toward the barn, like someone walking down the aisle at a wedding.

"We forgot to pray together first," Jean calls. "Come back and let's pray for guidance. We can ask for guidance, that's not wrong."

A few metres from the barn's sharp wedge of shadow, Daniel stops again. He turns, his eyes alight, his face beaming.

"I love you, Jean," he says, then he steps into the barn's shadow and walks through the open doorway. They see him, a dark figure moving in front of the thin seams of light. His silhouette looks up to the rafters, then down at the dirt floor. He turns in a slow circle, faces the doorway again. Alex can sense that he's no longer smiling but can't read the expression on his face.

Daniel raises a hand, waves to the woman. They see him lower himself slowly to one knee and bow his head. He stays like that for a while, then climbs to his feet again and remains standing where he is. To Alex he seems to lose his features, to melt into the darkness, as if he has become a part of the structure itself, burned to blackness but still upright, immovable. That or the interior of the barn has somehow gotten darker, Alex can't tell which. Either way, he can't say for sure the man is still there. Under the hot sun that deep darkness is beckoning. Vaguely Alex notices the desire to lose himself within it. To be swallowed up.

"Daniel," the woman calls. "Are you all right?"

There's no answer. Finally, after a long time, they see the man's shape materialize as he comes toward the doorway. He steps out into the daylight, looking just like he did when he went in. He hasn't brought the darkness with him. Nothing has changed.

Jean lets out a sound like a choked-off sob. She lowers the muzzle of the rifle, but Michio doesn't move and neither does Alex.

The man pauses just outside the barn doorway, looking up at the sky and all around him, as if he's surprised by what he's found out here. The look on his face is thoughtful, preoccupied. Then he catches sight of the woman and breaks into a smile.

"Daniel. Oh Daniel. Praise Him," she says, and the man starts moving toward her.

Michio murmurs in Alex's ear, "There's something . . ."

"Jean?"

It's the man's voice calling her, but it's not coming from his mouth. He's smiling, still walking toward the woman, but his mouth hasn't opened.

"Daniel?" Jean says.

"Jean," the voice calls again. As far as Alex can tell it's coming from the barn. The man ignores it. He's still walking slowly toward the woman.

"Back away," Michio says to Alex. "Now."

The woman turns on them, raises the rifle.

"Don't you move." She turns back to the approaching man. "Daniel, how are you doing that?"

"Jean, I can't see you. I can't find the door." The man's voice sounds thinner, farther away.

"I can see you, Daniel," the woman says. "I'm right here. It's okay. I can see you. Just keep going."

Another few steps and he'll be able to reach out and touch her. Then another figure steps out of the darkness of the barn. It's Daniel, or another Daniel, holding his hands out in front of him, pawing the air as if he can't see.

"Jean. Where are you?"

The first Daniel stops and turns. He regards his double for a moment. A shimmering broil appears in the air around him like skeins of escaping steam, then the living weave of him thins and puckers, collapsing in on itself where he stands, and when it ends, he's gone.

"Daniel? *Daniel!*"

The man near the entrance of the barn staggers a couple of steps forward, then sinks to his knees. The woman hurries toward him but stops a few feet away.

"Daniel, is that you?"

The man lifts his head at the sound of her voice. He crawls to the edge of the barn's shadow, then whatever strength has brought him this far seems to leave him. He wavers there a moment, his head drooping slowly until it's resting against the earth. The rest of him softly collapses. His eyes are open, unseeing. A bright coin of sunlight anoints the upturned side of his face.

The woman is making noises Alex has never heard anyone make before. She sinks to her knees, clutching herself.

And now there's something in the air. A sound or a pressure. Alex isn't sure if he can feel it or hear it or it's coming to him in some other way. Something is gathering, building, about to show itself. Alex has had the thought many times before, but this time it's more than an abstraction—he feels it in his blood, his bones, it's already inside of him, in the pause between each heartbeat.

He is going to die.

Maybe not here. Not now. But one day this being called Alex will just *stop*. All that he is, that he knows himself to be, will end. He will be gone. *Nothing*.

Michio strides over to the rifle the woman has dropped, picks it up.

"Come with us," he says to her.

She looks up, her face streaked with tears, her eyes hollow.

"We need to leave, right now."

A bird cries from somewhere in the trees behind them. Alex and Michio turn at the sound. When they turn back the woman has the handgun out of the holster and is pointing it shakily at Michio.

"What happened to him?"

Michio, still holding the rifle, slowly opens his arms.

"Put down the gun," he says quietly. "We can get out of here together."

"*What did you do to him?*" the woman screams. She's focused completely on Michio. Alex braces himself to lunge for the gun.

"We can't stay here. Come with us, please."

The woman's face contorts. She lowers the gun and collapses into sobbing.

Michio picks up the man's jacket from where it lies in the grass. He fishes in the inside pocket, takes out Amery's notebook, and turns to Alex.

"Let's go."

They return to the bridge to retrieve their packs. They haven't said a word to one another since they left the woman behind. Michio is locked in movement, driven.

As they're leaving the bridge there's the far-off crack of a gunshot.

They look at each other. They wait. Silence.

They walk without speaking until they come to a place where the dirt track flattens out and runs alongside a slough rimmed with nodding cattails. The water's surface is carpeted in bright green pondweed.

Michio stops here, raises the rifle over his head and hurtles it end over end into the water. When he turns to Alex his eyes are burning.

"That was your weapon she used," he says.

———

Late in the afternoon, the sunlight slanting dustily through the trees, they come out into a clearing. Before them stands a large house made of logs and stones, shrouded by towering evergreens. Alex is moving in an exhausted trance by this point, his head throbbing again, but he takes in the massive log walls, the stone pillars, the tall, mullioned front windows.

They step onto the wide veranda at the front door. Alex sets down his pack and drops onto one of the polished split-log benches. He notices a tremor in his legs. Ever since they left the burnt barn he's been resisting the urge to run, without any idea where he would run to.

"What is this place?"

"A Northfire executive had it built as a summer home," Michio says. "He didn't get to enjoy it very long. Amery and I sometimes stayed here when we couldn't get out of the Park before nightfall. This isn't where I'd planned you and I would spend the night, but it's almost as safe as the place I had in mind. There's never been much activity here."

"Activity," Alex says. "Is that what you call it?"

He has been trying not to think of what he witnessed at the barn. Whether something like that happened to Amery.

Michio has recovered his quiet detachment.

"You saw what activity means. That's why there are some areas we stay away from."

"Did you know what it would do to him?"

Michio doesn't answer.

The house is almost bare of furniture. There are no lamps or chairs in the huge, vaulted front room, only bare wood floors and a fireplace with a mantel of big, round stones. In the equally vast dining room and kitchen area there's a table, two wooden chairs, and an empty glass-fronted cabinet that probably once held dishware. The doorless cupboards are empty save for several empty plastic water jugs.

There's a third room on the ground floor, a den or study with two brown leather armchairs, their coverings cracked and peeling. Alex smells the books before he even registers they're there. The unmistakable fragrance of leather and dust and ink greets him and then he sees that the walls are lined with bookshelves that are still, to his surprise, filled with books. In ordinary circumstances Alex's curiosity would be piqued and he'd want to browse these shelves. He often dreams he finds himself in a house full of books, searching for a nameless, elusive volume he desires to read. But here, at the end of this day, it might as well be a wall of bricks. And maybe it is. Maybe that's what bookshelves really are. Walls between us and the terror of living.

Through a pair of glass doors at the far end of the room Alex can see a partially overgrown path of stones, leading to a small cedar-sided building nearly swallowed by red willow bushes that might have been an outdoor sauna.

In one corner of the room two thin rolled-up mattresses tied with bungee cords are propped against the wall, along with a large plastic garbage bag.

"This is where we'll sleep," Michio says, appraising the space as if they've just checked into a hotel room. "We can use those patio doors as an escape route if we need to."

He brings out his portable camp stove and gets started on their dinner.

Unable to sit still, Alex wanders over to the shelves. He finds mystery novels and thrillers, inspirational tomes by business gurus, books on politics, and biographies of famous people. He slides a book at random from a shelf and finds the pages tinder dry and riddled with holes. This is a den for other creatures too. He slides the book back in its place.

"The shelf just to your right," Michio says. "The book about Churchill."

"Yeah?"

"Have a look."

Alex slides out the book. Behind it is a hip-pocket-sized bottle of Canadian vodka. It's full and looks like it hasn't been opened.

"Amery found that when she was exploring one of the abandoned liquor stores. She never touched it, but she figured it might come in handy someday."

Alex unscrews the cap, sniffs, and is about to take a sip when he stops.

"I don't suppose you'd care to join me."

Michio looks like he's about to decline but then nods.

"I think this qualifies as someday."

Michio has made a vegetable stew from dehydrated pouches that they eat off paper plates. The food has no taste, but Alex devours it greedily and when he's eaten, he wishes there was more. The alcohol helped him calm down, but he needs something to fill him up, to remind himself he's still alive.

After the meal Michio folds up the soiled plates and packs them away in a plastic bag. Then he boils water and serves them both tea in metal camping mugs. They sit in the armchairs facing the patio doors like two old vacationers at a peaceful bed and breakfast in the woods. They sit without speaking for a while, then Alex can't help but ask, "Did you ever go to the burnt barn with Amery?"

"No, but she's been there on her own," Michio says. "She

says she's never actually gone in, and I believe her. It's always been clear there's something about that place, that it has some kind of power. You know if you give in to it you're not coming back. You must have felt it."

"I did. I've been wondering if she . . . you know . . . if she might have let that happen to her."

Michio sips his tea and ponders this. "Not there. Not the barn. She's smarter than that."

"But maybe somewhere else?"

"She's always taken more chances than I have. If we come across something new, something we've never encountered before, she wants to learn about it. She wants to get up close, to see things the way an animal might see them. To feel the danger, or the temptation, so she can understand it, learn from it. I've always told her, if she finds something when she's on her own, to come back and let me know. Don't go checking it out alone."

"Maybe she found something like that. Something she'd never encountered, and she didn't wait to tell you."

"That's what I'm thinking."

"So she could still be alive. She could be trapped right now, and maybe she can still find her way out. That happened once when we were kids. She got trapped when she was alone in the woods one time, and she got herself free."

"I know. She told me about that day. About the fox. For what it's worth, I think you did the right thing. The only thing you could do."

"Maybe. But I didn't do it for the right reason."

"Does that matter? I've told Amery many times, we can't save them all. Even she had to admit that, eventually."

"I just think . . . maybe she wouldn't have come back here at all, if it wasn't for me."

———

As the sun begins to set Michio leaves the study and returns with a full-length mirror in an oak frame, the glass cracked in one corner and flecked all over with black spots. He stands the mirror up just inside the entrance to the room, facing out into the dining area.

"We'll keep this here tonight," Michio explains. "The Visitors seem to get confused by mirrors. They'll stand in front of them, looking at themselves maybe, who knows. Sometimes it'll hold them in place until they vanish."

He unrolls the mattresses onto the floor, covers them with white sheets from the plastic garbage bag, along with one faded red wool blanket each.

Alex takes a small battery-powered camping lantern out of his pack.

"We can't have any lights on in here after dark," Michio warns him. "The Visitors are attracted to light."

"Like moths."

"Or people."

"Are we going to take turns keeping watch?"

"Amery and I always did when we came here together. I'll stay up, for the first few hours. Get some rest."

Alex doesn't expect to sleep, not after what they've witnessed today. But he must have dropped off, because suddenly he starts awake to find that night has fallen.

He's on his side, his face pressed into the sheet. He feels the wet cold against his face, his arm, and scoops up a handful of crystalline white powder that scalds his palm. This isn't his bedsheet. It's snow.

He's lying in the snow, somewhere outside, in the darkness. No walls, no glimpse of a horizon, only whitish grey swirling snow, sculpted into ridges and drifts by the driving wind. How did he get out here? And it can't have snowed like this. Not this much in so short a time. There's no sign of the log house. Nothing to tell him which way to go.

He squints into the dark. In the distance a small, blurry shape is labouring toward him.

He climbs unsteadily to his feet, shields his eyes, and now he can see a little better. It's a tiny person coming closer, their feet kicking up dim plumes of white. Or no, the person is ordinary-sized, it's just that they were so far away at first, he thought they were small. The person stumbles, falls, gets up again, labours on, getting closer and closer to him with each step.

It's a boy. He staggers over a blade-like ridge and pitches forward onto his hands and knees. This time he doesn't get up until he lifts his head and sees Alex in the distance. Then he climbs unsteadily to his feet and starts toward him. When he gets closer he stops and studies Alex with a confused expression, as if he expected him to be someone else.

The boy is lost, just like him. Alex understands this, even if he doesn't have any idea who the boy is or where he came from.

You shouldn't be here, Alex says to him. This is not a good place.

The next thing Alex knows the boy is clinging to his back, and he's trudging through the snow with this weightless burden, blinking against the streaming flakes. They might have been walking for a moment, or a long time, Alex isn't sure. He only knows this is what he has to do.

Then the boy speaks in his ear.

There. That's where I need to go.

Alex squints against the driving snow, just makes out the bare branches of a fallen tree. And something else, above. Like a flickering light in the darkness, something beats toward them through the billowing snow. A small black and white bird.

This is a dream, he says.

He's standing in the middle of the book-lined room in the log house.

Sleepwalking. Not something he's ever done before. He actually got up out of bed. But then again, the Park isn't like any place he's been before. Who knows what it's been doing to him? And who was the child? He knows it was only a dream, but he can't help wondering if the boy reached safety.

Michio isn't in the room. The mirror's still standing where he placed it, in the doorway. What if he was taken by something? He said he was going to stay awake. Surely he would have seen or felt it coming, whatever it was. Alex decides Michio must be here somewhere, in the house or outside, maybe doing a perimeter search like he did at the diner.

There's a soft thump from outside. Then another.

Alex clamps down on his fear and moves slowly, in a crouch and as noiselessly as he can, toward the glass doors. When he gets closer, he can see something there, just outside the doors, a dim, whitish grey shape. An eye.

He jerks back. It's an animal, right below him on the sloping lawn, grazing on the thick moss covering the low stone retaining wall alongside the house. An elk? No, smaller, with a white ruff, antlers pointed skyward like reaching hands.

A caribou.

The glade around the cabin is bathed in moonlight. The caribou hasn't noticed him. Head down, it goes about the business of feeding. Its antlers probably bumped the side of the house and made the sound he heard.

The temperature must have dropped over the last few hours. The animal's breath huffs out of its nostrils, plumes of phantasmal white in the cool fall air. Alex watches these brief, ephemeral galaxies appear, whirl apart, vanish, disclosing no meaningful pattern at all.

He wonders if this is a real animal or one of the Visitors. An echo. Or a copy.

Then he notices the rest of the herd, bunched together near the edge of the lawn. Six or seven dim spectral shapes, necks bending to the grass and lifting again.

Woodland caribou. He'd learned about these animals in his high school biology class. A critically endangered species even then. His teacher spoke about them in resigned tones, as if they were doomed beyond hope, their future already written and finished. The same story as always. Too much disruption of their habitat and food sources by human activity.

Then the humans went away, and they were left alone.

He watches the caribou feed and asks himself how they can live here. The same way animals have always lived with us of course. Expecting nothing, enduring everything. This terrifying place isn't new or different to them—it's simply another deadly enigma humans have created, which must be suffered. For them the Park *is* us: an unknowable, unstoppable fact. A hole in the heart of the world that is never going away.

The caribou steps back from the window, to feed on another nearby patch of moss. Alex changes position as well, to keep the animal in view. It must see or sense his sudden movement because with a jerk of its head it starts up and then bounds away into the dark. The others follow, a soft thunder that swiftly fades.

Somehow at this moment he knows he will never see his sister again.

He hears a sound and turns. Michio has come back into the room.

"A wave went through just now," Michio says. "One of the big ones. I went out to have a look around. Sometimes the stronger waves bring Visitors. And other anomalies. You met our antlered friend?"

"Yeah, but I scared it and the others away. Didn't mean to."

"They won't go far. They're much smarter about this place than we are."

"I'll watch now, so you can get some sleep. I think I'm done for the night."

"That's all right, I'll sit up with you. It's not long until dawn."

Alex is going to argue the point but changes his mind. After that dream about the boy, lost in a snowy desolation, he feels the need for some company. And what's rare for him, he wants more than anything to talk to a fellow human being. Even though he already knows the answer he can't keep from asking. "She's not coming back, is she?"

"No. I don't think so. I'm sorry."

Alex sits in one of the armchairs. Michio puts some water on to boil and when it's ready pours two cups of tea. He hands one to Alex and sits down across from him in the other chair. For a while they sip their tea, not speaking.

"I haven't been entirely honest with you," Michio says at last. "I told you when we met that Amery and I were just friends."

"And . . . ?"

"The last time we came here together, not long before she went missing, we stayed at the cabin overnight. I tried to convince her it was crazy to keep doing this. She told me the craziness was out there, on the other side of the fence. *We're fighting a war,* she said, *for the animals. For ourselves too. For the future.* I talked about my research on the clouds, how much progress I'd been making, and how what I was learning could be just as important. Maybe more so. She could help me with that, I argued, but she insisted the Park was where she could do the most good. We talked until we exhausted ourselves. Neither of us was going to win the argument, and I think we both had the feeling this might be the last time we'd ever see each other. I think I *knew* it, somehow, and it frightened me. I didn't want to lose her. I needed her to know how much she meant to me. And maybe she needed to let me know too."

He looks into his mug, and Alex is startled to see tears glittering in his eyes.

"We slept together that night," he says, then he looks up at Alex and gives a broken little laugh. "Neither of us saw that coming. The next morning, I went home on my own."

"That was the last time you saw her?"

Michio nods. Alex searches for words.

"The thing is," he finally says, "I know she isn't dead. I can't say how I know, but I do. I suppose you don't believe in that. In intuition or gut feelings or whatever you want to call them."

Michio shrugs. "A gut feeling can tell you the truth long before any other evidence does. Usually when it's a truth you don't want to hear. And sometimes hope is more than just another way to lie to ourselves. Sometimes hope is based on something real."

"That's it. She's alive, I know it. Just not *here*. Those people from the Church, they believed there was a purpose to all of this. I don't know, maybe there really is something more at work."

"What do you mean?"

"Maybe there's something that needed to be done. Or will need to be done. Something only Amery can do. Just . . . somewhere else."

Michio ponders this. A sad smile crosses his face.

"If it's needed," he says, "she'd be the one to try."

"You said you're keeping records, right?"

"Yes, an archive. Everything that happens here."

"Tell me about it."

Michio talks, and Alex listens, and an idea begins to shimmer into possibility in his mind. He wasn't a bystander at the diner, he was a witness. He still is. It can be his task now to keep records. To remember. He'll finish his decoherence project, his history of River Meadows set down on cards, but it won't be a game anymore. Or he'll make it more than a game. He'll work with Michio and he'll talk to the people at Aditi too, busy building their ark, and see if they can find a place in Sikandar's entanglement of worlds for River Meadows and what Amery learned here. He'll build his own ark, one made of words, and some day others might add to it with their own threads and scraps of memory. He can't see the shape it will take yet, but he knows it will speak of what happened to his family and this town, the lives lived here, the fever dreams of endless growth, the rifts torn open in things, the vanishings. Likely he'll never see the whole shape of this story he begins. He'll only ever know some of it, the way you know a cloud, or a life, a coming together and departing that has no real beginning and no end.

ALL-WEATHER NOTEBOOK No. 25

Sept. 6, 1:30 p.m., edge of the Northfire hot zone

Following a magpie for the last hour. Likely a fledgling from
that breeding pair I observed last summer. Something's wrong
with the bird, not sure what. It's been sort of hopping and
limping along the ground, dragging its tail, keeping it low.
Hasn't taken flight since I first noticed it. No idea whether the
bird strayed into one of the traps or some other animal did this.

The magpie knows I'm following. Whenever it stops moving,
I stop too. It waits for a few minutes, pecking half-heartedly
at the ground, and moves on again. I'm sure it would have
flown away by now if it could. Every once in a while it calls,
a deep, stuttering vocalization I haven't heard before. Either
calling for others of its kind or warning them away.

2 p.m.: The bird was hunkered down half-concealed in a
clump of dwarf birch on the edge of the Northfire hot zone.
It hadn't moved for almost twenty minutes and I thought it
was probably exhausted, maybe even dead. I moved closer
to get a better look, but I must have spooked it. The bird
suddenly took off running, flapping its wings like it was about
to fly. Then it disappeared.

It was just gone. Between one second and the next.

I need to get closer. Confirm what I saw, if I can. There's
something here Michio and I haven't met with before.
It's stronger than the burnt barn, I can feel it on my skin.
In my bones. It took the magpie, but where it took it is
hard to say.

I know what Michio would do. The sensible thing. You
can't help the bird now, he'd tell me, always the scientist.
Its injury was probably a natural event, just part of life
for an animal. It was hurt and afraid, and in its suffering,
it made an error. It went toward something it would normally
have stayed away from.

But it was me who made the error. Following the bird,
spooking it when I should have left it alone. Whatever
happened here, it was my doing. My responsibility.

Let this one go, Amery, my friend would tell me if he was
here. We can't save them all.

THE BOOK OF RAIN

TRANSLATOR'S NOTE

The story that follows was originally told to me by a bird, in the language known among animals as the Uttering. The storyteller, a female raven, was foraging for her nestlings and visited our field research station in search of food, but she lingered and eventually spoke with me at length. I asked her if I could record our conversation, and she agreed after I explained to her that my audiovisual device would preserve her words. *It's like the leaves that Bone Woman made marks on,* she told me once she had grasped what my making a copy of her speech meant. I asked her who Bone Woman was, and that was when she began to relate the narrative I have translated here.

I had already learned enough of the Uttering to have held brief, simple conversations with various avian species in the area, but never before had a bird shared with me such a long and involved narrative. Her name for herself was Speaker, as this was what she was most known for among her kind. I supplemented the recording with a written shorthand notation I had already devised for quickly transliterating non-human modes of expression. Despite Speaker's obvious facility with language, I had to pause and ask her many times to repeat certain words and phrases that were difficult for me, which she did with some impatience at my slow and halting progress.

On that first visit Speaker did not stay long, as she had to return to foraging for her young, her mate having recently lost a battle with a red-tailed hawk. We made it through only part of the story before she abruptly flew off. The following morning, she returned and resumed her narrative exactly at the point where she had left it. On her third and final visit, we came close to what I believe was intended as the end of the story. Speaker hinted then that there was a little more to tell, but she did not return to the research station. I never encountered Speaker again and I don't know what happened to her. I think of her often.

In the weeks and months that followed her visits, I began the process of translating my notes and the recording of her speech into human words. I am acutely aware that no translation can truly do justice to the performance of this story as I witnessed it. For a brief time during those three days, a window was opened for me on the universe as a bird sees it. I am grateful beyond words for this experience.

My colleagues and I believe this is the first time a human researcher has been gifted by a non-human animal with a story about the era of environmental collapse that the birds call the Broken Years.

In the last troubled decades before the breakdown of global human civilization, our own species was still in the early stages of grasping the full richness and complexity of animal communication. Systematic efforts to build bridges between humans and other sentient life had barely begun, with a few notable exceptions. We have evidence, for example, that something called a "Forever Ark" was in the process of construction, with the hope of bringing human and non-human worlds together in mutual understanding. In fact, we owe much of our own early efforts at interspecies dialogue to what little we were able to retrieve from this ancient feat of knowledge-gathering. It has recently been theorized that the Uttering was originally developed by human researchers some time before the Broken Years, perhaps as part of an experiment on animal learning. This nascent form of communication was likely taught to several individuals from one of the more verbally gifted bird species, such as a parrot, raven, or magpie. After the collapse of human societies, in the lawlessness and chaos that followed, the Uttering escaped captivity, so to speak, and was passed along among wild avian populations, where it ultimately spread to other animals besides birds. It is ironic when one considers the theory that our ancient human ancestors themselves may have acquired the faculty of speech by listening to, and imitating, the songs and calls of birds.

For the devastated animal populations of the Broken Years, a shared language might well have proved the most valuable adaptation for staving off extinction, as likely was the case for us in our prehistoric past. The Uttering would have been a means to foster group cohesion, relay messages, spread warnings, and share cautionary tales of past encounters with the animals' common enemy—humans. The conclusion that must be drawn is unflattering to our species' self-image but inescapable: the animals developed a common tongue not to speak with us, but to survive us.

One result of the long centuries of sundering and isolation is that the Uttering and its kindred tongues have proven notoriously difficult for humans to gain proficiency in, even now when we have taken the first steps to renewing our interrupted dialogue with the rest of the life that shares this precious, fragile planet. Most birds cannot speak our languages because they lack the necessary vocal apparatus for the kinds of sounds we make. It is admittedly not much easier for a human to imitate the trills, whistles, chirrs, head bobs, and wing flaps of the Uttering (hands make poor substitutes for wings). But if we are to work together with our fellow creatures to heal what has been so deeply damaged, it is up to us to walk in their world. To see it, if we can, with their eyes. To speak the Uttering and have it speak to us, as they do.

The birds I have communicated with believe that their language and the universe came into being at the same time, long before humans ever existed. I for one am not going to debate that assertion. After all, the avian storyteller who gifted this tale to me also employed the phrase "the Uttering" as a name for the earth, sky, and waters, and everything in them. It was difficult at times to tell whether her use of the term referred to the language or to the cosmos, or perhaps both at once.

One might well ask: Is this story true? Did these events really happen the way the storyteller related them? This might be a fable, after all, or a parable, if birds have the need or desire to make such things. We don't yet know. The only answer I can give is to suggest that the ancient epics we have rediscovered, the *Odyssey*, *Journey to the West*, the *Epic of Gilgamesh* are clearly not factual, but no one who has ever felt the timeless power of a well-told story would doubt that they embody deep truths about our kind. As for *where* these events may have happened, for now we must also leave the question unanswered. We know that during the Broken Years, animals in many bioregions gathered together in unpeopled areas for mutual protection. The "watersedge" of the story is clearly one such sanctuary. All we can say is that it might have been found, and perhaps still could be, not far to the east of the Shining Mountains, in the northwest of the continental landmass known once more as Turtle Island.

One further note about the name of the avian hero of this tale. In the Uttering a near-simultaneous combination of vocalization, head tilt, wing flap, and other gestures and displays is capable of conveying complicated statements with remarkable compactness. An idea that might take a long, tedious string of words for a human to articulate can be uttered by a bird in one near-instantaneous "burst." This is especially true of bird names, and it is why I have chosen to render the long string of signifiers "Noisy-curious-one-who-chatters-even-while-preening-and-keeps-on-asking-questions-when-adults-want-to-sleep" as the much shorter and simpler "Yap."

* * *

I am Speaker.
I speak the Uttering.
I speak it with you now,
human,
so you will hear
and remember.

I will go slowly.
Keep your ears open.

This is a story
from the Broken Years
of Yap the magpie,
of Bone Woman
and Star Boy,

and their journey
to the sky's teeth.
Our foremothers
carried this story,
they sheltered it,
kept it under their wing
through the Broken Years.
They passed it on to us.

They told of what the humans did
in those years
to the Uttering.
How they broke the Uttering.[1]

When they saw
what they had done
the humans made half-alives[2]
and sent them into the sky.
They sent those tiny, unseeable
half-alives
into the heaven sea
to take the shapes of clouds.

---

[1] Here Speaker uses the phrase "the Uttering" to refer not to the birds' language as such but to the rest of the world as well, the entire multifaceted web of life, the waters, the air, the earth itself; what some now call the great biotic symphony. For the birds, most things speak and can be spoken to, even objects or phenomena that are not conventionally considered "alive."

[2] "Half-alive" is my admittedly inadequate translation of the complex avian term for— and concept of—devices made by humans that appear to have some of the characteristics of living things but are not considered fully awake and aware beings. Vehicles, firearms, robots, and communication equipment fit into this category, as do, apparently, some animals and humans: those who are not aware of the Uttering or their place in it.

They thought those clouds
could bring rain,
shield the earth from the sun
to heal the Uttering.

But those clouds escaped.
They roamed
where they pleased.
They would not save the humans
from what they had done.

So the rains did not fall.
The earth burned.
Many animals perished.
Many humans died.

After a time
there was only watersedge,
the last green place,
the last good place.

There was water there,
there were seeds and berries
and tiny crawling alives[3]

---

[3] The birds use the term "alive" as an adjectival noun, mostly to refer to insects and other small living things. The actual term in bird speech is a complex utterance, containing many subtleties of meaning, which regrettably I was forced to render down to a simpler concept. As we have begun to understand, the animals' unique and intricate forms of communication are constructed not only of sound but of movement, gesture, proximity, and even orientation: which direction one's beak or tail is pointing can entirely change the meaning of a phrase. The Uttering, in other words, is danced as much as it is spoken or sung. And there may be other even more subtle conveyances of meaning within this language that we humans aren't aware of, because we lack the senses upon which they are based.

in the earth and the air.
Birds could live there.
They could find mates
for a season
or a lifetime.
They could hatch their eggs
and care for their young.
It was safe there
from the humans
and what they had done.

In that place
in that time,
our foremothers said,
Yap the magpie
came into the world.
Yap who went
to the borders of death
and beyond
to the sky's teeth.

Even nestled in the egg
Yap was a talker.
When his parents sang to him
the first teachings
all parents give
before their young
come forth from the shell,
even then Yap did
what no chick had done.
He sang back to his parents
from inside the egg.

When Yap was a fledgling
he liked to play games
and make mischief
with his brothers and sisters.
He played hide and seek,
pounce and chase,
and other games
he made up himself
like, Who can fly farthest
from the nesting tree?

It was always Yap
who flew the farthest.
He wanted to know
what lay beyond watersedge.
His mind flew even further
than his wings could take him.
It wheeled, winged, soared.
It travelled
to places he could not see.

Yap's grandmother
was the one who told him
about the humans.
Yap snapped up her stories
like ripe berries.
He could not get enough of them.
He asked his grandmother,
Where are the humans now?
Are there any left?
His grandmother told him
no animal in watersedge

had seen a human
for many years.

Yap asked his father
if he had seen humans.
They aren't anymore,
Yap's father told him.
They were stupid,
never learned the Uttering,
and they all died.

Still Yap dreamed
of meeting humans.
With the days he grew
and spread his young wings
to the air.
Smallest of his siblings
he flew first
from the nest.
He grew stronger.
He flew farther and farther
each day
until he could reach
the boundaries of watersedge.
There he met the terns
who of all birds
journey the farthest
across the heaven sea.

Yap asked the terns,
had they seen any humans
in their travels?

They hadn't,
they told Yap.
The humans left things,
signs you could read
that told you they were there.
The terns hadn't seen human signs
for a long time.
Not their many smokes,
not their dead earth-paths,
not their streams
filled with black poison.

If there are any humans left,
the terns said to Yap,
forget about them.
Let them die.

Yap was frightened
by what the terns told him
of human things,
but his grandmother's stories
had taken wing in his mind.
If humans still lived
it would be good
to know where they were
and what they were doing.

Yap wanted to be
the one to do that.
He could fly far.
He could search.
He could find

those terrible creatures
if they still lived.

Being Yap
he couldn't keep a secret.
He told his brothers and sisters
his thought
that he would look for humans.
He would be the first
to see them again
and bring back the news.

Yap's siblings said
he had batshit for brains.
No one wants to see a human,
they told him.
They hopped around Yap
making pretend human noises.
Ba kee kaka waa kook.
They called Yap names.
Bee-fucker,
they called him.
Turd-with-Wings.[4]

In that time
for three seasons of growing
the rains did not come.
The streams and ponds
began to dry out.

---

[4] For all its subtlety the Uttering can be a blunt, crude, even violent method of getting
one's point across. I have been told by several bird informants—though I have not
seen it demonstrated—that a certain word in the Uttering can only be "spoken" by
tearing out another animal's throat.

The birds and animals
grew thirsty.
They grew afraid.

If watersedge was no longer
a green place,
a good place,
where could they go?

One sungoing
in the last
of the Grasshopper song[5]
the crows spread the alarm
through the trees.
The call passed
among the birds:
humans had been seen.
Not far away.

From all over watersedge
birds came,
they flew,
they flocked,
all the chosen speakers
from the tribes and nations.[6]

---

[5] "Sungoing" is sunset, or more generally, evening, and also an indication of direction, in this case west. "Suncoming" refers to dawn or morning, and to the direction east. The season called "Grasshopper song" roughly corresponds to our month of Heartsummer.

[6] The birds have their own names for their many and varied species. One of the most difficult aspects of translating Speaker's story was to determine which species of bird she was referring to in each case. In the Uttering, for example, bald eagle is rendered something like "Snowy-headed-builder-of-the-biggest-nest." This was a fairly easy identification compared to some of the others. I cannot be sure in all cases that I have translated the Uttering word-concept correctly. The term "tribes and nations" is my unavoidably anthropocentric rendering of the birds' own concept of their distinctiveness from one another.

They came
to the gathering place
below the tall, lone pine
on the earth mound
at the shore of the marsh.

Bald eagle settled
on the top branch
of the tall, lone pine.
Horned owl
alighted nearby.
Raven perched
on a bare black limb.

All of the speakers came
to the heart of watersedge
to the tall, lone pine,
to the earth mound
by the water.

Hawk, falcon, nightjar,
ptarmigan, pintail, killdeer,
yellowlegs, ibis, grebe,
phalarope, swan,
blackbird, woodpecker,
blue jay, grey jay,
vireo, redpoll, swallow, pipit,
nutcracker, wren, warbler, dipper,
and all the sparrows.

You ask, human,
why the strong didn't prey

on the small and weak.
Listen.
When a gathering is called
the great treaty holds.
No hunting,
no killing
is allowed
when a worse danger threatens.
A bird who breaks the treaty
is driven from watersedge
and killed if they return.

Yap and his family were foraging
in the bunchberry meadow
in the ring of old birches
when the alarm came.
Humans!
Humans are coming!
It was Yap's turn to keep watch
from the treetops for danger
while his parents and siblings
searched and scraped below.
Yap didn't like keeping watch.
He wanted to play games
with his siblings.
He hated sitting alone
in the windy top
of a leafless birch,
keeping watch.

When the call came
Yap heard it.

He flew to his family.
Humans!
he told them.
Humans have been seen!
They are coming this way!

That's not our business,
said Yap's father.
Your uncle Thinks-It-Over-Twice
speaks for our clan.
He's going to the gathering.
You go back to watching.

Yap flew back up
to the birch top.
The wind shook him.
It ruffled his feathers.
It stirred his mind.
He couldn't stop thinking
about the humans.
He had to see them.

One of his sisters flew near.
Yap called to her:
You keep watch. I'm going.
And Yap flew off
to the gathering place.

Yap came there
to the gathering of the speakers.
He was small and nestled
in the tall grass

at the edge of the mound.
No one noticed him.

It was the turn
of the saw-whet owl
Many Lice
to lead the gathering.

Many Lice waited for quiet.
Then he puffed himself up.

The humans,
Many Lice said,
were not far away.
Two humans,
one tall and one small.
They had an animal with them,
one of those like-wolves
as the old stories said.

The humans were near,
Many Lice said.
They would reach the gathering place
by moonrise.

The birds all began to speak
at once,
their voices clamouring.
Some called for the humans
to be killed
before they came any nearer.
Send the red hill wolf pack

to hunt them down,
cried a grey jay mother.
She'd had many hatchlings
that summer.
Then we can eat their flesh,
she said,
and their blood
will feed the earth.

Many birds took up her cry.
Kill them!
Eat their flesh!
Scatter their bones!

While they debated
the old crane
Reflected Moon
came out of the reeds
from the last of the water
that had not dried in the heat.[7]
She came into the circle
of the birds.
She came walking slowly,
not speaking,
and all the speakers were quiet.
They made way for her.
Reflected Moon lived alone

---

[7] The old crane's full name was expressed by Speaker as "Resembles-the-shining-whiteness-of-the-skybird-reflected-in-the-water." The phrase also implies that the crane is thought to have lived almost as long as the moon—imagined as a bird—has been soaring across the night sky; a way of venerating her great age, endurance, and wisdom.

in the reeds.
She was the oldest
of all in watersedge.
She saw and sang
the deepest
in the Uttering.
In those deep places
she saw things
that were not
but would later come to be.

Reflected Moon
had not been to a gathering
for many lives of birds,
but this sungoing she came.
The birds were astonished.
What would she have to say?

Send out searchers,
Reflected Moon said,
to find the humans
and bring them unharmed
to the gathering place.

My hatchlings cry for food,
said the grey jay mother.
We hunt for it all day,
we scrape and peck and dig,
we find so little.
Why speak with humans
when there are young to feed?
The humans do not know

the Uttering like we do,
said Kinked Wing
the killdeer.
They do not speak the Uttering.
They open their mouths
and shit comes out.
Everyone knows this.

Have you seen a human?
asked Reflected Moon.
Have you spoken with one?

The grey jay and the killdeer
were silent.

My foremother's foremothers
passed down a story,
said Reflected Moon,
from the time before
the Broken Years.

Because of what humans did
to the Uttering
only two of my kind
still lived.
Only two.
We cranes were close
to leaving a silence
forever
in the Uttering.[8]

---

[8] A particularly resonant image for the idea of species extinction.

My foremothers say
it was a human
called Nightbird
who saved us.
She took our foremother,
the last of her kind,
from our home
before a great water rose
and drowned it.
She brought the cranes back
from silence.
That is why
I would let the humans come
and speak to them myself.

At moonrise
the rufous hummingbird
Stands in the Air
found the humans.
She led them
to the heart of watersedge
where the speakers
were waiting.

Yap was still hiding
in the tall grass.
He saw the humans coming.
They were impossible to miss
but hard to see.
They had no wings.
They walked
like no other animal.

There were two of them.
An old one—
his grandmother told him
humans called this a woman—
and a young one—
what they called a boy.
The woman's hair was pale
like moonlight through mist.
The boy was small
but he was not afraid.
He walked in front of the woman
to protect her.
Beside him walked their like-wolf.
When it wandered away
from the humans
and they called it back,
it came to them.

The humans climbed
up the earth mound.
All the birds waited.
No one spoke.

Reflected Moon
came from the reeds
to meet the humans.
She spoke to the humans.
She welcomed them
to watersedge.

The woman lowered her head
and spoke back
to Reflected Moon.

The birds were astonished.
A human spoke the Uttering.
She did not speak it well
and her accent was strange,
but her words stunned the animals
and made them quiet.

Reflected Moon
gave her name.

The woman
gave her name
in her own speech.
That name sounded like
mree hwit.

When the birds heard this
they chattered
with surprise and delight.
The woman's name sounded
like the starling does
when it mimics the calls
of other birds.
Mreehwit, the birds called.
Mreehwit. Mreehwit.

The woman looked around
startled by the commotion.
Then she understood.

She said:
If my name amuses you
you may call me Bone Woman.

That's my title
where we come from,
my son's child and I.
It means I am old
and have survived much.

Wanderer, the speaker
for the white-throated sparrows,
asked the woman:
How did you learn the Uttering?

The woman said:
I came from another place.
I was lost for a long time
in the Uttering.
You've seen a leaf
caught in a stream
where the water whirls
around itself?
I was caught like that,
like a leaf
in whirling water,
only the stream was time.
When I finally got free
I was here
in your time.

The birds did not understand.
How could someone be caught
by time,
which was the nest,
woven and unwoven always,

for the Uttering
that brought forth all things?
The woman made no sense
but they let her speak.

I have met many birds
and other animals,
the woman said,
in places far from watersedge.
Slowly,
travelling to many places,
speaking with many animals,
I learned the Uttering.

Snowbrows the goshawk
spoke:
You should have learned
not to come here.
You are lucky
not to have been killed
and eaten already.
I would enjoy the boy's flesh,
if not yours
which looks dry and tough.
Eating the boy
would be a good end
to this gathering.

The woman said:
We're travelling to the mountains,
the teeth of the sky
as you birds call them,

that rise toward sungoing.
The boy's father,
my son,
was to come with us.
A sickness grew in his lungs.
He died before we were ready
to set out.
It's only the two of us,
my grandson and I,
the woman said.
No one else
would come on this journey.
We have learned what we can
of the Uttering,
now we wish to speak
with the clouds
in their own tongue.
We seek those clouds
made of tiny half-alives.
We will go to the sky's teeth
and climb up high
to where the clouds live.
If we find the half-alive clouds,
if they will hear us,
we will plead to them.
For humans.
For all animals.

I am old,
the woman said.
I don't know
if I'll finish the journey
back to our home.

I have brought my grandson
so he may learn.
He has only thirteen summers
but he's strong and quick,
he sees and hears much.
He was named
Mee chee oh
for his father's father.

Again the birds chittered
at the strange sound
the woman had woven
into the Uttering.

If his name amuses you,
the woman said,
you may call him Star Boy.
That's the name I gave him
when he was a nestling.
He would look up
at the night sky
with wonder
and the stars would shine
in his eyes.

I name him Dinner Walking,
said Snowbrows the goshawk.
Why doesn't he speak the Uttering
as you do?

I learning to speak,
the boy said.
My grandmother teaching me.

I not good yet like her
so I not speak much.

That's wise,
said Snowbrows.

Brief Shadow the black swift
spoke:
You have far to go
if you want to reach
the sky's teeth.
There are many dangers.
I came to watersedge
from that place
when I was a fledgling.
I was bold in those days,
too bold,
too curious.
I flew too far.
I left my home
so far behind
I couldn't get back.
When I was close to dying
I found watersedge.
It was a good place.
I stayed.
I never went back.
But I know and remember
the way between here
and the sky's teeth.
It is long
and filled with dangers.

The woman said:
We've already come
many long days
and faced many dangers.
We have eaten
almost all the food
we brought.
But we must go on.
I see no choice.
If we do nothing
the young among us
and those who come after
will live in pain and hunger
before they die
far too soon.
One day perhaps all humans
will perish and be forgotten
by the Uttering.

Would that be a bad thing?
asked Snowbrows.
How many of our kind
have gone silent
because of you humans?
How many other creatures
who once filled the Uttering
with their music
have been forgotten?
There would be no birds at all,
nothing living,
if your kind still swarmed
the earth.

It seems only fair
you should suffer
what we have suffered.

Far-Off Thunder
the speaker for the bitterns
came forward.
He was slow of speech
and given to visions
of dreadful things.

Far-Off Thunder said:
Toward sungoing are strange lands,
bad lands.
There are animals there
who do not speak the Uttering,
who do not know the great treaty.
In those bad lands
are the hundred deaths
that came into the world
with you humans.
No song of ours
sings of them.
We do not go there.
We cannot live there.
We birds have watersedge,
said Far-Off Thunder.
You have your home,
you humans.
Go back to it.
Live while you can.
Face your time to die

with what courage you have.
This is our place.
The good place.
This is the nest
where life is uttered.
That is how it is
and how it always will be.

It may not always be,
the woman said.
We humans no longer have
a watersedge.
We no longer have a place
where life is uttered.
Once long ago
I lived in a place like this,
the river meadows
we called that place,
it is not far from here,
a few days' walk for us.
That place was green,
there was life there
until humans destroyed it.
Soon
I can tell you,
and I speak what is,
watersedge may no longer
be green,
may no longer be good
for birds and other animals.
We must go,
we must try,

or watersedge may become
like those bad lands
toward sungoing.

The birds were silent then.

Reflected Moon said:
Now that I see the humans
and hear them,
I understand what I saw
when I journeyed to
the under-sky[9]
the sungoing before last.
In the under-sky
I saw the place
where the humans live.
It is a place of dust,
of hunger,
of dying.
In that place was fire.
From the dead stalks of reeds
flames soared into the dark.
Then I saw
coming through the reeds
someone walking
not touched by the fire,
not burned by the flames.
A human, I think,
a small one
but covered in feathers.

---

[9] "Under-sky" is my rendering of the avian term for dreaming, conceived of by birds as
a place they fly to when they sleep. This is where Reflected Moon apparently had her
visions of "things that were not / but would later come to be."

The human called to the sky
in a voice I could not hear.
Then all at once
rain came down.
The fire went out.

When I woke,
Reflected Moon said,
there was a thorn in my breast,
the pain of knowing
a new thing,
a strange thing.
I know these humans have come
to do this thing
I do not understand
but that must be done
for all of us.

To all the speakers
Reflected Moon said:
Some of you
find fish.
Others, find nuts and berries.
We will feed you, humans,
so that you may go on
to the sky's teeth.

The woman thanked
Reflected Moon.

We will do more,
Reflected Moon said.

I am old.
My wings
no longer carry me.
I won't leave these reeds again.
If some of you
who are quick,
who are young and strong,
go with the humans
you can help them
so that they may live
to reach the sky's teeth
and do this thing
that must be done.
Will any go?
Who will go?

After a silence
Brief Shadow
the black swift said:
I will show the humans the way
to the sky's teeth.

Many birds spoke up then.
Many Lice the saw-whet owl
puffed himself up
and said that he would go.
Riverwalker
the speaker for the dippers
said he would go too.
Snowbrows the goshawk spoke:
if we agree it is good
then so it is.
You will need sharp eyes

and sharp talons
so I will go.

Wanderer
the white-throated sparrow
said they would go.
The flicker said she would go.
The eagle said so too.
The raven said so.
The blue heron said so.
The tern said so.
The pipit said so.
The horned owl said so.

When Yap heard
where the humans were going
he wanted to fly back
to his family,
to his nest,
put his head under his wing,
forget what he had heard.
But when those birds spoke up
Yap's heart took flight in him.
Then he took flight too.

He flew out of his hiding place
into the circle.
He flew around Bone Woman
and Star Boy.

I'll go, he cried.
I'll go too.

The speakers chittered
and mocked him.
They all knew him,
the young chattering one.
He didn't understand.
All he did was talk.

The woman spoke to Yap:
You remind me
of a magpie I met
long ago,
the one who led me
to your world.
We were companions
for many years.
It was she who taught me
my first words
in the Uttering
before she returned to it.
If you will come with us,
young one,
we will be glad.

Reflected Moon said to Yap:
Yes, you will go.
You will teach the boy
to speak the Uttering
as it should be spoken.
You love to speak
so that will be your task.

Sungoing was over.
It was time to seek refuge.

The birds flew off
to their nests and holes.
The woman and the boy
had no nest or hole
to shelter in.
They would sleep on the ground.
Yap stayed with the humans
to see what they would do.

Thank you for coming with us,
the woman said to Yap.

I thank too, said the boy.
I happy you teach me.

Yap said nothing.
He was alone
with humans
and they were not
as he had imagined.
For the first time ever
he couldn't utter
a single word.

The woman had a pouch
like the pelican's bill
for carrying things.
From it she brought out
a small shining half-alive.
She did something with it
Yap did not understand.

The half-alive began to speak.
It spoke like the crackle
when lightning sets fire
to a dead tree.

Yap hopped away.

Don't be afraid,
the woman said.
This is called a *chit-chit*.[10]

That's how other humans sound?
Yap asked.
Like a burning tree?

That noise not humans,
the boy said.
That noise just air.

The other humans are too far
for us to speak to them,
the woman said.
What you hear
is a storm speaking
a long way from us.
In that other place
far away
it may be raining.
Yap said:

---

[10] The story as it passed down from Speaker's ancestors may have lost the strange and hard-to-pronounce human word "radio" along the way. "Chit-chit" is my rendering of the nonsense syllables that Speaker used as a placeholder for the missing human word.

Can you speak to the storm
through that half-alive,
tell it to bring that rain
to watersedge?

I wish I could,
said the woman.

At suncoming
the woman and her grandson
began their journey.
They set out toward sungoing
toward the sky's teeth.

With them went many birds.
Brief Shadow
the black swift
knew the way
and led them.

They journeyed three days
toward sungoing.
The birds went with them.
The small and swift-winged
scouted ahead.
The high-flyers soared overhead
to watch for danger.
They found the best paths,
the easiest paths
for the humans to take.
The hunters found small alives—
rabbits, mice, fish—
to share with the humans.

Whenever they rested
Yap spoke with the boy.
He told him stories he had heard
as a nestling.
He taught the boy
how to see many things
by giving them their names
in the Uttering.

Sometimes they walked
on the stone-rivers
made by humans long ago.

Yap asked,
What were the stone-rivers for?
The boy told him
the old humans
had hollow half-alives
that carried them
where they wished to go.
Once the stone-rivers
were busy with many half-alives
rushing here and there
with humans inside them.
There were other half-alives
that carried the humans
through the sky
like birds.

Yap wasn't sure he believed
humans had flown like birds,
but he didn't say so.

One night the boy asked Yap:
How do birds always know
which way is suncoming
and which way is sungoing
even when the sun is hidden?

The sky-river,
Yap said.
That is how we know.
Humans can't see the sky-river?

The boy said they couldn't.
He asked Yap
what the sky-river looked like.

It's like a stream of water,
Yap said,
with many colours in it.
We see it
and feel it.
When you wade in a stream
to drink
you feel the water
tugging at you,
wanting you to go
where it goes.
That's how we feel
the sky-river.
On one bank is suncoming.
On the other bank is sungoing.
That's how we always know
where we are.

On the fourth day
from watersedge
they came to the sand hills.
There were no trees.
There were no tiny alives
to catch and eat.

As they crossed the hills
the sun scorched them.
Some of the birds grew afraid then,
remembering Far-Off Thunder
and his talk of the hundred deaths.
They turned back.
They flew back to watersedge.

The woman and the boy
went on.
Brief Shadow the black swift
led them.
Many Lice the saw-whet owl
went with them.
Riverwalker the dipper kept on.
Snowbrows the goshawk kept on.
Wanderer the white-throated sparrow
kept on.
The flicker kept on.
The eagle kept on.
The tern, the raven,
the horned owl,
they all kept on.

A cold came at night
like the heart of winter.

Those who kept on
found what shelter they could.
In the dark they called out
to one another.
Are you there?
Yes I'm still here.

The woman and the boy hid
from the sun's heat
under overhanging rocks
and under thorny bushes.
Yap stayed by their side.
He talked with the boy
and taught him the Uttering.

Snowbrows the goshawk
and the eagle
soared high and far.
They searched
for the gleam of water.
They found none.

At last
Riverwalker the dipper
found a trickle of water
hidden among stones.
They all came to it
and drank.

At each sungoing
if the sky held clouds
the woman would take some things
from her pouch.

She put those things together
to make a bigger thing,
another half-alive
like the chit-chit
but larger.
It had a face
smooth and dark like ice
that Yap could see himself in
and a tail
that fanned out
like the grouse's.
It had long legs
like the crane or the heron
but there were three of them
that it stood upon.[11]

The woman set the half-alive
on its three legs.
Yap asked her
if it was a bird
that humans had made.
This half-alive, she said,
speaks the language
of the clouds.

My son, she said,
Star Boy's father,
made this thing.
His father was my friend
in the time I came from

---

[11] It is not clear from Speaker's description exactly what sort of device this was, but we
can assume it had to be a crude early version of the technology we use today to add
our voices to the biotic symphony.

when those clouds first appeared.
He watched them
and knew it was possible
to speak with them.
My son never met his father,
but I made sure
he knew of him
and of the knowledge
he had gathered
before it was lost
in the Broken Years.

My son's body was weak
from birth,
but his mind was sharp.
His mind flew
where the minds of others
could not.
He watched
and he gathered knowledge.
He found the way
we could listen
to those half-alive clouds
and talk with them again,
if we were patient
and willing to learn.
He made this half-alive.
Now I am teaching my grandson
to make it speak.

That night the woman
showed the boy
how to tap on the face

of the half-alive,
like the sapsucker rapping
on the bark of a dead tree.

The boy tapped.
They all waited.
He tapped some more.
Then Yap hopped up and down.
I can hear it! he said.
I can hear the voice
of the half-alive.
It's like the sky-river.

The woman said:
We need to catch
some of those half-alives
in the clouds.

To eat them? said Yap.
Snowbrows said,
Like humans ate
everything else.

To speak with them,
the woman said.
To tell them about us.
To ask for their help.

The woman waited all night.
The half-alive did not find
any of those clouds
to speak to.

Then she brought out a thing
Yap had never seen before,
like many pale leaves
all gathered together.

She made marks
on the leaves
with a small stick.

Yap asked
what that thing was.

This is a book,
the woman said.
It's where we keep
what we learn
of the Uttering
and all that's happened
on our journey.

How can leaves hold
all of that?
asked Yap.
Leaves are for catching sun.
For catching rain.

These leaves have caught
much sun and rain,
the woman said.
But they catch other things.
When a bird sees tracks
of another bird's feet

in the snow,
they know who was there
and what they did.
The markings I make
in this book
are like that.
We set our thoughts
down here,
like tracks in snow
that do not fade with spring,
to remember what was done
and said.
We can even save the thoughts
of those who died
a long time ago
before the Broken Years.
A book is where we keep
our memory
so we do not lose it.

The next sungoing
they came to the end
of the sand hills.

As they travelled
the woman made marks
in the book
about everything they saw.
She asked the birds the names
for plants and trees.
She made marks for them
in her book.

When a bird fell along the way
she made marks for it.
The bird's name,
she said,
would be remembered
by the humans.

After many days
they came near a place
where humans once lived.
The woman called this place
a city.
Humans still lived here,
the woman said.
They were full of fear
and that made them dangerous.
They had no treaty
with any living thing.
Because they did not know
the Uttering,
they did not know
themselves
and all they did
was harm.

Brief Shadow
had seen these humans
when he flew over the city
on his way to watersedge.
These humans, he said,
hunted and ate anything alive,
even other humans.

Again some birds
would go no farther.
They were afraid
and turned back
for watersedge.

Yap was afraid.
He wanted to turn back too.
Now that he was so far
from his home
he missed his siblings.
He wanted to see them again.
That night he told the boy
and the woman
about his brothers and sisters,
the games they used to play.

I had a brother,
the woman said.
I miss him too.
I think of him often.

Where is he? Yap asked.

He lived long ago
the woman said.
in a place I cannot return to.
I will never see him again.

Was he like you?
Yap asked.
He was more like you,

the woman said.
He liked games.

At suncoming
they came near the city.
Snowbrows the goshawk
went ahead,
he soared high
keeping watch for those humans.

Led by Brief Shadow
the woman and the boy
took a wide path
around the city
so those other humans
wouldn't find them.

They walked at night
and slept during the daylight.
The like-wolf stayed by them.
Yap stayed by them.
The horned owl kept watch
with his eyes that could see
in the dark.

They walked one night
and the next.
They were almost past
the place of those humans.

The next suncoming
they saw Snowbrows returning.

He was still high in the sky
but getting closer.

There was a noise
the birds hadn't heard before.

Snowbrows fell
from the sky.
The humans had brought him down
with their half-alives
that spoke thunder.

He fell on a stone-river
where those other humans were.

The birds could not go
where Snowbrows was.
They didn't know
if he was alive
or if he had returned
to the Uttering.
They had to hurry away
before those humans
found them.

They kept on.
They travelled for two days
in the direction of sungoing.

They came to the place
of the hundred deaths.
Here the long-ago humans
had poisoned the earth,

the waters,
the air.
Here were things
from the Broken Years,
half-alive things
that could catch an animal
and tear the life from it.

Some of the birds
turned back.
They would go
no farther.

Bone Woman and Star Boy
kept on.
The like-wolf stayed by their side.
Brief Shadow kept on.
Wanderer kept on.
The raven kept on.
The horned owl kept on.
Yap was afraid
but he kept on.

While they journeyed
through the half-alive place
the raven disappeared.
They never saw her again.
If she returned to the Uttering
they do not know it.

They came to a forest
of black and dead trees.
The earth was white

with ashes.
Wanderer
the white-throated sparrow
stopped them.

Wanderer was gifted
in the Uttering.
They could hear the speech
of many things
other than birds.

This was a place of meetings,
Wanderer said.
A place of messages.
Many birds, many animals
spoke together here
with the water and the wind
about what was happening
far and near
and then moved on.

We must wait, Wanderer said.
Something's about to be
spoken here.
A message is coming.

They all waited.

No one's coming,
Brief Shadow said.
Or if they were
we missed them.

We got here too late.
Or too early,
Yap said.

Something came flying
through the dead trees.
A tiny, buzzing alive.

Wanderer snapped up the tiny alive
in their beak
and ate it.

This was our message,
Wanderer said.
One of the hundred deaths
is not far away.
It is a human thing,
a half-alive that walks.
It's coming this way.

Brief Shadow soared up high
and flew out of sight.
Then he returned.

I have seen the death,
Brief Shadow said.
It walks like a wolf
but it's a half-alive,
a human thing.

The birds did not understand.
The woman understood.

She called the half-alive
by its name
in her own language.

If it finds us we will die,
the woman said.
This death was made by humans
to hunt and kill
other humans.
It was made for a thing
we called war.
There is a human-made fire
inside of it
that keeps it hunting,
even though those who made it
are long gone.

Your like-wolf can fight the death,
Brief Shadow said.
It can tear the death's throat out.

The death has no throat
to tear out,
the woman said.
It has no life to take.
It will take our lives
if we don't escape it.

I've tasted the poison
the death carries inside it,
Wanderer said.
That was also the message.
I can feel it inside me

eating my life.
Before it returns me
to the Uttering
I will find this death,
I will lead it far away.

The woman and the boy
didn't want Wanderer
to do this.

Those leaves you make marks on,
Wanderer said to the woman.
Make your marks on the leaves
for me.

Wanderer took flight,
they shot away
through the trees.
They were gone.

Brief Shadow
the black swift
led the others away
from that place
toward sungoing.

Wanderer did not come back.
How they returned to the Uttering
the birds do not know.

As they went on
through the place
of the hundred deaths

the boy grew weak.
His skin was hot
but he shivered.
He couldn't walk anymore.
He wouldn't eat.
The place of the hundred deaths
had made him sick too.

The woman found a place
to shelter,
a hollow among the roots
of a fallen tree.
She watched over the boy.
He lay and shivered
and spoke broken words,
like one halfway
to the under-sky.
The woman sang to him.

The birds decided
to look for food and water.
Yap wanted to go too.
He spread his wings,
he hopped and called,
watching them fly away.

Stay with me,
the boy said to him.

I must go
help find food,
Yap said.
He flew off.

He searched
with the others.
They found no food
and only a little water
that was not good to drink.

They returned
to the fallen tree.

The boy lay still.
He had gone far
into the under-sky.
Yap was afraid
he would not return.

He asked the woman,
Is he coming back?
I don't know,
she told him.

What happened then
was strange.
It was Yap who told
our foremothers' foremothers
how he nestled
by the boy
through the night.
This time
he would not leave.
He would stay
as the boy had asked him.
It was then
he did what no bird he knew

had done.
He travelled with eyes open
into the under-sky,
to the place
the boy had gone.

In that place
Yap was alone
beside the fallen tree.
The boy was not there.
The woman was not there.
All around was snow
and darkness.

Yap knew then,
this was the home
of one of the hundred deaths.
It was very close.
If the boy was here
the death would find him,
it would have him.

It would have Yap too
if it caught him here.

Yap flew high
in the dark air
and circled,
calling the boy.
He felt the death
stir at his call,
the way birds feel a storm
lift their feathers

before it arrives.
It had heard his call.
It was on its way.

Then Yap saw
a tall human
coming toward him,
struggling,
stumbling
through the deep snow.

The tall human
had the boy
on his back.
He was carrying him.

Yap called to them.
He flew to them.
It was like flying
into a gale.

Then he saw
the man was gone.
The boy was alone.
He took a step.
Then another.
Yap flew to him.
The boy saw him.
He walked toward him.

Then Yap and the boy
were beneath the tree
with the woman

and the like-wolf.
It was suncoming.
They had travelled together
to that dark place
and returned.

Who was that human
who carried you?
Yap asked the boy.

I didn't know him,
the boy said.
He saved me.
He brought me
back to you.

The boy felt stronger.
He could stand
and walk again.

They went on
through the place
of the hundred deaths.

The next day
they came to a river
that flowed from the mountains.
They followed it.

It grew colder now
after sungoing.

The foremothers-in-the-sky[12]
came out with the stars.

The woman and the boy
had outer skins
they could put on
and take off
as they wished.
The skins kept them warm.

Still the woman grew tired.
She lagged behind.
She sat down often to rest.
They had to stop
and wait for her.

The next suncoming
she called the boy to her.
Go on without me,
she said.
I'm slowing you down.

I can't do that,
said the boy.
He took her hand in his.
He did what humans do
when they are moved within.
Water fell
from his eyes.
We have to go together,

---

[12] The aurora borealis.

the boy said.
I can't do this
without you.

The sun was warmer
that day.
The woman got up.
She kept walking.
She walked slowly
and rested often.
The boy waited for her.
Sometimes he helped her walk.

They followed the river
toward sungoing.

One night they heard
an owl's call.
That one is alone,
the horned owl said.
There are no others.
I must go to it,
she said.

She flew off
and didn't return.

The rest kept on then,
following the river.
Brief Shadow led them.
Yap perched
on the boy's shoulder.

After one more suncoming
they came to a place
where the river widened
to a long, shallow water.
On the far side
were the sky's teeth.
They rose up
taller than any tree.
At their tops
there were no clouds.

That night the woman
made another fire
beside the water.
She and the boy
sat close to the flames.

At suncoming they reached
the sky's teeth.
Before them rose a tooth
not so tall as the others,
but still a great stone
with many trees
on its sides
like blades of grass.
The tip of the tooth
was white with snow.

There will be clouds
the woman said.
They brought the snow.
They will come again.

Brief Shadow flew ahead
to find a path.
He came back down.
He'd found a way.

The woman and the boy climbed
and the like-wolf and Yap
stayed with them.
Brief Shadow would fly off
and then return
to show where the path was.

They climbed and rested
and climbed.
The sun climbed too
into the sky.

I will look for clouds,
Brief Shadow said.
He flew off
up the mountain.

The others climbed
and waited
for Brief Shadow to return.
He didn't come back.

They climbed some more.
The woman grew tired.
She sat down in a place
where water ran from the rocks.
She drank a little,
then she called her grandson.

I came here once,
I climbed here
when I was young,
she said.
I'm no longer young.
I can't go any farther.
She stroked the like-wolf's fur.
Ben will stay with me,
she said.
You go on with Yap.

She gave the boy the half-alive
to take with him.
The boy didn't want to go
without his grandmother.
She told him not to be afraid.
He would do well.
She would see him again
when he came back down.

Before he left
the boy found some sticks
and made a fire
for his grandmother.
I'll be back soon,
he said.

He went on with Yap.

As they climbed higher
it got colder.
The boy kept Yap warm
under his outer skin.

They came to a place
without trees.
The wind pounced
like the falcon
with sharp talons.

They found Brief Shadow
lying among the rocks,
cold and stiff.
He had returned
to the Uttering.

You must go,
the boy said to Yap.
Fly back to my grandmother.
It's too cold here.

I will stay with you,
Yap said.

The boy and Yap climbed on.
They found a hollow
in the rocks
sheltered from the wind.
Here they could rest.
There was a trickle of water
they could drink from.
Beyond this place was snow
and the point of the tooth.

There were no clouds.

The boy stood the half-alive
on its three legs.
He took off the skins
covering his hands.
He tapped on the face
of the half-alive.
Then he put the skins
back on his hands.
He waited.
He took the skins off again
and tapped some more.
Then he waited.

Yap waited with him.
They huddled together
against the wind.
Then Yap felt the air
change.
He felt his feathers lift
the way they did before a storm.

Clouds are coming!
Yap told the boy.

The boy looked up.
It was true.
Shining clouds
like new snow
were coming over
the top of the tooth.

The clouds rose over the tooth
then came down the side
where the boy and Yap waited.

The boy tapped on the face
of the half-alive.
The clouds
slowly came down
toward them.

One of the clouds
passed over them.
It passed so close
they felt its cold droplets
settle on them.

The boy tapped the half-alive.

The cloud moved away.
It moved on
down the mountain.

The boy tapped
and moved the tail
of the half-alive
to point another way
at another cloud.

That cloud moved away too
down the mountain.

Only a few small ones
were left.

They drifted
like moulted feathers,
lingered in the gullies
and hollows of stone
where the wind
let them be.

The sky was bare again.

It didn't work,
the boy said.
We have to go.
We have to get back
to my grandmother.

The boy
put away the half-alive
and started back down
with Yap sheltering under
the boy's outer skin.
Yap wanted only
to sleep.
He looked out
one last time.

Then he saw
another cloud
by itself.
A small cloud
not far away.

It hung
where water fell

with a roar
down the mountain's face.

Inside of that cloud,
Yap saw,
it was like the sky-river.

Yap saw it
and felt it too,
like water in a stream
pulling on him.

He stirred.
His wings beat quickly
against the outer skin
as if he was the boy's heart.
He flew out from the skin.
He flew around the boy.

That cloud,
he told the boy.
That cloud is speaking
like the half-alive.

The boy stopped.
He took out the half-alive.
He took the skins
from his hands.
He tapped and tapped
on the half-alive.

The cloud stayed
beside the falling water.

I have to go there,
he said,
where the cloud is.
I have to get closer.

The boy climbed
to the edge of the gorge
where water plunged
with a roar.
The rock was wet there.
The boy lost his footing.
He clung to the rock
and the half-alive slipped
from his hands.

It fell on the rocks,
its face splintered
like old ice.

The boy climbed down
to where the half-alive
had fallen.
He clung there
with Yap on his shoulder.
He picked up the half-alive.
He tapped and tapped
on its cracked face.

It speaks,
he said.
It still speaks.

The cloud hung there
beside the falling water
below them.
It stayed still
as if it was listening
to the water.

The boy tapped
the half-alive's face.
He waited.

The cloud
began to move.
It drifted toward the edge
where the boy waited.

The boy tapped faster
on the face of the half-alive.
The cloud moved closer.
It came up toward them.

The cloud rose
over the boy and Yap.
It stopped moving,
hung above them.
Its cold droplets
settled on them
like dew.

Yap felt the sky-river
pulling on him
from the cloud,
stronger than ever.

Yap hopped up and down
on the boy's shoulder.
He called to the cloud too.

The boy tapped some more
on the half-alive.
The cloud came closer.
And now
it did not change its shape
the way clouds do.
It stood in the air
over their heads
and the boy spoke to it
through the half-alive.

He spoke to the cloud
with its own speech.

Yap saw and heard this.
He told it to our foremothers'
foremothers.
He said it was a thing
that is.

Then the cloud rose up
away from the boy,
away from the side
of the mountain.
As it went up
it changed shape.

It looked like a tree,
like a hill,

like a bird
with wings spread wide.

The cloud moved away
through the sky,
getting smaller
until they could no longer
see it.

The boy put away the half-alive.
He left the falling water.
He began to climb
down again.

Did you speak with the cloud?
Yap asked.
Did it speak to you?

I think so,
said the boy.
I think it told me its name.
But we can't wait for it
to come back.
If we stay here, we'll die.

Yap and the boy
returned
down the mountain.

They found the place
where the woman was lying.
The fire the boy made
had gone out.

Beside the woman
the like-wolf was huddled close.

The boy bent down
beside his grandmother.
He called her name.
She didn't answer.

He touched her face.
It was cold.
She had returned
to the Uttering.

The boy stayed there
beside his grandmother
for a long time.

Then Yap said
they had to find shelter.
Sungoing was coming.
It was too cold here.
If they stayed
they would die too.

The boy covered his grandmother
with one of the skins.
Before he left
he took the things
she had carried with her.

He took the book
she made markings in.

Then the boy and Yap
went down the mountain.
Yap flew ahead
searching for shelter.
He found a hollow place
under the roots of a pine.

The boy made a fire.
They were warm again.
They slept.

At suncoming the next day
they set out for watersedge.

There were only
the three of them,
the boy,
the like-wolf,
and Yap.
There was a long way to go.
There were many dangers
between them and watersedge.

As they walked
a shadow dimmed the light.
They looked up.

A cloud stood above them,
not moving.
The only one in the sky.

Where they walked
it walked.

When they stopped
it stopped.

From the cloud
a few drops of rain
came down.

The boy held out his hand.
He caught some of the drops.
He shouted
and lifted his face
to the rain.

He shouted to the sky.
He danced.

The like-wolf jumped up
made its like-wolf noises.
Yap flew around the boy,
calling and calling.

The rain fell,
more and more drops.

Then after a time,
fewer and fewer.

Now only a few drops
were still falling.

The boy took out
his grandmother's book
and spread it open.

He lifted its leaves
to the rain.

On a leaf he caught
one of the last falling drops.

Where the raindrop fell
the boy made marks
with a stick.

He told Yap these marks
spoke his grandmother's name.

The boy told Yap
no matter how far
those leaves were carried
or who carried them
the book would remember her.

THE OTHERS

After we're gone, time will be an ocean again.

But right now, it's Wednesday evening. Tonight we're marking our nation's birthday, and in small towns everywhere people celebrate as they always have, by setting off fireworks. This year, with so much that has gone wrong, with so many dreams shut down and hope such an elusive quantity, a bigger, more encouraging display than usual feels called for. And so we've made sure the pyrotechnic spectacle will be louder and more dazzling than ever before.

In our town, the eruption of noise and light startles flocks of nesting songbirds: starlings, jays, and many other species, which rise up into the tumult and quickly become disoriented. While below there's dancing and singing and embracing, the birds, mostly unseen in the darkness, fly into electrical wires, water towers, and the sides of buildings, while others turn on one another in the frenzy, or are attacked by other, larger birds of prey. The fireworks go on longer than usual this year. The avian panic does not dissipate quickly but spreads to other flocks, up and down the countryside.

The next morning hundreds of birds of many species are found dead in the meadows and on the highways and streets. Still more continue to fall lifeless from the skies during the day in exhaustion.

Not knowing the cause, we're baffled and disturbed. Many are convinced it must be a portent, or at least a sign, though of what exactly, no one can agree.

ACKNOWLEDGEMENTS

Solomon's "Unattainable Border of the Birds" was originally told to a Russian anthropologist on the banks of the Wolverine River in Siberia by a storyteller named Yatirgin, circa 1900. Adapted from V. Bogoraz's *Material for the Study of the Chukchi Language and Culture*, translated by Barbara Einzig.

The story of Jean de Léry and the parrot was very freely adapted by me from de Léry's own *History of a Voyage to the Land of Brazil* (1578).

I'm immensely grateful to Denise Bukowski, agent extraordinaire, whose encouragement and perseverance were essential to this book from incubation to its finally leaving the nest.

Admiration and bows to my editor, Anne Collins, for believing in the novel and graciously readying it for flight with all its feathers in the right places.

Thank you to copy editor Tilman Lewis, designer Emma Dolan, and the team at Random House Canada.

Many thanks to John Barton, Shashi Bhat, Sven Birkerts, Paulette Dubé, Anthony Enns, Romeo Kaseram, and Becca

Lawton. I'm indebted to Jason Kapalka for a serendipitous writing retreat at Otter Lake, where the story began to stir within its shell. A tip of the hat to Bill Thompson for reading early versions of the novel and for all the writing walks and talks.

To Sharon, Mary, Conor, Ronan, Jason, Kailey, and my family near and far, thank you for your love and support. To the children of the future, may you live in a world filled with birdsong.

THOMAS WHARTON has been published in Canada, the US, the UK, France, Italy, Japan, and other countries. His first novel, *Icefields,* won the 1996 Commonwealth Writers' Prize for Best First Book in Canada and the Caribbean and was also a 2008 CBC Canada Reads pick. His next book, *Salamander,* was shortlisted for the 2001 Governor-General's Award for Fiction and was also a finalist for the Roger's Writers' Trust Fiction Prize the same year. In 2006, Wharton's collection of stories, *The Logogryph,* was shortlisted for the International Dublin Literary Award.

Thomas currently lives near Edmonton, Alberta.